UNHOLY
FIRE

WHITLEY STRIEBER

UNHOLY FIRE

A DUTTON BOOK

DUTTON

Published by the Penguin Group
Penguin Books USA Inc., 375 Hudson Street, New York, New York 10014, U.S.A.
Penguin Books Ltd, 27 Wrights Lane, London W8 5TZ, England
Penguin Books Australia Ltd, Ringwood, Victoria, Australia
Penguin Books Canada Ltd, 10 Alcorn Avenue, Toronto, Ontario, Canada M4V 3B2
Penguin Books (N.Z.) Ltd, 182–190 Wairau Road, Auckland 10, New Zealand

Penguin Books Ltd, Registered Offices:
Harmondsworth, Middlesex, England

First published by Dutton, an imprint of New American Library,
a division of Penguin Books USA Inc.
Distributed in Canada by McClelland & Stewart Inc.

First printing, March, 1992

10 9 8 7 6 5 4 3 2 1

Ⓡ REGISTERED TRADEMARK—MARCA REGISTRADA

LIBRARY OF CONGRESS CATALOGING IN PUBLICATION DATA:

Strieber, Whitley.
Unholy fire / by Whitley Strieber.
p.   cm.
ISBN 0-525-93415-4
I. Title.
PS3569.T6955U5   1992
813'.54—dc20   91-28475
CIP

Printed in the United States of America
Set in Melior

Designed by Steven N. Stathakis

PUBLISHER'S NOTE

Then Satan shall be loosed from his tomb, and go about spreading great harm. But they will be blinded to his work, and rejoice in it until come the waters of heaven to wash their eyes, and when they see what has been done among them, they shall be much afraid.

—Theologium Ioannes, Liber VI

UNHOLY FIRE

NIGHT RIDE

IT WAS THE LAUGHTER THAT MADE HER RUN, MORE THAN THE
dark, more than that gliding shadow.

The air swept like cold silk past her face. She heard
her own feet drumming on the pavement, felt the frigid wind
invading her lungs. His heavier tread drove her on; she knew
that she was losing ground. She'd been a damn fool, of course:
she should have called the car service.

Inwardly she raged at the man who dared invade her with
this terror. But she had a right to the aesthetics of the night.
Also, the party would be jammed—hot and stuffy and intense.
Melanie had billed it as the end of the club, as the Last Party.
As indeed it was—disease has sapped the courage of the bad.

She'd wanted to arrive very late and ice-cold.

She made a turn into Charles Lane, moving into the dark
of the warehouses there. Even in the ice-cold air you could
smell the memories of meat and spices, the things held on
racks in the old buildings, where heavy men came in the day

to do their trade. Now everything was brown and gray and shuttered with steel. A loading dock, sick with rot, lined one side of the street. Trash blew down the other, rattling past a couple of cars, parked or abandoned.

She turned, crouching down behind a derelict Chevy Camaro. There was nothing behind her but the wind. But was that really all—the outline of a naked window, the wind laughing in a broken eave? She stood up.

The shadow sprang huge, filling the street, and the laughter filled her, shaking her muscle and bone and very blood. She turned and scampered away like a frightened kitten, her puffball of expensive and politically fatal white ermine fluttering around her, tickling her cheeks with its elegant touch.

He was there, oh yes. Him. He. She could taste his enforced kisses, feel the brutal thrust of him. Her legs did not want to carry her, her feet to find purchase on the frost-bitten cobblestones. She jumped onto the loading platform. God, if only she had a gun. Just a little pistol, nothing much. Then she would stop, she would turn, she would empty it into that dark form. Rape is not sex. Rape is anger about sex.

Any cop: you were walking the street at three in the morning, you must have been looking for it. No, I was looking for the moon in the winter shadows, for the mystery of a single light in a skyscraper window. I wanted to enjoy the long voice of the wind. I wanted to feel the cold on my cheeks, I wanted to feel snug in my beautiful coat, oh God help me, help me now!

Close behind her he grunted, dragging his heavier body up. So much for the shadow, the whiff of the unknown: this was a hard, struggling man.

The Secret Club was along here somewhere. No matter the stature of the party, the entrance remained invisible.

Where are you, Melanie, whom I kissed in my youth? Where are you, friends I have abandoned? Where—

A light flowered behind her: a match. He'd struck a match. Why? There was enough light to see. She turned, and found herself transfixed by the evil blossom.

As soon as she saw the black long coat, the wide black fedora, she knew that this was no ordinary rapist. And this was not an ordinary match. He stood with it between his fingers—a hating, flaring rose of white flame.

As the flame died she got used to the light, and saw a flickering image of his face.

She screamed, the extravagant howl of a woman profoundly shocked. The bright, bulging eyes, the mouth—they were sensual, monstrously eager.

"No," she pleaded, "no!"

The match went *whoomp* and became a torch, tall and flaring, filling the street with the echoes of its flames. She was frozen by it, transfixed. He stood as grave as a bishop, holding his torch high.

"And always, woman, to be burned is thy fate in the consuming world."

What voice was that, like the grumble of leaves in the wind, and touched with the clammy threat of the not-quite-human?

She would have screamed again, but the torch sailed suddenly toward her, tumbling *whoomp*, a bright white arc, *whoomp* and it had a face and it had a name, it was Lucifer, *whoomp*, and she heard him say, "do wop." His voice was low and slow and extraordinarily sinister.

The torch exploded on the cobblestones, and she had to dart out of the way. She fought the urge to give up and face her oppressor with her fingernails.

You will not win the fight, if you stop running you will be raped or worse. This is real, Maria Julien, this is absolutely real.

She turned and clattered away, high-fashion shoes wobbling down the pocked loading dock.

He was now so close she could hear his ticking breath. A glance over her shoulder touched her nose with white blowing fur, and she thought angrily that she must be beautiful in the night. She must be incredibly beautiful.

He was a dark form . . . with that face. A chill pain as if

of a great blow racked her, made her stumble. She had not seen that, no, not a gargoyle, not that wet, spitting—

Since her earliest days she had dreamed in sweat and terror of the stranger behind her, but *his* face was a blur.

She dared not look again, no. It must have been her imagination.

"Where is it, where is it, oh God?" The terror had made her eyes go wet with tears that were now freezing and blurring her vision. She knocked them away, they could not be afforded, not now.

She moaned, listening to the admonitions within: It's not my fault, the rape is not the woman's *fault*!

If this was a rape. Something about it—the fire, the face of the very devil—belonged deeply to her, to the life she was living now. She could well believe that this thing behind her had come out of the hole that leads down.

But that was superstition, was it not? To believe in the devil is to create him. She did *not* believe, of course not. He was only entropy, the falling of the wheat, nothing more. He was not behind her.

Another black metal door, no handle on this one. She tried to remember back a year ago, when she'd last come here. Andy Webb, Laura Walker dead now, wearing silver lamé then, so quiet, so distant, so . . . sunken. "Where's the damn door, Melanie!"

Behind her, clop, clop, the sound of shoes on wood. "Get away from me," she screamed.

Her priests would expect her to pray.

Quite suddenly her hand closed around a familiar knob. The door was the same as ever, big and rusty and completely unmarked. Generally they left it unlocked. Melanie's bouncer, Clam, took care of anybody who didn't belong.

Maria slipped inside, pulled it closed behind her. From the bottom of the stairs there came blue light and the slow drum of music. This was not a rock club, this was not a jazz club. Something far more esoteric happened here. She went downstairs, her heels clicking smartly on the stone steps.

Behind her she heard the door open. So he'd seen her

come in. Damn. "Get Clam," she said as she came up to Melanie, "I'm being followed by a crazy."

Clam came, the former sumo wrestler. He had muscles like hard butter. Evidently the follower saw him too, because there was nobody on the stairs when he went to check.

"Jesus, God, I was nearly killed." The fire still flickered in her eyes. Do wop?

Melanie took her in her arms. The world of the night is not a large one, the people who know about places like the Secret Club are few.

Melanie offered some pills. "Cockroaches," she said.

"Pretty name."

"I don't know what they do."

"I'm in no mood for an adventure. And I don't do drugs anymore." The image of that face floated in the center of her mind. She could not even conceive of what it would look like pharmacologically enchanced. "I want something to drink. I've got to sit down."

"Baby, come over here."

"Hi, Maria," called a man in black silk. "How're your priests?" There was a sneer in his voice.

"Go to hell, Louie," she replied genially.

"I want some Holy Communion. I want to use it in one of my paintings."

"She nearly got raped," Melanie whispered as she gathered huge pillows. People made room for her, then, amid expressions of sympathy.

She sank into the pillows.

"Downer?" asked Leila Griffiths-Gordon.

"No, thanks. Nothing. Maybe a beer. Melanie, do you have any beer?"

Somebody handed her a Bud, half-full. She drank deep. She didn't want to be here, she'd been blown in like a leaf running ahead of the wind. No more did she belong in places like this. She had been drawn by the thickness of memories, holding the invitation with its dark ineffable portrait of Melanie and its scattering of poetry. Once such an invitation, such a party, would have made her damp with pleasure.

Then she heard the laughter.

"What's that?"

"You mean the drums?"

"No. Nothing."

There were so many reasons for her to hate herself, so many failures. But she was a new person now; the aimless, useless life she had lived before was behind her. She'd been too alone, too rich, too self-involved. Now this all seemed made of tinfoil and smoke. In her new world she was needed.

She was calming down a little. It was warm here, there was a lot of sympathy, there was a sense of safety.

She shuddered, exhaled slowly, letting the terror escape through her nose, her pores. She opened her ears to the music.

The drummers had been going since ten. It was now three. She watched their naked, working bodies. Drums at the Edge, they called themselves. There were people who had been dancing for hours, their faces deep. This was not a place of entertainment, but of meditation. Maria got up and twirled, letting her fragile dress spread out from her body. A man came up when she stopped, touched her face.

"You're amazing," he said. He was sheened with sweat, his skin stretched and fragile. His face lift was too taut. His eyes glittered, the pupils tiny from drugs.

"I'm an angel," she said, "let me help you."

"Then kill me."

Once she would have laughed, but now his request stabbed her in the heart: it was very possible that he meant it.

Melanie moved between them. "So glad to see you back," she said. No doubt Melanie was glad; Maria Julien had been a much-desired customer in places like this.

"The official last day is tomorrow, but nobody's coming in," Melanie said. "This is it." There were tears at the edges of her eyes. "Beauty weeps."

"What'll you do?"

"Go to my apartment and shuffle my papers. You'd be amazed how much paper ten years in the club trade generates." She looked around, her eyes flashing anger. "Taxes, mostly."

"You paid taxes?"

"If I had, there wouldn't be a problem."

Maria knew little of such problems. She had been born rich, her parents were both dead, she was alone with her money.

Recently she'd changed a lot of things about herself. There was a sense of life evaporating, of missed chances. She'd seen death, friends gone bald and thin and hundred-and-four fever.

People had tested the edge of love, never dreaming that they were also testing the edge of life. In those steam-hot rooms, amid the squirming others, one never thought of last things.

Human life is always serious. The party lamp might bob gaily, but it bobs in the wind, and the bit of foil on the dirty morning floor tells the truth.

She'd bought uniforms for the school band, set up a scholarship fund, arranged for flowers every Sunday at the church.

The Church: she had adopted a parish, in memory of her father. An image of him, like wax: his deceptively staunch face, his shot cuffs, his reek of cologne. So easy was his life, so soft. His only faith had been the Church, everything else had belonged to booze and South American whores.

Because of him she sought the Church when she sought meaning. He had taken his cancer to the Virgin, had taken money, had taken promises and regrets for his ill-lived life. He had died with a rosary between his fingers.

Her mind drifted to the exotic look of priestly clothes, the white of the alb, the white of the Easter vestments.

She wanted Frank's burly arms around her.

Now the drumming was getting on her nerves. She fought its hypnosis. A guy had once died of a heart attack while dancing here. Perfectly healthy. Cocaine and extreme physical exhaustion had caused his heart to blow up.

It was all hypnosis, and it could capture her, even now. She did not want to be in this stifling little room. She looked to the door, the dark stairs beyond. "Melanie, darling, send me a note when you've got your new place up."

"This is the end."

"Yeah, it is. But you'll have a new place going soon. I give you three weeks."

Melanie's shoulders were stooped, her hair slack. "I wish I was rich," she said.

"I know how you feel."

Her eyes grew hard then. "No you don't!"

Maria looked at her watch. Fifteen minutes she'd been here, standing in the middle of a dancing crowd with a bottle of tepid beer in her hand. She went to Clam. "Look, go up and see if he's gone."

He disappeared into the darkness. She saw the faint light as the outer door opened. He was gone five minutes. The music beat her ears, she watched a couple doing pure white lines, the drums sang.

"Gone."

She looked up, astonished. Clam was staring down at her, his fissured teeth showing. "You're sure?"

"Nobody there."

She flew back up the stairs, stuck her head out into the cracking cold. Had he ever been there? Yes, certainly.

Perhaps.

She was not halfway to the end of the street when she heard laughter. It wasn't loud, it might even have been mistaken for the cackle of an owl. But there was such intelligence in it, such . . . awful wit.

She ran. She did not look back. You can see something that awful only once or twice, then you cannot bear it. Memories of evil are themselves evil. The evil man might penetrate you with a nail and run away, and your wound might heal, but the evil memory will rot in your heart forever.

"Wanna do the strut," he said. His voice was a rich, hard whisper. It carried easily in the quiet.

He could certainly catch her, but he didn't. No, his pleasure was elsewhere. No doubt he would let her run until she fell and then he would come and take her up in his arms, and she would see close the wet bones of his face.

She ran down the empty middle of West Street. Where

are you, New York? Where are your cars, your people, your lighted doorways?

Did she secretly *want* this? No, no, no!

On he came, breathing like a machine. She skipped and skittered along, the damned shoes fighting her every step.

He took a swipe at her, his gloved fingers contacting the blowing fragile fur of her coat. She cried out, trying for a burst of speed, just managing to make it around another corner. Behind her, very soft: "do wop."

And all of a sudden she was in a crowd of men. Leather smells, bourbon and beer and strong tobacco. This was spill-out from the Boondocks, a gay leather bar she'd forgotten even existed. "Help me," she gasped, falling into the arms of the first man she saw.

There was immediate response. Behind the studs, the leather, the glittering silver skulls, there were sometimes surprisingly gentle people. Such men are the kindly ones of the night.

"Okay, sister," he said. She saw a spider tattooed on the back of his hand, saw a death's-head silver belt buckle as she sank into his arms.

"I love your belt buckle," she managed to say.

"It's okay," he said. Others crowded her, protecting her. "He your old man?"

She looked back. He stood just beyond the pool of light that surrounded this much more public club. "I don't know him from shit."

Then the attacker spoke. His voice was clear and young and high with madness. "The perfection of the Inquisition lay in the structure of its judgments," he said.

"Jesus," the men said. They watched him as they might a panther in a zoo. Remaining always just beyond the edge of the light, he began to back away.

She could have rested in this man's arms forever, gazing from the silver skull at his waist, up his enormous leather-bound chest, to that gnarled, hard face and those infinite eyes.

Her attacker left only laughter.

M
ARIA'S CALLING HIM TO THIS LITTLE CAFÉ FAR FROM THEIR
usual haunts made John Rafferty uneasy. She lived
at the edge and she was beautiful. For a priest this
made her two times dangerous. He sat in the last booth, staring
at the wall. He was on his second coffee; when she came he
would have a third, a fourth.

Why did Maria want to come here? The Café DeRobertis
didn't offer the elaborate pastries of the West Village places.
It was strictly hard, hot espresso and cappuccino, and perhaps
a *pignoli* tart if you really wanted one. Maria normally preferred places like the Caffè Reggio or Patisserie Lanciani.

He did not like this dark, private corner. "Go all the way
to the back," she'd said. "Don't watch the door. I'm going to
surprise you."

He was ripe for her and he knew it. At his age he ought
to be surrendered to God, but he was not surrendered. For him
the priesthood was a continual battle. Despite spending all his
life in the Church, serenity had eluded him.

All around him he smelled life, and the smell made him dizzy with regret. It would take no more than the slightest gesture for her to seduce him, and he knew it. Nearly forty years a priest, and he was about to allow himself to fall to a woman, and she less than half his age. But of course, why not? In a priesthood so full of questions, what did one more vow mean?

It meant a great deal. Despite the struggle, he had never broken his vows, never once.

He tucked his left hand under his right arm. He was sweating. She'd notice this, realize that it meant he was vulnerable. She wanted him, and that ought to make him damn mad. But it didn't; on the contrary, he found it touching. She wanted him in a girlish, sentimental way. He understood it, a little bit. He understood women a little bit.

Until he had gotten to know Maria, he had always felt inadequate to counsel them. His one coupling had been as energetic as it was brief, the result of his single successful seduction, a desperate affair in the last week of the last month before he entered the seminary.

Maria had taught him secrets of womanhood through the medium of poetry. "She walks in beauty like the night," "You, Beloved, who are all the gardens I have ever gazed at . . ." "Tell me not here, it needs not saying, what tune the enchantress plays . . ."

She had taught him of womanhood!

Father Samuel Dozier, St. Joseph's Seminary, June 1956: "You will come to the point that you will be willing to cohabitate with any female, I assure you. Your flesh will literally burn. You take your rosary and you pray it, you turn to Her, give Her your total and absolute devotion. She is there for every priest. She sees us through."

"You look like you're on your way to the electric chair," Maria said. She dropped down into the seat opposite. A wave of perfume came with her, that remarkable scent that followed her everywhere. As always, it intoxicated him, drew him into her soft authority.

"Extraordinary," he said. It came out quite unexpectedly. Her face shone as if with the Madonna's own light. Her lips were full and perfect; he found himself grateful even for the mischief in her eyes.

"Call me Mary Magdalen."

"Hush!"

The admonition raised her eyebrows. She could see the waitress coming, he could hear the tattoo of her feet on the tiles. "Father," she announced as the woman approached, "I love you." Then she turned and ordered a double espresso. "They make it right at this one," she said. "We ought to come here more often."

"No."

"No more discretion, John. We're coming out."

This was his vocation she was talking about, and she knew it. He heard the threat in her voice. He sparred with her. "There's nothing to bring out."

"I want to shout it up and down the streets! I want to hear you announce it from the pulpit!"

Maria was an exuberant woman, but also a subtle one. This outburst would have many meanings. Of course it had been designed to make him recoil in horror, to throw him off his stride. She subsided, though. She gave him a steamy look. "Your faith doesn't stand in your way."

"I'm not having a crisis of faith. It's a crisis of belief."

"Hair splitting won't save you. Your crisis is physical. You're getting old, and you've never known a woman. That's your crisis."

"My crisis is that I think the Church is dead wrong about a lot of things, but I still feel like a Catholic inside. That's my crisis."

"Ten thousand men have left the priesthood for that reason. The Church is dead wrong. Wrong about birth control. Somewhat wrong about abortion. Wrong about compulsory celibacy." She took his hand. Now she would make him her lifeguard: she was drowning. She raised her arches of eyebrows, fluttered her long lashes over those steady, cool eyes of hers. "I have to do it with you," she said.

"I can't."

"Just to hold each other while we're naked. It's not too much to ask."

"Far too much." How lovely it sounded. In all his life he had never seen a woman naked and in flower, but he could imagine, he could well imagine.

"Let's sneak off to my country place."

"Your car's not working. Remember, the top won't go up."

"So we'll bundle up."

"It's ten degrees!"

"But if I get the top working, you'll go?"

He could not bear going to her apartment, far less to her country house. He'd never entered either place. He saw Maria at Mass, encountered her in the confessional, counseled her at the rectory . . . and met from time to time in the public venue of the coffee shop.

He believed in his celibacy. He did not see it as a disordered artifact of the neurotic medieval church, but as a vital, living sacrament. He had offered up his manhood, and—as far as he was concerned—the offering was for life.

"I don't think you should tempt me."

Smiling, she dangled her hand before him. "Kiss it."

"No." He sipped his espresso.

"I dare you."

The hand was long and smooth, glowing in the dim light as white as death. She moved it closer to his lips. He could see the tiny serrations in the flesh, smell the soap and perfume. Without knowing he would do it, he inclined his head. His dry lips touched it, touched the skin. She turned her hand and pressed her palm to his lips.

He tasted her at last, just this little bit, and felt such an extraordinary feeling. His heart ached, not with desire or sorrow. On the contrary, there was gratitude.

Then the hand was withdrawn, the fingers brushing his lips as they pulled away. He thrust his head slightly forward, seeking to prolong the contact. "The lips are so sensual," she said.

"I know that. God made them that way."

She closed her eyes, laughed silently. Then she looked directly at him. "Why do you love me, John?"

"Because you're a human being—a most wonderful one."

She tilted her head, regarding him with curiosity. But there was also sadness there, deep and abiding. She spoke softly, almost a whisper. " 'As he paces in cramped circles, over and over, the movement of his powerful soft strides is like a ritual dance around a center in which a mighty will stands paralyzed.' "

Her voice had risen as she recited. The thought flitted through his mind that she would have to die if he was going to preserve his celibacy, and he blinked his eyes.

She laughed aloud. "You look so surprised!"

"Rilke always surprises me."

"*The Panther?* It shouldn't surprise you. 'Only at times the curtain of the pupils lifts, quietly—' " The waitress brought her double espresso. "Now I'm going to shock you, my dear, with two sugars. *Sucre.*" He watched the crisp measure of her movements, like a nurse performing intimate mercies. Suddenly her eyes met his. "I am so beautiful," she said. "You cannot imagine the effect my naked body would have on you."

Instinct caused him to reach out. She looked at his hand, the edge of a smile playing in her face. It was such a complex face, the eyes startlingly wide apart, the lips full but given to subtle expression. In Maria's face the difference between a smile and a look of sadness was not great. Her eyebrows would arch up for the smile, drop a bit when she was disappointed. She could blush, color rushing up her neck and into her cheeks. She was narrow but not thin, and her bones were big. There was in her eye that curious squint that is a mark of extraordinary beauty. Each feature, taken of itself, was only good. But the harmony of her whole face was a stunning thing to behold.

He had come here to accept this temptation, to help this woman find the place in her soul that would respect his celibacy, and thus his priesthood, and thus the Church.

But the temptation was real, and the temptation burned

in him. He had been too canny to wear clericals here, but he'd been wishing for a cassock to hide his excitement ever since the moment she'd sat down.

"You inspire me, you know that."

"To what? Saying the rosary? I consider Mary my rival."

"And a stronger one, too." He did not say, though, that he had quite intentionally left his rosary on his dresser. He realized that he had come here for the purpose of being seduced, and felt his eyes growing wet. If he made love to her, he would do so in an ocean of tears.

"It's so wrong of me to try to seduce you," she said. "But it's such an extraordinary pleasure."

"I suspected that."

"But aren't you sick of talking philosophy? Just sick of it? Making love is such a glad thing."

"Out of wedlock and in vows?"

"But when you do it, you know God intends it. You can feel the divinity of the thing!"

He relaxed. Suddenly she had taken him to safer ground. They had been arguing like this ever since they had met. The battle itself was heady with sensual implications. He would study her face as they talked, imagine his lips upon hers, or tasting the soft line of her neck, or lifting her naked breasts in his humid palms.

"You're red as a beet, John."

"I'm blushing."

"No, you're not, you're mad. I've made you furious!" Her eyes wrinkled shut and she laughed, throwing her head back and knocking it hard against the rear of the booth—which made her laugh the more.

He waited through it, and was surprised to find that she was quite correct. He would have really enjoyed giving her a good belt across her face. There was laughter, there was love, but he sensed that there might also be a part of her that was sneering at him.

Then why did he feel as he did about her? Perhaps because he detected beyond her love and her anger, an even greater good. Every priesthood is a fantastic essay into *hubris*. No man is good enough to keep all the vows, and it is prideful indeed to make God promises that cannot be kept.

So her destructive impulses had their place; she could be fairly certain that he was not the priest he pretended to be. On some level she knew that he deserved destruction.

She was extremely sensitive to his moods, and when she had recovered from her attack of mirth, at once saw that he was feeling suspicious of her. "I know many things, for I walk by night. I know those nameless terrors of which people dare not speak!" She was alluding to his enjoyment of vintage radio. That was from the opening credits of *The Whistler*.

"You don't walk by night. And you don't know any name-less terrors."

"Yes, John, I do." Her tone was so changed that he blinked in surprise. She regarded him coolly. "I really do."

He would have laughed, but her demeanor stopped him.

"You think I'm innocent," she said. "I'm not."

"That I know!" Some of her confessions, he suspected, had been part of the design of her seduction. He could never forget those words, "I touched him, Father, I inflamed him . . ." She never said who "he" was, though. At first he had thought the confessions false, but later he had realized that they were not. The dark man, as John had come to think of him, was quite real.

Once or twice she'd been bruised. "We pray together, late at night. We do it, and afterward we pray . . . and sometimes he gets mad."

Why did she want to corrupt a priest? This was certainly her motive, and it wasn't a pretty one. She was so sweet, though, one of the best people he had ever met. In her own way she was honorable. It wasn't an evil thing she was doing, not by her lights.

"Want to go to the Moon with me?"

"That again?"

"It's a beautiful place."

He had lived most of his life in New York. Although Prohibition was before his time, he thought that even then there probably hadn't been as many secret nightspots in the city as there were now. "It's for drugs."

"I think it's a perfectly wonderful place."

"Psilocybin in the *haricots verts*? I don't think so."

"Oh, John, you poor man. You can't die like this! Your soul will wander the world forever."

"How so?"

"If you die in unrequited love, your soul wanders between the winds."

"Not Catholic doctrine."

"No, it's Sioux, actually. But it's true. You can sense all the priests and nuns of the past wandering between the winds. I certainly can. My theory is, that's why the weather's changing."

A sweaty flush made him shudder. His body was desperate. He could hardly hear her, could hardly talk. "I never know when to take you seriously," he murmured.

She sipped her coffee. Her eyes twinkled. "I think somebody played a rather sinister prank on me last night, my dear." She paused, then continued. "Somebody who knew I was going to the Secret Club." She raised her eyebrows, her face demanding an answer.

At first he started to laugh, but there was too much of an edge to her question. "I went to bed at ten-thirty," he said.

"I was walking along Charles Lane down by the river."

"When?"

"About three A.M." She said it as if it was the most natural time in the world to be alone in that empty place.

"Well, now I'm not surprised. May I ask what happened?"

A flicker went through her face, of some emotion that he could not quite identify. "I can't really say. It *felt* like I was being followed by some kind of creep."

"Probably were."

"I saw him. He looked . . . odd."

"Probably was."

"I mean, *really* odd."

"So, tell."

"It'll sound too weird."

"To a priest nothing sounds weird. I once had a guy tell me that aliens had opened up a hole in his skull and stuffed an old baby shoe into his brain. You top that, I'll give you something."

"A kiss? A long one?"

"I love you," he whispered. There can be sweet pornography in the simplest words. She wrinkled her nose at him. He felt a burst of loyalty; he adored her. "I want to protect you."

"It was probably a hallucination. What do they call that when somebody who hasn't used LSD in years suddenly starts tripping?"

"Flashback."

"Yeah, that was it, my dear love. Flashback."

He seized her words. "My dear love," he said, "I don't know what I'd do without you."

Now there came into her face a look of kindness. Not tenderness, but kindness. He thought: If I don't make love to her, I'm going to perish. And he was scared. He was talking himself into it, he knew.

"You're lots of fun, John." Her manner had become offhand, as if he was expendable. She knew exactly what she was doing. The knot of seduction tightened a little more.

He saw that the situation had changed. No longer was he resisting and she tempting; now they were both seducing him.

There was a step he could take, a thing he could say, that would announce his surrender. How many words? He counted them in his head. Four words. He had to say only four words.

They were: "There are practical considerations."

A slow smile came into her face. Her neck colored, then her cheeks. He thought she presented at this moment the most perfect appearance of human beauty that he had ever seen.

"Let me kiss you on the cheek," he said. She let him do it, and he felt the softness there, and thought that physical beauty was truly the greatest miracle.

How stupid to fall in love with a woman so many years

your junior. When she was ten, he had been forty and already stationed at Mary and Joseph. She'd been skipping down the streets in cutoff jeans when he had been a priest for nearly a quarter of a century.

He closed his eyes, looked down into his empty coffee cup. "I treasure my vow."

"And I respect that tremendously. I do."

He tried to pray, but there was no ability to concentrate. He imagined demons pounding in him, crushing the simplest prayer.

"Let's go to my apartment now," she said.

"That'd be a big step for me."

"John, if you love me, would you leave the priesthood for me?"

"Leave—"

"John, you're in love with me! Don't you understand how precious that is, how little time you have left? You're old, you're staring at death! I wasn't joking when I said it was bad to die with love unrequited. Oh, John, the Church has gotten your whole adulthood. All of it! Reward yourself with the little that's left."

When the decline of the Church got under way in earnest during the seventies, John Rafferty had promised himself that he would never, ever become a statistic. "When I took my vows—"

"You took them for life!" She put her hands over her ears. "I know all that, Johnny. You've told me a thousand times. But I also know that you love me, and you ache for me, and I for you."

"A frumpy old man?"

"Look, you're not the handsomest man I've ever seen. But, John, you have a wonderful mind, a good soul, and a delightful sense of humor. I care a lot more about those things than I do about frequent erections." She covered her lips with her hand, giggled. "I bet I'd come in under a minute with you," she said. He felt his own face blush, this time. They'd never before spoken directly about . . . functional matters. "How about you," she continued, "how long do you think it would take you the first time?" She paused, rested her chin on her palm. "How many strokes?"

This was too much. "I have no idea."

She was not to be put off. "I'd be able to tell, by the degree of hardness. I'll bet you'd get terribly hard."

He thought again to defend himself with prayer, bowed his head.

"No! No, sir! Don't you dare start praying. Don't even think about it! In about one minute I am going to get up and take you by the hand, and we are going to walk together hand in hand all the way over to Waverly Place."

He was horrified. That would be suicide. "We'll give scandal!"

"Yes, we will—to Christos and those creeps. Most of the parish thinks we do it already."

"They honor their pastor!"

"They do indeed. They come to him for the sacraments, they whisper to each other that he is a saint—which I happen to believe is true—and they accept the fact that he has a lover much younger than himself named Maria Julien."

"That isn't—"

"Oh, come on. Reggio, Lanciani, Figaro—we meet in public all the time. I go to your Masses, you hear my confession. I go to the rectory, you take me out to Ennio and Michael's for dinner. Let's face it, the whole parish knows. And it doesn't mind, John! The Italians expect their priests to fool around. And the others—Village Catholics are different. New Rochelle this ain't."

"Except for Christos."

"Frank Bayley does a wonderful job keeping them in check."

That did it, he was convinced. He could become her lover without destroying his pastorate. His mouth had gone so dry that he had to swallow a few times before speaking. He knew what it meant for one's loins to be on fire. "I'm afraid."

She got up, took his hand. "Come on, Johnny. You're going to do just fine."

They walked through cold, golden light, the ancient light of the afternoon, passing down Stuyvesant Place with its memories of a village gone by, the houses of the merchants whose enterprise had built the city, then crossed beneath the facade of Cooper Union, where John often went for music or lectures. They went down Astor Place, passing the big new bookstore that had replaced the old National, where you had been able to get all the Loeb Classics in crisp new editions.

They went down Eighth Street, moving past the welter of shoe stores and leather shops that had come in recent years to clog it, replacing the bookstores and coffeehouses of the old village. Then they cut across an empty, windblown Washington Square, and he began to feel as if the sorrows of the ages were slipping down in the sunlight to rest on his shoulders.

He thought of the cross, the central image of his life: the murdered God to whom one John Rafferty had vowed himself, body and soul.

"The first thing is going to be a long, long kiss," she said. "I'll bet you haven't done that."

"I haven't."

They arrived at her building, a red brick apartment structure about fifty years old. It was elegant, with white trim and a lobby of marble.

She drew him quickly past the doorman, who looked at him with the canine eyes of one who knows.

The world became filled with details, the hiss of the elevator doors, the drumming of its fan, the soft creak of the cables as it rose. He noticed the line of dust in the groove that guided the door, he noticed the beauty of the carpet that filled the hall with deep blue silence.

At her doorway at last she raised her face and opened her mouth a little, and all of a sudden he was kissing her.

The sensations of the mouth to the mouth, the sweetness of her breath, the warm, the wet, and her hand holding his head, gently compelling him to continue.

The kiss, the kiss, the kiss.

2

S HE STOOD LOOKING OUT HER APARTMENT WINDOW, WATCHING as old Father John huddled off toward Seventh Avenue in his black overcoat and hat.

He was full of guilt now. She could imagine how he felt. Her heart suffered for him and with him. How she respected that man! What a noble soul, how lucky God was to have his love. "I will never leave you," she whispered, "I am the candle that is lit to speed you on your precious path." Her breath trembled against the cold glass. After a moment she drew a narrow line through it with a fingernail.

She watched him disappear into a whipping cloud of steam from a Con Ed leak. "Cold, old day," she said. It was nearly three. She picked up the phone, dialed the rectory. "Father Frank," she said when the curate answered, "he's on his way home."

"Intact?"

Now, what should she say? Frank had wanted John to be

drawn into the pit with him. But Frank was also a jealous man, it would drive him nuts.

What fun that would be. "The cherry is pitted, my dear." Oh, how wicked, what made you tell him that? What a wicked thing to do.

"I . . . He . . . I mean . . . he actually—"

She laughed. "It was very special."

"It was? In what way?"

"That's for me to know and you to find out." Oh, you slave driver, you devil, you shouldn't incite like this!

"I'm coming over."

"Oh, Frank, I'm simply exhausted."

"You're actually exhausted? He exhausted you?"

There was something genuinely frantic in his tone, and she felt a twinge of guilt. She shouldn't torment him so. She tried to be quite clinical about her relationships with the priests. But if she looked deeply into herself, searching for motives . . . well, then.

The Church appealed to her because of its inaccessibility and its mystery. The feminized vestments fascinated her. She loved to watch the priests swishing around in their cassocks and their chasubles. The whisper of the cloth, the dull scent of starch, made her curious and fed deep, deep anger.

It was wrong, she was convinced of that. The Church was a trap. It captured people away from the lusts and bodies God had given them to enjoy. The bird has wings and thus is meant to fly. The human being's genitals are the most prominent feature of the body, meaning that God intended man to love. The greatest lovers must therefore be the greatest saints.

She had gone into the catacombs, searched the crypt under the Vatican, gone far off the ordinary tourist paths. She had walked the streets of Nazareth, done the Stations of the Cross in Jerusalem, visited Lourdes and Medjugore and met some of the young people who had visions there.

She was not sure that she believed in the visions, but she certainly believed in the devotion. Her search had taken her far and deep. She knew the secrets of Christian and Muslim worlds alike, had crashed the Hidden Monastery near Rennes la Château in southern France, had risked death by beheading to enter the House of the Men in the deep Sahara.

She had her own ideas about salvation; she had tasted the mysteries of Kundalini and believed in the transformative value of sexual ecstasy. Her beauty brought her anybody she wanted. She had experimented with sexual contact with numerous fabled spiritual leaders. But they had all been easy. The priests were hard, especially Father John. Father John *believed*.

Well, that was quite impressive. Still, though, she did not think that he could continue his spiritual journey if his sexuality remained asleep. It was her duty to awaken him. These thoughts brought to mind an image of herself as the fairy godmother, and she laughed her rich, clattering laugh, the one that so delighted him.

Outside in the hall the elevator door opened. Her rescued priest was on his way down the hall. Even his footsteps were brawny. This man she loved fully, with her whole mind and body.

She was also terrified of Frank Bayley, and that made it all the more thrilling. Her bell rang. She did not go at once to the door. He hated waiting in the hall. He was always afraid that her neighbors would see him. She'd told him that some of them attended Mass at M. and J. It was a lie, of course, but what fun.

He tapped, not too hard. He was trying to be polite; she had instructed him carefully on this. She went to the door, leaned against it. He heard her, of course. In fact, she made certain that he would.

"Come on, Maria."

Finally she pulled the door open and this tall, remarkably handsome man in jeans and windbreaker strode in. "Thanks," he said.

"You've gotta remember who's boss."

"Yeah, right. Look, I have no more than half an hour."

She leaned against him, embraced his hard body. He was

only two years older than she. He could have been her husband. She'd toyed with the idea of letting him make her pregnant, but so far hadn't been able to picture herself as the mother
of an infant. At the present time John and Frank were children
enough.

"You want a quickie?" she asked. She lifted her face and
let him give her one of his delightfully clumsy kisses. A year
they had been doing this and he was still clumsy, still rough.
She felt him tremble against her. He was so big, yet so fragile.
When this man slept, he sometimes cried out in anger. "I never
want a quickie. I love you so much."

"What's next on your agenda?"

He looked at her. They were still in the foyer. "Why?"

"What is it—Mass? Confessions?"

He shook his head. "I leave my priesthood at the door."

There was a lot of priesthood, too. He was a popular and
successful curate. She put her arm around his waist and drew
him into the living room. What did he want today, what demand was to be made of his sacred prostitute? "Feeling kinky?"
She kept an appropriate instrument under her bed, ready to
use on him.

"Please don't start in on that."

She wasn't going to let him off. The most important thing
for this man was that he face his guilt. He was racked with it,
eaten by it, consumed. This fine young man was being eaten
from within as if by worms or acid. "You want me to heal you,
Frankie?"

"Like you healed John?"

She dug her hand down between his legs.

"Oh, God," he whispered. "Oh, God."

"Remember, Frank, when you were lying before the altar,
lying at the feet of your uncle—"

"Shut up!"

"Lying at the feet of Bishop Bayley, dedicating your life
—your *life*, my friend—to the service of the Lord?"

He looked at her in horror.

"Remember, Frank?"

"What in hell's gotten into you? You shut up about that."

She unzipped him, put her fingers in. "Where are we, morally?"

"Nowhere! If you must know, nowhere at all!"

She grasped him naked. "I believe that hell is the discovery that you've missed your life. We have to use the gifts that God gave us."

He leaned his head back against the couch, gave himself to the pleasure of her touch. She never ceased to be amazed at how much this poor man enjoyed the sensation of hands upon his body. Everybody needs to be touched, everybody has a right to it. We think of it as a gift, but it isn't. Somewhere there must be a law that says: Touch thy neighbor.

"Oh, Maria."

"Are you mad at me?"

"Of course not!"

"I mean, about John."

"You did him a favor. Just like you did me. Do. Are doing." He smiled, and the gentleness in the man emerged. "I could never be mad at you."

She continued touching him. Very gently, though, very softly. She imagined that her touch mirrored the softness of his soul.

"Oh, stop," he said, repeating a familiar refrain. It didn't mean *really* stop, she knew that. No indeed, not really. . . .

She laughed a little. "Let's go to the bedroom. I'll give you a lesson."

"A lesson in love?"

She stood up, pulled him to his feet.

She saw a little fear in his eyes, and thought that this was good. To a degree his pleasure depended on these anticipatory moments. He could not fully express his love without there also being some pain to relieve the guilt. The pain wasn't always physical, and it wouldn't be today. But to create the anticipation—that was the art of satisfying him.

"You come on, now," she said sharply. "It's up to the curate to finish what the pastor started."

"Won't you quit reminding me that I'm a priest! Won't you please do that!"

"No." She drew the jersey she was wearing off over her head. He came to her, and he was his sweet, gentle self. She undressed him. "Now look at you," she said. She took him gently between her fingers, squeezed just a bit. "On a scale of one to ten, I'd call this a twelve." He sighed, his own hands coming to her breasts.

They lay for a time touching one another. His eyes were full of mist. "Sad?"

He nodded. "Never leave me."

She stroked him softly, the velvet hot skin, then drew the skin tight at the base of his penis until it stuck straight out in the light, shining and purple. "Men are so naked," she said, "so much more naked than us."

He turned to her then, and she accepted the true fire of his kisses, hungry and intimate. Then, quite suddenly and expertly, he had entered her. She arched her back, delighted by the fullness she felt, and then the sudden bursts of pounding, followed by his kisses, frantic, luscious, and wet. How devoted he was! How he adored her!

Then he went to it full bore, pounding and shuddering and sweating, his eyes wild, his lips slack, and even so he remained a beautiful man to watch. Slowly but steadily the heat rose in her depths, a flower bursting open, a sudden spring day, and then she was weak from the pleasure and she saw it in her mind's eye, the great pounding deep thing inside her, and when she expended herself and lay quiet with him still pounding away, she thought that he smelled sour but he did taste sweet.

With each shuddering rush of him she intoned, "Bless me, Father, for I have sinned."

The instant he was finished he rolled off her. "How dare you!"

"I have a right to absolution. I want it now. Instantly."

"This is outrageous."

"You won't absolve me?"

"Maria, we've thought this out! We've discussed it! There is no sin."

So, he was making progress. Somewhere down this road, Frank Bayley would find his freedom.

"Maria?"

She kissed his chest, his neck, his lips, drove her tongue deep into his mouth. When she finally released him, he sighed. He clung to her. Above all, Frank loved to be kissed. To feel his trembling, to see his pleasure—one thought then of all the other priests who never gained this grace. There was a fantasy in which she was huge, with room for them all, and they all came to her.

"My angelic name is Zophiel. And I'm not a woman at all. My real form is male. I look like a Marine drill instructor." She dangled her hands in front of his face. "My hands are all warty."

He raised his eyebrows. "I don't place Zophiel."

"You don't know enough about our religion. It's all well and good to be able to do the rituals. But you need to know the myths." She opened her arms and drew him to her. Gently, insistently, she pressed his head down, farther down, until he was kissing her there, and she laughed a little in her throat.

The body is such an extraordinary thing, capable of such high sensations. Pleasure, pain, all so beautiful. She dreamed of yellow flowers smacked by the sun, the blossoms dancing in the wind. Sometimes she thought she was the most ancient creature on earth. "I am an angel," she said. "My name is Zophiel, and I am the Herald of Hell."

He kissed her inner thighs, running his tongue along the skin. "You're soft, angel."

"If you looked into my eyes right now, you would see my fire. My terrible fire."

He rose up. Their eyes met, and she was astonished at the shock, the pain she saw. She threw her arms around him. "No, baby," she said, "oh, no, baby."

But nothing she could do would comfort him, not all of her gentleness and all of her wiles.

He turned away from her, he covered his face with his hands. "Get away from me," he said.

She went into the kitchen, angry with him now, and snapped open a Heineken. Her priests, her children. Damned superstitious, guilt-ridden children. She drank deep, and then she cried.

He had the capacity to slink like a cat. She was startled when his finger touched one of her tears. "I want you to pray with me tonight."

That again. Very well, she loved the church when it was dark. She also believed in prayer, knew it was real. She would pray with him.

"I've gotta do a CCD class at seven, then we have a budget review at nine-thirty. Could you come at midnight? Is it too late?"

"Of course it's not too late. I didn't get in this morning until four."

"You're not tired?"

She regarded him. "Maybe I should be."

"You said John exhausted you."

"Well, you gave me back all my energy." She wanted him to be happy with her, but above all to be at ease. He smiled. It was a tight, complex expression that emphasized his teeth, and made her feel lonely and obscurely angry. She ought to stand him up tonight.

Instead she found herself kissing him. "Do your CCD class, do your budget meeting. Then we'll take the journey."

He left, withdrawing like a courtier before a princess. Sometimes she felt like an invader, somebody who had infiltrated the secrets of history. She had this man in her power, and so also the whole church he represented . . . at least, in a way.

He'd been jealous of John, indeed he had. Perhaps that was why she'd told him what she had. Probably was. She went through the living room, adjusted the flowers that stood in the vase in the foyer, then turned on the TV. CNN bored her. For a few minutes she watched an old movie on AMC. Lucille Ball yelled at some actor. They were young and fresh. She looked at her own hands. How did aging work? Was it some kind of monstrous disease that everybody had?

She showered and dressed and called Empire Szechuan on Bleecker, ordered her supper in. "Zophiel," she said, and laughed a little to herself. It sounded like the name of the wind.

There was a Hindu story about God entering the body of a pig and forgetting himself. So what did they do—they killed the pig. What about an angel? Could an angel enter a human body, then forget herself? What would the other angels do . . . kill the pig?

It was full dark when her food arrived, brought by a sullen man who stank of cigarettes. She ate the orange beef steadily, without really tasting it. On a sudden impulse she opened a bottle of Clicquot, drank a couple of swallows from the neck. It made her burp and she put it in the fridge.

She hated to kill time, she was terrible at it. There had to be something to do—make calls, fool with her money, anything. She did not want to go out and score, and pass the time cracked out. She'd done enough of that, more than enough. Look at the consequences: at twenty-eight she had the blood pressure of an aged trapeze artist.

She was trying to escape from a life that was worse than meaningless. The drugs, the hours, the endless sexual changes—it was a rush toward death. People wanted oblivion, and they wanted it forever. That was what all the glitter was about, and the music and the lights.

Finally she threw herself on the couch and turned on the TV in earnest. The picture hadn't even appeared before she was asleep. When she awoke she recalled no dreams. There was just the ordinary sense that she had been gone, and awakening was a return from farther mists.

She put her cashmere coat on over a sweatshirt and jeans, then grabbed her black monogrammed purse. She went down the back elevator to avoid waking old Tommy, who guarded the door and had to unlock the main lift every time the button was pushed from above. She passed through the humming fluorescent silence of the basement hall and out into Waverly

Place. The wind cut into her, the wind billowed the coat and made it snap, and the cold of it made her scream and laugh.

Thin traffic barreled up Sixth Avenue at high speed, the drivers making up for daytime's clogged frustration. She went around the corner on Washington Place, noting the empty lighted loneliness of the McDonald's and the news vendor banging his arms to beat the cold. There was an immense dark on the city this night, as if some great creature had enfolded it in huge cold wings. She bent her head into the teeth of the wind and wished she'd had the sense to put on a nice thick hat.

Then up Greenwich Avenue past the old Elephant and Castle with its memories of omelets and piping hot coffee at four in the morning. She never came here with John, for it had been part of her old life, the place of final repose. She had danced on a table there once, danced slowly, to a brooding Corelli trio of all things. In the days of the gods, she had danced.

She saw the old church ahead of her, the thick penile bell tower, the fat columns, the brooding great windows all dark now. How many voices had been raised there in the day? How many babies had been brought all astonished and how many dead had swept forth from her doors? "What candles may be held to speed them all," she thought, once the wife of a poet, now a poet's widow. Rich poet, rich widow.

Mary and Joseph stood like some sort of sentinel, a doorway into another world, brooding, sweet, dangerous, and as smart as death. She was gray and old and her roof was long and dark. There was a ragged cross high on her tower, and her bells rasped a throaty, rusted call.

She mounted the steps to the portico and brought out her key, and twisted it in the lock. The smell of candles burning and the silence caused her to pause in the doorway. All the lights were out, only candles would light her way.

It was eerie, the waxen faces of the great statues of Mary and Joseph that stood in their side chapels, the huge presence of the cross over the altar.

If ever a silence could be called charged—this was not

silence, it was a silent voice. You could not come here without seeing that there was something about it all that was real. Perhaps it was the distant roar of two thousand years of belief, the weeping of the faithful that made the statues seem alive and the candle fires to be dancing.

She was halfway down the aisle before she realized that there was another person present, and it wasn't Frank.

"John?"

There was no answer. She went forward, not expecting at all whom she found: the vicious leader of the parish fundamentalists, George Nicastro, dean of the Christos chapter.

As she passed him he hissed like a snake, and she caught the gleam of hate in his small dark eye.

The hell with him. The hell with all the woman-haters, the guilt-spreaders. The hell with them all.

"Get out."

She stopped, stunned by the sharp, hateful demand.

"I will not."

"You're a damned whore."

What an amazing creep, look at him in his too-tight suit with the shiny lapels and the clip-on tie. If she had ever known anything that suggested the reality of Satan, it was the Christos movement with its vituperative woman-hating, fear-ridden rituals and its tight, tight control over its adherents.

Satan is different from God. God is forever. Satan's secret is that his survival depends on our belief, which is why he hates us and why he cannot ever leave us. It was people like Nicastro who served that belief. Like cancer, evil is a dependent life form.

She walked down the aisle, determined to stay despite the eyes knifing into her back, feeling a pinch of anger that Frank had not been here to protect her from this madman.

"The Pharisee's place," he said as she knelt in a front pew.

Where was Frank? Had she come too late, too early? No, it was twelve, the right time. He'd seen Nicastro, retreated to the rectory. No, Frank had more courage than that. Frank would have stayed to protect her.

Wouldn't he?

"You must have a key," Nicastro whined.

Still she did not answer, could not. Her mouth had gone quite dry, because of what she was seeing before her. The silent, dried-up old ghost, Father Tom Zimmer, was standing just in the shadows beside the altar, standing and watching.

He'd been struck dumb years ago. Frank said he didn't believe it, they'd even laughed about it. A miracle in reverse —a curse.

She knew that he was staring at her, willing her to obey Nicastro's request. They hated women, they were full of guilt and fear. Why did men fear pleasure? Why not just enjoy yourself, express the gifts that God gave you?

She felt like a missionary from a healed world. Even the drugs, the parties, the empty nights were not worse than the awful state that had entrapped these men.

Nicastro could never be reached; his wife was like him, just as dry and terrible. Tom Zimmer was lost forever in the dark hollow of the priesthood.

"I'm going to stay," she said.

George Nicastro bent his head, enclosed himself in his prayers. When Maria looked up, Father Tom Zimmer had gone, disappearing as silently as he had come.

NIGHT RIDE

H E DANCED. TWIRLING UP AND DOWN THE AISLES, HE DANCED. *Poof*, out went some candles, *poof*, out went some more.

"Who are you?"

Her voice was loud, was sharp, and he smiled, how delighted he was that she was afraid. Let her fear lead her, then she would not escape.

"Eh heh heh heh."

There, that shut her up. Oh, raise your arms, raise them high, and twirl round and round, twirl like the flame dancing round the black wick, the flame of fire.

They confessed from the stake, the witch women did, while the fire tasted them and licked them where their victims had. Oh, the flames and the stake and the night: evil is not evil, good is not good.

Tap.

What's that?

Stop dancing.

She was getting up, tap, tap, and then the crash of the
kneeler going back. A deep, flapping rustle: her coat coming
around her body. Poor dear, she's had enough. "Do wop."

"Oh, God!"

Sing to me, O my love, sing to me of vows eternal. The
flame in his heart rose high, fire of truth and retribution, and
by its light he saw her groping along the center aisle.

He listened to her breathing, saw the ancient beauty of her
profile, the tilt of her nose, and the perfect line of her eyebrow,
and saw the eyes flickering helplessly in the darkness. Her
hands were out before her, fists, and she was making choked,
stifled sounds of fear through distended nostrils.

"Pattycake pattycake, baker's man, bake me a cake as quick
as ya can!"

He took the great gilt sun from the side table where it
stood, and went smartly down the aisle, passing the Marian
altar with its staring plaster virgin, holding the monstrance
out before him and in it the consecrated flesh of Our Lord. O
God, since when have you been used as a murder weapon?

Oh, so sad, though: "In the south the Inquisition against
witchcraft was incidental to the pogrom enacted against the
Jews. But in the north the Holy Office turned its attention to
this ancient faith, and burned to death most of its practitioners.
These were generally backward people living in the forests,
selling cures and herbs to make a scratch living. They would
be dragged into the towns and burned in screaming agony, and
their medical business given over to barbers with encrusted
scalpels and filthy bleeding pans."

"Who are you?"

He came closer but she did not see. Her eyes were opened
wide, she was batting the air before her, she was crying a little.
They carried them to the stake in carts, for nobody could walk
the distance to that terrible death. They had all seen it, they
all knew the absolute agony and the absolute humiliation of
it, the rendering of sweet flesh to a raw and crusted cinder.
They invoked their gods, the forest people did, and died as
witches.

Thus!

He popped up three feet in front of her, his eyes bulging, his face twisted into the biggest, brightest smile he could create.

Her scream was sharp and high and loud. He raised the monstrance, and she cringed away, she started to protect herself with a forearm, to stumble.

"Don't hurt me!"

"I hafta!"

So scared, striving for her life: "No, no, no!"

"I have a right."

Stunned silence, she must have heard the truth in his voice. He did indeed have a right. She should kneel, she should bare her neck to him. But she did not kneel, instead she denied him his right and struggled, fighting his iron hand, fighting the iron pressure of fingers that could crush bone.

She shrieked, her voice pealing, going high and frantic. She flopped like a fish on a line, her feet tapping the floor, her shoulders shaking, her head bob-bob-bobbing.

She was extraordinarily frightened of death, this one.

Delightful.

"All right," he said affably, "I'm going to go ahead and kill you now."

He hefted the monstrance and let her go. There was a surprised gasp, then she took off down the aisle. Oh, yes, off she went! He moved with the sweet air about his face, speeding in the dark, and when she reached what she thought was a safe distance and stopped to gasp for breath, he said, "Hi there."

She would have run again, back and forth in the enclosing walls, until she dropped. Such is the life force in youth, such is the force of beauty. Sigh, so pretty. Sigh.

He swung the monstrance. "Oh, no," almost a whisper and the cringing—

Pock: the sound of the skull caving in. A rush of babble: "Obalmah!" Voice deranged by the destruction of the brain. What did she think she was saying? Then she flew backward, her arms windmilling, and hit the floor with a wet thud.

Gone, no movement, the soul escaping through the hole in the forehead.

He wiped the base of the monstrance clean and returned it to its place of honor. One by one, he lovingly relit the candles.

At the last he painted her with gasoline, splashing it over the still body. Then he lit another fire, and held it high. He could smell the fumes all around him, and when he dropped the light she would burst into flame. It was time for the woman, the church, and the whole damn madness to be burnt. "She shall be consigned to the flames. He is consigned to the fire. He shall be burnt in the fire. At the stake. Take him, and bind him upon the stake, and burn him with faggots while he be yet alive."

Yet dead . . .

Then, in the sacred moment before the match dropped from his fingers, he was given a vision. He saw what he could do, what destruction he could wreak. How extraordinary it was, how very beautiful.

He put out his light, and stood a moment more, head bowed. He was breathless from the grandeur of what he had understood. What a vengeance he could do here! Calculated with precision, it would echo in all the world. Oh, dear Church, how I will hurt you!

How I will hurt you, old friend.

"Ad altare Dei," he whispered. "The church is burning." Then he said, "In nomine Domine." He folded his wings and bowed his long head, and went swiftly away. Behind him he left the dead and her smells, and the immaculate darkness.

3

A T SIX IN THE MORNING JOHN RAFFERTY'S EYES POPPED open. He hadn't needed an alarm clock in years. His life, his priesthood, drew him awake at once. He pushed a shuddering, guilty dream of Maria into the dark of his mind and rose from the bed.

He was in deep crisis, but he was no burned-out priest. For him prayer was real, the sacraments worked, a living and immensely sacred being known as Christ actually entered the bread when a priest performed the act of consecration.

Communion was a form of food, offering mystical union between man and God. John consecrated the host at least once every day, and was always astonished, and took it into his body every day, and each time felt like a little boy grasping an awesome hand.

He lived a life of miracles; he was always in awe. There was a difference for him, though, between the faith he practiced and the Church he served. He disliked and distrusted his cardinal, and thought the pope a disaster of historic proportions. Between them they had almost emptied the churches, at least in the Archdiocese of New York.

The cardinal preached that God was primarily male. John believed that God was a mystery. The cardinal used God as a means of controlling others; John strove to submit to the control of God.

But he was also a man of ritual and habit. He loved the sense of permanence they brought. For this reason he always followed the same morning routine. He got up, went downstairs in his old red robe and lamb's wool slippers, and plugged in the percolator. Then, while the coffee brewed itself, he did his breviary and dressed. As usual it was a cassock, which he preferred to the collar and suit. The idea of not wearing clericals at all during a workday was foreign to him. After he was dressed, he prayed, saying his rosary until the rattle of the percolator stopped.

This morning it completed its cycle at about the same time as always. It was six twenty-eight.

He sat at the kitchen table drinking coffee from one of the thick old mugs that had come with the rectory. Sometimes before he poured his coffee he went to the corner and bought a paper, but not this morning. Unless there was some tremendous news that needed prayer, or a notable Mets victory, he preferred the silence of early morning. As he sipped from his mug, he deliberately directed his thoughts away from the thousand problems to which he would later apply himself.

At six fifty-five he drained the mug, stood up, and went to the kitchen door.

He went up the sidewalk, turned the corner, and mounted the steps to the portico of the church. He loved the elegant, imposing facade with its white columns and big black doors. Mary and Joseph dated from 1845, one of the oldest Catholic churches in America. The only older Catholic church in Greenwich Village was St. Joseph's, over on Sixth Avenue.

He unlocked the doors, as he had done every morning at seven since a fast-food restaurant had replaced that fascinating old vintage record store on Morton Street. Before that they had left the church open day and night, but the fast-food place had brought with it a different kind of crowd. When he had started finding crack vials in the sanctuary, he had reluctantly had locks installed.

The precinct boys said the next steps were vandalism, theft, arson. "They ain't human, Father."

A church ought to be a kind of friend made of stone and mortar, offering shelter and the presence of God. Churches were vital: they were places where blessings were common in a world where blessings are rare.

The open doors were more to him than a symbol of the open arms of the God he believed in so deeply. In some cases they could be a necessity. Well he remembered a pudgy form huddled in a back pew a long time ago. He had just been ordained; it was long before he was assigned here as pastor. It was early morning, and dawn was filtering in the Marian window. He had heard a thin echo of sobbing, and had gone to the figure, placed his hand on the bent shoulder.

Then the poet Dylan Thomas had looked up at him, his face horrible with sweat and fear. He had shrunk away like a rat caught in the breadbox, shrunk away hissing, and left in a shuffle, the great door booming behind him.

The sins of my youth and my frailties remember not; in your kindness remember me, because of your goodness, O Lord.

Now he took the brass Medeco key from his deep cassock pocket and unlocked the doors. There was a little flourish of ceremony to it.

He peered into the dark nave and the small red eyes of candles. Morning light swept down the aisle, illuminating the bare altar and the wavy floor of ancient oak, and a bundle of black cloth on the floor. It was exactly seven o'clock.

Still tasting the morning's solid coffee in his mouth, John thought at first that somebody had left an overcoat behind. People leave all sorts of things in churches: wallets, coats, you name it. He'd once found a hairpiece, another time a very frightened kitten in a box with a note on it: "Good-bye, Fluffy." In 1972 Father Tom Zimmer had found a baby boy.

He saw there was a body, and thought then that he had discovered a homeless person who had defeated his nightly search and made camp in the aisle.

Dimly he was aware of a smell of gasoline, but the implication of danger didn't penetrate to full consciousness, because he had realized that he was looking at a dead woman.

He rushed to her, knelt beside her. "Lord God," he said. He pawed at her shoulder, attempting to turn her, to make the crosses of the Last Rite upon her. "I absolve you," he said, and was stabbed by sorrow that this had happened, and in God's house.

Finally his efforts shifted her weight and she rolled over. Her glaring eyes said she had suffered, and the awful damage to her forehead that she had been clubbed.

The damage and the blank inertia made the corpse horrible rather than pitiful, until he recognized the face. He threw his hands back as if her body was burning hot. His fingers reached toward her forehead, touching the horrible welts, the sharp edges of bone.

His mind tried to form a question, couldn't. Surprise rendered him empty of thought and captured his voice, reducing it to a trembling sigh, the sound of pain so intense that it was beyond outcry.

He stared. There were those perfect lips, lips he had kissed, now delicately parted, as if she had just scented a flower. "What candle may be held to speed them all," he whispered, looking in wonder at the deadness in the face. Her favorite line, and from Hilda Doolittle, her favorite poet, "But we know there is a mystery greater than beauty, and that is death."

One hand lay at her throat, holding the collar button of her coat with a gesture so delicate that it must refer to the infinite. How could such beauty be lost, how could it die?

Coming up from deep, deep inside him he sensed, then actually saw the great black wave of sadness. Her kiss! Her kiss had been sweet, the only sweet kiss he had ever known! He bent double, jammed in the belly by the shock. He felt himself falling, grabbed the edge of a pew.

Steady, there. Steady.

Details riveted him: the narrow golden chain come out from under her overcoat, the blue contusions radiating down into her eyebrows, the "MJ" embossed on her familiar purse. He heard the little noises he was making, was further terrified by his inability to form words. His mind sought back to better days, grasping for a life that had very certainly and very suddenly ended.

Christmases in the rectory, carols—she and the Communiellos and Father Frank and old Fluffy in Frank's lap, and Father Zimmer seeming to be aware of it all, and John so damn happy, as happy, he thought, as a human creature could be.

The cords of anguish whipped round his chest and tightened. He drew his fists to his temples and willed with all the power in him that this not be so.

Such a look in her poor eyes!

He raised his eyes to the altar where he had said so many thousand Masses, finally to the pulpit from which he explained the tactics of faith to his good parish souls.

Then he hurried from the church, forgetting to genuflect, forgetting to bless the poor ruin on the floor, forgetting everything.

He burst out into Seventh Avenue just as Mrs. McReady was coming in with her little Tiffany. They were on a novena, weren't they, cancer in the family?

"No," he said, "darlings . . ."

"Father?"

"Not now—no—"

She tried to go around him. "But you opened—"

It was *her* cancer, he remembered, of breast and lymph and bone, and she took her fear and suffering to the Virgin every morning. Now, like a barrier of ugly wire, the fact of the murder lay between her and her devotion.

"Our Lady won't mind—the church must stay closed today."

"I mind."

Helpless to argue or explain, he abandoned her, ran to the

corner and down the sidewalk to the rectory with its grim, wire-sealed windows. He rushed into the front hall, passing under the dim chandelier, and took the stairs two at a time.

"Frank," he shouted. Was that frail, quavering old voice truly his? "Frank!"

The curate appeared at the top of the stairs in boxer shorts and T-shirt. He was a powerful man, his shoulders huge and gleaming, his dark hair tangled with curls. A gentle nature, lots of good old-fashioned Irish sentimentality. "John?" Uneasy. Aware of a problem, just becoming concerned.

The thing that reassured you about this young man was his expression, so gentle, so determined. Yes, John had thought when they were first introduced, it's the face of a priest.

Old Zimmer, who had not yet suffered his misfortune, had approved too. "A good kid," the ancient priest had said. "He'll go far."

"Maria is dead in the nave," John said, and his heart went like a battering moth.

As if the announcement was a shot, Frank pitched back into the bathroom. John ran past, seeing the man capering within, drawing on his jeans, shaving foam still clinging to his cheeks. For an instant their eyes met, and John was shocked by the grief in that face.

John wondered what he should do about Zimmer. Would he care? Sometimes he seemed full of energy and awareness. Other times he was so passive that he appeared catatonic. Sixty years a man of God, John's theory was that he had become a living, breathing prayer. Once last year he had pulled the leg off a chair. Nobody had ever known why.

Father Zimmer wouldn't emerge from his room until eight. Let him find out then.

John went to the hall phone, thought at first to call directly to Captain Malcom at the Sixth Precinct, forgot the number and dialed 911 instead. "This is Father Jonathan Rafferty at Mary and Joseph Catholic Church. One of our parishioners has been murdered in the nave."

Behind him Frank cried out, his rough young voice high

with shock. He rushed up, half-dressed, grabbing John by the shoulder. "Murdered?"

John nodded, listening to the dispatcher at the same time. He felt as if a dirty film was clinging to him, like Maria's murder was a kind of contaminant.

"Address?"

How strange that a New Yorker wouldn't know that. "Mary and Joseph. Seventh Avenue and Morton Street."

"Number address?"

"God knows, it's just here!"

If they weren't opening the front, the priests entered and left the church by a door that led from the downstairs hall into the sacristy. From behind this door there came high threads of sound. John knew at once that the McReadys had gone in. "The little girl is seeing," he said.

"What?" came the voice on the phone, sharper now.

"I . . . The church is open—people are going in—I have to close it."

"Do that, but stay outta there."

"Why on earth—"

"The perp might still be inside."

Those words were fired into John's depth. He saw himself in an ancient fantasy from his youth, the priest in the burning church racing for the tabernacle to rescue the Blessed Sacrament within. The warning, the fantasy, combined to make his heart thunder.

It was then that he remembered the odor of the gasoline. "Don't go in the church," he told Frank as they both headed downstairs.

"No?"

"They think the murderer might still be inside. And I smelled . . . There's gasoline."

"Gasoline?"

"It stinks in there. The church is full of it."

"We've got to get them out of there!"

"Them?"

"The McReadys!"

As fast as he could John ran for the front entrance. He went up the wide steps, past the columns, pausing at the door. "Mrs. McReady!"

There was no reply. Silence fell. He was aware of one of those curious hushes that sometimes touch the city, as if some great passage has brushed every heart.

Frank, who had not been afraid to use the sacristy door, came out cradling the McReadys in his arms. Far from feeling jealous of the younger man's greater courage, John felt a glow of appreciation spreading within himself. Frank was much more than an ordinary priest. Look at him, tears pouring down his face, his whole body shaking with the anguish he felt— and still he was helping the McReadys.

John had realized that this would hit Frank hard, even though he was not close to Maria Julien. He was painfully sensitive. He couldn't run the AIDS group, and he could only take so much work with the homeless. But he was wonderful with the young.

He was sufficiently accepting and good-humored to act as counselor to the parish Christos group, a charismatic organization so extreme that John wouldn't tolerate it on church property. John couldn't stand them, and he was glad that Frank could, because they were strongly endorsed by the archdiocese and, of course, by Rome.

He pushed the door closed on the pews, the distant altar, and on Maria, then turned to his curate, who was now standing with his shoulders bent, his fists clenched against his temples, in an ancient posture of anguish. "God has her now," John said, "she's beyond suffering."

Frank looked at him out of red, devastated eyes. "I should . . . You—"

"I loved her like a daughter."

They threw their arms around one another.

The police came abruptly, in the form of three radio cars and a brown detective special with a portable red flasher stuck to the edge of the roof.

The men and women who emerged from the cars looked

more like a crowd of young technicians than police officers, and they set about their work with precision. First they unrolled yellow tape across the door of Mary and Joseph. Then two of them "controlled" the little knot of seven-thirty Mass regulars who had been gathering in the portico. The rest of the uniformed officers entered with guns drawn.

Faces looked to the priests. John's grief paralyzed him. He didn't want to deal with this. He wanted to go deep into his church and bow his head before God.

With a choked sound that might have been a cry, Frank suddenly rushed back into the church. He broke through the yellow police line, his feet pounding off into the dim nave.

"Frank!" The poor man was losing control. "Frank, stop!"

John started to run after, but a hand came onto his arm. "We need to talk to you, Father." This was a woman in a blue dress with small white hearts on it. She wore an open raincoat and had on a plastic rain scarf.

"Yes?"

Frank reappeared, and John saw that he hadn't lost control at all. His gray face was streaming tears, but he came out carrying a pyx with the Eucharist inside. He went under the tape again and down the steps, stopping in front of the parishioners. "We'll have Mass in the parlor," he said in a choking voice. Then he strode off toward the rectory, followed by a straggling line of people.

It should have been John Rafferty, of course, to take things in hand, but he couldn't begin to shake himself out of the hypnosis he'd entered the moment he saw Maria. How could that shabby little bundle in there possibly be Maria?

"I'm Detective Pearson," the woman was saying. "This is my partner, Sam Dowd." The man was narrow, his face all angles and edges. His eyes sparkled. John thought he might enjoy knowing a man with a face like that. Detective Pearson was beautiful in the most classic black Irish way: dark hair, an oval face, complexion like cream. Her eyes were quite shocking, so hard they seemed like jewels of some sort. They did not have the sheen of life.

The two detectives were asking him questions: When did you open the door, where did you stand when you saw her, were the lights inside on or off? Their voices were subdued by the looming closeness of the church.

John answered as best he could, watching as the last of the faithful disappeared into the rectory door. "The grace and peace of God our Father and the Lord Jesus Christ be with you . . ." he murmured to their backs. He envied Frank the celebration of that Mass, the strengthening food of that communion. Lord, forgive me and give me strength.

"Father?"

"Sorry!"

Detective Pearson reached up and touched his face, an impertinent, good-hearted gesture. "She was close?" When her fingers came away they were wet with tears.

"A parish is a family." Pearson gave him a quizzical look. "I'm her confessor. I consider myself her friend."

"So you'd know about her. But can you tell us?"

Obviously she made reference to the secrets of the confessional. "Are you Catholic?"

"Fallen away. Lapsed." She gave him a naughty, girlish glance. "Totally collapsed."

"Her confessional secrets wouldn't help you anyway."

"But there are some?"

"Well, of course." She had whispered, "I love you, you dear old man. You don't know what I am . . . how it feels." The stuffy confessional, the way she breathed the words, so that he could smell them. . . .

The lady detective was writing on a pad. Fallen away, one among the millions. During his lifetime he had seen the Church dwindle as in autumn. The garden now was bare and cold. Between him and the lovely young detective there was an ocean of failure, the black satanic water of the material world.

Why didn't she speak? Why not? What was she writing? No doubt he appeared confused. He was. Was she giving him time to collect himself? Kindnesses that acknowledged his age always made him uneasy. He tried to explain himself. "It's a

shock, you know." That voice again, so thin and fragile—could
it be his? Dried leaves.

"This is a hard neighborhood, Father."

"It's a complex neighborhood. Probably the most complex
neighborhood in the world."

"It's rough."

"More churches than any other neighborhood in New
York. More universities, more bookstores."

"Yeah. Look, do you know of anything she might have
been involved in—cult stuff, like?"

"No," he said in a dull voice.

The thin Mr. Dowd spoke. "So she was a good Catholic
girl—straight-arrow?"

How should John answer? Tell the truth. It seemed the
only sensible thing to do. "She was not. She'd recently returned to the Church after what I believe was a life of consid-
erable dissipation."

A wave of traffic blasted past. He motioned with his head
toward the dark entrance to the church. They followed him
under the crime-scene tape into the rear of the nave. Dowd
took a copy of the Sunday bulletin from the rack, peered at it.

"You're the pastor, the other guy is Frank Bayley. Who's
this emeritus, Father Thomas Zimmer?"

"Tom's retired. He's past seventy but he runs every day
and he's in excellent health. His only problem is, he's lost the
power to communicate. He can't speak. He can't even write a
message."

"A young guy, an old guy, and a stroke victim. That's all
you got for a big place like this?"

John snorted. "Tom's not a stroke victim. Nobody knows
what's wrong with him. But he obviously can't function as a
priest. He gave this parish the best he had, though, and here
he stays as long as we can give him the care he needs. As far
as Frank is concerned, I'm lucky to have him as my curate.
Frank Bayley is probably the best young priest I've ever had
the privilege to know. A truly wonderful young man."

"If you say so."

Kitty Pearson stared down the aisle toward the corpse, which lay in a pool of artificial light, surrounded by floods on spidery legs. A heavyset man was vacuuming the area around it with a small machine while others painted dust on the pews and worried plastic gloves onto Maria's stiff hands.

"For about a year she was the last wife of a poet, Kenneth Glenn. Ken was a parishioner. Do you know his work?"

Dowd shook his head. "A rose is a rose is a rose: Shakespeare. That's all the poetry I know."

Kitty Pearson announced that she wanted a cigarette.

"Not in here," John responded gently. " 'The black bricks of night/ the skin of rose-white/ damned by love's prison chant . . .' "

"She went by Glenn?"

"Maria Julien. Maiden name. I think he went through five wives before his overdose. She married him three years ago, apparently as a sort of lark."

Kitty's eyes questioned him. "Why marry him?"

"She was rich, she liked adventures. Being the wife of a dying poet apparently qualified."

"He was an addict?"

"He was."

"You know many addicts?"

"I founded our detox program before you were a mote in God's eye, my girl. This is Greenwich Village."

Dowd smiled, a softness there that suggested much to Father Rafferty. "Tell us about it," the detective suggested. John wanted to reassure him, to say to him that it was all right for him to express his gentler side.

Dowd, annoyance flashing in his face, repeated his question in a louder voice. "Tell us about drugs in the parish, Father."

"Drugs used to be an exotic sin. Now they're ordinary." He felt the familiar helplessness that made his chest ache with frustration. He wanted to slap these bland police faces, wake them up to his world as it was. He didn't see crime in drugs, he saw need.

"How can you keep a church going in a place like the Village?"

"Are you kidding? I do three jammed Masses every Sunday, and I could lay on two more if I had another priest. Mary and Joseph is very much alive."

Very deliberately Dowd kicked an expended amyl-nitrite container down the steps.

"They use the portico at night," John said dryly. "One of the reasons we lock the doors."

"So go on, Father, tell us the whole story. Is this lady the victim of some kind of drug hit?"

"Certainly not."

"Did she have any enemies?"

"The other four wives probably didn't like her a whole lot. Plus she was part of the club scene. Or rather, she had been. Maybe she had some enemies there, although I doubt it. Maria was . . . How can I describe her?" It started hurting again, hurting bad. How could he tell them of her intelligence, her wit, her attempts to seduce him? "She was a good young woman," he said at last. "My guess is that she somehow got in to pray, and lost her life to a mugger."

"Tell me, Father," Dowd said. "This woman is a fifth wife. Yet she's obviously an active Catholic. How does that add up?"

"Because he was divorced without an annulment, her marriage to Ken was never recognized by the Church. Once she left him and received absolution for cohabiting out of wedlock, everything was copacetic—at least that was my opinion."

"Copacetic," Kitty Pearson repeated. "That's a blast from the past."

A thin man straightened up from the corpse and came down the aisle. His loafers clicked on the floor. "I got it," he said as he approached.

"What's the story, doc?" Dowd asked.

"No sex, no robbery. Purse's still there, unopened."

"What did her?"

"A single blow, as far as I can tell. Caved in the skull. Penetrated the brain."

"Weapon?"

"You're looking for an instrument that has a lot of heft and a wide, disk-shaped base."

Kitty Pearson went quite red. "That really fucking narrows it down." She had a temper, John could see that. He waited, expecting an explosion. But she controlled herself. "Time of death?"

"Four to eight hours prior."

She thought a moment. "That puts the murder between midnight and four this morning."

Dowd regarded John. The sparkle was gone from his eyes. "So you close the doors when?"

"We do afternoon Mass at five-forty-five, then close up."

"She wasn't here?"

"No."

"And you're sure you locked the place completely?"

"It was locked this morning."

Kitty cleared her throat, drew her red porcelain fingernails down her cheek, leaving faint marks in the pale skin. Suddenly John saw that she was not simply temperamental. This woman was deeply, permanently, and profoundly angry. He wished that he could somehow convince her to pray. Lapsed Catholics distressed him. "Father, this lady couldn't have gotten in here without a key."

"She had a key."

"Prayer?" Kitty asked.

"Yes. For prayer."

"So you give out keys?"

"A few."

"To who, the parish saints?"

"She made a special request. She needed to pray."

"Why did she need to pray?"

"I don't know." He was ashamed of himself. But he was about two sentences away from admitting how close they were, and he did not intend to do that.

They were getting Maria onto a stretcher. When they lifted the body, the arms and legs didn't move. He hated the thought that they would break her at the funeral home if the family wanted a viewing.

They would probably bury her from here and expect him to officiate. That was going to be a hell of a rough funeral for him.

For each of us, comes the pale moment.

PROCEDURE

D OWD SAT WITH HIS KNEE AGAINST THE DASHBOARD, STARING at the parish bulletin. "Big operation for just two guys to run."

Kitty lit another cigarette. "Yeah." She didn't want to talk about the parish or the priests. They were only incidental to the solution of this murder. The fact that it had happened in the church was almost certainly an unlucky accident.

Sensing her disinterest, he folded the bulletin and stuffed it in his pocket. "I didn't know you were raised Catholic."

"Yeah. Communion, confirmation, the whole nine yards."

"I think I was raised in a religion. I mean, I remember seeing the inside of a church once in a while, so we musta had one. An occasional religion, I guess."

Kitty didn't want to talk about the burnt-out ends of childhood faith. "How are we gonna solve this crime, Mr. Dowd?"

"Go through the routine till something turns up. Unless you got a better idea."

Now that she'd opened the conversation, Kitty found that

she didn't want to talk about the crime either. In fact, she didn't want to talk much at all. The sight of the body had hit her hard. This was a woman her own age, maybe from a middle-class background a lot like hers. Most of the deaths you encounter in the Job have to do with the aged, the exposed, or the evil. A murder like this didn't happen every day, not even now, not even here. "Did you see her face?"

"No, I shielded myself from that appalling sight—except for the hole in her forehead and the look in her goddamn eyes."

Kitty watched the smoke from her cigarette curl slowly up. "And the smell of the gas. You couldn't miss that."

"No. Like he was gonna set her on fire and got disturbed."

"Not at that hour, he didn't."

"So why didn't he burn her?"

"Because we don't know the answer to that question, we don't understand this case. Let's not forget that."

Dowd shifted, began paging through his notes. He took notes, always. They had a lot of open cases. Everybody had a lot of open cases. He never quit, though. Deep inside Sam Dowd there was a sense of outraged justice. He just couldn't leave a crime alone, no matter how much official apathy he encountered, how many lying witnesses, how much defeat.

She felt his eyes on her. "I knew this was gonna get to you," he said. "Soon's I saw her."

"She was so damn scared." The clay features had been marked by terror, the dead eyes glaring, the lips parted in that complex expression that so often touches the faces of the murdered.

"Shit, I wish you wouldn't smoke in the car."

"Addictive personality. Runs in the family."

He cleared his throat. "Okay, what we got? This is a crime of passion. Nothing stolen, her purse is beside the body."

"Maybe the M.E.'ll give us something," Kitty said. But she knew that the M.E. wouldn't call, not unless there was some amazing discovery like poison in the tissues or something completely crazy like that. But there wouldn't be. The head wound would be the only insult. "This is gonna be a shitty case, Dowd.

Lots of press 'cause it's a church. No goddamn suspects. Gonna be like that damn boutique over on West Fourth last year. Random crime. Zero evidence, and working it'll prove worthless. We're gonna lose."

Dowd sighed. "You're always so depressing. Look, lady, you and me happen to have a very damn good record. We top the division, and don't forget it."

"I'm not a competitor by nature."

"No, I guess not. A thirty-three-year-old lady who's had her gold shield for three years already and is one of the hottest homicide dicks going. Not competitive, no ambition. Just serving your time."

"Well, maybe not quite."

Again he paged through his notes. "Maybe forensics'll turn up something useful."

"Somebody walked up to her and brained her. Period. There probably wasn't even any physical contact."

Dowd looked at her. "When I was a kid, I sold encyclopedias door to door. Made a fairly decent buck, too. If I hit a hundred houses a week, I'd sell three. I mean, somebody was gonna like all the color pictures the sucker had. It's just a matter of working the routine. If there's an answer, we'll find it."

He told the encyclopedia-salesman story at least once a week. *The Collegiate American Encyclopedia.* "The winner is the guy who doesn't quit": Sam Dowd.

"You still got any?"

"What?"

"Encyclopedias. Every time you bring that moronic thing up, you sell me a little bit more. Got nine million words, covers everything from aardvark to zilch. Now I find out it's full of color pictures. So that does it, I just love color pictures of Grand Coulee Dam and the interior of Woodrow Wilson's summer home. You gotta get me one, Sam. I'm sold."

He shook his head. "It's cold in here, lady. What say we go back to the office and do a prelim? Chief's gonna want some kinda shit to feed the press."

She looked up at the church. "I haven't been in one of

those things since I was about fourteen," she said. "I was very pious. Then all of a sudden, I wasn't."

"What happened?"

"I had an unbelievable knock-down, drag-out fight with my mother about Vincible Ignorance. We came to blows. Like a couple of cats! Jesus, we fought. To punish her, I never set foot in a church again."

"What the hell is Vincible Ignorance?"

"Damned if I know."

Sam started the car, pulled into traffic. Kitty leaned back, wishing she had a cup of white coffee to go with her cigarette. Today had not begun well at all. Would it get worse? That wasn't really the question, not the true question. The true question was, how much worse?

F RANK BAYLEY DESCENDED INTO A SAD AND SECRET HELL. HIS
heart was broken, but he dared not appear more than
professionally grieved. He'd sinned with Maria, violated
his vows, ground them into the dust. Then he had stood before
the faithful members of the parish and the Christos community
and pretended.

The great stone of grief that burdened his heart had much
to do with broken vows, and much also to do with the fact
that his beloved was dead. She was dead! How was this possible? And in the church, right in the middle of the church!

He'd done morning Mass in the rectory, done the curate's
Mass at noon, then worked with his Spotlight on Faith group,
then done his Confraternity of Christian Doctrine class in the
evening—all as usual.

Now it was late and he was sweating and could not sleep.
Fear followed sorrow, wave after wave, again and again. They
would fingerprint her apartment, find out that he'd been there.

His eyes popped open. He wanted a drink. No, he wanted

something stronger, some kind of oblivion. Valium. Something stronger. He could call the doctor in the morning, get a prescription. "I can't sleep, doc, not with this terrible tragedy . . ."

After midnight he heard laughter, and it was a savage sound. It came sailing down Seventh Avenue, echoing off the buildings, penetrating his cozy little room, dragging him back from a fitful sleep. Only human beings laugh, and that was what was so disturbing.

As ugly as it was, the laughter brought sad memories. Laughter had been the lubricant that put him at his ease with Maria. "Come on, Frank, don't be afraid, I'm only a woman." She had slithered in the sheets, her skin hissing against the pale cotton. "Come on over here," she had said with laughter in her throat, "and let me undress you."

She had said, "I don't *believe* in celibacy. It's my sacred mission to make you whole."

She had said, "You're so damn beautiful, Frank Bayley."

She had said, "Oh, break me, break me in half, you big beautiful guy!"

Oh, break me.

He sat up, then went to his window. Yellow sheets of rain drifted through the streetlights. A squad car hissed down Morton, its occupants no doubt heading for a coffee break at one of the all-night diners nearby.

Other than that the street was empty, which left the issue of the laughter. Had it really come from outside, or had it been in the rectory?

He listened, but there was no sound of movement in the halls. The old priests were sleeping the sleep of eternity. Tom muttered, John snored heavily.

Frank crossed the hall, stepped into John's room. There the old man lay, snoring toward oblivion. Frank touched the side of his head. The snoring stopped, started again. Frank rubbed his cheek along the prickly stubble of John's beard.

When he groaned, Frank stepped back. Poor old guy, he'd been such a faithful priest. How had it felt for him, with Maria?

She'd been a living miracle, capable of creating sensations that actually brought you close to the divine. Had she done that for John?

His smell hung in the air, the distinctive waxy odor of elderly skin. The old guy's bedstead was iron, his walls bare but for the cross and the picture of Our Lady. It was a seminarian's cell, austere, unutterably drab.

He was deeply identified with his priesthood.

Had he viewed Maria as a seductress . . . as someone evil? If so, then what might he have done after she had seduced him?

What indeed?

No. Not that man. John was not capable of such rage.

Not unless it hid deep, deep inside him.

Frank looked down at John's sleeping face. He wished that he could touch their grief away, could soothe the old man's loss even if he could not soothe his own.

Lightly he touched the bags under the eyes, then he ran his finger down the fissures that lined the mouth. Sixty-plus years of smiling had made those lines. That sweet little smile! It made the heart ache.

Frank had a secret mission in this parish, charged to him by the cardinal himself. "One day you will replace John Rafferty, son. He's been down there forever and he's clinging to it with all his might. But we need a change."

He was to do it with love if he could, without if he had to. Poor old fella, he just couldn't say no. Queers, abortionists, you name it—Rafferty's church swarmed with excommunicants, to whom he dispensed the Eucharist without a blink.

The old man turned his head, smiling slightly in his sleep. Look at him! He'd suffered the agonies of the damned today, and yet that little smile remained.

For a man who had gone through the seminary in the strict days before Vatican II, he was a curious mix of annoying traditionalism and dangerous heresy. He wanted the Latin Mass back, but he also wanted women priests. He agreed that abortion was wrong, but he thought people ought to have a choice.

As for birth control—his attitude was that overpopulation was so dangerous that contraception was the lesser of two evils.

These were certainly defensible positions, but they were not *Catholic* positions. John's vision of the Church was entirely his own. Mary and Joseph might as well be a separate religion.

Frank bent close to the sleeping figure, touched his fingers to the side of the neck. He could feel the light vibration of the snores communicating through the paper-thin skin.

Finally he withdrew, wondering what urge had drawn him into this room in the first place. Was it kindness, wanting to comfort the old guy with a touch? Was it anger, even hatred? How did he feel toward the pastor he wanted to supersede?

John would never quit, retirement age and the twelve-year rule be hanged. He'd either be taken out feet first or he would be removed. Eventually, no matter what, the archdiocese would have to act. He was too individualistic, too self-willed. The priesthood, after all, was the cardinal's army, not a debating team. Men who disobeyed were nothing but trouble.

After nearly a quarter of a century of decline, the Church in America was on the move again. Quietly, behind the scenes, parish populations were growing again, Masses were being added, there were fewer priests leaving, more seminarians signing on.

The confusing tide of theological liberalism was waning. People needed certainty, they needed authority.

John would disagree, of course. He would say that they were coming back because they loved God, and could not live without him: "People bear the cardinal and his certainties. They do not like them, and they do not believe."

Frank was the new, stronger, more faithful Church. John was the Church of the sixties, lost in questions and disputes.

Frank practically choked. He'd actually been thinking of *himself* as part of the Church. But he wasn't. His Church was Maria Julien, and his god was dead. As long as Maria was alive, he'd been able to pretend, to play her game. But the games were over now, he had things to face, and he was sweating.

Somebody just busted her head in.

Frank stood in the doorway twisting his hands together. They were powerful, like the rest of him. He'd played football in high school and he relished his memories of bulling through the line, pushing them aside like they were toys.

Maria would have helped him. He remembered her arms coming around him with yearning, and remembered the reassuring sense that she had simultaneously communicated, that things were under control. "Sleep now," she would say, "I'll protect you from everything."

John had lost a dear companion, but Frank had lost the anchor of his soul.

He strode across the hall, went to the bathroom to splash some water on his face.

He gripped the edge of the sink, blinked his eyes. Breathing hard, he stepped back. He wanted to fight, but there was nobody there. Whom could he hit? How could he repair himself and his life?

Sinner, repent. Let Jesus heal you. He *wants* your sins; they taught you that. Then why doesn't it feel like that?

He needed to phone Maria, talk to her, listen to her, be reassured. "You can always confess your relationship with me. Go to a church where you aren't known. It's not a real problem, Frank."

He decided that he could use that drink. As he went downstairs, the ancient clock chimed. A glance at its face, dimly lit by reflections from the streetlights, told him that the hour was two-thirty.

He went into the front parlor, opened the liquor cabinet. There was some of that nice brandy Zimmer drank. That would be just the ticket right now.

As he took the bottle down, he noticed that his hands were shaking like leaves. He realized why: he was absolutely terrified. Just the idea of murder being done here was enough to make the whole place seem sinister and faintly unreal, like some sort of shadowy stage setting.

As he poured his brandy into one of his own cut-glass

snifters from home, he noticed that he had stuffed his feet into his running shoes instead of his slippers. Running shoes, pajamas, brandy in the wee hours—he was far gone.

Rain spattered against the top of the high front windows. Frank went to the curtains, parted them. Towers of rain marched down the street. The weather report had said that it would freeze and turn to snow.

Maria is standing naked in her candlelit bedroom, her arms open, palms out, in the posture of the Madonna: "John may be seeking God in my heart," she says. "But you're young, Frank."

In the middle of his thoughts, standing in the dark rectory parlor, Frank Bayley realized that somebody was watching him from the top of the stairs. He saw the shape against the landing window. "Father?" There was no answer. He realized who it was, and felt suddenly the chill of the night. "Father Zimmer?"

The other priest looked silently down. Frank went forward, started to speak.

—You go into the church late, Father Tom. You do it often. You've seen us there, me and Maria.

You?

NIGHT RIDE

H E WAS MOVING ALONG WEST STREET NEAR WHERE THE OLD Hellfire Club used to be. The dark warehouses told nothing of what was transpiring within. Now the rain-swept Hudson was in view, and tottering at the edge, a shabby old wreck in a soaked wool coat and a scarf for a hat.

The sight of the filthy creature drove a white-hot needle of hate deep into his brain. He approached him, smiling.

A quavering voice called, "Somebody there?" Couldn't the old bastard even see?

Then they were circling one another. Within himself he laughed. "We aren't dogs," he said. He reached out and touched the man, who staggered back, gasping.

"Don't hit me! I give! I give!"

"Shut up," he said. It was such a mild voice, so kind.

"I give! I give!" The old man groped, staggered.

He saw that his victim was blind. Very well, this was going to be an easy one. He cleared his throat. "The way the Inquisition worked was remarkable for its simplicity and effectiveness. An accusation raised the presumption of guilt. To deny was to admit. So if you said to the tribunal, 'I didn't do it,' you were tortured until you changed your story or died. When you admitted your guilt, you were consigned to the flames.''

"What the hell izzat you sayin'? You a teacher?"

"Dance with me."

"Oh, Lord."

"Yes, him too. How about let's do the strut? Do you know the strut?" It was an old dance, an old, old dance, none of them knew it anymore, none of them!

He took the old man in his arms and did the strut with him, and it was as if the stars embraced the two of them. The old shit stank of sour skin and tobacco, and he started crying.

Too bad he was such a stiff dancer. Maybe it was fear. Better give him some encouragement. They used to encourage the *penitentes* on the way to the stake. "Agony is nothing to be afraid of, my friend."

The old man pulled back at the waist, shaking his head from side to side. His arms went around the man's middle and he could not get away. He whispered as they danced, formal words from his earliest days:

> "They was two great big Black Things a-standin' by
>   his side,
> And they snatched him through the ceilin' fore he
>   knowed what he's about!
> And the Gobble-uns'll getcha if you don't watch out!"

The old man said, "Lordy me." He sounded awed.

Old Momma Mooney, who had taken care of him, would recite that poem, and he came to know that the Black Things were real, and where they lived. They lived in a hole in the center of his chest.

He took his blind dance partner closer. There came a groan. He dug into the kidneys. The groan changed to a wheezing scream. Now, that must be painful. That must be positively inquisitorial!

The question! Put him to the question!

"Tell me, do you believe in the Communion of Saints?"

An agonized shriek.

Then he had the rope around the body, and he was wrapping once, twice, holding it up against a light pole, and then the gasoline, gurgling with the restless gurgling of all the rivers of the world. Then . . .

He stood quietly. Golden threads of pleasure trickled along his skin, causing him to tremble. He pulled his hat down to shield his eyes from the inferno.

Out on West Street a car slowed. White faces peered toward the spectacle of the *auto da fe*.

The fire sighed and crackled in the wind, the flames rich with the secrets of history.

"The Church never officially approved of human sacrifice, but it has forever been part of religion. The public destruction of human beings has been connected throughout history with piety and worship.

"What was the Inquisition really about? This can only be approached in a most oblique manner. When the last inquisitorial palace was entered by secular authorities, the remains of monks were found sealed up in the walls. That was in Lisbon in 1823."

How did an *auto da fe* sound, with—say—fifty heretics all burning at the stake at once? And what about the smell?

"The unconscious purpose of the Inquisition was not to stamp out heresy or paganism, it was to offer up the bodies of the innocent to those hungry gods that religion really serves, who have lived in man's dark heart forever."

He swept up Bethune Street, past the silent pile of the Westbeth artists' community, through the ghosts that crowd the night. Ahead a cab passed, and he glimpsed within it painted faces. Their makeup was too bright, their dresses too sheer, their radiance haunted his heart. Lucifer, thou art fair.

Too bad they were in a cab, maybe one of them would have liked to dance too.

He adored the extreme styles of the young, the daring stiletto heels, the leather skirts, the breasts wobbling with silicone. He would have liked to see the rainwater sluicing down their hairless arms, to smell their dense perfume.

By dream light he had learned secrets. For example, it is better to be the predator than the prey. The owl is superior to the rat, the tiger to the man.

He walked now like a god, he knew all the night places. But he avoided the glitzy celebrity scenes, the rock clubs, the teen hangouts where pulsing youth made him feel like a mummy. He was interested in the true night, the secret night, and he favored the hidden societies of the hurt, the places where the broken people went.

Toward dawn the people of the night would end up in certain coffee shops and diners. He stopped into a familiar spot, a diner on Eighth Avenue and Thirteenth Street, and went to the counter. There were a few people here and there, hunched over coffee, some eating a little breakfast.

At one table was a group of outsiders, kids from Jersey shoveling back bacon and eggs before returning to their jobs as tax attorneys and car salesmen.

Everybody was down off the drugs and booze and sex of the night, everybody was kind of loose and drowsy now. The place reflected the special softness of evil men grown tired. A smoky blues ballad played on the juke; it was perfect. Night people had a sure instinct for atmospheres.

The waitress was pouring coffee. She was tall, perhaps forty, with full lips and an eye that regarded you with innocent appraisal.

Doin' the ole strut had had its calming effect. The day man's time was coming again. Okay, that was copacetic. He could handle that.

Dawn was not far off, and the day man was dreaming those dreams of his. Soon it would be time to descend.

The waitress came over. "What'll it be?" She was not afraid of him, shocked by his face. No, the day man was far advanced in him—but not entirely in control, not just yet. He looked her up and down. "Lick me."

"You're kidding."

"Hell no. I'll come under the counter and you can get to work."

The hard black counter reflected their faces.

She shoved a menu in front of him. "I got coffee or tea, buddy." She met his eyes. He was amused when she tried to look deep. After a moment she turned away.

"You got any cherry pie?"

"Cherry, apple, lemon."

"Gimme cherry pie and coffee."

She poured the coffee into the standard thick white mug and cut the pie. "You want it hot?" she said over her shoulder.

"Sure."

She stuck it in the microwave. He picked up a book of matches from the counter, lit one. He let it burn down to his fingertips. Interesting.

She set the pie before him, then leaned close. He saw suddenly how her skin languished in its paste of makeup, and how her eyes were watery with exhaustion. "If you want me, mister, I hafta tell you, I'm available. If you're just bullshittin', I won't be offended. I know what I look like. Fifteen years on the street, I'm all used up."

"Me too."

"No, you ain't sold yourself for money. I was a flower child. The Woodstock generation! That pretty little girl in the pictures, the one with a braid of flowers in her hair, that's the kind I was. Very was."

In her face he saw the beauty of the ages. She was Mona Lisa, she was Venus, she was Helen of Troy. He hated her so much he thought he was going to literally choke on it.

He lit a match.

"Hey," came a voice, "you got feet, or should we call the coroner?"

She scampered off to take an order for steak and eggs. He sipped his coffee. The music stopped, the atmosphere became quieter, more reflective.

At the table full of outsiders, there were changes. The two clean-cut young men had gotten up and were dancing together, their hands clutching each other's buttocks. The girls ignored them, sat talking with animation over the remains of their scrambled eggs. Two boys, two girls, clean and fresh. They were country-club people. Shuffle, shuffle, the country-club boys danced to the silence, round and round.

He finished his coffee, and, feeling the weight of the coming day, paid his check. The waitress made his change with blank efficiency. Too bad he hadn't encountered her on the street. Walking out the door, he pulled another match from his book and lit it. Too damn bad.

5

J OHN KEPT HEARING MARIA SPEAK HIS NAME, SEEING HER IN THE
street as he went about the business of organizing her funeral. Mrs. Communiello, who had mourned a husband,
two brothers, and her parents, could not have been more indifferent to John's suffering. Her eyes were deep and sour, her
top lip dusted by a mustache. Once she had been full of laughter, a long time ago. Life had extinguished her light. "The dead,
they don't mean nothin'. You ain't gonna hear from them again,
unless you crazy." Betty's wisdom.

Sometimes you would come upon her when she was
crying, and she would rage at you, spitting Italian curses. When
she arranged flowers, she sang. She had a tiny dog named Ippi
that she loved.

John intended to cherish his grief, but not to let it destroy
him. Instead he considered the details at hand: the funeral
arrangements. Get through the next day, the next hour, the
next minute.

There was an unfortunate little mystery to contend with

too. In one way that was good: it helped deflect his mind from the dark, numb emptiness that wanted to engulf him.

Maria had talked about brothers and sisters, an ancient parent, told family stories, gone ruefully to an occasional Christmas or Thanksgiving gathering, visited the elderly mother at an old folks' home in Pennsylvania, gotten and sent birthday cards, all the rest of it.

But none of it was real. He'd discovered that she had no family. The afternoon after her death the police had tried to find them, but she'd had no sisters and brothers. Her parents were dead.

"That can't be true," John had said to the detectives. "She had a family. She talked about them all the time."

"She didn't have any family," Kitty Pearson replied, "unless we consider you. And as for friends—they aren't exactly lining up to be counted."

She had provided a chronicle of her big complex family. She'd worried about their indifference to the Church. At one point she'd even said a novena when her youngest sister was considering an abortion.

He had counseled her, commiserated with her, learned to care about her people. When she made her visits to the nursing home, he prayed to St. Anthony of Padua for a good journey and to Our Lady for strength and wisdom.

He was exquisitely confused by the news of her deceit. Curiously, he kept finding himself assuming that the whole family had been killed together.

When she'd made those alleged journeys to Pennsylvania, where had she actually gone?

Before now John had never personally felt real grief. When his mother had died at the age of seventy, he had experienced a kind of lonely sweetness in his heart, for she had been so good. She died with an almost comical expression of surprise on her face, one that had made him think heaven was wonderful to see. His big old lion of a father had been brought low by cancer, and that had been very hard, but the faith was so strong and so simple. Toward the end of his last hour he'd said, "Well, hell!" Then he'd been very quiet, barely breathing. His eyes flew open, he said "Lord?" and he died.

The most awful part of Maria's death for John was that he had to continue to go about his duties as if he wasn't a stricken man. He could not say, "My lover is murdered," but that was how it felt.

He'd hoped that Frank would give him support, but the murder had made this cheerful, open-hearted man withdraw into himself. He moved about like a ghost, startling John more than once with his sudden, silent appearances. "Don't do a Zimmer on me," John had pleaded. Frank didn't even laugh.

The morning after the murder the chancery called, but Monsignor Hanratty's questions only concerned plant security. At least they didn't know what the whole neighborhood was now talking about, which was how close John had been to the murdered woman. Everybody knew. Hell, they'd been a fixture in many of the local coffee houses for years.

The *Post* ran a big headline: "CHURCH OF BLOOD." More than the article in the *Times*, their lurid story caused a sensation in the parish. Fortunately it failed to mention the relationship between John Rafferty and Maria Julien. He sighed, feeling as bitter at the sensationalism as he was relieved by the fact that they hadn't gotten the whole story. Give them time, he thought sadly.

Today John had to face the funeral. The rosary had been bad enough, DiMarco's small chapel a foolish mistake. But how was he to know the whole parish would turn out? He'd changed to the small one on the basis of the fact that she had no family. The crowd had come to mourn not only Maria but also their priest and, above all, their poor parish. They'd come to share their grief, and he had seen such faith and support in their eyes that he was left feeling conscience-bound to address the scandal of his relationship with Maria publicly.

He shaved and brushed his hair and threw on his cassock. Then he went down into the aroma of coffee and bacon. The moment he appeared, Betty took a cover off a plate and put his breakfast before him. He stared down into bacon and eggs and toast.

"Betty, thank you."

"Eat it."

This must be her way of acknowledging his pain, to prepare an especially elaborate meal.

Frank looked up from his own plate. His eyes were red, his face gray. "You slept hard," he said. "It's after seven."

"You look like you didn't sleep at all."

"Night thoughts. But let's worry about you. I'm not the one who lost family."

Well-intended as it certainly was, Frank's solicitude only made John feel worse. Kindness can be terribly isolating. Tom Zimmer ate like a machine. Once he had been a man of enormous strength, and now he was all wire and bone.

If he appreciated Betty's cooking, he gave no indication. He might as well have been eating just this breakfast at just this time every morning for the past fifty years. Maybe Tom was silent because he was a saint. But look at him slashing into his eggs: John reflected that the silence could also be because of anger. A man has to love, John, or he'll miss his life.

Had Maria brought the truth into this rectory, and died for her effort? Was she a demon or a heroine?

John sighed, wishing not for the first time that the resident zombie could be sent to an institution. Now, that was cruel. This was Tom's home. "I've gotta open the doors," John said.

"I did it at seven sharp."

"You need to eat, Father." Betty hung over him like a great hovering bird. She was hard-fat, fifty, a huge woman given to silent, intense rages. John had seen her twist a candlestick into two pieces. He had seen her petting that fragile little dog of hers with the love of a mother and the touch of a surgeon.

Betty would sometimes stare into the fireplace and mutter what John thought might be curses or words of love.

He ate heartily, knowing from experience what it would mean to Betty if he refused the food.

"Ah! Look!" Suddenly huge arms enfolded him, he found his face pressed into a pillow of bosom. "The father, he weeps!" It was not a kindly gesture. He had the feeling that she was laughing at him. She would not let go; John finally had to pull away.

He got up. "I've got to do the seven-thirty."

"I opened the church, I'll do the Mass."

John was swept by an absurdly disproportionate wave of gratitude. "Thanks!" Ordinarily he never gave up his Masses, but this time he was grateful.

"Gotta get a move," Frank said as he rose.

John watched him leave. The moment that there was silence, he heard a word whispering in his mind, "murder," soft and sweet. He shook his head, he didn't want to think about it. But murder—the word had a blade in it.

If only he had been able to give her the last rites, then he would know she was in heaven. Oh, that she might see the face of God!

When I die, let her be waiting.

He cut an egg, watching the yolk spread. He had work to do. It was like dissecting her life, when all he wanted to do was forget. But somebody had to empty her apartment, somebody had to gather the debris of a life and consign it to a dumpster. He thought he ought to go and have a look.

"You finish?"

"Finished."

"Good. I'm outta eggs."

What about the way I feel? Shouldn't there be more than this? He wanted sympathy, not an unkind, grappling joke of a hug.

He returned to his room, took off his cassock, and put on some street clothes. Roman collar or not? Nowadays it was certainly an issue. Once it had been a source of pride and special protection.

More than once while on the street in his dog collar, he had heard the crucial words: "Father, I need a priest." He wore it.

As he left the rectory he put on his long black raincoat and his sad old fedora. One of these days he'd have to get the hat cleaned and blocked, if he could ever find a cleaner who would do it. Maria had claimed she knew of somebody, but she'd never taken the hat.

He had a job to do, and there was no time like the present, especially when the duty was as painful as this one.

He could not let some cleaning crew come and throw her life into a dumpster. She deserved better than that.

He crossed Sixth Avenue, headed down Waverly toward the distinguished old building where Maria had lived. The streets were bursting now with life, the news vendor on the corner of Washington Place selling his *Posts* and his *Timeses*, angry traffic jamming the avenue, people going in and out of the McDonald's on the corner.

He loved it all, considered every bit of it a sign of the spreading grace of the Lord. The newspaper blowing in the street, the little girls in their uniforms off to Our Lady of Grace School, the boys in blue overcoats behind them, the panhandlers jingling their cups, the smell of coffee and frying bacon sweeping past on the wind, a garbage truck roaring to engorge itself with the refuse of yesterday, and over all, the benign and hopeful light of the sun.

In such a day, in the presence of all this bursting life, he could not be gray and full of grief entire, so he raised his head, and stepped more lightly, and whispered the name of the Lord.

Then he was at the building. He paused at the doorway, went in. He introduced himself to the doorman, not the same one he had seen before. "I'm Father John Rafferty. I've come to see about Miss Julien's things."

The man nodded. "It's such a shame!" His eyes were empty. Maria had been much beloved.

"A great shame."

He gave John a key. "She was the most beautiful girl I ever seen. Beauty like that—who'd kill her?"

"You have to wonder."

"An animal, I say!"

"No, actually, animals don't do murder. Except rats."

"A rat, then! A sewer rat!"

John took the elegantly paneled elevator to the sixth floor. How well he remembered this whispering carpet, the sound of his tread. And there, there at that door—the shrine.

She stood glowing, her face raised again, and he tasted the taste of the kiss, and tears poured down and he was blind and had to stop and shake them away.

He was in an agony of grief as he worked the key into the lock of the eggshell-white door. He went in, moving with the exaggerated care of a man in a museum, then pulled the door closed behind him. He was standing in a small, surprisingly formal hall. There was a drop-leaf table to the right, above it a colorful abstract that looked to be of the first quality. A small, very fine Oriental carpet covered the floor. There was an odor, also, a familiar one. To the left was the explanation: a tall jar stood open. It was filled with superb handmade potpourri, the scent of which exactly matched Maria's perfume. It was a meticulous, elegant touch—so painfully, perfectly Maria.

That smell! Patchouli, ginger, citron—here was the essence of the woman he had known. This scent, and the books in this living room—these were his Maria. He moved among them like a ghost. There was the familiar and well-thumbed Richard Hugo, and there the Ginsberg they'd both read from so often, there the Osip Mandelstam and that fabulous Carolyn Forche, *Gathering the Tribes*. John took it down, remembering. She had leaned across the tiny table at Lanciani just a couple of days ago . . . her face had caught the afternoon sun, and she had blinked her eyes. "Memory becomes very deep," she had whispered in that tiny, bake-sweet room. Then she had read:

"*She is a good woman, walking*
in the body of a twisted bush . . ."

How odd it is that words can sometimes capture the drift of the eternal.

The room that was Maria, was so quiet.

How could one person possibly kill another when lives are so rich with meaning and so expressive of the presence of God? How could they do it? Her skull was crushed. It must take an awful courage to destroy another person—or an awful inner numbness.

He didn't want to, but standing there in the middle of her place, he gave way to hate for her murderer. "God," he said, "I want you to strike him down into the depths of hell." His voice was thick and dry, and he felt suddenly the bitter, impotent rage of childhood, the anger of a tiny boy who has been made to do something he despises.

He pulled down a volume from the shelf: *Juliette*, by the Marquis de Sade.

His disquiet deepened. While they had embarked on such projects as turning prayer into an art form, she had been coming back to this graceful apartment to read de Sade. Novenas, meditations, experiments in constant prayer—and perversity.

He got to his feet. He hoped that her interest had been purely intellectual. Telling himself that there was no reason to assume prurient intent, he put the book back. Now he took a deep breath, consciously calmed himself. He kept wanting to call her, to say her name. There was a powerful sense of something missed. He was homesick for a marriage he had not lived.

His heart was sick with grief, but he continued to explore. To be among the artifacts of her life was in one way a relief. He could not bear to stay; he never wanted to leave.

Her bedroom was a delight of femininity. How often he had wondered what it would be like to awaken beside her. And this would have been the bed, this four-poster with its lacework spread.

On her desk he saw a few bills—phone, Bloomingdale's, garage. She had a superb 1960 Mercedes convertible. In all the years he had known her, he had never asked what she did for money. Now, looking through the papers, he was asking.

Everything on the desk was ordinary, right down to the

notice from the History Book Club that needed attention if she wasn't to receive a biography of Stonewall Jackson in the mail.

He opened the bifold door of the closet. The familiar clothes were all there, and he sobbed aloud to see them. He hung on the door, his eyes closed.

Then he saw leather. He pulled out a garment: it was an odd thing, a leather robe with a hood. He recalled the detective's question on the first morning: had she been involved in any sort of cult activity? He pressed the strange robe back into the closet.

"She was a good housekeeper." He turned fast, shocked by the voice. There stood Detective Pearson. She smiled, came forward. "I'm not surprised you're here, Father. We've already found out about you two."

"You followed me?"

"Not exactly. Mrs. Communiello didn't know where you'd gone, so I made a guess. Good guess." She lit a cigarette, inhaled deeply. "Nice bedroom," she said.

"Yes."

"Decorate it together?" Her voice insinuated, and that made him mad. Why had she come here, sneaking up behind him? How dare she! She blew smoke into the room. "The will's been found. It was in her safe-deposit box over at the Chemical Bank on West Fourth. You should be very pleased."

"Pleased?"

"Don't act. You're not good at it."

"Act? What do you mean?"

"She left you two hundred and fifty-five thousand dollars and a thirty-thousand-dollar insurance policy and the entire contents of this apartment."

He found the edge of the bed, sat down.

"Father, you'd best tell me anything that's on your mind." From under the bed she drew a wide belt studded with golden rivets. John had seen such belts on display in the windows of sex stores. She smiled a thin smile.

"You wanted to pick up this stuff, didn't you?" She snapped the belt against her thigh. "Can't say as I blame you.

But we got here first." John heard her as if down a long-distance wire. Love nest. Kinky sex.

His first impulse was to defend Maria's good name, until he realized the threat to his own priesthood.

The whole neighborhood knew that he enjoyed Maria's company. Entirely helpless now, without even a ghost of a response, he looked blankly at Kitty Pearson. He was touched by the beauty in her face, there with the anger and disgust and that deep hurt he had seen the first time he laid eyes on her. "My only indiscretion was to be her friend. I did absolutely nothing wrong."

"Look, Father, I've got to do a job, and sometimes it's not a pleasant job. You seem like a nice man. From what I hear about you on the street, you're a good priest. A hell of a good priest. But the victim, she died in your church, at a time when it was locked. She left you everything. You had some sort of relationship with her." She lifted the belt, letting it swing against her thigh a little harder. "Maybe a very sensitive, unusual one."

This was worse than mere exposure, far worse. "You think I murdered Maria?"

"I wish it was that easy. Officially, you're gonna be a suspect, yeah, but it's nothing to have a cat about." She paused, tossed the belt on the bed. In her gesture there was dismissal, in the flash of her eyes, contempt.

"I didn't do anything, not make love to her, certainly not . . . not this other thing. I've never been farther than the door to this apartment before. I made a terrible mistake loving her, being her friend. But I had to, for the sake of her soul. This may look perfectly awful, but I've done nothing wrong."

She was staring at him, a solemn, accusing child.

He tried to make a case for himself. "I came here to see what there was left of her. I'll have to attend to it, you know."

She nodded. Her eyes revealed anger, and behind it disappointment.

"Please believe me, because we're talking about my survival. My priesthood is my soul. If you destroy my priesthood, you destroy me."

Her chin tucked into her chest, she gave him a hard look. "I think you should be ashamed."

"Oh, no." But his throat was dry, his voice only a whisper. He felt horribly sick. De Sade, leather, a studded belt—this was so ugly, so sordid, so incredibly sad. Maria was some sort of pervert—maybe even a whore with a specialty.

He remembered her lovely face. He did not want this policewoman to see him crying, and so he left the apartment, creeping out, he knew, like a guilty man.

She stood watching him go, smoking reflectively.

He went down the elevator with a young professional woman of a very different sort, quiet and self-possessed, even elegant, with her hair in a graceful wave. He caught her noticing his collar, and smiled a little. He almost recognized her, but then, he almost recognized half the permanent residents of the West Village.

Outside there was a tang of smoke on the air, the remains of some fire. He'd heard sirens in the night, hadn't he? How small is the flame, tiny in the dark, transforming the lilacs of life into memories.

He thrust his hands into the pockets of his coat, leaned into the wind, and headed home.

6

ON THAT SAME MORNING, THE MORNING OF MARIA'S FU-
neral, Frank said early Mass. He had to drag himself
into the duty; John was beyond doing it. He was no
actor and the institutionally tragic demeanor he had adopted
was hardly able to conceal the true depth of his sorrow.

The ordeal of saying this Mass was made much harder the
moment he realized that Tom Zimmer was going to attend.
Normally Tom's habits were extremely regular. He attended
eight-o'clock Mass on Sunday morning. He never went to daily
service. And never until today had he sat right in front of the
altar.

An inner tension played in his cheeks, drawing the skin
so tight that he might have been made of wound wire. John
had offered the opinion that this man was a saint of some kind.
Frank had a different idea, and—he felt sure—a correct one:
Tom Zimmer was not sane. Those eyes were malevolent, not
mystical. There was hunger in them.

Frank continued the service, trying to avoid looking at

him. He raised the host. "This is the Lamb of God, who takes away the sins of the world. Happy are they who are called to his supper."

Now it was done, this bread filled with the living Christ. But look at Zimmer! He was smiling! Why the hell was he doing that? And why so sardonic? Did he know about Frank and Maria? The mad were sometimes incredibly perceptive. The way he crept around like a thief, he could easily have followed Frank to Maria's building. The rest would have been a series of correct assumptions.

Frank fought to regain his concentration. This was the crucial moment, the magic. "Lord, I am not worthy to receive you, but only say the word and I shall be healed."

And how about you, Tom? Are you healed? Or did you enter this church in the deep of the night and find Maria here . . . ?

The soul of Tom Zimmer seemed to reach out for attention. For a moment he could not help returning the man's stare. Tom was quite horrible to see, quite bizarre, with that tight skin and those razor-sharp bones and his tiny age-filmed eyes.

Frank had once seen him catch a moth by its fluttering wings. His hand had shot out and suddenly the creature wasn't there anymore. There had been a faint crunch as he destroyed it, the flick of a wrist as he tossed it into the roaring parlor fire.

Frank detached himself from Tom's ensnaring gaze. His eyes sought solace, found it quickly in the faces of his own people, Christos, who were seated in the second and third pews. There was love there, love and kindness and . . . These were the faces of watchful dogs.

Frank came back to his work, concentrated once again on his Mass. "May the body of Christ bring me to everlasting life. May the blood of Christ bring me to everlasting life."

He went around the altar with his chalice and began giving out communion. "The body of Christ," he said to George Nicastro. "Amen," and he hurried back to his pew. Then to a man of fifty, "The body of Christ," another muttered "Amen."

They came forward like flashes of light, each holding out his open hand.

The last of the communicants returned to their pews, the last prayers were said.

"The Mass is ended, go in peace."

Then he was back in the sacristy divesting himself, and Joe Carlotto was hurrying off to his law office, his acolyte duties completed. He was one of the more moderate members of Christos, and his influence was much appreciated. He kept the firebrands like George in check.

Frank looked at his own face in the mirror over the tiny sacristy washstand. He was startled by just how much he had changed since the murder. There had been youth in his face before. Now there was something else—something used and so sad that it frightened him. He turned away.

Attending this funeral was going to be a very, very difficult experience. He would have to fight against the woe that the sight of her coffin would bring.

He went through the sacristy door into the rectory, thinking to find a little privacy before the service. Betty Communiello would be upstairs cleaning by now. The kitchen would be empty. There would probably be some warm coffee.

But when he pushed through the swinging door, he wished he'd gone to a coffee shop instead. At the kitchen table, a steaming hot mug of Mrs. Communiello's sullenly hoarded coffee before him, sat Detective Dowd.

"He aska me about the father," Mrs. Communiello said. Her voice was low, an accusatory chant. "I tell him, this place fulla crazy. A priest here, he kill himself in 1968. Hang himself in the rafters, right above where that lady get hers." She glared from Frank to the detective and back. "Father John—he been-a sleepin' with her, this guy say." She laughed. "Suppose it's-a possible? Anything's possible!" And she laughed the more.

Frank did not like the drift of this. There was a queasy stirring within. "What is this about, Detective?"

"We got word off the street that Father Rafferty's real close to the lady who died. The people run the coffee houses, they seen 'em in there together all the time."

The irony of the situation was immediately clear to Frank. "You don't think he . . . did something wrong?" Hypocrite.

The detective shrugged. "You ask me, that guy wouldn't kill a cockroach if it was eating off his plate. But we hear these stories, how they hang out together in this coffee house or that one. So there's a relationship we don't understand. And she left him a lotta money. Is that a motive? Usually. In this case, considering he's a priest? We don't know yet."

This was an incredibly delicate, complex situation. Frank realized at once that any breath of scandal over this terrible and very public affair would cause the chancery to make its long-delayed move against John . . . and he would gain the pastorate.

He must not allow himself to get sucked up in the scandal. His queasiness resolved itself into cold fearful knives inside him.

The detective, who had become involved with pouring himself another mug of coffee, finished stirring it. "Look, maybe Father John was fooling around a little bit. She was a beautiful woman. A real looker! Hell, I envy him, if he was gettin' a piece of that."

"That seems almost absurdly unlikely to me." He fell silent because his grief was threatening to shake his voice. He had remembered her words over the phone, "The cherry is pitted, my dear." He could not even begin to touch the murky and tremendous passions that those words had stirred in him.

Betty snorted. "Seems unlikely," she repeated, her voice full of derision. She had been with priests too long. If he ever came into this pastorate, Frank here and now resolved to retire her.

But at the moment it seemed imperative to say something to neutralize her obvious contempt for her employer. "John Rafferty is a dedicated priest, Lieutenant."

"I'm a sergeant, Father. The lady is the lieutenant."

"Sorry."

"We want to find out who killed the deceased, not necessarily who loved her, you understand me? Unless there's a connection—which there often is."

"Yes, of course."

"So you fellas just go about your business. Keep prayin'."
He downed his coffee in three huge gulps. "And we'll see what
turns up."

Frank was aware that the detective was evaluating
him. "I've got to say my morning prayers, then we have the
funeral."

"How long have you been working here?"

"I was assigned to this parish in September of 1986." How
deft the man was. All of a sudden Frank was being questioned.

"Rafferty?"

"He's been here since the second Crusade."

"I'm sorry, I don't know the Catholic calendar."

"He came in the sixties. Say he's been here twenty-five,
thirty years. Way past the time he should."

"You meant the Crusades—as in hundreds of years. You
were being funny, right?"

Frank's mind seemed to turn in on itself. He saw Maria
in apotheosis, brushing her hair before bed, and he heard the
whisper of the brush in her black tresses. He must have made
an involuntary sound, because the detective gave him a narrow, calculating glance. "Do you think we oughta be suspicious of anybody you could name?"

"The crime was committed by an outsider."

"The church was locked—"

"People have keys! The place is pushing a hundred and
fifty years old!"

"But it's a Medeco lock. That ain't a hundred and fifty
years old. In fact, we ran the serial number. It's four years old."

"Very impressive, I'm sure. All I have to say is this: no
priest was involved. Do you hear that—*no priest!*" Did his
voice sound as shaky as he felt? No priest, indeed? Not even
Father Tom?

There, the thought was on the surface. Tom Zimmer could
have been in the church that night, and Frank sensed that he
was full of violence.

Priests do not break their vow of celibacy . . . except they do. They do not commit crimes . . . except they do. They never, ever do murder—except they do.

Dowd shrugged. "Somethin' went down in that church that left a lady dead. And she was a friend of one of the priests. Close friend."

"I will not hear it! I will not!"

Dowd shrugged, openly insolent. Frank could have decked him. The detective continued. "A lotta priests are very unhappy men. You find out you can get two hundred grand by just offing baby doll—"

"This is absolute conjecture. A fantasy."

Dowd sighed a long sigh. "I've gotta tell you, Father, that church locks up tight. We didn't find a single loose window, not an open door." He pulled his lower lip in, showed his top teeth. "If it wasn't a priest, it was another insider. Believe it."

Without another word he left. He went out the back door, drawing it softly closed behind him. Frank watched him disappear down the narrow alley. Betty began to rattle her coffeepot. "Cops drink this stuff like it was water. Sonembitches!"

The thud of the front door closing announced John's return. His expression told Frank that he'd had trouble as well.

"I've got to call the chancery," he said. "I think I have some sort of a problem."

"Detective Dowd just left—"

"Frank, I'm in trouble. They think I was her lover. And she left me a lot of money."

Betty stopped working, remained motionless, bowed as if praying to the kitchen window. There was a smile on her face, Frank could see it.

"So Mr. Dowd told me," he said. A new misery had presented itself. The police would talk to doormen, to neighbors. It was possible that they would find out that Frank had visited Maria.

Of course, they might not. He'd been damn careful. His key to the building had let him get past the doorman unnoticed. But she'd contrived for him to be seen in the hall once or twice, as a joke. Would that turn out to be fatal?

"PRIESTS IN LOVE TRIANGLE WITH MURDER HEIRESS."

That would be the most polite of the headlines.

But murder . . . to take a heavy object and slam her face. No.

The door slammed again, the deacons and acolytes arriving. The funeral was only a few minutes away; there would barely be time to vest.

"I went to the apartment," John said. "Detective Pearson apparently followed me there."

"The deceased is being brought in," one of the deacons said. The translation was that the two of them were late. Without another word, John left for the sacristy. Frank followed his pastor.

They vested in silence, using white at John's request. Frank drew his alb over his head. A few years ago they had gotten new albs which made the traditional amice and cincture unnecessary. He kissed his stole and put it around his neck, then threw his chasuble on with a neat toss of the head, causing it to flutter down behind him.

John, who wouldn't be caught dead in the more streamlined undervestments, was still fussing with the knot on his cincture while the deacons were putting on their dalmatics and preparing to enter the sanctuary.

Finally all were ready, and they lined up for the entry. John coughed self-consciously. "Let's go," he said in his rumbling whisper. Bells were optional in the church, but required at John's Masses. That was the traditionalist in him, the part that Frank truly respected. As he entered, he pulled the cord and the tinkling brought everyone in the nave to his feet with a great rush of sound.

As he had feared, the sight of the coffin cut a raw wound in Frank's heart. Inside the simple gray casket was the dearest person he had ever known. A single choked sound was all he uttered, though.

John had stopped. He was staring at the altar. Frank followed his eyes, and was also surprised by what he saw. Not only the altar but also the whole sanctuary was choked with

flowers. Not even the funeral of Don Frederico Manzini had
been so richly endowed with flowers. The coffin, a simple gray
box chosen by John, was decked in a fragrant array of garden-
ias, roses, and other blossoms. The Altar Society women had
blown the budget for the rest of the year. In their zeal there
was a peculiar meaning: they loved their pastor, and knew
how much Maria had meant to him. Without reference to the
moral implications, they were expressing their feelings.

As he went up to the altar, John's chin lowered in his
characteristic posture of disapproval. He didn't believe in
flowers for the dead, not a man who was struggling to feed
hundreds of homeless each week.

Frank was almost undone, and he was grateful for the
blossoms. Now he understood why flowers are offered at funerals: the elegance of their death provides consolation.

Oh, woman, where have you gone? Now that I have tasted
of you, how can I keep on?

Almost in a state of hypnosis, Frank watched the coffin,
his eyes hungry for some sign. Woman is the quintessential
other, the symbol of everything the male hides in his
darkness—his softness, his tears, his vulnerability. The merry
laughter, the immense strength, the remarkable needs, the
tempting voice: "You can kiss me, Frank. I'll tell God this one
doesn't count."

The funeral Mass proceeded in all its gravity, in all its
grace. Frank looked to the peaked ceiling, the huge oak beams
supporting it. The beams were so ancient that they were literally irreplaceable. There was not now an oak on the entire
North American continent large enough to provide such
beams. They were painted also in a very old way, as if there
were vines twining around them. The painting was faded now,
which only added to its beauty, the twining green vines with
their little pink roses, reminders of the first rosary, the one
Mary gave from her own blessed hand, which had been made
of rosebuds. So it came to be believed that the Hail Mary has
in the other world the scent of a rose, and he thought himself
that the Paternoster must smell of the lily of the valley.

What a remarkable place this was, its lines so elegant, so graceful, its materials so rare. There was here a sense of peace mixed with that of loss. There should still be oaks so great. There should still be craftsmen capable of repairing the magnificent marble baptistry and repainting the roses faded on their vines.

And the stained glass, the great glory of it, the glass itself imported from Germany more than a hundred and fifty years ago, the drama of the Annunciation in one window, the glory of the Visitation in another. The windows lived, in them the Virgin walked forever, her feet light on rosy dew, her bearded old husband straggling along behind, and her babe in glory at her breast.

Mary in her altar, Joseph in his: M. and J. probably married more Catholics than any other New York church, even St. Pat's. It was a favorite location, and John routinely granted permission for other priests to officiate here.

How cruel a funeral can be, how slow it all seemed to him as he prepared to enact the familiar ritual.

The altar boys had once again overloaded the censer, and it gushed suffocating incense during each veneration of the altar. When he'd been an altar boy they'd mixed sulfur into the incense and substituted whiskey for poor Father O'Dell's sacramental wine. They'd been scamps, real devils.

The gospel was read, but Frank heard not a word. Only when John began his homily did he awaken from his sorrows. There were TV cameras in the back of the church, and their lights rose as he ascended the pulpit, adding a sense of moment. He looked proud and strong and good up there, his hands gripping the rail.

What was he feeling now? How could he find the strength for this? Monsignors Quindlan and Hanratty from the chancery sat immediately below him. The detectives were there, watching in their unpleasant way, their eyes restless. Hanratty's bald head was red, the veins pulsating. Quindlan wore his familiar affable expression. Apparently not even the funeral of a murdered woman was enough to change it. Maybe nothing was.

Then John spoke. "She was a friend—of the Church, of this parish, and of mine. I was informed earlier this morning that she left me a substantial sum of money. It will go to Catholic Charities, and to our many parish programs. When I found her dead here in this nave, my first impulse was to hate the person who took this precious and beloved life. As many of you know, Maria is special to me. I am not ashamed of it, and I make no secret of it. I was her confessor, she my confidante. When I think of her—so dear to my heart . . ." He paused. His great pain was obvious to see. "When I think of how life will be without her . . ." Again he stopped. It sounded too much like he was speaking about his wife. Far too much.

The pause grew, and Frank began to hope that there wasn't going to be any more.

An inner battle was fought by the choking, diminished man in the pulpit. At last he raised his eyes. The battle was won: he continued. "I will miss you, Maria Clarissa Julien. We all will. And now, as Christians and Catholics, we must turn to the issue of forgiveness. Most humbly and before God we thank you, whoever murdered our sister Maria, for this precious chance to forgive. In Christ our Lord . . ." Again he stopped talking. The tears pouring down his cheeks said that this time he could not continue.

Frank forced his face to absolute wooden blankness. This was a disaster. God only knew what the TV people would do with this. Poor John, poor Church, poor priesthood!

John returned to the altar and went on with his Mass. To Frank, the church, the congregation, the coffin seemed to drift into the far distance. And look at Quindlan now, look at the calculation in those pleasant eyes! This was the mistake that was going to cost John his pastorate.

To his own horror, Frank discovered that there existed a traitor in him, and the traitor was elated.

No. He had to confess the feeling at once.

The bells rang again and John raised the host for veneration. During communion, Dowd and Pearson came up to partake of the sacrament.

The two monsignors also came down the aisle. They were certainly making their position in this clear, by not co-celebrating the Mass.

When communion was ended, John approached the coffin with his deacons and made the final farewell. First he anointed it with the still-belching censer, then he took the aspergillum from the head deacon and sprinkled holy water the length of the catafalque.

"Give her eternal rest, O Lord," John said. He departed then from the established Song of Farewell. His voice rang deep and true, its timbre filling the church. "Now let her be remembered by the poem she loved the most." He closed his eyes.

" 'What candles may be held to speed them all,' " he said, and his voice was harsh with sorrow.

> *"Not in the hands of boys but in their eyes*
> *Shall shine the holy glimmers of good-byes.*
> *The pallor of girls' brows shall be their pall;*
> *Their flowers the tenderness of patient minds,*
> *And each slow dusk a drawing down of blinds."*

He stood there, his head shaking a little, the echoes of the words trembling in the air. "There will be no procession and no Rite of Committal," he said, "here she will leave us. It is time to begin the forgetting. I will not hear scandal of her, for I loved her." At that, Quindlan coughed loudly. The TV lights made the pale flowers on the coffin shimmer.

John's voice dropped to a husky whisper. "I loved her. Hear it! It's true. And my heart is filled with pain! Oh, yes— the priest is weak."

He turned and strode out, leaving Frank and the deacons and the acolytes scrambling along behind. Frank watched that narrow back departing, the vestments flying. He was so shocked that it took him a good few seconds to go along behind.

Sometimes a great man comes to flower in the wrong place, in the wrong way. He hated to pity a man he respected so much. "The priest is weak!" He'd actually *said* that. He'd said it on television!

It was true, of course. But you must not say it! John would argue that priests are people, why should they be held to impossible standards?

The priest is weak.

PROCEDURE

KITTY PEARSON REGARDED BEING SINGLE AS A HOBBY SHE didn't have time for. When it was late and she was alone, she would sometimes find herself wanting to be loved. But not usually. Usually she thought about her cases when she was alone. She was tired now, and feeling a little mean, because she'd been up all night thinking about Maria Julien. She'd smoked too much and that was disgusting, and she'd drunk too much coffee so she was edgy as hell. Despite all the cigarettes, she'd also consumed a pint of Elan chocolate frozen yogurt and at least twenty graham crackers.

As she moved through the unutterably dreary precinct house with its tiled walls and linoleum floor, she sucked in her gut, compulsively trying to conceal the effects of the food.

Dowd was walking back and forth in the squad room, his new shoes creaking like old shutters. Did he realize how often he bought new shoes when they were going nowhere with an important case?

When he looked at her, she saw that his eyes were also

hollow. "There's an incredible DOA been found on the Twelfth Street Pier."

"Murdered?"

"Manual strangulation. But then he was tied to a lamppost and set afire with gasoline."

"Still not the same M.O."

"Not quite." He dropped into a chair, stared at the ceiling. "Blind man. John Doe. Indeterminate age, elderly. Vertebrae crushed like paper. And burned. No soot in the lungs, though. At least he was dead before he was torched, thank the good Lord."

"Poor old guy."

"I don't want this to happen in our precinct. This is gonna be a hell of a lot of trouble."

"He musta been strangled by a gorilla."

"Gorillas don't strangle. Anyway, there aren't any running wild in Manhattan."

She looked at him. "Possibly not." She was ready to drop the matter of the strangled derelict. Criminal activity has substantial habitual content, and it would be highly unusual for the same murderer to use two different methods of killing. Also, sequential killers were extremely rare outside of the movies.

Only there was the burned victim . . . and there was the gasoline-soaked body of Maria Julien.

Dowd wadded up the Xerox copy he'd been reading and tossed it over his shoulder. "So," he said, "back to ground zero."

"I thought about priests all night, Sam. Priests and money and kinky sex. You know what I concluded? Rafferty's pitiful, and he's disgusting as hell. But that man didn't murder anybody."

"I agree. Neither did No-Say-Um or Bayley. No motives."

She pulled out a cigarette, lit it, talked around it. "I found out last night I got a thing in me about priests. I remember the priests at Mount Carmel, Father Palmer and Father Moore. They were holy men. Now, these guys, they're running around in dog collars all right, but they answer to the call of the studded leather belt." She took a long drag, reflecting that the devil definitely introduced the tobacco plant. So good, so unsafe.

"Only Rafferty. I read Bayley as a straight arrow."

Kitty couldn't help but laugh a little bit. "Here we are, chewing over the priest angle 'cause we got nothing else."

"We got a few things."

"A dead lady in the middle of a big empty room."

"Locked room. This is a locked-room mystery, remember."

"Murder mysteries. I hate that crap."

Sam gave her one of his sad-dog looks. She hated that look also. It came with the shoes. "Captain Malcom stuck his head in a little while ago."

"Okay."

"The chief's gonna press-conference the case at three."

Seeing her eyebrows ascend, Sam tossed the *Post* into her lap. "CHURCH OF BLOOD." The story was four lines long. "They could have added a fifth line," she commented. " 'Police experts believe that the case will never be solved.' "

"I put in a forensics order on the blind guy, ha ha. Sort through the ashes."

"Waste of manpower."

"Crossing T's and dotting I's. Chiefs are interested, remember."

This was the worst possible doom that could befall a detective. A spotlighted case with no out. "We get anything from the neighborhood canvas?"

"A lady thinks she saw the door of the church hanging open one night last week."

"But not the right night?"

" 'Course not."

"Okay, good, that's real useful. What else?"

"The church is haunted. A psychic wants to spend the night in the choir loft. Malevolent entities abound."

"So we tell Captain Malcom, we say, 'Give the chief the following brief for his press conference: there is no official

word. The police are stumped.' And we question all the personnel in Maria's building: who enters and leaves her apartment? Name names, if they can."

"I hate to remind you—"

"I know goddamn well they were questioned, Sam. But
we do it again, and this time we do it hard. Break 'em."

"Due process."

"ACL you, you stupid fuck." She glanced at her watch,
stubbed out her cigarette. "First stop, the back door of 158
Waverly. Midnight-to-eight crew's just now getting off. Time
to go tell 'em we can revoke their green cards."

"What green cards?"

"My point exactly."

7

THE MEMORY OF MARIA'S MURDER CLUNG LIKE GREASY SMOKE to the graceful old church and all who were connected with her.

Frank's days were made of public smiles and secret tears, and that awful hollow in the center of his chest.

Right now he was jogging hard, working off the frustration of seeing John on the Channel Five news at six. His devastated face had filled the screen: "The priest is weak!" The media bastards loved to hurt the Church.

In fifteen minutes he had his Christos group, the one bright spot in a day that had included arguing with the finance committee, chairing a Knights of Columbus executive meeting, gently rebuffing a delegation from a group called Lesbian Irish Catholics, who wanted to use the church for woman-centered rituals.

And then he had taken the AIDS group. Above all duties, he hated that one. Their pain was almost more than he could bear, and normally John dealt with them. "The Lord sees us through," Frank had said, looking into those solemn, sick faces. The men of the group sat holding hands.

"We're worse off than the damn martyrs," the group secretary, Jerry Edwards, had replied. Tears then followed one and another down his cheeks; he'd just been told that his Kaposi's sarcoma was now uncontrollable. "I went through *hell* for the first twenty-five years of my life trying to face the fact that I'm gay." The tears had stopped him, as he contemplated where his courage had led him.

"Come on, guys," Frank had said, "we gotta make a circle here." You cling to them and listen to the wind rip their lives apart. He'd told them a story. "When I was a kid we went to Rome. St. Peter's! I saw a statue there of one of the popes— it's famous, but I forget—he's sitting on a throne with the world between his legs, and under his feet there's a serpent, and it's struggling but it cannot consume us! It can't get us because we're in here, in the Church—we *are* the Church—and we are going to defeat death."

"Oh, no, Father, I am not. I am not!"

"Your soul will go on, Jerry!"

Suffering like theirs was part of what makes good priests so desperate: God, listen to me! My people have awful problems! God, they're suffering terribly! Listen to me! Listen to me!

He ran harder and harder, letting the smooth working of his muscles relax him, concentrating on the rich and steady strain. Maybe his only alternative was to open the whole Maria thing up to his spiritual director the next time they were scheduled to meet. He could tell every single detail, get himself back right with the Lord.

As he rounded the corner onto West Fourth Street he slowed down. He grabbed his freezing cold towel from around his neck, wiped his face as the sweat crystallized, then went up the stairs to the Nicastros' handsome brownstone. Too bad John wouldn't let Christos meet at the church. Too extreme, he said. But that wasn't the cardinal's view, and it certainly wasn't Rome's view. Father John would have done well to play a little diocesan politics, then he wouldn't be on such shaky ground.

Well, one thing was certain, the next hour was going to be Frank's one winner all day. The Christos gang was really wonderful. They were trying to live in the manner of ancient Christians, in deeply pious cooperative groups.

He let himself into the house. He'd long had his own key, since this place was almost a second church for him. He said Mass here three times a week, in addition to weekly meetings of various kinds. And there was always a place for him at George and Maureen's table, whatever the meal.

There was something of a bounce in Frank's step as he entered the living room.

He was greeted with a smattering of "Hi, Fathers." As he dropped his backpack in the corner and pulled out his Christos *Ritualis*, he looked across the twenty faces.

They were not smiling.

Lead enclosed his heart; they must want to talk about John and his televised humiliations. So the good hour was going to be another bad one. If this day ever ended, it was going to be with a major drink and some deep, deep sleep.

George spoke first, and as usual he got right to the point. "Father, we're terribly upset about Father John."

Frank was not surprised, but he would have hoped that something else would concern them more. "What about the murder? What about the welfare of the parish?"

"I think I know how to solve the murder," George said. "The main issue is now Father John."

Frank tried to hide his astonishment. Solve the murder of Maria Julien? *Solve* it? "Have you told the police?"

George blinked, looked away. "I'm doing what I have to do. Now let's talk about Father Rafferty. His heresies and his scandals are our primary concern."

Frank felt an inward groan. He wanted to be at home in bed in the dark. "Yes," he said as he took his seat, "it's an unfortunate business." He thought of his tiny room with its old oak dresser and its iron bedstead. Small, but it was private

and he had made it into a little home with nice yellow curtains
and a vase on the dresser where he sometimes put a few flowers. He wasn't there, however. He was here, and the fury in
George's eyes was startling to see. "He strikes at the integrity
of the priesthood."

"What he did or didn't do—"

"The degree of sin isn't the key issue. He's brought on a
media inquisition."

Jenny Conrad went over to the television, punched buttons. They had made a tape of Ernie Conners on Channel Five:
"Popular Greenwich Village pastor Father John Rafferty buried
a very special friend today." A sneer in the handsome anchor's
fruity voice, a wicked little twist in his charming lips. Then
came John in the glaring lights: "I loved her. Oh, yes, it's true."
Back to the newsdesk: "Father Rafferty has been pastor at Mary
and Joseph since the sixties. Since it's normal for pastors to
rotate every twelve years, we asked Archdiocesan Personnel
Director Monsignor Robert Quindlan why Father Rafferty had
been allowed to keep his parish so long." Quindlan's big round
face, as sticky as a scoop of ice cream: "Father Rafferty was a
Village institution." Back to John, tears glistening in his eyes:
"Oh, yes, the priest is weak!"

"All right," Frank said. "Obviously I've seen it." He felt
sick inside.

"He's so sweet and simple," George snarled. Absently he
picked up a book. "Like one of these naughty little mice." He
tossed his daughter's Beatrix Potter story aside.

Maureen Nicastro spoke in her soft, curiously intense
voice: "What we want is for you to lead a delegation to the
chancery. We want to present a petition to the cardinal asking
for Father Rafferty's removal."

Frank knew that the blood was draining from his face, he
felt the vertigo that always accompanied moments of extreme
intensity. "I—"

"You can do it, Father," Maureen said. She held out a
sheet of paper. He took it between numb fingers. "There are
seventy names, Father. All parishioners in good standing."

"In excellent standing," her husband added.

Joe Bowers put in a word: "Because of the murder, a small scandal is being magnified. And if she was killed in a lovers' quarrel—"

"Hold it, now, Joe. That's going way too far."

"If she was killed by his hand—"

"Oh, come on!" A terrible pain seemed to split his head. "Come on," he repeated, his voice sinking.

"*If she was!* Then it will be a scandal for all the world."

Frank was at a loss for words.

George Nicastro had gone white, he was sweating. "She was a harlot, she deserved what she got."

There were snickers. Maureen Nicastro went crimson. "Now, George!"

"Well, perhaps that's a little extreme."

The snickering went to a round of laughter. "George for pope," somebody shouted.

Frank put his hand on the man's shoulder. "I know how you felt about her, George."

"She was a whore and a harlot and she's better off dead."

Frank loved them and respected their faith tremendously. But their intensity was just plain scary. He was a big man, but not tough inside, not like these people.

To play football, he had to reduce the opposing players to anonymous uniforms or he would be unable to hit them hard enough to win.

Conflicts like this made his head throb, his stomach churn. He had a moral obligation to defend his pastor. That was what Mother Church needed right now, and that was what he would give Her. "It's perfectly normal and moral for a priest to have female friends. Women need priests too, and not just in church. They need counsel and friendship from their priests. Of course they do." He looked to Maureen, to Jenny, to Linda Evans. "Everybody needs their priest, everybody has a right to private contact with him."

Linda spoke. "That's not the point, Father."

"We've investigated," George said evenly.

Their eyes were drilling into him. If they'd been at the

apartment, watching, then he could be the one on trial here.

"The doorman saw her come home with an elderly man the afternoon before she died."

Frank almost gasped with relief. They'd caught John with the Sister of Mercy.

"They went upstairs together. The man the doorman described was Father John."

Frank cleared his throat. "This is grave news." The taste of hypocrisy in his mouth was like a thick, foul oil. The guilt was like a shivering blade.

They watched him, their faces mixing hurt with suspicion. "The collar is sacred," Joe said with quiet conviction, "you do not violate the collar."

"Did he?"

George gave him a hard look. This was a man who could turn against you in an instant. "Father, we respect you for defending your pastor. You have to do it. But the man went to her apartment. Come on, Father Frank." Behind his words there was something close to a sneer. Frank realized that he knew. He was simply hiding his knowledge from the others.

He knew!

Maureen spoke. "Every priest who falls takes some part of the Body of Christ down with him."

Frank's head was thundering, his stomach lurching. "Every priest who falls," he repeated faintly.

"The hand of Satan," Jenny said.

Frank looked at her out of eyes hazed by agony. "Not that, don't bring that in."

Jenny came to him. She was at the edge of age, but her eyes were young and wide and warm. "Satan hides, Father."

"Meaning?"

Joe Carlotto leaned forward from his place in the middle of the thick couch. "He hides, Father. He seems not to exist. But he does exist. We're talking about the acts of Satan here."

"I don't see that."

Maureen giggled, the sound like a misfortune to fine glassware. "Because he's hiding from you, Father."

Frank swallowed hard. If there'd been a bottle, he might

have taken it by its neck and chugged until he fell. He recovered himself enough to remember that there was a logic that could preserve him from the hideous experience of appearing at the cardinal's door with their petition in his hand.

He remembered the snicker of the belt, the flash of pain, the laughter, the rising of his member, his poor pitiful twisted needs mocking him. He wanted to creep from the house of this pious man. "Remember," he said, "Lord, I am not worthy. Remember that. Who casteth the first stone . . ."

A number of these people had memorized the whole of the New Testament, every word. "He that is without sin," Joe said, "let him cast the first stone."

"Exactly."

George spoke up. "It does not mean that the guilty should go unpunished, Father. It means that the sinful should attend to their sins." Always the lawyer.

"If we take such a petition to the cardinal, it suggests that we know something the press and the public don't. The papers will go wild. We'll make things worse."

That stopped them, because it was true, and thank heaven he had found the wit to say it. Where was this headache from? It was the worst he had ever known. He wanted to scream, to drive a nail into his skull, anything to relieve it.

George seemed to be staring at him. He stirred in his seat, remembering the sense of entrapment brought by childhood guilt. They would put him in a hard chair and question him until he squirmed. Then he had to wait there for the punishment. He would sit on the hard chair, twisting and turning, listening to the fan whirring overhead, watching Momma finish her ironing before she came to hurt him.

He managed to look around the room at them, to recall that he loved them all. Love sustains. "We have to let matters run their course a little longer." His voice was stronger, his head hurt less. "If the worst has happened—if, God forbid, this was not a random murder—"

"You think I'm right?"

"No! No, I do not, Joe. By no means. There are a lot of

other possibilities. But it wasn't Father John. He's devastated. No man could imitate emotion like that." He wanted to just be with someone who would treat him kindly.

"The voice of wisdom," Maureen announced. "Father, you are so full of grace, sometimes it just amazes me." She looked around the room. "Father Frank is right. We don't petition openly."

"We've got to act," George said. "This community cannot remain silent."

"I agree with that," Frank announced. Then he was afraid. He shouldn't have spoken at all.

"Letters," Jenny said. "Like the Dignity campaign."

"That didn't work," George snapped.

They had organized a letter-writing campaign against the Homosexual Dignity group's continuing use of Mary and Joseph even after the cardinal had evicted them from church property. "It worked," Frank said. "The chancery called him on it."

"Dignity still meets in Ami Hall," George said. "And we do not." His voice was acid. These people hated John. *Hated* him.

George had a ball-point pen in his hand. He had jammed the tip into his palm so hard that it seemed to Frank it must draw blood.

"George . . ." Frank gestured, his tight expression revealing his concern and confusion.

George smiled at him. For a moment he thrust even harder. Then he drew the pen away from his hand.

"Jesus felt that pain," Maureen said.

"That's why I do it, Father. To feel what He felt."

"I say we write letters. We can get thirty letters from Christos."

"Some of the sympathetics will write too."

"Our last letter-writing campaign *failed*."

"George, it didn't fail. It put John in a very much more fragile position. If you want to get rid of him—"

"And see you made pastor, Father!"

"Be that as it may. In any case, your letters are certainly read." He tried to give them a knowing look. "And they have a very definite effect." A few letters would be much less troublesome than a formal petition.

The meeting continued. They wanted to do their own Spotlight on Faith program. Fine. They wanted more Christos confession sessions. They wanted benediction in Latin. All fine.

"When can we use the church—officially?"

About a third of the parishes in the archdiocese had Christos groups. Only one group was not allowed in its own parish church.

"That's still a no."

"Him and his harlots and his heresies! We have a right, we're recognized by Rome!"

"We've been over and over this, George. I just can't change his mind, and the chancery will not force a pastor on a matter of parish policy like this."

"We've accepted this, Father, up until now. But now it's obvious why he doesn't want us. He's a sinner, given over to Satan body and soul. So he spurns us. We are not going to let this continue much longer. We will take our place."

Frank didn't like the sound of this, either. They were getting ready to go into full rebellion. He dared not look at his watch for fear of seeming unconcerned with their problems, but he sensed that it must be pushing toward nine. He hoped that they would end the meeting promptly.

"Frank, if he doesn't let us in officially, we're just going to start using the place on our own. We want some of our rituals in the church!"

Frank realized that he could not resist this. A head of steam had been building among these people for a long time. They saw that John was vulnerable. No matter what, they were going to move against him.

It was deserved too. He had no right to prohibit a group approved by Rome. "They don't fit the parish," he had said. "We're different in the Village." By which he meant more open-minded, more tolerant, kinder than Christos.

Well, it was true enough.

"I say we move confession into the church on our own. Just do it!" Joe was always one to act.

There were murmurs of approval. "Can we, Father?" Maureen's eyes were hopeful.

Frank nodded. He could not deny them. He'd just have to cope with John. "Next confession," he said. There was a noticeable lessening of tension. They were a little on edge with Frank. They knew that his position compelled him to support his pastor. "If he tells you to shine his shoes, you get your brush," George had said.

Group confession was absolutely exclusive to Christos. It bound the members to one another very deeply. To see the way they participated in each other's most private lives was profoundly moving. It was one of the greatest strengths of the movement, and Frank approved of it completely.

A silence fell, and Frank saw a chance to look at his watch. There were only ten minutes to go. "Let us pray," he said. They all went to their knees. He led them in the Nicene Creed, then in the Christos Prayer. His voice quavered, he was full of fervor, asking God for deliverance.

But there would be no deliverance, not unless he told the truth. He raised his eyes, looked across the little crowd of bowed and faithful heads. "By my hand I bless them, by my voice I bless them. I call God's love upon them, I draw Christ into their bodies."

I am a liar and a cheat and a hypocrite.

The meeting ended. He begged off coffee and doughnuts, claiming that he was tired. "I've got two loads to carry," he said. "Father John's too grief-stricken to work."

They bundled him up then, hustled him out, and sent him on his way with their love and their prayers. He went through the cold streets, wishing for the crowds of summer, passing few people, feeling the icy wind working at his collar.

He was not like John, a man eaten by the history of the place, but in his five years at M. and J. he had learned something about every family and every house on all the streets hereabout. There was the McCafferty house, he was a theater director, she a doctor. They had bought their brownstone in 1971; it had become their major asset. They had three children, they were pretty regular at M. and J. Two doors down had been Mary and Richard Ames. A divorce, now the house was jointly owned by three gay guys. One of them, Eddie Stevens, went to M. and J. every other Sunday like clockwork.

He passed the houses, the sad and happy ones, the indifferent houses with their indifferent windows. He was conscious of the secrecy of life in houses, so ordinary that it reveals itself as a mystery. Life huddles inside while all the cosmos wheels at the door.

He passed the neon-spattered card shop on the corner with its Hallmark sign in the window and its rows of sweet cards and moving cards and shocking cards, and little Annabelle Garrity who was the third one in a year trying to make the place pay.

Then there was the rectory, seeming somehow stronger, more solid than the other houses. It was the gray stonework, perhaps, or the wide inviting stairs, or the taller windows. But it was also grim, and there was too much security screen to make it look welcoming.

He went up the steps, unlocked the door, and closed it behind him. Like a fugitive on the run, he leaned against the door, shut his eyes, breathed deep.

It was wonderfully quiet here, blessedly quiet. He didn't turn on any lights as he moved through the house: he wanted the dark.

Then he was in the parlor, standing by the old sideboard, taking out bottle and glass. He poured half a glass of Cutty and leaned back in the best easy chair the parlor had to offer. Too bad there was no fire. He'd have to get Lupe to lay one.

Silence settled at last. His sorrow seemed to seep from his pores and spread around him like a gas. He thought of Maria as she was now, lying in the dark and stillness of the grave. He would never go there. He considered her soul, shining somewhere. Could she see him, hear him? Dared he pray to her now, ask for strength and forgiveness?

His mind returned to the Christos meeting, to George Nicastro's impeccable faith. He saw George's eyes, brimming with that brittle intensity . . . a hard man to love. His fervor made him ugly, and one feared his mutinous heart.

If they knew, how they would despise me. . . .

From upstairs there came the sound of one old priest snoring and the other one walking. He listened. He would wait down here until they were both asleep. He could not speak one more kind word, offer one more reassuring smile.

Tears came, and he allowed himself the luxury of their tickling passage down his cheeks.

Back and forth the man upstairs walked. A long time ago his uncle had walked thus, back and forth, Bishop Edward Francis Bayley of the dark swinging cassock and the starving eyes.

A life can be defined by its losses, but that isn't absolutely necessary. There are also gains. "You're not a priest until you restore your vows." No, not true. Actually, it was worse. He was a priest, but a soiled priest, a broken priest.

"Maria, you broke me."

—No, I broke myself.

A man alone, weeping in the midnight, touching the final bottom of despair—this was Maria's legacy to the world.

Poor world.

NIGHT RIDE

I T WAS TIME TO INCREASE THE PRESSURE, TO PREPARE THEM TO
be broken on the public wheel. It was time to smell the
smell of fire and listen to the fall of words: they would
think, after this, of abandoning the parish.

That would only make its ugliness more famous.

A long, slow surge of darkness built from deep within
him, like a storm fattening just below the horizon.

Cool air . . . naked skin . . . There was that time, he was
eight, it's high summer, and he is lying on the roof as usual,
watching the stars. They are on the porch below, and he can
smell the tangy odors of Mother's cigarette and Dad's cigar.

He cannot quite hear their voices, only the trouble in their
tone.

Momma is crying and he realizes who it is they're talking
about. Then the night wind rises, and the whisper of the leaves
drowns everything.

When they'd come home from Mass they'd found the rabbit. And why not, you didn't hide it. Now it's gonna cause a

lot of trouble, but when you did it you had fun, it was neat to watch, it made you feel all full of thrills and peace.

The next morning they call you into the living room. Dad is wearing a dark suit, Mom a somber dress. It's as if they've dressed for the occasion, and you get the willies.

It is there on the floor, in a paper bag. You can smell the burned hair.

Momma: "We know that you didn't mean it."

You: "Oh, Momma, I sorry, I sorry!"

Dad comes to you, folds you up in the ocean of his arms. "Satan, leave my child!"

You go to confession, you go to Mass, you join the altar boys, you devote your childhood to the Lord.

But it doesn't leave you. It can't, it's part of you. Instead it hides down deep inside you, and this becomes the pattern of your life.

Sometimes you think about your sister's rabbit, and it's fun. You think about the blue flames all over it, and the way it moved while it was burning.

In your dreams you walk the night . . . and once a girl you love appears at school marked by ugly bruises.

She had screamed when she saw him, "I hate you! I hate you! I hate you!" Oh, yes . . .

Actually, the only thing that made him act as he did was the very slightest quirk of personality. Nothing anybody would notice. Nowadays people like him were called sociopaths. He lived in a world that was fast becoming impotent before its own violence. Sociopath, indeed. What did it mean?

He went to attention, his arms at his sides, his fists clenched. His whisper was as sharp as an electric discharge. "The accusation itself raises the presumption of guilt. And you have entered a, um . . . let's see, here . . . rescript number seventy-four, case twenty-three-eighty-one . . . ah, you have entered . . . a denial of guilt! Very good. Guilty as charged, the denial is the proof.

"You are hereby condemned by this Court of Inquisition to be bound over to the secular arm, that you may be taken upon the killing ground and there consigned to be burnt."

He fled like a leaf along the sidewalk. The night was clear and hard. At this small hour a few stars penetrated what remained of the city lights. He liked the mean jewel-eyes of the stars. You fake it during the day, then you sleep, then comes the time when the stars welcome you.

When he arrived at the church it was black dark; he unlocked the door and went in. Like a spider stringing his web, he left the big door open a crack. Fe fi fo fum.

He threw off the loose street clothes and stood in his tight underthings. When he moved, the leather creaked. Sucking in his gut as far as he could, he notched the belt tighter.

The floor was cold under his feet, the air tickling soft against his skin. Gooseflesh withered along his thighs as he moved to the center of the nave.

He inhaled the deliciously sickening aromas of the church, filling his lungs with the scents of spent candles and dust, and a touch of incense from that hilarious funeral.

The street outside was silent. Wind boomed softly in the choir loft. Darkness had transformed the familiar old altar into a lair of gleaming shadows. The cross above it cast a mean shape across the first ten rows of pews.

He looked along the severe lines of those pews, where the people sat at Mass time. It would be fun to pop their heads like balloons. He could see a great red arrow pointing at this church, seeking to transform it into myth. From this one small lodgment he could build a great destruction. In six months the whole world would know of the priests who loved and killed.

He stretched, he gloried in the feel of the church air against his skin. On one side of the church was the St. Joseph altar, on the opposite the Marian. Churches were so mysterious, so filled with vision. You could sense something looking at you in churches.

He went first to the St. Joseph altar.

The statue stared at him. It was alive, of course—after midnight all statues were alive. He looked up into the balding, bearded visage. Question: Do you tell ole St. Joe first, or just *do her?*

He went up to the statue. It stood on a marble pedestal

high enough to make it easy to kiss the foot, which had been polished by the lips of the ethnic faithful.

"You want to dance?" he asked. "I know you're a guy too. But what the hell, I think bald Jews are cute! C'mon, do the strut with me!"

St. Joseph didn't move. But then, he never did. "Ah, too bad," he said, "fretting about the Five Sorrowful Mysteries again, eh? Yeah, I can see that. No man whose son was Scourged at the Pillar would want to dance." He aimed, he spat. Scratch one kissing toe, at least until their handyman came along with some Kleenex.

He pirouetted. "Oh, Mary," he called, turning around, raising his hand, extending his first finger as if remembering something. "Oh, Ma-ary!" Like a ghost he drifted across the rail that separated St. Joseph's little sanctuary from the rest of the church. Directly opposite stood a seven-foot-tall statue of the Virgin Mary, her body encased in a blue plaster robe.

He got to within fifteen feet of her altar before he was compelled by her sheer majesty to hurl himself to the floor. He lay there, feeling his erection crushed against the hard old oak. For fully a minute he lay without moving, staring straight into the planks.

"Sorry, babe," he told a knothole. "Gettin' hit by an attack of worshipitis here. But I think I can still kinda ooze along." As his face dragged against the floor his mouth was pulled open. He left a sheen like a snail.

Finally a kneeler hove into view. He had reached the Marian altar. He rose to his knees, took a deep breath, and in a clear and strikingly pure voice sang the *Ave Maria*. The words echoed in the sorrowful air, filling him with memories of the time when his heart shone with faith.

Ave Maria, gratia plena, Dominus tecum, benedicta tu in mulieribus.

His hands were clutched together in a fist of prayer, the song swelling from his throat. His one voice set the whole hollow of the nave to ringing, and any who heard it would have thought an angel had descended . . . until the fine old Latin collapsed into laughter.

He knelt rigid in the silence that followed, his skin touched by sweat.

Outside a siren rose, a deep horn bleated frantically. A fire engine, no doubt on its way to some arson job. Like rats, the people of the small hours were working. He visualized the tired men with their bottles of benzene and their rags, creeping through the basements of the city in pursuit of insurance dollars.

"Preserve them, St. Sixtus." Was that the right saint? Or was it St. Christopher? No, he'd been canceled. Now he was just plain Mr. Christopher. Or rather, Mr. Christophers, since he'd turned out to be three or four different people.

How dare they tamper with St. Christopher! What about the statuette makers, how were they going to handle the loss? You couldn't just flip a switch and start spewing plastic Jesuses out of a St. Christopher press.

Sinuously, slowly, he slithered across the marble rail that separated the Marian altar from the rest of the nave. A few candles guttered in the holder. He blew them out: the hell with the old ladies and their pointless, absurd candles.

But for the flickering of the Sacral Candle near the distant altar, the church was entirely dark. "To darkness," he whispered, "and to me. . . ."

The shadows brought vastness. The church had no roof, and the sky had no stars. This place was in direct contact with the infinite.

He climbed up onto the statue's pedestal, running his tongue along the smooth plaster feet, grasping the rough body of the snake on which they trod. "Dance with me, Henry," he whispered as he pulled himself higher and higher up the statue. It was covered with dust, and he sneezed once, the sound echoing sharply all around him. Then he prayed, "Dear Virgin, bring me a nice fat rabbit tonight." Fact: The Catholic dictionary defines a rabbit as a living being sacrificed to God. Read that "victim."

He tongued her face furiously, stopping from time to time

to raise more liquid. It seemed to him that the stars had come out inside his head.

Soon enough, he heard the rattle of a fool coming in. "Thankyew," he snapped, and clambered down the statue.

With a hiss a match was struck far back near the doors. There was an old face wobbling in its light, some parish elder attracted by the chance the open door offered to make a few more useless Acts of Contrition. The older they got, the more frenzied their attempts at atonement.

Leaping off the statue, he crouched low. He skittered along, his arms out before him, a spider-shadow. Before he was halfway down the aisle he heard the breathing, shallow and unsatisfactory. Emphysema or lung cancer, advanced.

He flew like a hawk, with the grace of a condor, a bird of prey, a carrion bird.

When he touched her she gasped. Her dream-skin was dry; this was a bony old her with lots of floppy skin on her flailing arms. Instead of screaming, she sort of whistled. He took her hands behind her and together they floated up the aisle to the sanctuary. Before the altar he forced her to bow, taking her hair in his fist and bobbing her head.

He might not say much, but he was a man who wanted every word to count. Limit yourself to saying only what is important. He cleared his throat. "Hippity, hoppity, happy Easter day! Say your litany, Hunca-Munca—no, she's a mouse. Jesus loves me Jesus hates me Jesus isn't sure!"

Her shrieks were bubbly and cracked.

You couldn't actually laugh out loud at an execution, could you? Let's see, would that be a mortal or a venial sin?

Laughter was fine during torture, of course. But not while you were killing. Then you were kinda grave, kinda stern, and just a little condescending.

He got to the pulpit, bringing her with him. The pulpit was his favorite spot in the church. Here the damn priests got to talk loud and not say shit.

He flopped her over the front of the pulpit, gathering the collar of her coat in his fist. Sunset and evening star . . .

She trembled, she tried to reach around behind her. When that failed, her hands came up and started working at his fingers. They pulled, then they flapped, then they fluttered like frantic moths.

"Do *wopwopwop!*"

As softly as a song at evening, her soul slipped away. "How lovely you are," he said. Then he giggled a little, dropping the inert heap. He jumped down after it.

He landed lightly, now alive with the special strength that comes from sacrifice. He was energized by the finest, rarest drug of all.

He believed in killing hard, but he could never do it hard enough. His dream was to do somebody at the stake. The sparks, the screams, the magic!

He saw in the glow of the transept window the first lines of dawn.

Time to fold your wings before the coming of the sun, dear boy, and clean up this mess! Heavenly days, you can't leave old Mrs. Rabbit in here. One more like Maria and they'll shut the place down. That wouldn't do, not just yet.

Rollemup rollemup, markem with B, puttem inna oven fer baby an me? Nah, too late to incinerate. Gotta dropper inna dumpster.

Too bad, fire releases the soul.

Swiftly he left the church, and swiftly discarded his burden, stuffing her into a dumpster a block away. A little ritual: three candles, one on the forehead, one on the belly, one at the toes.

The striking of the match was a fine sound, and so fair the flames.

He left her like that, with her candles guttering in the winter wind, her skin as warm and as sweet as that of some ancient baby.

Then home went the hunter, home from the bloody hill, do wop, wop, wop.

"Hunca-Munca, indeed. Can't you get anything right, man? Hunca-Munca was a friggin' *mouse*, not a rabbit!"

As he talked, he listened with amazement to his own voice. An ancient voice.

By the time he was finished, the Village was just beginning to groan awake. Fish stores were being stocked, garbage trucks were roaring along Bleecker and Christopher and West.

All was well when he arrived home. He fell into bed like a stone, and the sleep that came was as deep and black as old rotted water.

He would keep picking away at the church, again and again, until its putrid entrails were laid open. Then he would hurl them forth into the face of the world.

8

I T WAS ALMOST IMPOSSIBLE FOR JOHN TO CONCENTRATE ON
morning Mass when he knew that Monsignor Robert
Quindlan was waiting for him in the parlor. This was the
first early Mass he'd done since the murder, and he'd been
eager to let his routine do what it could to fill the hole in his
life. Then Bobby had decided to pay a visit. He kept trying to
find pleasant reasons why the archdiocesan director of personnel would be here, but there weren't any.

He knew that he was in trouble over what had gone out
over the television, and that it was serious.

To make it even harder to keep his attention where it
belonged, during the consecration he began to notice an odor.

"Before he was given up to death . . ." he began. Then
what? He hesitated, grabbed for the next words. He forced his
mind away from all distractions, compelled himself to continue the eucharistic prayer. As he distributed communion he
smelled the odor more and more clearly. Finally he recognized
it: urine. Some filthy pig had pissed in his church.

After Mass he went into the sacristy and removed his vestments, then returned to the nave to investigate. It didn't take long to track the source of the odor. The fluid was puddled in front of the pulpit. It was crystalline around the edges, something done in the night.

He searched the pews, moving row by row down the center aisle, thinking he might find a sleeping derelict. But the only person there was Jerome White, secretary of the AIDS group. He was praying intently and quietly at the St. Joseph altar.

John finished his examination of the church, even looking in the confessionals and struggling up to the choir loft, which was dusty from disuse. The choir usually stood near the altar with the guitarist nowadays, as the organ hadn't worked for at least ten years.

He was leaving when he decided to go say a prayer with Jerome. He knelt down beside the narrow, trembling man. These days Jerome almost always had a low-grade fever. Doubtless he was cold in his thin jacket. John made a note to make sure the AIDS group had decent winter clothes. These men had mostly been successful professionals. But the disease had ended that for them. A lawyer with AIDS has a problem getting clients, a doctor with AIDS can't hang on to his patients.

John put his arm around the man. "This old cave is cold, Jerome."

"I shoulda worn my overcoat."

"You have one?"

"Of course."

"Well, if you have a friend that needs one, we've got about five down in the clothes room, for emergency cases. If you guys decide to organize a raid, the keys are in the key box in my office."

Jerome nodded, then raised his eyes. At that moment they both saw something on the foot of the statue. John looked harder. He was confused. At first he thought it must be a pigeon dropping, but that was obviously impossible. "Excuse me," he said. He went into the niche and realized immediately that somebody had spit phlegm on the statue's foot.

His church had been intentionally vandalized. He took out his handkerchief and cleaned the statue. Some of the old-world elderly kissed the foot; he would tell Lupe to clean it with Lysol when he told him about the urine.

He wondered if he ought to inform the detectives. There was a whiff of madness here, just like the stink of gasoline that surrounded Maria's murder. Of course he would inform them. This might be vital evidence, if it was some demented sequel to the killing.

He racked his brain, trying to think of who might be able to get in here undetected. The Knights of Columbus had a key. The Altar Society had one. Betty and Lupe had keys, as did both of the other priests. And Maria, of course. Always Maria.

He had to ask himself another question, in clear conscience: Could it be one of the other priests?

No. Frank was a big soft bear, gentle and sensitive. And it wasn't Tom either. John had done his growing up in M. and J. when Tom had been a vital part of the work force. He was a devout man, a bit abrasive, but always willing to fulfill his duties. And he loved the Lord. Even now Tom would come down here to pray . . . at all hours.

After divesting himself he returned to the rectory. He leaned into the parlor. "I'll only be another moment, Bob." The personnel director, who was sitting on the edge of a chair with his overcoat still on, nodded his big head without smiling. John went to the phone in the parish office and called the detectives. Dowd, who was apparently second in command to that difficult young woman, answered their telephone. "This is Father Rafferty. There's been some vandalism in the church."

"Yeah?"

"Somebody urinated on the pulpit and spat on our statue of St. Joseph."

"You want to report it?"

"Well, it isn't very important in that sense. But I thought—you know—you're investigating a crime in the church . . ." He didn't know what else to say. The silence on the other end of the line quickly became unnerving.

Finally the detective spoke again. "Has anything been touched?"

"I cleaned off the statue with my handkerchief."

"Leave the rest of it. We'll come over and take a look."

He hung up, feeling gratified that he seemed to have done the correct thing. It wasn't five minutes before the detective's car was again parked in front of the rectory. Quindlan was growing impatient, and stood in the doorway of the parlor. John noticed that his beautifully tailored overcoat was still buttoned.

"You look like a hit man," John said.

Quindlan did not smile. "I've only got a little time."

"Then you'll be delighted to know that I've got to take the detectives over to the church at once."

The director managed a curt nod, then picked up his *Times* with an elaborately annoyed rustle.

The two detectives came up the front steps, Dowd stomping to ward off the cold. John led them into the church, where Jerome still prayed, and showed them the puddle before the pulpit. When Kitty Pearson shone a small flashlight at its base, something that John had overlooked became immediately obvious. The wood had been pounded so hard splinters were gouged out of it.

Kitty directed her light toward the floor, where there were particles of wood, some of them floating in the urine.

"Whoever peed there also kicked the bejesus out of the pulpit. Excuse me. Or does 'bejesus' qualify as a curse?"

John didn't see how anybody could kick that high, and said so.

"Hung over the top," Dowd commented. "Had to." He squatted down and gathered liquid into a tube, capped it, and stood up. "We'll take another look around," he said.

John didn't know whether to stay or go. Recalling Quindlan's grim mood decided him. He would linger as long as he reasonably could.

Kitty moved among the pews. Her face was a white blur in the shadowy nave. He really ought to leave more lights on, but it was so darned expensive. The finance committee had discovered that to light the church for twenty-four hours cost seventy dollars. Frightening.

She was saying something, but he hadn't heard. "Excuse me?"

"You can go. We're fine."

So he wouldn't be able to delay facing Quindlan. Too bad.

The chancery did not approve of John Rafferty. The problem was simple enough: he disagreed with the cardinal about certain key issues, and his management of his parish reflected that. Sometimes in the dark of the night he thought that the only thing preserving his pastorate was the shortage of priests. But the light of day told a different story. The cardinal was a practical man, and he knew that John was having success at Mary and Joseph.

While waiting, Robert Quindlan had fired up a cigar. The aroma had spread like memories in the silent air. John's father had smoked cigars, and that odor had hung in the house all during his childhood.

He and Bob were of the same generation; they'd gone through St. Joseph's Seminary a year apart. In those days one left the seminary full of innocent certainty. The graduate possessed the truth of God, and the authority of His Vicar on Earth bound the faithful to accept your rule.

In those days this rectory housed six priests, and they were all busy. Deacons were unheard-of. There were thirty altar boys on the roster and plenty of eager kids waiting to replace anybody who didn't know his responses or came late to Mass.

Bobby Quindlan had been a cheerful seminarian with red pockmarked cheeks and a ghost of his mother's brogue. She looked and sounded like old Mother McCree, and rumor had it that Quindlan had gone to the seminary to escape her razor tongue. Rumor also had it that he'd once given her a pipe for Christmas, all unaware of the fact that this was an odd gift for an American boy to give his mother. There are parts of Queens that will forever be Ireland.

What Quindlan did well was follow. Where his cardinal

led, he betook himself also, pockets full of cigars, neck bulging out of his collar. Abortion? Perish the thought. Birth control? Remember the Eleventh Commandment: "Thou shalt not use diaphragms, IUD's, condoms, birth-control pills, or anything of a similar nature that may be invented in the future. And no damn foam, either!" And as for homosexuals—well, God had certainly responded to *their* prayers, hadn't he?

"You don't smoke, do you, John?" Quindlan asked as he worked on his beautiful cigar.

"Not unless I'm successfully tempted."

"Laudable." He puffed hard, getting it fired up. "So where do you spend your passions?"

"I offer them—"

He held up his hand, talking around the cigar, which now dominated his face. "It's a rhetorical question. We all offer everything up. Maria is a bad business, John. That coverage was . . . wow. Spectacularly unfortunate."

"I know that, Bobby."

"A real bad business. I've even heard the phrase 'degrading to the priesthood,' but I wouldn't personally go that far."

"Thank you."

"What I have to tell you is, I think you're gonna have to throw it in. The cardinal's ready for a change at M. and J."

It was just as if a huge hand had shoved him hard in the middle of the chest. He'd known that this might happen someday, but he'd always hoped that day would remain in the future.

His mind blanked, his heart started crashing, he felt dizzy. The words that emerged came from his deepest truth. "You'll kill me."

"What?"

"I said . . . I don't know what I said."

Bob gave him a long look. "You've been down here too long anyway. I'd have thought you'd welcome a change."

"Oh?" He'd refused to believe that they would actually take his parish from him. The cardinal had the right, of course, but that sort of thing just wasn't done these days. He grabbed for whatever support he could. "There'll have to be a meeting of the personnel board, Bob."

"Well, not actually. If we have a resignation, things can just roll along on a business-as-usual basis."

"Tell me this isn't real."

"The cardinal loves you as a priest. But he thinks it's best for M. and J."

He considered his homeless, his gays, his spiritually unwanted, and thought: Where will they go now? But he asked, "Who's going to take the parish?"

"We're going to put your curate on."

"He . . . he's unprepared." Now, John Rafferty, was that charitable? Here you are trying to cut the other man's throat.

"We don't agree."

"We've both been questioned hard by the police. Attacked, really."

"I know it. He's been on the phone to me, and to the cardinal too, as I understand it."

Now, that was peculiar. What would a lowly curate like Frank be doing with direct access to a Prince of the Church? "I didn't know he had a private line to the cardinal."

"Well, he does. You know, the cardinal and that uncle of his, Bishop Bayley, go back donkey's years. They've been friends since their seminary days."

This was a real surprise. Why hadn't Frank ever mentioned that he had access to the cardinal? He'd always downplayed the fact that he was Bishop Bayley's nephew. "An old man in an old house in an old part of Chicago" was the way he had described his uncle. John was uneasy with this revelation about his curate.

Quindlan continued. "You and I are two priests trying to extricate ourselves from a big mess and preserve the dignity of the Church at the same time. Two *friends*, I might add, although I'm sure you don't feel that."

"Oh, come on, Bobby, don't get defensive just because you have a rotten duty to do. I still love the kid that bought his mother a Kaywoodie pipe for Christmas."

Bob chuckled. "She enjoyed it. Y'know, John, the reason the cardinal's left you down here so long, let you do your own thing and all, is that you fit this place. You do a damn good job. But you're getting on, and Frank's a good man too. You practically raised the boy. You should be glad to let him take over."

"Don't tell me when I ought to be happy. Getting my throat cut is not going to make me cheerful."

"At least admit that young Frank deserves a shot. He's dynamic, and this parish is unique. I don't want to put one of the usual crowd in down here. I suppose 'crowd' is the wrong word these days, but somebody could be found."

John did not want to challenge Frank's fitness for the job, except on grounds of experience. To do more than that would be outrageous. And in any case, Quindlan would see it as a ploy. So he took a more guarded approach. "I question this whole decision, I have to tell you. I think it's hasty."

Bob reached down and pulled a folder out of his briefcase. John could see New York City Police Department forms inside. The chancery could observe every detail of the investigation. If they really wanted to, they could probably call the shots.

"John, you can't blame me for being sensitive. The kinds of headlines that are apt to show up any day—priests in dutch for sex—they really hurt a lot of good people and good work." He fell silent. John saw the darkness in his expression, the great sadness. The man had faults, but the man loved the Church. He gestured with the report. "If this stuff gets out, it's gonna gut us. What was going on? They talk here about 'sadomasochistic implements.' "

"That has to be something explainable. She wasn't involved in anything like that."

"I should hope not." Quindlan gave him a steady, direct look. "You're going to do a retreat. A month with whatever contemplatives we can find, far enough away from here. Then it's off to a new challenge in Catholic Charities, where a man like you is much needed."

"I'm a pastor!"

"You're long overdue for a move. You have one of the best charitable outreach programs in the archdiocese, maybe the best. We've got less than half the number of Catholics involved in volunteer work that we did twenty years ago. You might be able to improve that, John, with your drive, your passion, and your extraordinary motivation."

"I'm not an administrator! I'm a pastor. I say Mass, I give out communion consecrated by these hands! That's the definition of John Rafferty."

Bob sucked on his cigar, closed his eyes. "It's a big parish. We've had complaints."

"From the Christos people, I know. To them I'm a heretic. And our homeless men dirty up the neighborhood. My gays are an offense to the Lord. The AIDS patients ought to have separate-but-equal holy-water fonts. I know the whole disgusting drill. If you have an ounce of fairness in you, you'll leave me in my parish. Let me die here." Suddenly he felt quite terribly bitter about the whole mess. "It won't be long."

"Are you ill?" Bob asked, his face registering very real concern.

"No, actually, I'll probably live to a hundred."

"Frank told me you wouldn't fight."

It crossed his mind that he might be able to scare them. "I will, and if he was any judge of his fellowman he would have known it. You must realize that this is going to make a hell of a stink in the parish. I don't want to toot my own horn, but I'm very far from being hated around here."

Bob went back into his briefcase and pulled out another memo. "We've received dozens of letters since your television appearance, most of which plead and beg for your removal. You should read them. People love you, but they also love M. and J. You're tearing the place apart."

"A few people are always disgruntled."

"More than a few. The Church of the sixties is gone, John. M. and J. is a remnant of the past."

"And Frank's supposed to bring it into the neoconservative present, I suppose. A great task even for a very strong young man."

Quindlan pressed the point. "So you do approve of him."

"Frank is a wonderful person. But he is not the pastor of Mary and Joseph parish, not yet."

Bob leaned forward, put his hand on John's knee. "I'm afraid he will be soon." He must have learned the gesture from the movies.

John drew away. "You're ordering me to step down? Firing me? I want you to say it. Make it official."

Bob looked down at his hands. This was painful for him, John saw that. "John," the director said, "there has to be a personnel-board meeting on this if we're forced to fire you. If you resign for reasons of health, we can protect you."

"From what? The press? You'll excuse my impertinence, but you can't even protect the cardinal from the press."

"I'm talking about the law, John! If there should be something like an arrest warrant issued in your name."

"Oh, for God's sake, that's the silliest thing I've ever heard!"

"Look, buddy, I want to be straight with you. You are a very real suspect."

"But there's no evidence. There can't be any!"

"A secret love affair, a will leaving everything to you? Of course they're suspicious."

"But it's ridiculous! I . . . I'm incapable of killing."

Bob covered John's clenched fists with his own big right hand. "I know that, old friend, believe me I do. And so does the cardinal. But they don't. If there was an indictment, it would be a great tragedy for the Church, whether you were ultimately convicted or not."

He had told the truth, and now there was no escape. He didn't see how he could even play for time. "So what you're saying is that if I resign quietly you'll get the NYPD to call off its hounds."

"We'll try, John. No promises. But we have a certain amount of influence there, obviously."

"I'm the one who's being destroyed for not doing a single thing wrong!"

Quindlan got to his feet, stuck his cigar into his mouth. "I assume from this that you refuse to resign."

"Categorically."

"Then we will inform you in due time about the date of the hearing to which you are entitled."

9

FRANK STOOD BEFORE THE MEMBERS OF CHRISTOS WEARING his cassock, a white surplice over it and violet stole around his neck. He was violating John's direct orders doing this; Christos was not allowed to carry out its rituals on parish property.

But it was time to assert a little authority. He had Monsignor Quindlan's explicit permission to do this.

He was surprised to find that his vestments embarrassed him a little. Why? They were so automatic a part of his wardrobe that he hardly even thought of them.

Maria was there, tall in her hooded cloak.

"Worship before me, my little priest."

—No! I don't want to think about you! I can't!

He cleared his throat, squared his shoulders. "Let us all be mindful that we are in the presence of God. Brothers and sisters, we assemble in the presence of God seeking His mercy for our mistakes and failures."

Frank surveyed his small congregation. They were his people, and he loved them dearly. There were the Bowerses with their three children, the Conrads, Jack and Martie Glenn, the Nicastros, the Kellys, the Evanses, Jenny Poole.

Pat Kelly had on his face a raptured, distant expression. His wife, Tricia, was looking downward with such intensity that she might have been counting the cracks in the floor.

Behind the radiance of the faces Frank saw darker, more complex emotions. They were afraid, of course. This rite always did that. Open confession is a tremendous personal challenge.

In the apartment it had been more intimate, in a sense more distant from the presence of God. But here—until this moment he had not realized just how much being in the church would change things.

When he spoke, his voice filled the nave. "Let us now reflect for a few moments, calling to mind our offenses and failures, singling out those for which we are most sorry."

He fell silent, waiting. After a long moment Linda Evans stood up. "I confess that I took the name of Almighty God in vain. I confess that I suffer constantly from the sin of envy, that I am a jealous woman, that I have since my last confession desired a man not my husband." She sat, then knelt, bowing her head.

"I confess that I cheated on a contract, am cheating on the contract, and don't know how to stop cheating on it." That was Pat Kelly. Nicastro gave him an odd look. Recently they had become partners in the commodities futures business. George was a wealthy man, and an extremely ethical one. Pat was less so, on both counts. Frank hoped that there wasn't going to be trouble between the two of them.

The confessions continued. Randy Mills, who was fourteen, confessed with bright red face to masturbation. Deborah Kennard, who was forty, did the same.

Then there came from the gloom at the back of the nave a tremulous voice: "I confess to the sin of righteous anger! I confess to the sin of wanting justice! I confess to thinking that all of these other confessions are very shallow indeed. Father, I pray for absolution!"

Frank was not too surprised to see John Rafferty come into

the lighted area closer to the altar. His face was dripping with sweat, his eyes unfocused.

He was very much surprised, however, when he saw that John was inebriated. If John wasn't outright drunk, he was awfully close. "Father—"

"You came to me as a thief, Frank. *As a thief!*"

"No, Father, I did not."

John peered around at the assembled parishioners. "My God, it's Christos. What's going on here, some kind of pagan ritual? Christos! I've heard you sacrifice pigs!"

There was a collective intake of breath. George's eyes grew hard. His wife covered her face with her hands. Others stirred, mumbled.

Frank rushed down off the altar, seeking to somehow contain the poor old guy. But John unexpectedly gave him a hard shove. Astonished, Frank slipped backward, fell. He let out a whoosh of air, recovered his breath, and regained his footing just in time to avoid a pratfall. John was not a violent man. He must be suffering terribly.

Nicastro and Kelly came rushing out of their pews, grabbing for John's arms. "Shame," Nicastro muttered. Then Kelly, "He's loaded."

"I am not loaded," John said, "you are mistaking sadness for drunkenness." He looked at Frank. "Young man, you have broken my heart."

Nicastro tried to put his hand on John's shoulder. "Don't you dare touch me, you weasel!"

"You're drunk! Get out of here!"

"I am not and I will not."

Recovering himself, Frank intervened. "The Blessed Sacrament is in the Tabernacle, John."

"I won't offend Jesus. Jesus belonged to the people." He spread his arms, an expansive gesture. "Punish me, O Lord, if I am annoying you." Then he dropped his hands, dropped his head, the waiting penitent. At last an eyebrow came up. "See? He doesn't want to punish me."

"John, this isn't you. This is booze." Frank spoke in the mildest, most calming tone he could manage.

John moved toward the pulpit. Surely he wasn't going to ascend. He mustn't try to give a sermon, not to these people and not in his present state. "John, let's go back to the rectory." Frank said a silent, fervent prayer for him.

"I want to talk to you about your sins. 'I took the name of the Lord in vain, I masturbated, I cheated on my wife, I screwed my business partner.' Please give the Lord a break. These sins are trivial. Don't you people realize that sin is an actual event in the life of a soul? You sin, you etch something ugly onto your immortal soul. You lessen yourself."

How eloquent he was, even in his cups. "John!"

He ignored Frank, looked out across the small congregation. Despite it all, his presence commanded. "You're here to confess? You've brought your sins? 'I masturbate.' That's not a sin, where's the sin in that?"

"John, for the love of God!"

"Open your mind, young man! Nowadays we console ourselves that Satan is just a symbol. Ha! My faith tells me different. If you're going to have a rite like this, at least do it well! Real sins!"

Jenny spoke clearly and with pride. "Our sins are real, Father Rafferty. And so are yours."

"If you want to know sin, you've got to know Satan. So what is he? George, you're the leader of this group—do you know what Satan is?"

"An evil spirit."

"A glowering spirit with horns, à la the fourteenth century? Or is he the anger in some furious, incest-scarred kid out to murder the world? Come on, don't just stare at me! What is he, *what the hell is Satan*?" He glared at them. Their pale faces were fixed, it was like a room of wooden people. "You mean you don't know?" He stopped, his eyes full of fire and love. "Satan is the unseen one. The truth is we *never* see our sins, not the real ones, the ones that hurt others and hurt them bad. Those sins proceed in the dark, and so does their author. That's why he's called Master of Darkness."

They shrank away from him. Maybe, Frank thought, it was for the best that he expose himself in this unstable condition.

Maybe it was best that he not even make it to Catholic Charities. Frank figured that the chancery now had grounds to retire the poor guy, and maybe—given this—it would be the best thing.

John had slumped into a pew. At least he wasn't going after the pulpit anymore. "You," he said to Frank, "I trusted you." He bowed his head and was silent. But then the voice started again, an awful, brown muttering. "It is he who keeps the faith forever, who is just to those who are oppressed. It is he who gives bread to the hungry, the Lord, who sets prisoners free, he who raises up those who are bowed down, the Lord, who protects the stranger and upholds the widow and the orphan." He looked again at Frank. "Do you know that, young man?"

Frank shook his head.

"That, my boy, is from the Common of Pastors, Psalm 146. Do you know the Common of Pastors? I thought not. You should read it, commit every word to your memory and your blood! This wonderful place, this parish, is about to be turned over to you. You brilliant thief!"

Frank drew the line there. "No, Father, I'm not a thief. I love you, you know that. I'd love to see you stay on. But your public indiscretions have hurt the Church. That's why you lost your parish."

"Be quiet, son. I'm not good at saying things like this, and I can only do it once."

"Now, Father," he cautioned, "remember the faithful."

"Look at me, Frank."

"John, I beg you—"

"Look at me!"

Quite intentionally Frank looked away—and was at once ashamed of his action.

Predictably, John became furious. "You can't look into my eyes!" His voice was shrill. People were scared and ashamed and embarrassed. Look at poor Maureen Nicastro, her hands knotted together, her head bowed.

He might intimidate the faithful, but Frank would not be intimidated. "You're the one who opened this church to the gays, the abortionists—"

As he had hoped, his forthright tone encouraged the others. Martie Glenn spoke, her voice like a flag slapping in the wind. "You give communion to Dr. Peter Morris. I've seen you do it."

"Pete's been part of this parish longer than I have."

"He supports Planned Parenthood. He has *done* abortions!"

For the first time Frank saw hate in John Rafferty's eyes, real hate. "That's my business," the pastor growled.

Martie, God bless her, got damn mad. Frank held his breath. "That doctor is an excommunicant. And Jerome White, the theater producer? He's an open homosexual. He commits sodomy and doesn't confess it!"

"How the devil do you know what he confesses?"

Her voice went up an octave. "There! You took the name of the Lord in vain! You're not worthy to be a priest, let alone a pastor."

"As I recall, the devil is not the Lord. It's no sin to take his name in vain, child. And as far as Jerome is concerned, I'm proud to be his pastor and his confessor. He's dying of AIDS. Would you deny the sacraments to a dying man?"

Frank cut in, attempting once again to gain control. "If he was excommunicant, yes." John fell silent. They both knew canon law, which on this point was crystal clear. Frank pressed his advantage. "Father, I want you to go to the rectory and let us continue with our service."

"This is a Rite of Reconciliation?"

"Yes."

"With public confession?"

"Yes."

"Not an approved rite. You're all in mortal sin."

Frank cleared his throat. "The Holy Father gave Christos permission to conduct confession in this manner as long as the rite was restricted to initiates."

John surprised him by getting abruptly to his feet. "Not being an initiate, or an interested party, or the slightest bit in sympathy, I didn't know about this little liturgical perk. What fun. Sort of a confessional-group grope, eh?"

"Go ahead and despise us," Pat Kelly said. "We're still the future of the Church."

"The future of the Church is in the streets. You wear the wrong uniform." Like all the men, Pat was wearing a dark suit.

"The sixties ended twenty years ago," Pat replied with admirable conviction. "Or hadn't you noticed?"

"We feed fifteen hundred homeless men and women a week in this parish! *They're* the Church! Who knows, maybe some days we feed Jesus himself. Because I can assure you, when He comes back, He will come among them."

That set George off. "He will come in glory!"

"What does that mean? In a gold-plated Infiniti? The glory of this world is the humble man."

"Let us proceed," Frank said softly. "Are there any more sins to confess?"

There were none.

John started in again, just when Frank thought it was over. "My worst sin was probably to tell a little boy that he should obey his mother. I committed that sin right in that confessional over there." He pointed to the dark wooden closets along the north wall. "I knew his mother drank, she'd told me. I knew she beat the child. Spankings, she called them. Instead of demanding that she seek counseling, I arrogantly believed that confession was all she needed. Now the mother's long dead and the son's a tortured soul, separated from his wife and the daughter he's all but beaten to death. The wife is ill of cancer, and if the worst happens, the daughter is going to end up in the custody of this abusive man. And it's because a foolish priest thought the confessional could be a substitute for the psychiatrist's couch." His composure failed him. His eyes shut tight, tears started, his words sank to a rumble of sobs.

Frank regarded his people. "Go in peace," he said. His voice was barely a whisper. Then he put his arm around his friend and led him to the privacy of the rectory that was their home.

PROCEDURE

T HE YOUNG MEDICAL EXAMINER STOOD AT THE HEAD OF THE dissection stand dictating his conclusions into a microphone. His eyes were almost as glassy as his patient's. It had been nearly forty-eight hours since the subject cadaver was located in a dumpster in the Village, and the odor of chemical preservatives was strong. She had been thoroughly autopsied, and her organs were now piled in her open chest cavity in plastic bags. She probably could have been a good deal colder, but the more you refrigerate, the more you spend.

Attempts to identify the corpse had failed. There weren't even any laundry marks in the shabby clothing. No relatives had come forward.

Pearson and Dowd were here because the woman had been manually strangled by a killer strong enough to break her neck, the body was found near Mary and Joseph, and fire was involved to the extent that the corpse had been decorated with lit candles. They were here because they were two very careful, very nervous detectives.

"This is the corpse of an approximately seventy-year-old female Doe, who expired due to strangulation asphyxia. She is a Caucasian, undeformed, no prominent scars, blood-typed at O+. Her internal organs show no sign of disease process other than extensive but nonlethal levels of arteriosclerosis and some arthritic changes to bone typical of an aged carcass. The liver is enlarged, but not grossly. Hemorrhagic evidence confirms death by suffocation, and contusions about the neck are consistent with injuries inflicted by the violent and intense application of finger pressure. It is therefore my opinion that this woman was the victim of lethal murder accomplished by hand strangulation."

The young medical examiner pushed the microphone away, drew the rubber sheet up over the Jane Doe, and left the room. Kitty lit a cigarette to cut the stink of formaldehyde. "Let's get outta here," she said.

Sam hesitated. He waited for her to notice what he considered obvious. She didn't, which was unusual and, he thought, a measure of just how frightening this case was getting. "Ah, perhaps we ought to take her shoes," he said.

She still didn't get it. "What the fuck are you talking about, Mr. Dowd?"

"Well, in view of the marks on the pulpit . . . If she was strangled there . . ."

"Never tell anybody that you're smart. They wouldn't believe it until they actually saw it." She called an orderly to remove the shoes, bag them, and sign them out.

"Did the old guy on the pier have any shoes?" Kitty asked. "I mean, intact."

"If these don't fit the marks, you mean."

"If there are marks from more than one pair of shoes. Maybe it's part of the M.O. He does them in the church, then takes them out and burns the bodies."

They drove together to the church.

"I wonder why the hell it's happening now?"

"Guy got bored, Sam. Or he changed hobbies. He used to play bridge, now he kills people."

"It's like he was suddenly triggered. Something happened in his life that set him off."

"Unless he's been picking and choosing very carefully. Normally he kills them and burns them so thoroughly that there's never any I.D. He's been doing it for years. Now he's old, weak. He's starting to slip up."

"Father No-Say-Um?"

"He and Rafferty are both old."

There was no record of similar crimes anywhere in the country. There were bludgeonings and stranglings aplenty—even in churches—but the fire part of it was unique.

They arrived at the church, shoes in hand, at five-twenty. There was a small pack of citizens toward the front, so they went up into the choir loft. "Don't listen," she whispered, "you might catch Catholicism."

The priests were having some kind of subdued cat fight in front of about fifty people. These people sat rigidly, in neat rows, never moving, never coughing. Their stillness communicated an obscure malevolence. Kitty thought of the Church of history, with its inquisitors and its dogmas and the long, hard years of its power.

The priests were arguing. Father John seemed distraught, Father Frank conciliatory.

"I think they're probably arguing about Vincible Ignorance," Sam Dowd whispered. "I've been told that Catholics get very hot under the collar about Vincible Ignorance."

She decided to ignore this. "Listen to 'em and you might learn something. I think Rafferty's been fired. I think the kid got his friggin' job. No wonder he's seizuring." She wanted a ciggy, but she thought it best not to light up until the natives had departed the area.

Once the place was completely empty of Catholics, she stuck a Carlton in her mouth and lit it. She burned off a quarter of the cigarette on the first puff, and began to feel a bit better.

They went downstairs and through the silent nave, their footsteps echoing in the broad space. The stained-glass saints glared down from their windows, which cast a muddy blue

light across the rows of pews. It was not a place of death, not
precisely, but the two cops instinctively moved closer together.
Now that the congregation had gone, there was no longer any
feeling of electricity. Instead of peace, this church communicated only silence, and it was a brooding silence, a watching
silence.

With the efficiency of the practiced team that they were,
Sam and Kitty went about fitting the shoes to the marks on
the pulpit.

Kitty was the first to speak. "This is real."

"I know it."

"This is a bad boy did this."

"Very bad boy."

"And all we know about him is, he's got strong hands and
he likes fire."

"Big hands."

The two detectives did not linger in the church. They were
silent, they moved quickly. "A crazy man can get awful strong
when he's in the mood. So we're looking for big hands, but
not necessarily strong ones."

"Point taken and remembered."

They got into the car, Dowd driving. He made a turn onto
Sixth Avenue. "Let's make another visit to the priests."

"To my mind, this crazy business makes them less suspicious. I could understand a crime of passion. Priests have
passions. But this—it just doesn't fit."

"You don't think one of them could be crazy?"

"It seems unlikely."

"I'd make a case that No-Say-Um's certifiable as we
speak."

"But there's no violence there."

"Look, *if* this is being done by a crazy priest—and I freely
admit the if—then we got a very, very cunning nut on our
hands. Very cunning. We can assume that there's no sign at
all. None."

"That's a point, I gotta admit. Maybe we oughta put the
priests under a little pressure, see what happens."

"What's to be gained?"

"If one of 'em's crazy, maybe he'll set a fire or something."

"We should be so lucky."

They went then to silence, each deep in thought. They shared an unspoken urgency. Because they could not crack this case, people were dying.

They had a very bad boy on their hands, very bad indeed.

10

K ITTY PEARSON TOOK A LONG DRAG ON HER CIGARETTE. JOHN
watched Frank's hands shake as he poured her coffee.
"I'm glad you weren't busy," she said cheerfully.

"At eleven o'clock at night, even priests get left to themselves," John replied. "In the ordinary course of affairs."

The three priests were all present, as requested, sitting
around the big kitchen table. Kitty looked pleased with herself.
The inscrutable Mr. Dowd lounged against the wall beside the
refrigerator. Frank drank coffee mechanically, Tom Zimmer
looked expectantly from face to face, John appeared worried.

"We were sitting in the back this afternoon," she said.
"During your . . . episode. Remarkable."

"You weren't in the back of the church," Frank said.

"The choir loft, Father. People never look up. It was a
lovely show. Very moving. What was it all about?"

"It was private," Frank replied. Outsiders had no business
spying on Christos. He controlled his anger at the intrusion,

went to the issue at hand. "May we know the reason for this visit?" he asked. "Surely it isn't the coffee."

"No, it is," Dowd replied. "We love your coffee."

Tom smiled, made a cooing sound in his throat.

"Does he sing?" Kitty asked.

Tom's grin grew broader. He was so thin, his face was so bright, that he looked quite horrible.

"Sing," Frank said. "He won't even write messages."

"It's not a disease?"

John intervened. He'd known Tom since before Frank was born. He was the one to explain about Tom. "It's not a physical disease. He just stopped talking." He looked at his old friend. "There is a tradition of silence in the Church. My own belief is that Tom is praying all the time, for all of us." Tom's face, which had returned to its usual impassivity, gave no indication of whether or not this was true. John wanted to tell them about what he saw in Tom Zimmer's eyes, the goodness and the love and the determination. But they wouldn't understand, they would never hear the man say Mass, they had never confessed their sins to him, taken the sacrament from his hands, listened to him weeping in the night, seen him dance the tango with Betty Communiello in the old days, when this was a happy place. "He was very alive. He loves life."

All of a sudden Dowd moved. He shot toward John like a striking snake, his hands out before him, his lips twisting into a snarl. John fell back, almost knocking over his coffee.

Then Dowd had him by the wrist. Their eyes met. "A roach," the detective hissed, "crawling on your sleeve."

John snatched his arm away, brushing frantically. There hadn't been anything there. He had eyes, he could see.

The detectives were scaring him. He felt his heart start to go, felt his breath come faster. What were they doing? Why this hideous atmosphere of menace? "May we help you?" he asked. How lame he sounded, how guilty!

Kitty took a box of kitchen matches out of her purse, stuck a cigarette in her mouth. She lit a match, held it out while it flared. Her eyes went from face to face. John was hypnotized by the flame, watching it, listening to the hiss.

Then he found that she was staring at him. She lit the cigarette. "You should know that there's been at least one more murder in your church."

The coffeepot exploded against the floor. Frank bent down, his hands fluttering about, trying to somehow capture the mess.

Kitty laughed. "I'd help you," she said, "but I've been finished in the kitchen since I was about twelve."

John grabbed a cup towel and went to Frank's assistance. As the mess got cleaned up, Kitty continued. "We got a stiff in yesterday morning, a lady who'd been choked and deposited in a dumpster down on Bethune Street."

"Read about it," Frank said.

"She was surrounded by candles, she was strangled like another victim, a bum who got offed down on one of the old piers."

John had seen that one on television. Hideous. As he listened, his mind went to his poor beloved church, to her grace and her beauty. She was a little old, perhaps, a little in need of a face lift. But she was beautiful, if you knew how to look! Oh, yes, and she gave love.

Deep in Frank's guts something made a nauseating lurch. The room was stuffy and overheated. He concentrated on cleaning up the mess.

Tom looked from face to face with the beady alacrity of a bird.

John thought that he could not stand it, not another moment of it, not anymore. They'd come here in the middle of the night with this news to frighten and intimidate. They were watching to see who cracked, who couldn't bear it.

They thought that the murderer was right here in this room. Were they right or wrong? Wrong, his mind said, they had to be wrong! He looked at his colleagues, wishing that the truth appear graven on their foreheads, or that the Lord Himself give some sign.

There was no sign: Frank's forehead was gleaming with sweat as he cleaned up the last of his mess. Tom was dry and old and probably less alert than he appeared.

At that moment something gave way deep inside John. The situation, the grief, the terror: all converged toward a single blazing point of flame. Grief swallowed him, fear set him afire. He wanted to die, to take a kitchen knife and plunge it into his own bowels, to end this agony of a life at last.

Kitty took a long drag on her cigarette, blew some smoke in John's direction. She seemed entirely oblivious of his state. "We compared Ms. Doe's shoes to the indentation marks on your pulpit. Conclusion: Ms. Jane Doe was choked to death by somebody standing in the pulpit, holding her over the front. As she died, she kicked and peed. Suffocation panic."

With exaggerated care Frank pulled back a chair and sat down. He wished to God he hadn't spilled the damned coffee. It looked so . . . nervous. The steam rising from Kitty Pearson's cup, her noisy sipping, made him feel extraordinarily uneasy, as if her every innocuous gesture hastened some dreadful conclusion.

"Jesus deliver me," John whispered. A terrible inertia seemed to possess him. Like Frank, he found himself mesmerized by the detectives. He felt like he had been holding on for a long time and now he couldn't do it anymore. He was going to let go and he was going to fall, and down there it was black and the only light came from the ignition of matches.

"We want to have a look around the rectory," Dowd said. "Obviously there's the possibility that whoever's committing these crimes in the church might gain entry during the night."

John was appalled. Frank looked as frightened as a little boy caught at some childish crime. Forgetting their battles and his own bitter anger, John put his hand on his friend's shoulder.

"Nobody's accusing you," Kitty said.

"We know that."

"You look accused. Frank does."

"No, I . . . That strangulation . . . My hands . . ." He turned them over and over in the hard kitchen light.

"Do you have a door that leads into the church from here?"

"Yeah," Frank said absently.

She pushed back her chair. "We need to take a look." John could not stop looking at his hands. He'd thought often of the miracle that comes through a priest's hands, at the immense kindness of the God who has created that miracle.

Now his hands were claws, he imagined them come around an innocent neck . . . No.

It just wasn't possible. He would never, ever commit an act of violence. He had held dying children with these hands, had given aid, relieved suffering, given comfort. "I never murdered anybody!" He looked in horror from face to face. "Was that me? Did I say something?"

Kitty put her chin into her palm and just watched. Dowd was like a cocked gun.

"We want to look over the premesis," Kitty said. "It's not particularly secure, and you probably oughta make sure nobody can get in here at night from the church."

John ordered himself to stand up, to walk. But he did not stand, he did not walk. Instead he slumped back into his chair. He didn't want to do this, he'd fought this for days, but he couldn't stop now, there was no way, the sorrow of it, the horror, the ugliness—he bawled like a baby. He covered his face, trying to hide the shame, he shook his head, shook away the humiliating tears.

Kitty put a hand on his shoulder. "I know it," she said. Just that. And he saw that it was true. She knew, oh, she knew it all.

He hung his head, letting his shoulders shake with the convulsions of sorrow.

Frank came to his rescue. "I'll show you around," he told the detectives.

He took them to the door that led in from the sacristy.

She examined it. Thick oak. She pulled it open. There was the faintest glow in the gloom of the place—that one candle they always left burning in a Catholic church. She could smell the heavy, sullen air of the church, could smell the death.

She closed the door quickly. "Lock this." She threw the deadbolt, then rattled the door. "You have a monster on your hands, Father. Put simply." She shook out another cigarette and lit it.

Frank hungered to come right out with it, to ask her the question that was now destroying John, that was roaring in his own head like the voice of a storm: "Do you think it was one of us?"

Dowd answered. "We don't know who committed the crime."

They returned then to the kitchen. John now sat huddling over a mug of coffee. Tom Zimmer had slipped away.

"Where's Father Tom?" Dowd asked. "Turn into a pumpkin?"

"No, actually he turns into a glass slipper at night," Frank snapped.

Dowd might have laughed. Not now. "If you want to know what we think, we think that something really horrible is happening here. We don't know whether it just started, or it . . . surfaced. But it's damn bad."

John was simply too stricken to talk. He stared, listening to them as if they were actors. They were detectives contending with a particularly ugly crime. But John had a different perspective. His ideas about evil were careful and considered and very definitely did not involve a real devil.

But he believed in evil, all right. Nobody could be a priest for a week and not realize that there is something evil and it is huge and it is strong and it slides through the world like an illusion.

He could see how these lurid crimes would be magnified by the press, how they would loom like a great crushing shadow over the whole Church, causing more thousands to quietly stop going to Mass, quietly forget their contribution envelopes, quietly abandon the habit of prayer. "I hope it wasn't a priest!"

"You always hope the perp is innocent. You want a happy-ever-after. But it ain't usually real happy."

"What if I said the killer is in this rectory, Father Frank? How do you react to that?"

Frank regarded Kitty Pearson. "Is it some sort of test question?"

" 'Course it is! I wanna know who the hell is doing this! How do you think it feels—every day this guy stays free, we play games with somebody else's life. That bum, now this old lady—they died because of me and my partner and all the other cops working on this. We weren't smart enough, we weren't fast enough—and so they are dead. So this is an interrogation. Damn right! We got a monster on our hands! Is it one of you? We wanta know!"

John could not listen to any more of this. There was in that woman's voice the hardness of tempered steel. To hear those bulletlike phrases barking out of that sweet, soft, gentle mouth, to feel the washing grief, the sense of Maria's presence caused by Kitty's dark hair and her cream-pale skin—he just could not stand it anymore. "May I go to bed?"

"Tired?" Dowd asked, his tone saying that every little detail counted.

"He's distraught! Look at him! And I don't blame him. Why couldn't you be a little gentle? He loves this church. He's given his life to Mary and Joseph. Now it's going to become an attraction on the ghouls-and-goblins tour."

"Goblin," Kitty said. "Goblin . . ."

"What's that supposed to mean!"

"Nothing. Except it's an interesting word. Goblin. Something that gobbles, devours. The ones who manage the night."

They did not stop John when he left, and he was so grateful he could have kissed them. He tried not to glide, he tried not to run. Everything had to be casual, calm, as if he was back in control of himself.

He entered his room, shut the door. Privacy at last. He found himself wondering where she might live. Now, why would he wonder that? Perhaps to gain some perspective about her, some focus. Hadn't she referred to Brooklyn? Maybe. He threw off his clothes, dropped onto the bed.

Kitty Pearson. Single. Brooklyn.

He took up his breviary and turned to Night Prayer. Red

letters stared at him: "Trustful prayer in adversity." *Father, into your hands I commend my spirit.* "In you, O Lord, I take refuge. Let me never be put to shame. Lord God, be my refuge and my strength."

He lay back, the breviary still in hand. A wave of shivers passed over him. There came to mind the image of something crawling up out of the muck, of an old trapdoor opening. A *creature* was loose, loose in the church, stalking the halls of the rectory.

"Out of the depths I cry to you, O Lord, hear my voice! If you, O Lord, should mark our guilt, who would survive?" The breviary fell from his grasp, he felt a weight of great hands upon his shoulders, his chest heaved. The dark, profound words of the psalm beat with the beating of his heart. "My soul is longing for the Lord more than the watchman for daybreak."

NIGHT RIDE

THE MOST COMFORTABLE PLACE THAT GEORGE NICASTRO knew was Mary and Joseph church in the velvet middle of the night. Tonight he'd come in at eleven, and stayed most of the night. He'd slept a little, furtive, dream-tossed naps, but on the whole he'd prayed.

Behind these doors the voices that oppressed him were silent. Elsewhere he heard insults inside his head: "You're a pig, you're a liar." There were screams, the howling of the damned. He was never at peace, not even in his dreams.

This was the antidote. When he was a little boy his father had brought him to this very church and knelt him in a back pew and made him pray. For one hour each day they had prayed together.

The old prayers drifted in and out, mixing with thoughts and sleep and memories.

Tonight he was alone, although that was not always the case. Sometimes Father Tom came in and prayed quietly near the altar. Occasionally Father Frank would kneel beside him like Daddy had. He thought that comradeship in prayer was the deepest, finest friendship human beings could experience.

Every so often he would encounter another parishioner here, and that was good. The word was going from lip to lip that Nicastro sometimes prayed all night . . . and Christos was growing.

He knelt in a back pew, relishing the darkness. There were a few candles flickering before the Marian altar, and the light of the sacral candle was steady and true. He could see the huge shadows of the statues of the Virgin and of Joseph. What had their lives actually been? He'd been to the Holy Land, ridden the busses that raced through Bethlehem and Nazareth, contemplated the Stations of the Cross in Jerusalem.

These thoughts brought him to regard the cross that dominated the sanctuary. He looked toward the shadowed face, the pitiful visage of the murdered God. It had always seemed to him that the cross was a symbol of tremendous rage.

He began to whisper the Our Father, letting the words slip sensually from his mouth. ". . . who art in heaven, hallowed—"

He stopped, suddenly aware of an odd effect. It was as if somebody was whispering in exact unison with his own voice. But there wasn't anybody here. When the priests came in through the sacristy, the door into the rectory banged, echoing across the nave. Any parishioner with a key would have to open the front door. That made even more clatter.

". . . thy kingdom come, thy will be done—"

The effect was so convincing that he looked around him. The pews were empty; he could not see into the shadows over by the confessionals, or toward the door that led into the crypt.

He prayed very quickly. "OurFatherwhoart—" Then he relaxed. The other voice had kept up with him perfectly, and was therefore an echo. He'd never heard it before, which was strange, considering the amount of time he spent here, but there was now no question in his mind that it was a natural phenomenon.

He bowed his head and closed his eyes, and said his prayer so softly that the echo didn't take place.

When he opened his eyes he noticed at once that there had been a change. At first, though, he wasn't certain what it was. Then he realized that the candles in front of the Virgin were out.

Had there been a breeze, perhaps? Some errant gust? There must have been; he dismissed it from his thoughts, continued praying. He wanted to be close, very close to the Lord. It was in the fortress of the Lord's love that he would find protection from the demons and the voices in his head. "You filthy snot, you don't believe a fucking thing!"

"Our Father, who art in heaven—"

There it was again . . . whispering. But he'd been praying silently. Yes, he had—hadn't he?

He held his hands to his lips. In his mind he prayed: ". . . hallowed be thy name, thy kingdom come . . ."

It must be the wind. Of course, the wind could boom in the bell tower, the wind could weep through chinks in the old stained-glass windows. Now the wind was tricking him, trying to make him believe that the voices had gotten free, that they were somewhere in the church.

He noticed that the candles in front of the St. Joseph altar had also gone out. All that remained of them was a single red glow, like the eye of a rat caught in thin light.

The increased darkness was actually reassuring. This was absolute confirmation that the wind was responsible. Still, though . . . perhaps it would be best to call it a night.

He had long known that his voices were not a mental thing. He didn't need a psychiatrist, he'd been raised right and nobody in his family had ever been crazy. The voices weren't something out of a psychology text.

He prayed well, and they hated him for that. If God heard a man's prayers, so did the devil. He sent his demons. He did. "You filthy son of a cocksucking whore!"

"Glory be to the Father and the Son and the Holy Spirit!"

There, he said that one right loud, and there was no whispering and no echo. The reverberations of his voice faded. Faint street noise reasserted itself, subdued because of the late hour. At that moment the church was filled with huge flickering reflections of flames. George jumped up, he cried out—then he saw that the sacral candle was flaring; it had grown to white, angry incandescence.

He could hardly bear to look at it, but he stared anyway in fear and awe, his heart thundering, his eyes squinting against the glare.

Then it was gone, the flame reduced to a dull orange point.

George was thunderstruck. He fell back to his knees, staring in amazed delight.

It had been a sign. He'd had a sign from the Lord. He was wanted, he was loved, his work with Christos was noticed and appreciated.

He got out of his pew, went forward. Without the candles it was so dark that he had to feel his way. He had to respond somehow to the call of the Lord, he would go to the altar, prostrate himself.

Then he smelled something new, something quite peculiar. Was it . . . ? What? A petroleum derivative . . . kerosene or charcoal lighter or . . . something stronger. Gasoline.

He inhaled deeply. Yes, it was there, most definitely.

The thought crossed his mind that the flaring of the sacral candle might not have been a sign at all. He became wary. He was here alone, murder had been done in this place.

Then he heard a new sound, quite distinct and quite wrong. He heard a whisper, as if of silk or the swishing of a cassock. It came from somewhere in the dark, he could not sense the direction.

He turned around, all thought of the Lord evaporating in the certain knowledge that the sacral candle had been sprayed with gasoline. Behind him there was only thick dark. Again he turned; he could hardly see the altar. It was thicker, darker shadow, nothing more.

The rustling, whispering sound went down the side aisle, moving with a swiftness that did not seem natural. Why did he hear no sounds of exertion?

For an instant he caught sight of a figure, moving with the swiftness of a snake, racing in total silence along an old floor notorious for its creakiness.

He had to get out of here, and at once. He turned, and feeling from pew to pew, hurried down the aisle to the back of the church.

He was digging in his pockets for his keys when he realized that there was somebody near him. He didn't see a soul—indeed, could hardly see the door three feet away. But the atmosphere became thick and charged, and he felt as the mouse must feel in the eye of the cat.

Fear twisted his throat. He looked up, seeking for the eyes, the face. Who was this? He wanted it to be one of the priests —yes, that was why the black, of course. Tall and silent. "Father Tom?"

He reached out, trying to make some sort of contact. The figure did not move. Where was the face, why couldn't he see the face? "Father John?"

Silence. He thought then that this might not be one of the priests. Very well, he would just leave. Fine. He had his key now, all he had to do was step up to the door. Thrusting the key before him, he took the step.

But the air was hollow, and the bulk of the door resolved itself into something else. For a moment George was profoundly confused. He waved the key about, then he waved his arms, seeking contact with the solid surface that should be there.

Nausea overcame him as he understood that he had not gone to the back of the church at all. He'd gotten turned around. He was not at the door; the bulk ahead of him was the altar.

He was so awfully afraid now that he came near to gagging on his own tongue. Then somebody spoke, a voice so very dignified, so full of quiet authority, that George was left completely nonplussed, possessed by the most urgent question. "They walked two by two," the voice said, "carrying tapers and wearing the *sambiento*." Then the voice whispered, very softly, with a sneering lilt, "Do wop, wop, wop."

Outside the wind blew, a horn honked three times, a siren rose on the distance and then dropped away.

George snatched at the tears that were pouring from his eyes. He felt a terrible sickness, he was going to retch. He was beyond movement, beyond thought, a little boy standing naked in the middle of the dark.

He noticed a coldness against his inner thigh and reached down. He was appalled to discover that his whole front had been soaked in gasoline. He was dripping with it!

He'd felt nothing, heard nothing. How could it have happened? He tried to escape, turning from the bulk of the altar, then walking, then running, the tapping of his own feet rising to a crescendo, a thunder. The aisle seemed longer and longer, the doors farther away. He'd never get there, never, and he knew that there was movement behind him—fast, effective, the furtive rush of the rat.

Behind him he heard a sound: *ssst!* It came again, then there was a rising flare of light. Instinct turned him—and he was face-to-face with the most incredible thing he had ever seen. The face was hideous beyond words, leering and loose-lipped, the eyes glaring, pupils tiny, the nostrils distended.

Only a glimpse he saw, then his own chest grew a rose of fire. For an instant he looked down, horrified at what was happening, then high blue blades of agony sliced into his exposed face. He jerked his head back, his skin spitting like fat dropped into an overheated skillet.

He stumbled, fell, lay for a moment absolutely still. The deepest part of him had been thrust back to infancy by the sheer fury of the assault. His little silent inner self was waiting to be saved. The bush of fire grew from his chest. "And the flames would consume them and melt them, and so they would be taken, after much clamor, to their deaths."

No salvation came, and the inner child began to feel the pain of the fire. He saw it not as flames but as a furious horde of rats gnawing into his chest. He could see their gleaming backs, feel the tearing of their teeth, hear his skin pop and his bones crack.

Then there was another great sound, a hissing that filled the church, the rafters that flickered with his death, the awful shadow of the cross. He saw then the interior of the flames themselves, never perceiving the careful hands that were spreading gas over his body, nor noticing that he was lying upon a large fireproof blanket, and he did not see the dancing.

How he danced! Round and round, in the light of the flames, dancing with the rhythm of the flickering, the high bird-shrieks of the victim his only music, and fine it was, this old music: the very sound of the sacrifice.

George Nicastro's hands came up to his chest, the fists turning to black molten balls. His legs rose next, as muscle melted and tendon shrank, and the awful knowledge left the eyes like light rising into the night sky, the lark pinned by the sun.

He danced high, sailing from one end of the church to the other, leaping the pews ten rows at a time, moving in a blur of black cassock and damp, gleaming skin. He laughed and sang, "Rollemup, rollemup, markem with B, puttemina oven for baby an' me!" He leapt so high that he touched the very rafters where George had seen himself die, and the cross, its banal Jesus glaring down.

He would break it, though, he would eventually break the core of the thing. Then the evil souls of history would return to the world and choke the living on the sorrows they brought.

From one little church, a whole world would be made to shudder and rattle.

Earth would fall into his hands, for he was huge and could hold her between his palms. As she came tumbling out of the stars, he would catch her. In his fiery belly there was enough room for the whole world.

By the end of an hour the fire had died, and the bones lay in a crust of greasy ash and melted buttons. He folded it all very neatly and took it down for more profound incineration.

Thus the night ended. The earth turned her face toward the sun. The six-o'clock bell tolled its deep-throated call: all's well, the night is done.

The night is done.

PROCEDURE

"**M**ISS PEARSON, THIS IS JOHN RAFFERTY." HIS VOICE WAS unfocused, blurred. A civilian might have thought him drunk; Kitty knew the sound of terror. "Please come," he said, "hurry!"

"If this is a police emergency, dial 911."

"No, not exactly. But come. Come fast!"

They were about to go off shift; she and Dowd had done the twelve-to-eight to observe the church. No stakeout had been ordered yet, but they'd still wanted to get a sense of the place late at night. It had been a quiet night.

"Something's up," she said. "We gotta move."

It didn't take long to get from the Sixth Precinct to the church. On the way over they heard the bells tolling seven. She thought: It's calling us.

As Dowd pulled the car over to the curb, Father John came down the portico steps, his cassock flying in the wind. It was a sunny, freezing cold morning and he shielded his eyes as he approached the car. "Come inside," he said, "quickly!"

They followed him into the church.

Kitty practically collapsed. She had never smelled anything so horrible. It was as if somebody had decided to roast
a turkey with the feathers still on, and then let it burn. Sam
coughed, bent his head. Father John rushed up the aisle.
"Here," he said, "look!"

He stood near the altar, rendered to a shadow by the haze
of smoke in the air. Kitty tried to follow him, then she stopped.
The odor contained burnt hair, seared meat—it was too vile.
Gagging, trying to get the oily taste of it out of her mouth, she
sank to her knees.

Sam came down beside her. "Hey," he said.

"I'm okay. Just surprised as hell." She forced herself to
stand up. "How can you handle it?"

"I work beside a smoker, remember."

"Funny."

They went down the aisle together, approaching the tall
priest. He seemed relatively unaffected. When they got close,
she saw why: he'd used the old mortician's trick of dabbing
Ben-Gay under his nose.

"Somebody burned something," he said.

"Really," Kitty gasped back. "I'm surprised."

"Burned meat," he said. His face was gray, his skin dripping with sweat. Despite his apparent composure, both cops
knew that this man was close to clinical shock. "Look up," he
added.

They followed the priest's gaze. The rafters were all black
with soot. There had been a big fire here, that somehow hadn't
burned the floor. She knelt down, felt. "Still warm," she said.

"It's damaged too," Father Rafferty added. "You can see
where it nearly started on fire."

"Somebody built a fire in here?" She could not have been
more amazed. They'd been sitting out in their car drinking
coffee when this happened. She decided not to mention their
stakeout.

"They cooked something," Father John added. "Burned
it. I know the smell of a burned roast."

"You discovered this?"

"As soon as I opened the church."

She had remembered the gasoline that had soaked Maria Julien's body. "Are the other priests accounted for?"

"What do you mean?"

Sam picked up her train of thought. "Father Frank and Father Tom," he said quickly, "where are they?"

"Why, getting dressed, I suppose."

Sam was the first to move. He raced off across the sanctuary and into the sacristy. Kitty wasn't far behind him. They reached the door into the rectory at almost the same moment—and practically ran into Father Tom, who by chance was entering the church.

He staggered back. "Jesus Christ," Sam snarled. Behind Zimmer, Father Frank stood as if waiting his turn at the door.

"You're all right," Kitty asked, "both of you?"

"I'm fine," Frank said. "I can't answer for . . . What's that smell!"

"The church. It's filled with smoke."

Frank's voice rose. "A fire?"

"No, somebody burned something, I guess on a fireproof tarp."

Tom Zimmer's eyes at first widened, then became as small and black as withered olives. Frank pushed past them. Tom hesitated, then faded back into the rectory.

"Call for forensics," Kitty said. "We're gonna want to know everything we can about that smoke."

"You think—"

"This is the scariest, sickest crime I've ever encountered."

They went out to their car and put in the call.

"Now," Kitty said, "the question is, which one of these guys is our maniac?"

"You're suddenly sure it's one of the priests?"

"Nobody came or went. Nobody."

"After eleven-fifty, remember. We weren't here before then."

"Hell," she said, "the floor's still warm. It was done while we were here. Had to be."

"I wonder who he burned?"

"We'll find out. Maybe not right away, but we'll find out."

"You really believe we could be dealing with one of the priests?"

"Father Zimmer. Did you see the look on his face just now? He was . . . I don't know how to describe it."

"I think you could charitably say that there was not a lot of compassion there."

"He wasn't even scared!"

"He's a fragile old man. Hell, they're all fragile old men."

"Frank's not."

"He's the only one that seems human to me," Sam replied. "The other two—Jesus God spare me in a dark alley."

"Father John's a sweetie. And he has a great rep. People think he's a saint."

"He had a girlfriend with a whip under her bed!"

"Maybe that's not the whole story. Maybe he's as innocent as he says he is." Kitty didn't know what to think and she didn't care to speculate. She was frantic now, she knew another human being had died horribly last night, knew it as sure as she was a police detective, and she was almost beside herself.

Voices were raised in the church. "That's forensics. I'm going back." She marched into the church, and was greeted with an astonishing sight: Father John and Father Frank were prostrate, lying side by side before the altar. "Christ!" She thought they'd been overcome by fumes. "Fathers!"

They did not move. But they weren't in any danger. They were praying, praying with all their hearts and souls, to their God for the deliverance of the parish they loved and the great religion that they served.

They knew the stakes here. The crimes that had already been committed in this place would be remembered along with those of Blackbeard and Jack the Ripper and John Wayne Gacey.

But these were worse crimes, in a very particular way. Usually criminals do not attack an institution with their crimes. It's insanity or greed or a broken soul that leads to crime.

These crimes were a brutal, naked assault on the Church itself, an attempt to wound Catholicism. It would not be a fatal wound, of course, but it would be a severe one.

It's a priest, she thought. A priest who hates the Church.

She looked down at the two men lying in the aisle. She listened to the clatter of the forensics guys getting a ladder so that they could reach the soot deposits on the rafters.

"Fathers?"

"Not now," Father Frank said.

His voice was so deeply gentle, she could not believe that he was a criminal. And as for Father John, he looked about as dangerous as a gerbil.

"Shit," she said to Sam as they watched the techs working and listened to the priestly mantra at their feet, "what if there's somebody living in the walls?"

11

JOHN DRAGGED HIMSELF UP TO HIS OFFICE. THERE HADN'T BEEN any morning Mass, not with that stench clinging to everything.

He was drained; he wouldn't have minded going back to bed. His cell was not an inviting place, though. He'd never decorated it, not like Frank. You wanted to enter Frank's room with its colorful curtains and its attractive bedspread. He had stayed with a seminarian's gray blanket and iron bedstead. The only decoration was a large cross, which he would gaze at in the night, gaze in wonder.

Thoroughly miserable, he called Lupe and told him to come over and air out the church. Services had to be held as soon as possible. Somehow, M. and J. must survive.

He dropped into his office chair and then wished he'd stopped in the bathroom for some aspirin. He ached all over, not just his head. What sleep he'd gotten must not have been deep enough to work. And the smoke had done its part. It was the most disgusting thing he'd ever smelled. He rubbed his cheeks, and found that the prick of his beard hurt his left hand. It was more than slight; actually it hurt a good bit. He looked at his hand. There along the side was a burn, not a bad one, but very definitely a burn.

Was it coffee, this morning? Possibly, but he hadn't noticed. How about last night? He didn't recall burning himself.

Tina Signorelli, the parish secretary, gently reminded him of an appointment waiting downstairs.

He went down, wondering what he would say, how he would ever find the grace for poor little Joanie McReady and her terrible problems.

She had been standing at the window in the parlor. The instant he entered, she practically threw herself at him. "Father, I won't take up much of your time. I've just got to talk to you, I've got some awful news."

"Oh, honey, I'm sorry." He sat across from her. He had baptized her, watched her go from innocence to blooming girlhood to this, a tired thirty-five, cut by gray. As a girl, she'd been a quiet, sweet little creature. They'd had Mary and Joseph school then. He never would have closed it, except that his sisters had quit. Whatever gave them the idea that opening a drug-treatment center in Harlem was a more important ministry than teaching young Catholics? The center was long since closed, and he didn't know what had become of the Teresian Sisters.

"Father, Dr. Gentile—"

"I thought Pete Morris was your doctor."

"He's my internist. Dr. Gentile is my oncologist at Sloane-Kettering. He told me yesterday that I've got another probable primary in my right lung, and my pancreas is involved."

"Oh, Joanie, I'm so sorry."

"I've heard a million 'I'm sorrys' and they don't help. My problem is, I'm suffering a hell of a lot more than Jesus *ever* suffered, and I do not enjoy the privilege of a direct relationship with God."

"Of course you do."

"Father, behind all the doctor bullshit is the central fact that I am dying and my little girl is going to be left to *him!*"

"Your family can help."

"My mother's senile. When I die, she goes to the state. All Tiffy's gonna have is her father."

"Joanie, we've been over this before."

"But now it's certain! I'm going to die and he is going to get my beautiful little girl baby!" She drew herself up, sucking in her narrow cheeks. "He won't put her up for adoption. He refuses!"

"But he is her father."

"You know why I got my annulment! He's an alcoholic and he cannot control it. You know what he did to us, how hard he hit us! I had to protect her with my body, I had to lie on top of her and take it, or he would have beaten my baby to death!"

What could he say that would help this poor woman? She was absolutely right: Christ had not suffered like this, at least not physically. He considered the condition of the father to be his fault. He should have gotten Brian and his mother into counseling back when the boy was ten. He had not done that, and the option had certainly been open to him.

"Joanie, I'll promise you to refer Tiffany to the Catholic Home Bureau, if he doesn't take custody."

"Oh, no, Father! Don't let him get her! For the love of God, this is worse than the cancer! Please, Father!" She opened her hands, pleading.

What could he do? Take the case to Family Court? If a finding of incompetence or abandonment was handed down, only then could he refer the child to the Home Bureau. She would go to a healthy, nurturing Catholic foster care facility, but not unless the court could be moved to deny the father custody. There was tremendous weight of precedent in favor of the natural parents.

The suffering of this woman, dying slowly and in agony, knowing that her daughter would be left in terrible peril, was almost too awful to contemplate. What should he say to her?

Nothing would comfort her. Should he counsel more prayer? She was in the church every morning as it was.

"Father, don't just sit there staring at me! I'm not a creature in a zoo!"

"I know that, darling."

She sank to her knees in front of him. "Please promise me you'll help her. *Personally*, Father! Find somebody to adopt her. Find a good family, please, I know you can do it!"

He remembered Joanie as a child going primly along the aisle with her hands folded, her eyes down, her little hat bobbing on her head. Tiffy was a larger girl, full of mischief, a freer spirit than her mother had been.

He said a prayer, almost wordless: Grace, please. . . . "Get up, Joanie. Let's stop calling this your problem and call it our problem, okay? We'll solve it together."

It shocked him to realize that he was lying. He'd be long gone by the time Joanie died. This was going to be Frank Bayley's problem.

She came back to her chair, leaned forward. "I'm sorry, Father." She took his hands. Her skin was cold and startlingly dry, her grip was harrowing. "I have to have your promise."

He could not tell her the truth, he didn't have the strength. Maybe he'd find some way to hang on here, anyway. Maybe it wasn't over yet. "Of course I promise."

"No! I want more than that! Say, 'I promise to find adoptive parents for Tiffy McReady, to get her away from her daddy.' Father, say it!"

"I promise to find adoptive parents for Tiffy. To do what I can to protect her from her dad."

"What'll you do? Tell me exactly."

"I won't let her father abuse her. I'll counsel him. I will visit their household, and if I see evidence of problems, I will report this to Family Court and get a social worker for her."

She fairly screamed, "Father, this is not what I want!" Then she was consumed by a ripping cough that left her face as white as chalk. "Sorry. This is . . . Excuse me . . . Oh, my God, it hurts! Oh, my God!" Her hands shaking, she pulled a bottle of bright yellow pills out of her purse, threw three of them into her mouth. "The fact that it'll only get worse makes the pain much harder to bear. Oh, *God!*" She began shaking uncontrollably, going into some sort of seizure.

He went to her, put his arms around her. Was she dying here, now? "Tina, call St. Vincent's! Tina?" Naturally, she'd chosen the moment to step out. "Tina!"

Then Frank was there, moving like some enormous humped primate, and he took Joanie in his arms. He carried her to the couch and laid her down. There were yellow pills all over the floor. "What are they?" he asked her.

"Dilaudid."

"They don't prescribe that, do they?"

"The painkillers they prescribe for me aren't worth a shit. I buy my relief in Washington Square Park."

Gently Frank stroked her forehead. "That's all right, as long as you didn't take too many. Did you take too many?"

"It's not the Dilaudid, it's the disease! Just let me be, I'll get myself together."

"Sure you will. Now, you just close your eyes, you rest. You're safe with us."

"Tiffy gets out of school at two-thirty. She'll want me, she'll . . ."

"The sisters will take care of your little one," he said. His eyes met John's, telegraphed a question: Why is she like this?

"Joanie's been told she's dying," John explained.

A great howling cry burst out of her and John Rafferty saw human pain raw and exposed. Her torment reached out to them both and included them. John's mind brought forth the image of a hot, stony hill and a bent little naked man choking out his last on a cross made of a couple of tree limbs, his lips drooling with blood and mucus, feces smearing his slowly kicking legs.

Frank gave him a long, searching look. They each knew what was in the other's heart. "We can't cure her, Frank."

He nodded. His eyes were wet. "She's sleeping. Just like that."

"Those pills are heavy stuff."

"She needs heavy stuff, John."

Her breathing was soft and regular, but on her face there was an expression from war. John put his hand on her cold, clammy brow.

"We better let her sleep," Frank whispered. "I doubt if she gets much good sleep." Silently Frank bent down and gathered Joanie's pills into the little bottle, closed the lid, and carefully put it into her purse.

John looked down at her, thinking that she would struggle and suffer a little longer, and then Frank would be burying her. He knew the scene: the three-hundred-dollar coffin from DiMarco's, gray or black, the quick Mass in the empty church, then the long, stifling ride out to the cemetery and the interment.

He made a mental note to call the husband, and to see if he couldn't convince him to put the daughter up for adoption. That would be the best way, a good Catholic family who would love her and help her to forget.

Then he remembered. "The daughter's going to be your problem, Frank."

"Yeah. A terrible problem."

"Maybe you can convince the father to give her up. I'm sure the Home Bureau has a wonderful family just waiting for her."

"I'll study up on the kinds of sentences given to child beaters. Maybe I can scare the father into doing what's right."

"In your confession rite—this situation was what I confessed. Brian McReady is the child who got abused because I was too arrogant to get the mother to go into counseling. It's my fault, Frank."

"The sin of pride is a subtle business, John."

"What does that mean?"

"The McReadys' problems are bigger than you. It's pure egotism to lay claim to the whole catastrophe."

"You know, you'd actually make quite a good pastor. There was a lot of diplomacy in that answer."

"Then call Quindlan, tell him. Spare yourself the ordeal of the board."

Suddenly the fires of defiance flared in John again. He thought of Christos. A Christos priest was just too conservative for M. and J. There'd be havoc! He clapped his curate on the shoulder. "One day you will," he said, "but not just yet."

Tina came in and reminded him of the Hall baptism. He was apprehensive that the church wouldn't be presentable. But in the event, all went well.

Then he made a call to the roofing contractor, did some paperwork concerning incinerator repairs, and then noon was on the way.

Frank stuck his head in John's door. "I'll take the twelve-thirty Mass," he said.

"Yeah? Was there ever any doubt?" It was the damned curate's Mass. Frank took it every day.

"I'm the pastor," Frank said gently. "You should take the curate's Mass." His voice was taut, the gentleness forced.

"The hell! I'm pastor until the personnel board hands down its ruling."

"That isn't what Monsignor Quindlan told me."

"He hasn't got the authority to tell you anything, young man. The full board has to pass on it if I refuse to resign. And I refuse!"

"How arrogant you are."

"Arrogant! You . . ." For once John Rafferty was at a loss for words.

"I think 'arrogant' is the right word. You're openly defying the cardinal. *And* the Holy See, which has a hand in this."

"Oh, so now you're the pope's fair-haired boy too. Speaking of arrogant."

"Christos has a very special relationship with the papacy, and so do Christos priests. His Holiness considers himself our patron within the Church. And I'm not in the least arrogant about it. We're simply doing what we do best—"

"Stealing a parish from a good man!"

"Oh, John, come on. We're friends. *Good* friends. You're

compromised in this parish, and you know it. But you can do good work at Charities. Think of it! With your energy and administrative know-how, you're going to accomplish wonders. The bottom line is, the changes are going to help more people all the way around, and that's what this church is about."

"I'll say this for you, Frank. You *want* a parish. I suppose I should be pleased you're not burned out like half the other priests in the archdiocese." He had to laugh a little, comparing Frank to some of his more abrasive and straightforward elders. "You come off like the sweetest guy this side of heaven. But you're pretty slick, my friend."

Very deliberately Frank turned and put his back to John. He stared out the window. "You're not my spiritual director," he finally said. What bitterness a subdued tone can convey.

On the street a girl of about fourteen was giving a tiny boy a tongue-lashing in what sounded like Greek. The sun alternately blazed forth and disappeared behind fast-moving clouds.

Slowly Frank's gaze returned to his surroundings, resting at last on John himself. John could see the anger, the fury there. He found it confusing: Frank's rage was out of all proportion to the situation, and very out of character. Frank might be pretty political, but this kind of anger wasn't part of his makeup.

Indeed not—his broad smile quickly reappeared. But it was all false; John saw that now for the first time.

"John, I love you and I don't want to hurt you."

John just looked at him.

12

I T WAS NEARLY THREE IN THE MORNING AND FRANK WASN'T
asleep, because he was afraid to sleep. He was terribly
worried about the parish. There had been six people at
noon Mass today, where there were usually thirty. Next Sunday was going to be a disaster.

Unless the killer was caught, and caught soon, M. and J.
was going to stop being a parish and start becoming a tourist
attraction. He could hardly imagine what the papers were
going to look like tomorrow, when the latest outrage was
reported.

First there was Maria's death—a more-or-less-conven-
tional murder, except for that gasoline. Then there was the
homeless man on the pier, strangled and burned. Then the
woman inside the church, also strangled, left in the dumpster
surrounded by candles.

Now a body had been burned inside the church.

Frank saw the subtle escalation. This was not only about

murder, it was about destroying a parish and wounding the Church itself. In some strange way, it was about fire.

He intended to spend the critical few hours before dawn in the church, and to keep doing that until the criminal was caught.

This morning he'd lain beside John on the altar steps, thinking only one thing: God save her, God save M. and J. The words had gone through his head again and again, while the police technicians murmured among themselves, scraping soot from the rafters.

At two this afternoon they'd been told that the soot contained human fat. John had taken the call, then gone into the downstairs toilet and vomited. Frank had felt greasy, and showered.

Just thinking of it made him want to shower again. He went into the bathroom, threw off his pajamas and turned on the water. It was a nice sound, the shower. You had your best privacy there, better even than in your room.

He stood with the water pummeling him, trying to find some sort of oblivion. Eyes closed, he breathed deep.

Then he heard a sound. He listened—behind the roar of the water, hadn't that been a scream? And those other noises, they were thuds. Loud, hard thuds!

He turned off the water.

Silence.

"Hello?"

Not a sound. Imagination. He returned to the shower, trying to enjoy himself, to clean himself. He thought of the burned man, the unknown burned man, and he began washing himself, getting a thick lather of soap over his whole body. His eyes closed, he felt for his Prell, he shampooed. That smoke—would he never stop smelling it?

Just when he was covered in soap and shampoo, he heard another scream. This was loud and protracted and loud. He jumped out of the shower and went to the bathroom door. Pushing soap out of his eyes, he threw the door open.

The place was dark and quiet. He cursed the idiot drunk

who must be screaming in the street. He cursed himself for being so nervous. Then he told himself to calm down. Throwing curses was not very priestly. Say a prayer.

He shut the bathroom door with the Hail Mary on his lips.

When he stepped back into the shower, it was ice cold. He stifled a shriek of his own, gasped. Damn that ridiculous old water heater! Damn this ancient rectory! And above all damn that cheap old pastor who would not replace a thirty-year-old appliance!

He danced, he jerked, he forced himself to rinse off. Some shower—at the moment it wouldn't have been hard to convince him that hell was cold.

He hopped out of the stall, feeling the sort of blind, savage rage that he most disliked in himself. He took pride in his gentle nature. As a kid he'd beaten a few of his friends pretty badly when he was in this state. He could not quell it: the only way to deal with it was prayer.

That was what he needed now—prayer. He had a good reason to go down to the church, beyond even the need to guard it. He had to pray this feeling right out of his system.

He leaned against the bathroom wall. In his imagination he saw the intruder, a shadow moving with the spastic accuracy of an insect.

Then he heard footsteps, real ones, very soft. They were coming down the hall. He listened, toweling himself with a vigor just this side of pain. Then he wrapped the towel around himself. He thought maybe one of the other priests was waiting to use the toilet. John would have said something.

"Tom, if that's you out there, rattle the doorknob."

Nothing.

All right.

"If anyone's there, say something."

There was only the sound of the shower dripping. Frank looked at the door. He looked down at his own body, drew the towel tighter.

Absolute silence.

Goddammit!

He put his hand on the doorknob, thought better of it, and first turned out the light. It took a few seconds for his eyes to get used to the darkness. He was furious now, with the sounds, with the silence, with the whole damn situation. He didn't like being scared. Being scared made him damn mad.

Again he grasped the doorknob. With a single swift motion he turned it and pulled the door. The hallway was black and silent. He lunged for the switch, found it, and flooded the hall with light.

Empty.

Fuck this, fuck it! He hated this fucking place! When he went for the bathroom light his damp fingers got a shock. With an oath he snatched his hand back. He hammered at the switch, got another shock. Then he was slamming at walls, dancing around, kicking—and all of a sudden the shower door was dissolving in a spray of glass.

Ah, fuck!

He reached down to get at the mess, threw his towel over the shards, started cleaning them up. He'd just scooped them up in the towel when he noticed a pair of feet in the doorway.

He looked up.

There stood Tom Zimmer in his robe and slippers.

"I had a fucking accident!" Frank snarled. Once he would have lunged at the guy, given him a nose he'd never forget. Jesus, help me, he said within, exactly as he'd been taught at the seminary.

The anger faded.

"I had a little accident," he said. John was now standing behind Tom.

"Are you hurt, Frank?"

"No. I heard our resident ghost in the hall and I . . . got scared. I slipped . . ."

"I'll clean it up, you go on back to bed."

"Thanks, John, but I think I'd better do it." He set about the work, using two cloth towels and some paper ones from the roll under the sink. The two older priests soon returned to their bedrooms.

Back in his own room, Frank put on his sweatsuit and running shoes. He went to John's open door. The priest lay with his face turned to the wall. He appeared to be asleep, or trying to get there.

As Frank moved along the hall and down the stairs, every creak made him stop for a moment. He was like a creeping rat. The image distressed him.

Tom Zimmer certainly wasn't sleeping. He opened his eyes as soon as he heard Frank on the stairs. He lay still, his body coiled. His first thought was to leap out of bed at once, but his natural instinct to caution made him hesitate.

He waited, listened. What had Frank been doing up? What was going on?

They'd said that the killer operated late at night.

Frank had thought of entering the church through the inside door, but he was afraid of its squeaking. He pulled the front door open and slipped outside. He would go around, quieter this way. Wind swept out of the north, bringing with it long billows of cloud that glowed brown in the city lights. He went down the steps, moved away from the rectory, going up the street toward the front of the church.

For a moment Tom wasn't certain that he'd heard the front door close, the sound had been so small. The dead quiet that followed, though, told him that nobody was moving in the house. Frank had indeed gone out.

Tom knew a lot of things; people drop their guard around a silent man.

It was a thing of God's, this extraordinary and blissful affliction. He'd been making a valentine for his sister on the afternoon of February 8, 1983, when he had realized that his body was filled with light. You can't see inside yourself, but he could feel it, and when he closed his eyes he was no longer in darkness.

The light had stayed, it had become his friend. Nobody

else knew it was there, but *he* knew. It felt so good that he could not speak. He just couldn't get to the words. The light was his friend, holy light. And so it had remained, ever since its coming. He now prayed to the light inside: Oh, God, help this boy.

He threw back his covers, dragged some corduroy pants on over his pajamas, and pushed his feet into his one pair of loafers. He pulled on a thick Irish sweater and took the stairs two at a time.

As he left the rectory he saw a shadow slipping around the corner onto Seventh Avenue. Tom followed, fighting his overcoat on in the hard, frozen wind.

Frank leaned into the wind's steady pressure. Briefly he wondered if the police were watching. He found that he didn't care. He had work to do in that church, and he intended to do it. He moved up the crooked slate sidewalk, past the dark bulk of the church.

When he turned the corner onto Seventh Avenue, the wind hit him hard. The weather was changing again. Low icy clouds were coming down out of the north. Tomorrow they would banish the sun, driving the city deeper into winter.

He went up the steps to the portico, then unlocked the church. He entered.

Tom's old bones were not up to cold like this. He was going to pay dearly for being out here. He hunched his shoulders, shivering almost uncontrollably. He realized that Frank was going in the front of the church. Now, why would he be doing this at four in the morning?

The light in him knew. The light in him grieved. Protect the Church, the light said. Save her!

God had struck Tom Zimmer dumb so that he could see things that human beings weren't supposed to talk about. He could see demons in their panicky swarms, and the angels who smote them with fiery swords.

Satan had a lodging in Frank Bayley, Tom could see the

dark of it. When Tom prayed for the poor priest, he could see into the hidden world of the soul, where the demon was caressing Frank with its long arms.

In his youth Frank had adored the sensation of wind over his naked skin . . . summer wind.

He and another boy had been sleeping out in the backyard. The breeze had freshened, and Frank had been awakened by its sighs. The wind brought the scent of flowers, and with it pale thoughts.

As if stripping before an audience of fascinated girls, he had dropped his pajamas to the ground. He'd stood naked, his skin white in the moon crescent's glow.

Then he had crept through the sleeping neighborhood, walking across the Pellys' patio and sitting for a time in one of their pool chairs. He gathered his nerve and went down the alley to a very special house. The Cutler twins were the most beautiful girls in St. Agnes School. He stood before their open window and looked down at the shadowy form of Jennifer Cutler. She was sprawled in a summer nightgown, her long white arm dangling off the side of the bed. He was twelve, he was naked, it was magic.

Then their dog had barked and a light went on in their parents' room. His flight back to his camp had been full of the most delectable fear.

Kevin, half-awake, had asked him what was going on. "I'm cold," he said, and Kevin had cuddled close and embraced him. He felt no excitement as his friend's arms caressed his nakedness. Afterward, though, he'd been afraid, and the fear had lasted for years.

To keep from being seen, Tom remained close to the wall. Frank was in no hurry. He moved slowly up the block, slouching along.

Tom began to pray: O God, free this good young man from the trial that confronts him. Take me for thy evil abode, Satan. Come into me.

Frank unlocked the door and entered the church. What if he
met the murderer here? Well, maybe that would be best. He
shocked himself; this thing was so far gone that he was actually
ready to die.

There was still a distinct sharpness to the air in here, a
nasty, awful stink of burned hair. There were no candles lit
before the Mary and Joseph altars, and the sacral candle guttered fitfully.

In the dark, the church felt huge.

He went to the place in the aisle where Maria had died,
and dropped to his knees. "I am a guilty man," he said softly.
"God, give me strength."

Tom, now standing behind Frank in the foyer, heard every
word. I hear thee calling, O Satan, in the anguish of thy fall.
The power of God was such in Tom that he could sometimes
call the angels to the defense of the good. He could call the
smiting angels of God, yes, the smiting angels, with their red
swords and their cries.

Frank crouched, his hands clasped on his chest, feeling for the
first time the fire that had been burning within him. "You are
a guilty man," he said, "guilty, guilty, guilty!" His voice
echoed in the church. In it he could hear his youth and his
sorrow and . . . a sadness as bleak as the moon.

What did he sense within? The stirring of a snake, spiritual
nausea. It was a moment of breathtaking loneliness. "I'm going
to confess! No matter what, I am going to find the strength and
I am going to do it!"

A voice seemed to echo with his voice, whispering as he
spoke. He jumped to his feet, looked quickly behind him.

For a moment Tom feared that he'd been seen. But then he
saw the eyes, and realized that Frank wouldn't be noticing
anything. Tom knew that emotion, knew it well. God was ever
wise: this boy had been chosen as the field of battle not because

he was weak but because he was strong. It was not evil that had drawn Satan into Frank's heart, but a tiny flaw in his goodness.

Why would Satan bother to destroy the weak? As it was, their souls trailed behind him in long, cold lines.

Frank teetered as if on the edge of a cliff. At the bottom of the precipice was something so hideous that he could hardly believe it was a nightmare, far less that it was real.

Satan has a body, Satan has thought and form and substance! No, his form is guilt, his substance despair, his body the rubble of destruction.

"Leave me! *Leave me!*"

Tom heard this, and knew that his instinct to come here had been a true one. This boy had lost so much, suffered so terribly. God, please just give him a little help.

But instinct told him that God would not. No, this was up to humankind. Frank could only be helped by one thing: a man of faith.

Tom was such.

As the odd sounds around him faded, Frank regained his composure. Somebody passing in the street had chanced to speak at the same time that he did, and the sound had carried.

But this feeling, this black maw that had opened up inside him! This was entirely real. It was here that the fear of confession lay. It was here that the terrors of the night flew wild. Maria had died at this very spot. Here exactly she had snared the mystery. She had suffered, you could see it in the eyes, the way her brows were knit, her face frozen in preternatural horror. Oh, yes, she had suffered.

And I'm stirring! My body is *stirring!*

Oh, no, God, don't let it be like this, don't let me have such evil, perverse, terrible feelings. God, save me, please save me! You are the resurrection.

He fell to his knees again, began to crawl toward the altar.

Please, please, I feel *it* inside me, I've got to be made clean, it has arms like an octopus choking my soul. Oh, God of forgiveness . . .

Tom watched him creep up to the altar, heard his dismal, inarticulate murmuring, sensed the awful presence, noticed that the sacral candle guttered and flashed as Frank drew closer.

When Frank reached the altar, he opened the tabernacle. He put his hand inside.

Tom acted.

A hand came down hard on Frank's shoulder, knocking the host from his fingers. "Oh!"

He whirled around. And there was old Tom Zimmer, of all people. He stood like a great shadow, his face partially hidden by a black hat. "Tom?"

The fingers dug into his shoulder. There was extraordinary strength in them, they were like spikes. Frank winced, drew away.

All at once Tom snatched up the host, ate it with an expression of defiance on his face, then turned and went marching off down the aisle, his steps resounding through the silence.

He went into his room, took to his bed. He would not confront Frank about this, not now. But the message was clear, and the message had been delivered: I know you, Franklin, and I will fight against you if you presume to take the host into your filthy maw. I know you, Frank Bayley, I know you well!

Frank was desolated. But Tom had been right, you don't put the host into a vessel as unclean as he was. And here he was consecrating, taking communion, pretending to a purity that he neither felt nor possessed.

"You're right, old man. Quite right."

All he needed now was the strength to confess. God help him, the strength!

The evil within him stirred once more, then seemed to relax. His nausea sank away. He looked down at himself, at his own body. It's real, and it's within you. Real!

Nonsense, Satan was a concept, not an actual physical presence. Satan wasn't inside Frank Bayley or anybody else. There was something else there—a condition of the soul that leads to destructive impulses. For want of a better word, he would call it darkness.

Very well, Satan was only a concept. Darkness, however, was not. Darkness was real, and darkness was right there, in the sweet center of his soul.

PROCEDURE

KITTY AND SAM HAD BEEN WATCHING THE CHURCH. THEY were backed up by two stakeout teams. They'd seen Father Frank go in, and they'd seen Tom Zimmer follow him. Neither man had come out, and now it was nearly six.

Sam favored the direct approach. "I say we confront 'em. Keep the pressure up."

"All things come to him who waits."

"That's philosophy, Kitty. You don't believe in philosophy."

"I believe that we've gotta be damn careful here. What if zeroing in on the priests is a mistake?"

"It isn't, kid. Take it from your partner."

She looked at Sam Dowd. "What we have here is a worst-nightmare situation. A crazy who leaves almost nothing behind. Most of 'em are sloppy as hell." She gazed at the church, sipped her coffee. The car was too hot, the coffee too cold. "Looks like a prison. Nice inside, though."

Dowd played with a piece of loose vinyl on the steering wheel. "I hate the place. It gives me the profound creeps."

"They're good men, Sam."

"Back to Mother Church, lady? Is that it?"

"It's not impossible."

"I wish there was an operation to dig the sentimental crap out of a person's brain. You can't think right with that shit rotting in there."

"Once a Catholic, always a Catholic."

"There could be a very wild-assed crazy living in that rectory! Or two of 'em, considering what we saw here tonight."

"Father Tom and Father Frank working together. Now, that would be a good story." She tried to imagine Frank Bayley or Tom Zimmer actually throttling someone with his bare hands. She gave it up. "I just wish it was somewhat believable in some little tiny way. But it isn't."

Dowd watched a Brownie ticketing an illegally parked bread truck. A pigeon landed on the warm hood of their car, fluffed its wings. "I'd hate to be a bird, have to live outside in the cold all winter and eat cigarette butts."

Kitty cracked the window and tossed one out. "Here, piggie." She thought for a while. "Too bad we don't know what happened in there."

"Father No-Say-Um knows. Maybe we ought to question him."

"If pitchers could talk."

"It's 'if walls could talk.' 'Little pitchers have big ears' is a different proverb entirely."

"Well, thank you. Your trenchant criticisms are always appreciated."

"I'm glad."

"I'm glad you're glad!" She wanted to defend the priests. She put another cigarette in her mouth. "I think we can assume they returned to the rectory via the inside door. I guess they're guarding the church, making sure somebody's in there during the critical hours."

Sam gave a long sigh. "I gotta admit the partners-in-crime

theory sucks." He glared into the first gleam of dawn—which, given the clouds, would also be the last. "Well, maybe we'll get a break. We're about due one."

"We don't get breaks, Dowd, we're cops."

Nobody came to the church, not even when they rang the bell for seven-o'clock Mass. It remained silent, closed, and grim.

13

J OHN KNELT IN THE CHURCH HE LOVED, SILENTLY WAITING FOR the hour when he would go uptown to confront the personnel board over losing it. It was two o'clock in the afternoon, the doors were locked, and his heart was empty of prayer.

The murders in the church, his anger, his guilt—it all weighed on him. He felt impotent to solve his problems.

During the morning he had avoided Frank, staying away from the table when he ate breakfast, keeping the door to his office closed. He was terribly upset and confused about Frank. The man was a traitor. You just couldn't interpret what he'd done in any other way. He hadn't been given this parish, he'd damn well taken it.

John thought the less of himself for wishing misfortune on his curate, but he simply could not stop himself. If you'd asked him a week ago if he was even capable of hate, he'd have said no. Thus falls the sin of pride.

Despite his efforts to turn away from the emptiness left

by Maria, she came back now. It was with shock that he realized he had unconsciously chosen to kneel in the pew where she had died. "Maria, if you're here, put your hand on my shoulder." Now, wasn't that asinine, even to think such a thing? Still, the old church was a place where ghosts might walk.

He leaned back against the hard pew. Idly he picked up one of the new missalettes. He ran a good parish, very well organized and very active.

When somebody coughed behind him, he practically expired of apoplexy on the spot. "Good Lord, Tom, where did you come from?"

Tom's lips spread with a faint dry sound. His throat worked. He looked very much like he was trying to speak.

"Tom?"

The eyes were desperate, the eyes were awful to see.

"Are you scared, Tom?" The eyes became wet. "We all are, buddy. We all are."

The man was a living, burning volcano. But John couldn't help him, not now, not in this state. Anyway, Doc had examined him thoroughly, he'd been to specialists. Diagnosis: God works in mysterious ways.

As much as he wanted to stay with Tom, to give him some comfort, John could not wait longer. As he got up, though, Tom grabbed his wrist.

"If you've got something to say, say it. Try!"

Tom shook, his mouth opened, tears poured, sweat popped out all over his face. Then he let John go, slumped back into the pew. He sat with his head bowed. The tears made a small sound, dropping on his lap.

"Here . . . here's my notepad." He put the small spiral notebook down on Tom's knee. Then he tried to maneuver his pen into the old man's hand. "Come on, Tom! You can do it!"

The pen fell to the wooden seat of the pew, making a small clatter.

John picked it up. "Sorry, Tom! God be with you." As much as he wanted to stay, he couldn't. He must not be late to his board. For all he knew, they'd seize the opportunity to take their vote without his being present, and it'd all be over before he got there.

Rather than go through the rectory and confront a possible clutch of staff there to wish him luck, he decided to retreat directly to the street. He unlocked the main door and stepped into roaring traffic and blazing sunlight. He buttoned his overcoat and adjusted his ancient fedora to a jaunty angle. He pulled his black gloves onto his hands and went down the steps to Seventh Avenue. This was not going to be his last duty as pastor. No way. Somehow he was going to win. God was on his side, had to be.

As he passed people he recognized, he nodded and smiled, touching the brim of his hat for the elderly women, who appreciated that sort of thing. He crossed Seventh, leaving M. and J. behind him. Maybe there'll be a miracle, he told himself. Then he knew it, with mystic certainty: there *would* be a miracle.

By the time the F train came clattering into the West Fourth Street station, he had changed his mind again. His mouth was parched, he was moving with the deliberation of the infirm.

This morning Mrs. Communiello had joined Tom in the land of the silent. He should have discharged her long ago, but how could he: nearly thirty years of service, and she always did her work.

Tina had told him, "I said a rosary for you, Father." Trish had wished him well in her solemn way. Even old Lupe, his hands full of light bulbs for the choir loft, had come up and yelled, "They are retardation mental who do this thing!"

Frank had spent the morning closeted in the parlor with Maureen Nicastro and the Kellys. John had heard enough of what was being said to know that they were already revising the Sunday liturgy, in preparation for Frank's takeover of the parish. They were that confident. Why George Nicastro was not lording it around the rectory with them, he did not know. Probably on a mission to Rome, the way they talked.

A man came into the subway car selling *Street News*. He stood in the middle of the car explaining the fact that the paper was the special publication of street people. Then he gave today's date, the time, and a brief weather forecast. It hurt to see the poor earnest soul with his papers and his useless information, and that hopeful grin on his face.

The doors opened onto the Second Avenue stop and John rolled out with the crowd, his intention to buy a *Street News* thwarted by the subway schedule.

The gray sky made Manhattan look washed out. People huddled along in the wind, their faces covered by scarves, their heads down. The parish soup kitchen had distributed eighty-seven hot lunches yesterday, the clothing program had given away every scarf, glove, and overcoat it possessed. They should have opened Ami Hall as a temporary shelter tonight, but they just didn't have the resources. You needed more than beds, you needed guards. Homeless people were not necessarily nice people.

Crossing the street, he stepped into a hole, filling his left shoe with freezing slush. He went staggering into the chancery building, his foot sloshing.

They made him wait in an anteroom like a little boy seeing the principal. He sat there, his collar eating into his neck, searching along the beads of his rosary. He was reminded of nervous seminary days.

"Father?"

"Oh, Pete. Hi."

Pete Garrison smiled a thin smile. They had been distant classmates at St. Joseph's. Pete had been a big, humorous redhead. Now he was hairless and looked as if somebody had attacked him with an air pump.

Monsignor Robert Quindlan sat at the head of the long table in the grim conference room. This couldn't be the only place at 1011 Third for conferences. With its gray walls and Formica table, it looked like it had been decorated by the City Department of Corrections. John was shown to the seat opposite Bob. Head of the table, place of honor. There were murmurs as he sat, but no smiles.

Before each man was a Xerox copy of the *Post's* infamous "CHURCH OF BLOOD" headline. Toby Johnson had already drawn a doodle on his, appropriately enough, of a cross and a rather graceful lily of the valley. There was a TV on a cart, with an ancient and enormous VCR under it. Surely they weren't going to make him sit through the torture of his moment of fame.

They were, and he did. In the dazzling TV lights he looked like some sour old vampire. His effort to contain his grief had made him strident. His voice was as tight as wire: "The priest is weak!" The cut of it made him wince.

He wanted Maria with him now. A priest's only loves should be God and the Church.

Maria would have been an effective advocate. Christos might write fifty letters; Maria would have orchestrated a hundred. She would have won. Afterward the two of them would have drunk each other's eyes across the little distance they had by silent consent established between themselves.

John was brought back to the meeting by a curious golden light that seemed to enter the conference room. Perhaps it was only a shaft of sunlight reflected off the office tower across the street. But it seemed to him to bring with it spiritual implications. He briefly had the feeling that somebody—or something—great was searching about in the hearts of the men present. Then, very distinctly, a hand touched his shoulder.

"Well, John, if you have anything to say . . ." Bob Quindlan met his eyes.

"Am I to take it that I'm just here for the formal opening of the veins?"

"Oh, hey, wait a minute," Toby said. "You know what we were talking about before you came in? We were trying to figure out how to get you to go over to Charities and do an important job that suits you perfectly. We don't want to open your veins, man. We want to motivate you!"

Father Richard Joseph spoke up. He was ancient beyond belief, Father Joseph. He probably predated Spellman, if that was humanly possible. His parish used to be something big up in Westchester. "Everybody's hurt by these things, John. Think not of the pastor, think of the pastorate. All we're asking of you is that you withdraw from the front lines. I know it's hard for a soldier to accept a desk job, but sometimes that's what has to be."

"I don't think I should go. I don't want to. And it's the wrong time for a replacement to come into my parish."

Bobby reached across the table, couldn't quite touch his hand. "You've been down there for a thousand years, John. I'd think you'd welcome a change."

"You have to resign, John. For the good of your people. Not to mention the Church at large."

"There's been curial interest," Bobby said. "Rome has investigated, and Rome has responded." He pulled a fax out of his briefcase, which was on the floor beside him. " 'We regret the misfortune that has befallen this worthy priest, and wish that he devote his substantial energies to the work to which Cardinal O'Connor directs him. Please express to him that he is remembered in the prayers of this Collegium.' " He looked at John. "That is from the papal secretariat, initialed by Cardinal Thomasini."

"You guys sure know how to make a fella feel like an ingrate. Am I supposed to be grateful that I'm being pushed out? I've tried, but I just don't have that kind of gratitude in me. I'm sorry."

Bob Quindlan shook his head. "I can't reach you, John. Look. Let me try another tack. We need priests, we're desperate. And a priest like you—you're worth your weight in gold. Double your weight. I'm worried that you'll leave us, to be frank."

"Then don't throw me out of my parish."

"John, the media is eating us alive! Not to mention—I hate even to say it—not to mention the damn police. I know it's profoundly stupid, but the fact is that you had motive and opportunity, and they can be quite unreasonable about things like that."

"You already hit me with this, Bobby. I still don't see how my going to Charities will change a darned thing with the police."

"It'll take you out of the front lines."

"So you won't have to risk lurid television coverage of a pastor being arrested for the murder of his lover. As absurd and outrageously unfair as that would be."

When he lowered his head, Bobby now had three chins. "The welfare of the Church must be my first consideration, always. In the eyes of the public, indictment is tantamount to conviction. Even if you're innocent—which I'm sure you are —the damage would be done."

John could not deny the fact that Bob was right. If the worst happened, things like his arrest and arraignment would be much less damaging if he was out of the public eye.

Joe DiMarco spoke up. "I'm sorry, John. I love you, and we didn't come here to destroy anybody. If you won't give us your resignation, we're going to move to the formal vote."

There was no ballot box. Bob Quindlan simply asked if anybody on the board objected to the personnel director's decision.

He had not one single supporter. He'd known some of these men for thirty years, played golf with them, commiserated with them, even counseled a few of them. Now they were united against him, and the bitter part was that they'd made him see the sense of their position.

"All right," he said. He hoped he sounded better in the pulpit. "I'll go. I won't make any more of a stink than I already have. But I want some terms. I want another month in the parish. Then I'll go where I'm sent."

Bob nodded, then pushed his chair back. He went to a side table, picked up a phone. Although he spoke quietly, it was obvious that he was clearing the matter with somebody. He turned to John: "I'm sorry, but we want to do this immediately."

"Was that the cardinal?" he asked as Bob put the phone down.

"Hardly. The cardinal's in conference with the Manhattan borough president at the moment, discussing unrelated matters. That was Frank Bayley."

"He's a fine young man, but he'll throw the parish into total confusion."

"John, I have sixty-one open positions for priests on my books, including four pastorates. I consider myself lucky to have that young man. He actually *wants* your parish. Which, by the way, is already a bit of a shambles."

John went to his feet. He raged inside at this direct insult, then grabbed his anger and offered it up. "I'm being retired because of an imaginary indiscretion, not genuine incompetence," he said with a mildness he did not feel. "My parish is not a shambles, it's a triumph." With exaggerated care he pushed back his chair. "I'm not mad at you guys," he managed to croak. "I'm . . . It's just the situation! I'm sorry."

Carefully, holding his head up, shaking the tears from his eyes, he turned and left the conference room. He closed the door softly behind him.

This was it, he was finished. His first impulse was to tell Maria, which reminded him that he was absolutely alone in this world. He had only his God, and right now his God might as well be in a coma for all the interest He was taking in John Rafferty. He went down the long hall, stood in the slow, stuffy elevator, went out into the lonely streets.

He wasn't pastor of Mary and Joseph anymore. Frank had won. What about his gays, his homeless, his staff? What about Joanie McReady, she'd suffer the agonies of hell when she discovered that Father John was gone. She relied on him. He was needed, didn't they *see* that?

He had reached Fifth Avenue and was passing Saks when he suddenly decided that what he wanted was something to cheer him up. He went inside. John hadn't been in a department store in at least a quarter of a century, and the variety of things on display amazed him.

No wonder there was so much materialism in the world. Look at all the material!

He went into the men's department, looking at the fine suits, the neckties with their gaudy, complicated prints.

Then he saw hats. He pulled off his old black fedora. It

had been a miserable ghost of itself ever since it had blown under the Number 6 bus last March.

"Have you got any like mine?" he inquired of a clerk in a pin-striped suit.

The young man smiled. "May I see it?"

John gave him the fedora.

"Did you get this at an antique clothing store?"

"I bought it new . . . at Wormser's, I believe."

"Wormser's! They've been out of business for . . . God, mister . . . for years."

"Perhaps the hat is a bit old."

"Twenty years, maybe thirty. Why not try this Christie? It's a little more elegant than yours, and I think it does wonders for your face."

The young man might as well have been speaking Urdu for all the sense he made to John. He fitted the homburg onto John's head. In the mirror he thought he looked a little like Leonid Brezhnev.

"It's really great on you," the young man enthused.

"Nothing is great on me, young man. But I think it might keep the rain off my bald spot." He bought the hat.

When he returned to the street, the thin light had finally failed. An ocean of people headed south, moving toward Grand Central Station, their shoes knocking on the concrete and new ice.

He walked off through the gathering gloom with his new homburg firmly on his head.

14

The sound slipped so easily into Kitty Pearson's consciousness that she realized she was awake only when it was repeated. She listened again. Cobble Hill was a good neighborhood, but intruders were always a possibility.

The sound was soft, with a steady rhythm: swish, swish, swish. It would continue for fifteen seconds or so, then stop. If it had been summer she might have identified it as leaves brushing against a window screen. But the limbs were bare. There was also a sweet smell in the room, very faint.

Her clock read three-twenty. A hell of a time to be awake when you were coming in on the eight-to-four. She turned over, pulled the quilt up, closed her eyes. But her mind began to idle slowly, reviewing things that ought to wait until dawn.

She didn't like a situation where she had a crazy out there on the loose and all she could do was wait for a break. Even Captain Malcom was starting to leave notes about it. "Where's the production on the church case, Pearson?"

She tossed, felt a finger of cold air against her back, readjusted the covers. The church, the priests, the rectory: she thought of the nave as it must be at night, dark and forbidding. She could imagine the statues and the candles and the silence.

There is a special sort of surrender connected with faith. She could remember her own childhood piety, kneeling in among the smelly rows of Xaviers in their brown plaid uniforms, Janie O'Krent, Phyllie Gordon, Sally . . . who? Candles and incense and the drumming of the ceiling fans . . . singing *Tantum Ergo* and *O Salutaris Hostia* on Friday afternoons. Fish day. And the piety! The swelling breast of love, the novenas, the May altars, *Our Little Messenger* full of poems about the seasons and stories about the martyrs, and the great poster of the two little children at the edge of a cliff, being protected by their guardian angel.

Confession: "Bless me, Father, for I have sinned, it has been one week since my last confession. I spoke harshly to my cat, Father . . ."

Such a lot is lost. "Oh, Christ," she muttered. She threw the quilt off and sat up. There were three alternatives. She could turn on the TV and stare. She could go in the kitchen and glom cookies and feel lousy about it. She could sit here and smoke and molder. "God damn."

The Korean robe Sam Dowd had presented as a peace offering after some forgotten spat was slung over the back of a chair. She slipped it on, making a mental note to tell the damn landlord yet again that the heat sucked after midnight. Shuddering from the cold, she went into the kitchen.

It wasn't anything specific that drew her toward the kitchen window. Maybe she sensed that the darkness there was thicker than it should be. She went to the sink, leaned over and close to the glass, pressed her face against it. She cupped her hands beside her head to shut out reflections.

For an instant she saw nothing; then there was a flicker of movement and a sickle moon appeared as if somebody had pulled away a black card. With the movement there came a faint creak.

Realizing that somebody had been peering in at her—that

she'd been for an instant face-to-face with a prowler—she jumped back. Another woman might have screamed, but Kitty Pearson was long past that sort of thing. She was an effective cop who had taken her training seriously. Moving with carefully contrived languor, she returned to the bedroom. The instant she was out of sight of the kitchen window she lost the silk robe and pulled on an overcoat, then thrust her feet into a pair of Weejuns. With her snub-nose .38 in her right hand and a good flashlight in her left, she moved into the hall.

These fucking addicts were too dumb to know when to stop. Odds were the dickhead'd still be out there with his putty knife or whatever he was using to try to spring the lock on the window. Asshole. He hadn't noticed that there were screw bolts in the ends of the window frame. Springing the lock wouldn't make a bit of difference.

That swishing noise had been him working his blade into the crack between the upper and lower sash. Swish, swish, swish. What a turkey.

As she moved down the hall, she began to feel a sense of calm pleasure, like a professional gambler approaching a blackjack table. You never knew what you were going to come up with on something like this. Maybe she'd get a wanted man, a big crook. Of course, it could just as easily be some twelve-year-old kid on his first gig, but a good gambler doesn't overstate the downside.

She was careful and smart. This was her job, she knew exactly how to do it. She didn't turn on the light, and she went down to the first floor rather than step out onto the deck.

She ought to warn Mr. Florenz in the downstairs, but he was liable to ruin everything by having a fit, so she decided to let him continue his beauty sleep. If shots were fired, that'd be his alarm call.

Using the sleeve of her coat to muffle the sound, she released the deadbolt on the door that led into what was billed as a garden but was actually a grim little yard that featured a fantastically ill-groomed and ancient apple tree.

The air outside was shockingly cold. She stepped into the

well of stairs that led up to the yard. Best to go slow, there were lots of leaves around here and the silence was absolute. The least crackle would be heard.

The door had made a faint sucking sound as it opened, and she decided to leave it ajar. If the perp went inside, she would get him for sure.

What if he was carrying? So, let him carry. If she saw a piece, she'd blow him away and fuck the warning. After six years in cops, it was about time she got a notch. She took a long step up, skipping the three stone stairs. Now she was directly under her deck. Its wooden steps were to her right. Ahead was a clear view of the apple tree. She waited, fairly sure she was invisible in the deep shadow cast by the deck above her head.

She wanted to hurry, but she took her time. Let him make the first move. If he was in the yard, she was going to see him when he tried to leave. If he was still on the deck, she had him.

When she moved out into the yard, she was surprised to find that the deck was empty. She went up, looked around. There was nothing on it but the two very corroded metal chairs that had probably been sitting there since before the Second World War.

She'd missed the guy. Well, no matter, it was goddamn tit-freezing cold and she was just as glad to be able to go back inside.

She returned to her bedroom, got a cigarette, and lit it. Swish, swish, swish.

Jesus H. Christ, that guy was a significant asshole! She thrust her feet back into her shoes, put on her coat, grabbed the pistol and the flashlight. There was no sense in being quiet, this nerd was obviously totally strung out or he wouldn't have come back here three minutes after making his escape.

She stormed downstairs and out into the yard, turned on the light, and directed it up onto the deck. "Freeze, prickface!" For a long moment the black-clad figure at the window didn't move. "I've got a gun, asshole." Very slowly he started to turn his head, as if trying to peer over his shoulder. "You move even a little bit more and I'm gonna blow your balls from here to fuckin' China." She climbed the ten steps from the yard to the deck.

He was a big sonembitch, and he was dressed all in black. Very scary. "Okay, stud, spread 'em," she said. Strung out or not, a guy dressed all in black with black gloves and ski mask and all was probably a pro.

The next thing she knew she was in the air, flying backward very fast. There was no sound; she hadn't seen the perp even move. But he'd hit her, all right, a body blow so substantial that it lifted her off her feet and sent her sprawling against the railing of the deck.

The flashlight went in one direction, the gun in the other. She was aware of their sliding clatter, and then the distinct thud as the gun hit the ground below. Her one thought was to get down there and recover her piece before this crazy got to it. Her back hurt but she pulled herself to her feet and vaulted over the railing, her coat whipping around her legs.

She hit on all fours, then dived in the direction she had heard the gun fall. Where the hell was it—he's going to jump—he's coming down!

She felt cold metal, she had it! "Freeze! Police!"

Nothing. She'd expected him to be right on top of her, but he wasn't there. For a moment she was completely baffled; then she caught a movement in the upper reaches of her field of vision.

At first the black shadow moving up the side of the house simply didn't make sense. Then she realized, with astonishment and awe, that it was the prowler. He slid up the wall like a great black spider. "Jesus!" The cry was completely involuntary, drawn out of her by the fact that she was looking at an impossible act.

She raised the pistol, then thought better of it. You weren't going to hit a moving target fifty feet away in the dark, not with a snub-nosed .38. It was a good gun only if you stayed within the envelope of its possibilities.

Without a sound he reached the roof and swung over the edge. "Good God." Once she saw the top of his head bob up, then he was gone. There were eleven houses in one direction, six in the other, all connected by shared walls. He could go in either direction, let himself down to the street on a fire escape, or go out through a house if that option presented itself. There was absolutely no point in giving chase, and anyway, it was as cold as a long night in Alaska out here.

What she had to do was get on the horn to the Job *insta-mente*. She was returning to the house when she smelled the sweet odor again, and this time she knew what it was and she almost fainted with terror. Her hands were shaking so badly she could hardly reach out to feel the wall where the odor was coming from.

It was wet, dear God, it was wet.

She rushed up to the deck surface and was absolutely horrified at what she found.

A five-gallon can of gasoline had been emptied over the deck, splashed on the back wall of the house. That had been the source of the swishing sound—gas being splashed out of the container. Then she saw that a neat round hole had been made in the bottom of her bedroom window, no doubt while she was on the prowl.

Her heart was beating hard now. It was him, he was here, he was trying to burn *her*. How had he found the fucking apartment? Cops don't list their numbers or give out their home addresses.

She ran inside, pounded on Mr. Florenz's door. "Mike, get outta there!"

"Who—"

"It's Kitty, there's gasoline all over the back of the building, get out right now!"

Click, click. Door open a crack. Mr. Florenz's peculiarly boyish face was peering out, his bald pate shining in the hall light. "Kitty?"

"Somebody just poured gasoline all over the deck. They're trying to torch the building."

"Torch?"

"As in burn it down."

"Surely Mrs. Selby wouldn't—"

"Nah, it wasn't a real-estate scam. It had to do with me."

"Oh!"

She vaulted the stairs to her own place and dialed 911, told them she was an off-duty, and communicated what they needed to know.

The fire department arrived amid much neighborhood agitation and many shouted questions from up and down the block. Behind them came a squad car containing the predictable super-nerd. The burnt-out ends of the rookie class went to backwater precincts like this, and the nerd of nerds would be the one who drew the graveyard shift.

"What seems to be the problem, miss?" he said as the firemen invaded her apartment.

"I'm not a miss, I'm a gold shield," she growled. She wanted a cigarette. Considering the fumes, though, that would obviously be a big mistake. "The problem is, some asshole just tried to burn me to death."

PROCEDURE

THERE WERE SEVEN MEN PRESENT AND ONE WOMAN. KITTY was used to it. She looked from face to face, determined to speak in a clear, steady voice, the voice of a professional. She was going to hide the fact that she was scared to death. No way would the plainclothesman Hal Hawkins, or Captain Malcom, or Captain Brill hear her terror. Sam she couldn't hide from. Sam knew exactly how she felt.

"We got a very sick guy here, and he knows where we live," she said.

"Where you live," Sam murmured.

Captain Malcom: "Is there any chance we're dealing with another perp? Unrelated case?"

"None," Kitty said. "The gasoline is the signature."

"Okay, so our man knows who we are, and where we are, but we can't at present return the favor." Malcom raised his eyebrows "Any suspects?"

"He's big, he wears a commonplace black wool jacket, and he can climb walls unassisted."

"Means?"

"I saw him go up a sheer wall without so much as a fishhook to gain purchase."

Sam spoke. "Forensics pulled suspect fibers out of chinks in the brick. Just like she says, the guy went up the wall. There was no indication whatsoever that he used grapnels, ropes, or anything else. He climbed a fucking wall with his bare hands."

Captain Brill spoke. "First off, we move you, Kitty. You find a safe house, stay with a relative. Get the hell out of there. Don't even go back for your girdles."

"Captain Brill has a sense of humor, Sam. Make a note of it. As far as moving is concerned, I've already done that." She consulted her notebook, flipping pages. "Suspects: very few. We've interviewed the three priests, found a half-assed motive for one crime on the part of Father John Rafferty, but no linking evidence. And none of the priests looks like a sequential killer. The building custodian is an elderly Hispanic with bad arthritis. We've followed up on everybody else with keys and found a collection of elderly ladies and gentlemen, some with teeth, some without."

Silence fell. Dowd broke it. "We haven't yet located the weapon in the Julien case. The other two were barehand stranglings. With crushed vertebrae. And then there's the dead unknown, where we got nothing but carbon scrapings."

"What a fucking mess."

"We've had the church under stakeout. Aside from normal movements, nothing. Two of the priests went in at three o'clock yesterday morning."

"That's not suspicious?"

"One alone—"

"I get your drift."

"One of the priests had a leather goddess. I found leather implements in the Julien apartment," Kitty added. "Caught him trying to take them out, as a matter of fact."

Malcom chuckled. "That's sweet. I love it."

"The oldest priest is mute. Can't talk, can't write."

"Crazy?"

Kitty nodded. "And also at least seventy-five. The guy on

my deck was strong and fast. The strong young priest is a straight shooter. Father Frank. He's the good guy in this."

Malcom looked from face to face. "So what we got is, we got shit. Am I right?"

Ruefully Kitty nodded.

"And the perp knows where we live, and is willing to come after us."

Kitty nodded again. "Very definitely."

"I think we oughta get a search on the rectory. See if we can find matching fibers."

"What if we do? The fibers are commonplace. If one of these guys owns a jacket from the Gap or Sears or Penney's, for example, it's gonna have matching fibers."

"So we got no probable cause for a search anyway, is what you're saying?"

"That's right, cap."

Malcom shook his head. "Shit. Maybe we can get somebody's permission. The chancery. They're all over this thing. If I make a couple calls, maybe they'll let us do it."

Kitty thought about that. "It sounds like it's still illegal search."

"The Church owns the property, not the priests," Malcom replied.

"Landlord, in other words."

"Not exactly. The priests aren't tenants. They're domiciled at the sufferance of the owner. I think we'd have a good search, even without a warrant."

"If we get a matching fiber, then what?"

Malcom looked at her like she was a moron. Then he blinked.

She held her ground. "What, Captain? Make an arrest?"

The captain glared at her. "If I get the cardinal's permission, I want samples off every coat in the place. And nobody on the premises is to know." Kitty realized that he, also, was afraid, which made it all that much worse. "If we find any gasoline hidden anywhere, we take prints, arrest the man who's been touching the can."

Sam gave him a sidelong look. "Then what?"

"You bring him to me and I break the fucking bastard!"

"A priest?"

"Don't give me that, Sam! This shithead is no priest, whether he wears the collar or not."

Hawkins spoke up. "Lemme see if I got this right. We go in, we look for fibers, we look for gas. We print gas cans."

"Exactly."

"Well, what do we do to match the prints? Priests ain't gonna be in no prints file."

Kitty did not want to see this fall apart. "We'll check with the chancery. Maybe they keep them on file."

Sam smiled. "I'm sure. And mug shots." There was general laughter.

"I wanta get this guy," Kitty said. She could hear the scream in her own voice. Everyone in the room was looking at her, regarding her with frank curiosity.

It took her a moment to realize why. There were two big tears rolling down her cheeks. She was that scared.

"Fuckin' allergies," she muttered, and headed for her locker to wipe her face.

15

I T WAS TO BE ANOTHER SLEEPLESS NIGHT FOR FRANK BAYLEY. He lay staring at the ceiling, miserable and afraid. This time he'd been awakened by footsteps outside his door. Were they imaginary? Most probably. Or if not, it was simply somebody going to the bathroom.

These terrible days had left him feeling as if something deep inside had collapsed. He was always tired. Even the little bit of sleep he got seemed useless. There were nightmares and black patches. Long black patches, and in the middle of the black patches, there were screams.

As much as he hated to do it, he was going to have to get up and check the hallway. How could someone—anyone—connected with Mary and Joseph be this wicked?

He heard the movement again. His heart began rattling in his chest. Careful not to allow the springs to squeak, he rose from the bed.

Frank went to his door, listened. Nothing. He wished to

God he had a phone in his room, he'd call the police right this instant. "Who is it?" he asked. His voice was hoarse.

The response was silence.

Tom waited. He had prayed all day and into the night, had purified himself, had entered the heart of the light.

I was made for this moment, O God, I see it now. All these years, all this glory, and now I see it, I see thy plan, O God, I cast myself before thy will.

He closed his eyes. The light within him was bright now, bright indeed, brighter than the sun.

Now I must confront thee, O serpent. He felt the light inside him, felt that it wanted to spread, to fill the world.

The moment was coming. He clasped the handle of the door.

Frank heard sounds, felt the doorknob moving! Oh, God help me. I don't want to die like this. "John," he called. And then thought: What if John is the murderer?

He felt a firm grip on the knob. Tremendously powerful fingers were turning it, rattling it against the lock, and the lock was creaking. He could hear the steel of it bending and popping as the tongue was forced back.

Now. Tom flipped on the lights, held the cross before him, and shouted out words that had been etched into his very soul: "I abjure you, ancient serpent!"

Frank drew himself up, tossed a lock of brown hair out of his eyes, and said in a high, squeaking voice, "Father Zimmer!"

"By the Judge of the living and the dead—"

"You . . . you're talking!"

Tom's voice was dry, it was mealy, it was hardly there at all. "By the Judge of the living and the dead, by your Creator and the Creator of the world—"

"Excuse me? I didn't quite catch that."

He tried to enunciate, to gain some volume. "By your own

Creator, by Him who has power to send you to hell—" The words sounded like mist falling on wet leaves.

"I'm not hearing you, Father."

He cleared his throat. He was too weak, he'd waited too long! But the volume of his voice shouldn't matter. Perhaps his faith was as weak as his vocal cords. With a silent prayer in his heart, he tried again. "Depart immediately with fear and with your army of terror. Depart from this dear servant of God, Franklin Patrick Bayley, who takes refuge in the bosom of the Church!"

Frank had cupped a hand around his ear. "I just don't quite . . ."

Tom thrust the cross at him, the cross of love, the symbol of the greatest power in the universe. "Begone! Anathema!"

Very gently Frank took the cross out of the old man's softened grasp. "Now, Tom," he said, "you've got the wrong devil." He tried to laugh, but it didn't work, not with all the guilt and the hypocrisy and the sin festering in him. Tom was right in one way: he had smelled Frank's sin.

He led Tom to his own room, and Tom went with him.

If only it was this easy—an exorcism. Yes, my friend, there is a demon in me, but it isn't the demon of murder. . . .

Frank replaced Tom's cross on the wall beside his picture of the Sacred Heart of Jesus. "Your Palm Sunday fronds," he said, picking them up from the floor, "they must have fallen down when you got your cross." He replaced them too.

When he felt the strong hand on his wrist, Tom could not resist, even though he wanted to. It was terrible, he couldn't fight! He struggled within, but his body went along like an obedient sheep. There was an electricity coming through the man's hand, controlling him against his will. Tom wanted to fight! He wanted to fight the demon!

All he could manage was a stifled, scared noise through his nose.

———

Frank gathered Tom up and hugged him close. "Poor old man," he whispered, "you need to get some sleep." He lifted Tom off the floor and began carrying him to his bed.

His hissing breath was scented with the cheddar cheese of a frozen dinner. "Hey," Frank said affably, "you ate my Lean Cuisine macaroni and cheese for supper."

When Frank had taken the cross just like that, Tom had panicked. It didn't work, none of it, not at all! But why had he been silenced, then, if not to prepare him for this great confrontation? He was supposed to exorcise Frank, but it didn't work! It did not work!

He heard his own pitiful gasps, hardly screams at all, as he was carried by this large, strong, and entirely unruffled man.

To carry a struggling human being is a revealing act. You feel the heat of his skin, smell his sweat, taste his tears. "Come on, old man, you've got the wrong guy." He laid him on the bed. "You get some sleep, you'll feel a lot better in the morning."

Tom went slack, fingers feebly worrying Frank's lapels, tears pouring from his eyes.

During his years of silence Tom had hoped and prayed that there would be some purpose. But it was all meaningless, just one more bit of random suffering in the world. The light in him wasn't the light of God. He was just a neurotic old man. Frank didn't need exorcism. It had all been a fantasy.

He wept in Frank's arms, bitter and long. "There," Frank said, "there, it'll all be over soon. . . ."

What to do, how to help the poor distraught old priest? What did Tom believe? That Frank was the murderer—or had this simply been an attempt to exorcise the demons of lust? "Tom, if you know anything about this crime, you must, *must* tell the police."

He wanted to shake the old man, restrained himself with great effort. The eyes were big and wet.

"Tom, please, I know you can talk! You were talking just now."

The eyes went unfocused, then rolled back into the head.

Just like that, Tom slept. Whatever had possessed him to act in this way? What did he know?

Frank watched him until he was sure that he was sleeping, then slipped quietly from the room.

16

WHEN JOHN HEARD MARY AND JOSEPH'S FAMILIAR BELL
toll noon, he checked his watch against it. The morning had passed so quickly that he had assumed the carillon was out of adjustment.

Now that his duties were suspended, he had spent three hours doing little more than observing Frank Bayley in his glory. Frank hurried about, full of bustle and cheer. He was on the phone, then dashing down to another meeting with the newly formed steering committee—all Christos people, of course.

John was staring at the wall when Tina put a call through to his office.

"John?" It was Bob Quindlan.

"I'm still here, if that's why you're calling. I can't figure out where to go."

"I've got good news," Bob said affably. "You've been booked onto a retreat at archdiocesan expense."

"You're a fool to put him in charge. He's too young. Plus he isn't sleeping nights. I hear him."

"He's on edge, John, just like somebody else I could name. And who wouldn't be? I'd be worried if he wasn't."

"He'll crack."

"I've had two calls from him this morning. He seems in fine form, especially considering the problems you're having down there."

"Well, maybe he is in fairly good shape. Hopefully. I'm not, I must admit."

"Take the retreat. After that we'll talk. Hell, I wish I could send all three of you guys on a nice retreat."

"But I'm the lucky winner. Whee."

"You take the Albany train, get off in Rhinecliff. If you leave at noon you'll be at Holy Name Center by four."

"Twenty-two years can't be packed up in an afternoon."

"But a bag can, Father. Have your housekeeper do the heavy packing. I'm sure Frank'll agree to have your things sent on when you're in a permanent billet."

"What's Holy Name Center? I've never heard of it."

"A retreat house frequented by the likes of Bishop Tucker and Woodward Ames, among other luminaries. We bought you a ten-day special. After that, you'll live in the hospice until we can make appropriate arrangements closer to Catholic Charities."

"So I'm to be incarcerated in the retirement center to make sure I jump at whatever dismal job you're cooking up for me."

Bob chuckled. "Nothing of the kind."

John was not the sort to slam down phones. Rather, he placed the receiver carefully in its cradle. Then he sat staring at the blank wall across from him. For twenty years he'd planned to put a picture up on that wall. He opened his desk drawer. Paper clips, Bic pens, an unlabeled computer diskette, a ruler, his personal appointment book. He took out the book.

It was filled in partly by Tina's neat hand, partly by his own scribble. Today was February 26. Two days to Ash Wednesday, amazing. It was already the beginning of Lent.

He'd had a Pre-Cana conference scheduled for tonight, four couples. There was a finance-committee meeting at six. Confessions at five. The roofing contractor was due here at two. Frank Bayley was going to be a busy boy. You could be sure they'd get him a bright young curate within a matter of weeks. An ordinary pastor could wait years.

He turned the pages, February 27, 28, March 1—an endless list of duties and obligations. The deeper he went into the calendar, the fewer notations there were in his own hand. Then he saw "March 1, Maria b-day. Dinner? Lent???" He'd wondered how you celebrated birthdays during the season of atonement. Eat a cake sprinkled with ashes? Give a hair shirt?

He closed the appointment book and dropped it into the trash. Why not? He wasn't going to have personal appointments anymore. The sense of finality grew in him. He was sitting here for the last time, meaning to pick up a print for that wall for the last time, looking at his schedule for the last time.

There came a tap at his door, very light. How odd, nobody in this rectory tapped. They either hammered or—more usually—just barged in.

Tom was standing in the doorway. His eyes were hollow, he'd aged a thousand years. "Yes, Tom. Come on in."

"Fff—"

He was trying to talk! "Come on, Tom, you can do it!"

"Nnn!"

"Frank, he's talking!"

He leapt into the room.

"I think he's starting to communicate! Listen!"

But Tom had fallen silent again. He was staring at Frank. Veins throbbed in his neck.

"I might as well tell you that we had a contretemps last night. I think Tom's . . . old, I guess, is the most polite word. Right, Tom?"

"What happened? What kind of a fight could you have with him?"

Nobody spoke at first. But the silence needed filling, and

Frank finally did it. "Not a fight. A sort of confrontation. He tried to perform an exorcism on me. To be blunt."

John looked at Tom. "Tom?" His eyes were practically bulging out of his head. His face was stricken. "Tom, can you tell us why?"

"Uuh—gglll—"

John shifted his gaze back to Frank. "And you have no idea?"

He shook his head. "When you called, I thought maybe he'd told you."

"Grunts."

"You could hear the words of the exorcism. Just. But I have no idea what he was trying to accomplish."

John wanted to say: Maybe he knows you're a hypocrite and a thief—but he let it lie.

Tom was still struggling to speak, but there was only an awful, stuffed gobbling sound; then the old man slumped and hung his head.

John thrust one of the Bic pens into his hand. It dropped to the floor. He wanted to slap him, force him. Look at him, it broke your heart! "Mmmsss" he said, "msss . . ."

"Mss—miss? Is that 'miss'?"

He nodded furiously.

He will miss me. How touching. "I'll be around," John said. "It ain't over until the fat lady dances, right? You might even find me back on station soon."

Tom clapped his hands onto both of John's shoulders, then embraced him. The emotion involved was the greater because it was silent. Twenty-plus years they'd been living under the same roof.

After a long, pregnant moment Tom turned abruptly, as if he could bear no more. His shoulders stooped, he struggled off down the hall.

Frank looked after him. "He said a good bit of the Rite of Exorcism."

"Is there something you need to say, Frank?"

"Implying what?"

"Well, he's seen something he doesn't like."

Frank shook his head. "He's senile," he said. "I've done nothing to justify his behavior."

John nodded. "I guess."

Frank turned and left the room. As had been the case all morning, John found himself enveloped in deep and uncomfortable silence. When he was in this office he was usually going at high speed. He'd filled a lot of blank space in his life with tight schedules and backed-up meetings.

Where do you go, old man? Take the retreat, go to the hospice . . . and hope they don't just leave you there?

The cardinal had pretended to accept him, but the cardinal was pretty firm on the notion that priests ought to back the party line. John didn't really think birth control was a sin, and went easy on it. The cardinal would have noticed that. He thought of abortion as a tragedy, not necessarily a sin and certainly not a crime, and he said that from the pulpit. The list of objections was probably pretty long.

They were going to bury him alive.

He might be sixty but he *felt* forty-five. He couldn't hack it in a retirement home. But he also couldn't hack it outside of the clergy. He had to be a priest. That was what he was, heart and soul.

He looked around him. Anything to pack in here? Aside from the desk set given to him at his ordination, there was nothing he really considered his own. Well, maybe the leather blotter holder that had been on the desk for the past twenty years. The thing had sort of absorbed his presence, so maybe it was his too. But the rest of it—pencils, paper clips, calendar, notebooks, the files in the drawers—all belonged to the parish.

He went out into the hall, planning to go to his room and get ready. The whole rectory was tomb-silent. Frank's office door was closed; Tom had probably gone down to the church to pray, as was so often his habit when it was empty.

John regarded the place; he was hungry for details to cling to, things to remember.

His eyes fell on something he'd seen every day of his life

since he'd come here. He looked up almost in wonder at the picture of Our Lady of Guadalupe that hung on the wall. The old picture had probably been there for a hundred years. Good-bye, Lady.

So, where to go, if not the retreat? A hotel? He had barely fifty dollars in his pocket, another hundred in his account at Citibank. Maybe he ought to get a hotel room and order in a steak and a bottle of Black Bush, the only serious drinking whiskey worth the name. Then he'd eat steak and drink until dawn.

He looked at the face in the darkening old picture. Did it mean anything, really?

Oh, yes, indeed it did. That he knew.

Frank stuck his head out of his office. "I heard the floor creaking." He laughed a little. "I guess the moral is, if you're gonna lurk, lurk softly."

John went into his bedroom and closed the door. Then he did something he rarely did, which was to open the bottom drawer of his dresser and reach in behind the sweaters and pull out the ancient pint of whiskey he kept there. To him this was a ritual potion, and in fact this very bottle had been slipped to him by his father, "for the bad ones." It was easily thirty years old. There hadn't been very many bad ones.

He pulled the cork and put the bottle to his lips. The old whiskey was a wonder: merciful fire. It might be for bad times, but it surely recalled some good ones. His dad, his grand-mother, his mother, the warm life of the Raffertys.

They would sit together in the library of the big house in Morristown, sipping Black Bush and talking of the affairs of the day, the controversies surrounding Cardinal Spellman and the archdiocese. Always, the archdiocese. They were Big Cath-olics, were the Raffertys. When Spelly wanted a night off, he might show up at this house, and spend his time shooting pool with the old man. He was small, full of pepper and good hu-mor. Unlike other cardinals John could name, Spellman had been invested with startling majesty. What he blessed was blessed, what he condemned was condemned.

But Spelly was gone to dust, and Terry Cooke too. This had been the City of God once, and now look at it—crime was everywhere, the churches were bones. The godfather had replaced the cardinal. The Powerhouse was no longer a cleric's mansion on Madison Avenue. Today's Powerhouse was a social club in East Harlem.

The Black Bush whispered, the Black Bush sang: Why not just toss in the towel? You could spend the rest of your life traveling. You could crawl the brothels of the world, make up for lost time.

He corked the bottle, looked down at it in his hand. Why do priests drink? A very short question with many long answers.

He returned the bottle to its place, threw himself down on his bed, clasped his hands behind his head. But he didn't linger there long. No sense in delaying. The time had come, and it was now. Time to hit the road.

He threw a cassock, a dog collar, three pairs of underwear, some shirts and socks, a suit and his toothbrush into his old black suitcase. He filled it out with his precious *Imitation of Christ* and his much-thumbed Hans Kung, *On Being a Christian*.

He flicked through the pages of the Kung. The post-Christian world—empty and disoriented—mystified him. He thought that it was impossible to discover oneself without religion, that all human experience, properly lived, involved a return to God. Without the journey toward the divine that religion represented, people began to glorify raw needs. Longing for resurrection into the Mystical Body of Christ degenerated into hunger for a Mr. Taco.

He closed the suitcase. Well, look at that. He was ready to go. He did not pray, weep, plead. But for the single coal of sadness at his center, he was empty of remorse.

Well, almost. It was just that he had been so comfortable here! How often had he slept in another bed? That retreat back in '72 or '73 . . . the Florida Vacation in '81. That was it. No, when his mother had died he'd spent one night at home. Perhaps he'd been away a total of ten nights in all the twenty-two years of the pastorate.

Now he was going to pick up this suitcase and go out into the street and that would be it. He just couldn't, but he had to. He had to, they were making him. *Making* him.

He decided that he would beg Frank to let him stay awhile longer. Couple of weeks, what would it matter? Jesus begged.

Frank was sitting at his desk, and at first seemed perfectly normal. Then the thought flitted through John's head—the amazing thought—that he was dead. But no, the stillness, the gray, waxy complexion were not signs of *rigor mortis*. He was breathing, his mouth slightly opened. "Frank?"

If only Quindlan could see this! Deep in his throat he was making little noises, as if some kind of internal dialogue was taking place. There was about it a sense of false prayer, piety spun from bad stuff.

He bent closer. The eyes were open, the skin was as tight as steel. "Frank?"

"You fucking piece of shit, get out of my face!"

The sheer ugliness of the words made John shrivel inside. He was thunderstruck; he'd never heard such from a fellow priest.

The man regarded him with evil pins of eyes. "You have your instructions," he said. Wooden though it was, his tone still conveyed a whipping sneer.

John backed away. For the first time he felt fear. Until now he had thought of Frank as being disturbed by the crimes that had been committed in the church. This went deeper than that, though. Far deeper. There was obviously no point in begging this man for anything.

Thus, with a burst of drama, does the movie end. The old man walks off down the empty sidewalk with his valise in his hand. Fade to black. The lights come on, people get up licking the popcorn salt from their fingers, brushing hulls off their laps.

But what happens to the old man? The road ends, night falls, he gets cold.

He got his suitcase and went down the front stairs. In the foyer he paused. For the last time as a resident of this place he looked up the handsome sweep of the staircase . . . toward that stranger inside.

He went through the front door, pulled it closed behind him.

Now what? Go down the steps, walk to the corner. You can't easily get a cab on a side street in Greenwich Village, you've got to be out on an avenue. Behind him there was muffled laughter.

Maybe it came from one of the other buildings, but he thought not. He thought that Frank was watching him go and laughing.

The afternoon was hardly advanced, but in February even the noon hour has a wan, exhausted quality. It was not as cold, though, as it had been earlier in the week, and he walked with his head up.

The moon stood full in the sky of day, something he'd always been told portended death. Two gulls wheeled high, searching the sad, glittering city below them for garbage. A girl came down the street in a red patent-leather coat with an artificial fur collar. She was perhaps twelve. Her face compelled hope, as the faces of children will. He had the troubling thought that he might never perform another baptism.

He passed the little girl, reached the corner, again raised his eyes to the light. What difference did it make if people saw him, what was so wrong with an old man looking at the sky? He saw the tops of the buildings that lined the avenue, their spires, their oceans of mysterious windows, the heavens dotted with gulls. It might be worth a diet of garbage to live so free.

Lowering his gaze, he returned to the shambling life of the avenue. He took a deep, shivering breath. His first impression of the weather had been wrong. It was still bitterly, relentlessly cold.

It just wasn't in his nature to obey blindly, especially when he thought the orders were wrong. Perhaps that was a failing, but the priesthood is not an army.

He didn't go to Grand Central and set out for the retreat center. Far from it, he went precisely where he knew he shouldn't go, but the only place he really wanted to go.

He went straight to Maria's apartment. If he was ever going to capture his portion of happiness, it was there that he must start, among the shadows that remained of his truest and deepest love.

F RANK WAS LITERALLY SHAKING AS HE WATCHED JOHN LEAVE. He was appalled at himself. How could he *ever* speak in that manner to an older priest—or to anybody? How could he—and especially to that worthy man?

As he watched John struggle up the street with his luggage in his hand, he felt leaden sorrow. He could not wait longer, he had to tell the truth about Maria Julien and his role in her life.

Every Catholic priest has an adviser, known as a spiritual director. This individual may be another diocesan priest, but more ideally he will be connected with one of the orders and thus more or less aloof from the politics and society of the diocese.

Frank put his hand on the phone, felt the cold plastic of the instrument, lifted it to his ear.

He dialed the Martinist chapter house where Father Richard Hidalgo lived. He was a popular adviser, and a good one, and Frank was glad to hear his voice.

"I thought you'd laicized," Father Hidalgo joked.

"Father, I'm desperate."

"Aren't we all. Desperate enough to come tomorrow morning at nine?"

"Father, now."

"I'll shift a few things around, Father. You remember the subway stop? Fifty-ninth Street, and I believe that you should now take the A from West Fourth. The D's become a local."

Frank took the train. In the event, it was the D and it did indeed cost him some time. An elderly man selling Street News came in, offering a brief rundown on the weather. He moved close to Frank, his old eyes eager. "Street News, Father?"

Words burst out of him: "Get a job!"

The old man blinked. "My résumé ain't too good," he growled. "Seventy-five years old and hooked on T-bird."

Fingering his collar, Frank shrank into his seat. He'd expressed his true sentiments, but he shouldn't have, not like that! He should have bought the paper, spread good example, brought a little credit to the collar. People were eyeing him, and their looks were not pleasant.

Okay, all right, he had to fight this thing. He could still taste the acid of the rage that had burst forth when John had appeared in his office. Poor guy, all those years going up in smoke. The image of that old man hauling his single tattered suitcase up the street would haunt him until the day he died.

I sinned, and so you're suffering! I owe you, John Rafferty, in God's truth I do.

He was confused to find himself laughing. He couldn't help it, the sound just came pealing right out of him. The old newspaper salesman turned to him, his eyes narrow, looking for the joke.

He jammed his mouth shut, tried to appear nonchalant. The woman next to him got up and moved away.

I laughed! But what part of me? And why? Yes, what was so funny—

A great rolling guffaw thundered out of him, filling the rattling subway car, causing every head to turn. Frantic, he fingered his collar, trying to hide it from the eyes of the crowd.

—I'm having a classic nervous breakdown.

—I've got to have help.

—Father Richard, please be there for me.

Dark and forbidding without, the interior of the Martinist house was best described as comfy. There had been a school here once, connected with their enormous old church. But the school had gone and the church's people had moved away, disappeared, evaporated. The Martinists had been left with their headquarters and their memories and their crypt.

But these were good men still clinging to this order. A hell of a good bunch of men. Frank rang the bell, got buzzed in by Father O'Dell, who remembered him and gave him an enormous smile, one made the merrier by the delightful complication of wrinkles that defined his face.

Here was a man of ancient faith, entirely secure in his journey. Only with difficulty did Frank manage to control the impulse to throw himself into his arms. He would have knocked the frail old priest senseless.

He mounted the steps two by two, and there standing at the top of the stairs was the man he had relied on for advice for the past ten years, who had gently and persistently directed him toward the Lord.

He had betrayed this man, lied to him, abandoned his advice, besmirched his beliefs. As he moved toward the portly, smiling priest, he experienced the most dangerous outcome of great sin, which is its tendency to isolate the sinner in a prison of self-hate. One strives to present a pretty face to the world, and so must conceal the darkness.

Such things were not easily concealed from Richard Hidalgo, who had seen his share of spectacular sins and great personal crises. "Frank—do you mind if I just state plainly that you look like hell?"

"I know it." Father Richard's office was unchanged, the books in their glass cases, the ancient desk with its rack of pipes and its enormous leather-covered ashtray, the green-shaded lamp on the desk. Frank found the whole tatty dimness of it enormously comforting.

Father himself was one of those men spared the ravages of the years. Instead of growing grizzled and ancient, he had become ethereal, as if he was going to turn into a ghost without actually dying. "It's been eighteen months, Frank."

"As long as that? I hadn't realized."

"The last time you were here, we were talking about a Lenten observance you proposed to undertake." He made a little sound in his throat, as if the memory somehow amused him. "According to my notes, you were going to keep the Jesus Prayer for the forty days." He fired up his pipe. "A zealous undertaking indeed."

"Father, I'm in terrible trouble."

"Which is why you look like a dead dope addict, I gather."

"I . . ." Suddenly it stood before him, ready to be exposed: his sin, his terrible evil. The next few words would end his pastorate, compromise his priesthood irredeemably. What would Bishop Bayley think? His beloved uncle, the man he most admired on this earth and the finest Catholic clergyman he had ever known, would be shattered by this.

You gave me my vocation, and I spit on it. I spit on my vows, spit on my own consecrated hands, and now here I am asking forgiveness.

—You cannot be forgiven, said the silence.

The old priest smiled a moonlike smile, his eyes searching the face of the younger man.

—You cannot be forgiven, said the wind that indifferently tapped the window.

"Father, I—"

"A woman, Frank?"

Oh, it would be so easy, so easy to nod yes. Just nod yes!

Father Richard blinked. "Another priest?" His voice dropped. "A boy?"

"There have been murders in my church." No, man, tell him. *Tell him!* "And I'm upset about them. They haven't been solved."

"Ah, but they will be. The police are good at that when they put their minds to it."

"I suppose. But there was a scandal—"

"I saw poor Father John on the tube. What have they done? Fired him?"

"And put me in as pastor!"

"We reap what we sow—pardon the cliché, but it's quite a true one. Father John consorted with this woman—"

"He's a good man."

"Of course he is." He relit the pipe. "But you're a good man too. The Church has need to encourage its younger men." He smiled. "John will manage. He'll pop up somewhere once the scandal dies down, all confessed and contrite and ready to start again." He looked for a time at his hands, perhaps remembering similar cases from the past. "Unless he leaves us, of course."

"That mustn't happen, Father!"

"It may, and if it does, you're not to fret yourself about it. Your way is quite clear, young man. You get down there and get to work. Throw yourself into it. You're going to find all sorts of skeletons in the closets. Old pastors always leave fascinating problems to solve. The great thing is, throw yourself into the work! That's the cure-all for a devout man. I presume you're not having any trouble in that direction."

A vivid memory of Maria's long, soft thigh interrupted the pious response that this statement engendered. She would flex like a delighted cat . . . so incredibly lovely, so utterly perfect . . .

The deeper sin was to identify her femininity as the source of his own wrongdoing. There is nothing evil about woman; the evil comes from thinking it is so.

"Very much intact," he replied at length. "My devotions are very much intact."

Father Richard sat for a moment, reflecting. Then he smiled, and the pipe went to a jaunty angle. "The old men have the problem of death, the young ones the problem of life. And prayer is here for us all."

"Yes, Father." The moment extended. Frank could tell the truth, there was still time.

Father Richard suggested that they pray together.

The very image of piety, Frank bowed his head. The moment passed. He had imagined that Father Richard would be more acute, more demanding. He had come here to get his sin dragged out of him. Instead he got only the beatitude of a smile. It was not enough—although, of course, it was far more than he deserved.

He felt as if he was spinning out in the empty air, spinning and just starting to really fall, and there was nothing at all between him and the deep, deep beyond.

The pit.

NIGHT RIDE

TOM HAD BEEN LYING IN BED LISTENING TO THE RADIO WHEN he took him. He put him down on the floor of the basement, knelt on his chest, then reached across him to the black iron door of the incinerator. It made a dry creaking sound as he opened it.

What the hell do you know, old man? What *do* you know? What were you going to tell those fucking priests?

Tom was watching him blankly. He'd taken him from the bed, shown him his face, and that had made things easy. Tom had been shocked senseless. His eyes were open, but his body was like plastic. Fear can be a useful tool.

It was nearly ten, and he wondered how safe he was doing an incineration now. The smoke was thick, and they were already sensitized to the fucking odor of it around here.

Tom whined as he bound him hand and foot. "Not talking now, are ya?"

Tom shook his head furiously.

"We think we understand God, but it turns out we're off. *Way* off, right?"

Now Tom nodded.

"You know who I am . . . or rather, who it is that I—shall we say—inhabit?"

He shook his head.

"But you *might* know and you *might* start talking again. So here we are."

He shook his head harder. He'd understood where they were, he saw the incinerator.

"I can either choke you and then burn you, or just burn you."

He caressed the dry old neck. Tom drooled. Then there was a dripping sound. The old man's sphincter had failed. It was a common fear response. "They usually gave the condemned an enema before garroting them. I don't think they did the same when they burned them. What need?"

The Inquisition believed in very, very tight ropes. So he twisted the two ends of the rope around Tom's wrists until his hands were fat purple claws. Tom made a gasping sound, then a moan, then he uttered a loud cry.

This was the inquisitorial moment, one of his life's deepest pleasures.

He made his decision.

He lifted Tom by his shoulders, then shoved him into the maw. The old man cried and croaked and struggled like a fish in a creel. His feet were kicking as the firebox door was closed.

Now he could either light the fire or he could wait and do it after Tom had been overcome by the gas.

Gagging started. He sang to him a little song, to bide the soul on its journey:

I will build my love a tower,
by yon clear crystal fountain.
And on the tie will pile
all the flowers of the mountain.

He went to the shelf where Lupe kept his box of Diamond matches, took them down, and returned to the incinerator. From inside there came the steady thumping of feet, and solid gagging. There was a sharp reek of vomit.

He lit the match, and how nicely it ignited. And, oh, the consuming whisper of the fire. He touched the match to the fire hole. The burner started with a low, decisive boom.

The thunder of feet and arms smashing about in a confined space, the great gulping shrieks of a man beyond agony—and then the silence.

The soul departs so sweetly.

From upstairs came Tom's radio, still playing: "Remember me, O my darlin', remember me . . ."

He looked into the firebox, at the complex shadows in the deep orange flames. The radio crooned, and more distantly the city muttered in its flight.

As he gazed into the fire, looked at the flickers against the walls, fear began to move like a smoke through him. His instinct said that the cops were close. He knew how it worked. They probably needed only forensic evidence to connect him to some aspect of his crimes.

He'd missed getting that police bitch, missed by an inch!

The flames were clear now, a series of blue spikes in a black cage of bones. He turned the white control knobs and the fire died with a last pop.

As he mounted the stairs, his spirits lifted. By the time he had reached the hallway again he was feeling much more cheerful.

Now he was going to go up and get his gas-soaked clothes and his can of fuel, and everything that he'd used, and he was going to hide them well. He knew just the place.

He went into the bathroom, but did not turn on the light. The mirror was the reason. You do not look. You do not weep.

He took a drink of water from the sink, then opened the hamper. Everything was there, just as he had left it.

And why wouldn't it be? He was far more intelligent than the absurd little insects that pursued him.

They had only the brief dim light of their minds. He had the whole night at his command, and the torches of Lucifer to sail at his enemies.

He would win. Of course.

18

J OHN WAS SITTING AT THE KITCHEN WINDOW WIGGLING HIS FIN-
gers at the cat on the sill across the air shaft when an elderly
woman appeared, glanced at him, and dropped her blinds.

For a moment he was affronted; then he understood. He
had given offense: he was an invader. Privacy is essential in
a crowded city. He'd been stealing from the woman, exploiting
her pet for his own pleasure. He was embarrassed, and moved
away from the window.

He had gotten here at one-thirty this afternoon, hungry
and wanting his lunch. Mrs. Communiello usually slapped
some sandwiches together for lunch; he wasn't used to finding
his own meals.

He'd opened the fridge, stared into the bright light, caught
a rancid whiff of elderly milk. It had taken him some moments
to understand that he was looking into a treasure chest of exotic
provisions. There were tins of expensive caviar, bottles of
Smith's Lager from England, a selection of what must recently
have been fabulous cheeses. He recognized a Camembert, a

fine cheddar, some Gruyère, goat-cheese buttons with sun-dried tomatoes in a covered dish. There was a good deal of mold.

White-bean salad in a plastic container had been in much better condition. There was also a bottle of *vinho verde* and a French white he thought might be pretty good.

And so another of Maria Julien's mysteries had revealed itself. She'd had a fictional family, there was that strange leather cloak in her closet, and now she appeared to be a secret gourmet.

What would be next—a collection of impressionists hidden under the bed with the studded belt?

All the secrets were making him throw barriers up around his sorrow: what had been raw grief was reducing to a sort of dull pain in the center of his chest. She had cared about him enough to leave him money, and that was very thoughtful, but he had accepted enough charity in his life to understand that gifts of money are often used as a barrier.

He'd explored her apartment, feeling like a burglar or a fugitive of some sort. Thinking back now, when the apartment was dark and the world was silent, those first few hours had a special quality to them: terrible pain, but also a sweetness that he perhaps would never forget.

He'd opened a beer, drunk it in a few swallows. He was looking for some sort of anesthesia. Getting blind drunk was a possibility.

But the beer, the silence, the slightly overheated apartment, had combined together to make him sleepy. He had gone into the bedroom and stood looking at the bed, wondering if he should use it. Finally he decided to lie just on the bedspread, without getting between the sheets. Soon, however, he'd begun to feel cold. He'd opened the closet, looking for some more substantial covering than the thin spread.

Inevitably the leather cloak had drawn his interest. He'd pulled it out. With a defiant flourish he'd wrapped it around himself, raised the hood. Enclosed in the leather stink of Maria's secrets, he had lain back on the bed. What had her body known while it was wrapped in this thing? What had she done? "It's possible to go to hell," he had shouted. "Goddammit, Maria, it's *possible!*"

He'd turned over, pushed his face into the pillows. Somewhere in the dust and tickly feather scent he could smell the lingering odor of her hair. Then he'd turned aside, he couldn't bear it, he lay on his back. The leather cloak spread out around him. He had opened his legs, cupped his genitals, feeling the mild pleasure of his own touch. His usual defense mechanism operated: before more happened, he had fallen asleep.

It had been a hard afternoon's sleep, full of dark, unremembered dreams. He was glad he was finally awake. He wandered to the bookshelf, trying in some way to conjure her by remembering favorite titles.

He saw a familiar volume and grabbed it: *Notes on Thought and Vision* by Hilda Dolittle. They had read it again and again together, this was a bible of their relationship. "Christ was the grapes that hung against the sunlit walls of that mountain garden, Nazareth. He was the white hyacinth of Sparta and the narcissus of the islands. He was the conch shell and the purple-fish left by the lake tides. He was the body of nature, the vine, the Dionysus, as he was the soul of nature."

He cradled the little blue book in his two hands. How Maria's loss weighed on him. He felt as if he had lost his one chance to really live life. If only he'd lain down with her, just once. He could have confessed it, all would have been forgiven.

And he would have known. He would have *known!*

There was a bottle of cognac on a table, beside a vase of withered flowers. He grabbed the cognac and drank deep of it.

Then he doubled over, fighting nausea, his lips tight, forcing himself to keep it down.

"God, talk to me. Say something! Give me a sign! Just something simple—the rumble of thunder, the calling of a bird in the night . . ."

The immortal thought of Meister Eckhart mocked him now: "We should contrive not to need to pray to God, asking for his grace and divine goodness . . . but take it without asking."

Turning on more lights, he went back to the kitchen. He took a spoon and ate some of the caviar.

> O look, look in the mirror,
>   O look in your distress;
> Life remains a blessing
>   Although you cannot bless.

Hadn't they recently published a book of Auden's secret German poems? He'd have to get that, yes, he'd go over to Three Lives in the morning, then he would sit in here with a cup of coffee or go over to the Peacock Café on Greenwich and drink espresso and indulge himself.

That would be in the later morning, when the hard New York sun reveals what other light conceals. He ate caviar and drank glass after glass of water from the tap. Maybe the salt'll give me a stroke, he thought. What a way for the Saint of Seventh Avenue to die, by gorging himself on beluga.

He took the white wine out of the fridge, uncorked it, and drank. The cold settled into his deep belly. There was frost on the windowpane. He took another long swig of wine, listening to the bubbles flow back into the bottle.

He should never have come here, he wasn't strong enough to bear this, not nearly strong enough.

She'd had a secret life from which he had been entirely excluded. Therefore she didn't love him, she couldn't have, not if she hadn't trusted him with her life. "We are married in our souls . . ."

He dashed into the bedroom and grabbed the big leather cloak and put it to his face, inhaling the sharp scent of it. "I would have done it if you wanted me to," he whispered. "Sure, it's nothing," he said. A wan smile came into his face when he glanced toward the mirror and saw his own narrow figure.

He threw on the cloak. There, this was what it weighed,

this was how it felt. He wanted to possess it, to make it give up its memories.

He clutched it to him. "Your secrets," he whispered, "your beautiful secrets."

Oh, my dear woman, where are you now? She'd died without absolution, and even then her confessions certainly hadn't included anything about black cloaks and leather belts. She'd been such a wholesome girl! She even looked wholesome, with that perfect, blooming skin.

Where are you now, Maria? A sin is like a deformity, something we want to hide. He'd always agreed with C. S. Lewis that hell must be very tiny, because the souls within it are so turned in on themselves that they are small beyond vanishing. Satan, of course, imagines himself to be huge, to surmount the world. This illusion is his only weakness, and usually it is not enough to thwart him.

All the pit and the fires and the desolation could probably fit in the palm of a man's hand, all the sins of the ages.

He knew what he had to do. He should have done it days ago. He had to pray for her, he had to plead with God on behalf of her soul, he had to call her out from the fallen depths.

Now that he had realized that this was needed, there wasn't another moment to waste. He drew the hood up and went out into the hall. The leather was heavy, but it felt good to be bearing a weight she had borne.

The deep blue carpet hissed under his feet, the elevator clicked and whispered as he went down, the doorman looked up in astonishment, his eyebrows raised, to see such an apparition coming *out* of his building. The devil take the doorman: this was his place now, he'd inherited.

Here he was, a midnight crazy stalking the streets in a leather cloak. But it was her symbol and so he was proud to wear it. Let the damn thing be proclaimed to the world. He was sorry that it wasn't ten o'clock of a Sunday morning. He might have said Mass in it.

He crossed Seventh Avenue toward Village Cigars. A man coming down Christopher Street focused his shadowy attention on him for an instant. But when he saw an aged face in the cowl, his interest faded like winter twilight.

> *Oh stand, stand at the window*
>   *As the tears scald and start;*
> *You shall love your crooked neighbor*
>   *With your crooked heart.*

Alone in the pale streetlight stood M. and J., its windows blacker than black.

He mounted the familiar steps to the familiar portico, touched the familiar handle. The brass knob turned: the lock wasn't even set. Odd, but never mind. He was going to go in there and pray until he was dry of prayer.

"I'm coming," he breathed, "I'm coming."

He pushed the door open, stepped across the old boards, peered into the silent nave.

He entered the dark.

NIGHT RIDE

A T ELEVEN THE BELLS TOLLED, BOOMING OUT INTO THE RAG-
ing night streets. The city rushed its clock-sprung way,
none heeding the call.

He whispered. "Ooohhh, 's dark! So dark in here, Johnnikins." Very soft. "But I got darkeyes, I et my carrots!"
So-o-o soft. "Peekaboo, Johnnikins, you're kneeling right over
there . . ."

YOU FUCKING LOVER BOY!

He felt like an earthquake, the cracking of the sky, the
falling of the stars. He emerged from his hiding place behind
the Plaster Virgin and began moving across the church. He
skipped and clapped, making it a babykins dance. "Rollem
up, rollem up, markim with B, put 'im in the oven for baby
and me!"

John's contemplation was completely shattered. He raised
his head, looked wildly about with his tear-filled eyes. A voice
singing—a child. But where? His eyes were long used to the
dark, and anyway the church was hardly pitch black. Its

stained-glass windows glowed sick yellow from the streetlights. He didn't see a soul, the place was empty.

Killing can be like making love; soldiers know it. Your warm
trigger in its cradle of finger-skin, the bursting sigh of your
bullets . . . the distant, lurching figure, and you know what
he feels—an electric shock as your steel splashes into his
muscle.

Your killings return like soldiers marching back from their
melted worlds.

From his churning depth there came the stranger's voice,
as surprising, as sweet as a bell on a snowy night. Gently the
wind blew, the cradle rocked. . . . Oh, how charming you can
be, dear nightmare.

Prisoners were often so weighted down that they could
not even raise a hand to protect themselves from the rats. Those
who died during this ordeal were said to have been freed by
the Evil One.

It is ordinary for him to live in bad men. They are his
mansion. But when he achieves lodgment in the good, then
the heavens ring with sorrow.

Do *wopwopwop!*

There it was again—a sort of muttering, bebopping child's
prattle. John went rigid. Obviously the church might be dangerous . . . but surely not at this early an hour.

The murderer didn't come until after midnight, and for
the manifest reason that the streets were still well populated
before then.

He slipped along the aisle, flying quickly and quietly toward
his victim. He'd take the remains to the basement, burn them
down. He'd be working the incinerator overtime, taking a
hell of a chance doing it so near midnight. Officer-of-the-Law
Pearson would eventually notice that smoke.

Fer sure.

He had to work fast, do the execution, empty and clean the incinerator, hide a load of bones . . . oh, my!

Soooo solleeeeee!

If only he could see somebody, then he could know that this wasn't a trick of acoustics, people out in the street. He looked out across the empty pews, trying to find a specific direction for the sound.

It seemed to coalesce out of the air, though.

Turn to prayer, man. That's your strength. Trust your God, you've given Him your life. "Our Father, who art in heaven . . ." The words slipped easily off his lips, whispered into that muttering quiet. So his faith was still with him.

Good, excellent, clutchem hands, bow the head, he's praying again. He could smell John now, he was that close.

What fun.

Only when the new sound stopped did John realize it had been there, under the muttering. He thought about it . . . and it came again. A hissing noise. Yes, as if somebody was sliding stocking feet along the floor.

How extraordinarily sinister.

And probably nothing more than a radiator leaking steam.

He didn't need sight now, in fact it was an impediment. So he closed his eyes, relying instead on another vision, made of memory and knowledge and a thousand impressions too subtle to identify. He moved forward with infinite care, toward the scent of leather that surrounded the old fart. He would place one foot far ahead of him on the floor, then stretch until the other one was even.

They laid him in the casket and placed a wedge of wood between his legs, then hammered this wedge until the bones split and the marrow ran out upon the floor. How holy, how

Roman, how Catholic. He had to be taken to the stake lashed in a cart, for he could not walk at all.

Do wop, wop, wop, he-e-ere I come, ready or not!

There was definitely something moving toward him along the floor. A rat, a cat?

No, it seemed larger than a cat.

When the sound of movement stopped, he peered anxiously into the dark where it had been. Was there a thickening of the shadows there? Yes, he decided. That was it, he'd had enough, he drew the cloak onto his shoulders and rose from the pew.

His muscles became iron springs. He could smell the musty, sour odor that identified elderly terror. It was amazing how much old people wanted to live. His only passive victims had been young.

Johnnikins came into the aisle. He'd realized what was happening, and he was trying to escape.

Too late, dear, do wop.

John was hurrying toward the doors when he saw that there was a shadow pressed against them. He stopped, stunned and horrified. How could anybody move that fast?

He'd head for the sacristy. But no—Frank would have been certain to lock it from the rectory side. Even he wouldn't be foolish enough to forget that. There was another door, though, the one at the back of the sanctuary, that led down to the crypt.

From the crypt he could connect with the basement of the rectory. Would Frank have locked the door at the top of the basement stairs?

John would find out.

He was mildly surprised when John turned around and went back into the church. But the surprise wasn't born of any fear that he might escape. He was more than willing to run a little race. All he had to do was instill more fear. Real terror robs a man of his good sense and his effectiveness. "Wanna do the *strut!*"

My God, what was that? A voice like falling leaves, like rushing water, yet also like the scream of a child. What the hell *was* that? John couldn't help himself, he started running, he dashed blindly toward the altar, forgot where he was, blundered against the step that led up into the sanctuary.

There was somebody crouched on the altar. He could see the shape clearly against the pale marble of the tabernacle, his tabernacle. He looked up toward this person, his eyes swimming with tears, his breath ripping in his chest. The man's head was long, his face was . . . Oh, no. Surely John's eyes were playing tricks, the dark was making him see things. But that face, that face—spitting, pop-eyed, hardly even human—was the face of a gargoyle.

The sun in the morning would make Mother's canary sing. It was so happy. Oh, so happy! So, so, *so* happy!

It was a slow and intricate process to defeather a living bird. Too much pain and it died, too little and it wasn't any fun. He liked to have fun, in the sunlight, in the golden morning. "Tweedle tweedle, tweedle-dee," he sang. And oh, boy, John betook his ass outta there! Whee, he was flyin' all the way back down the aisle. "Wanta do the strut," he shouted after him. He stood up on the altar, tall and naked and stiff as steel.

"Help! Help me!" John's chest was burning, the words came out faint and dry. It was like a nightmare where you scream but it doesn't work. Every muscle in his body was quivering, he felt light-headed, he felt the floor wobbling under his feet. He'd never seen anything so horrible, never heard anything like that voice.

It was at the altar, it was blocking the entrance—where could he go? There wasn't any place to go. If only he could get to the lights, then he could flip the switches, but they were in the utility closet under the choir-loft steps. To get back there, he had to pass all the way across the vestibule.

He dived into the nearest pew, threw himself down, pushed the kneeler up, and began to scramble along the floor. He tried to be quiet but it was useless. He forced himself under the pew and into the row behind. Then he waited.

This was fascinating, it was a real hunt! He danced down the center aisle, singing. "Mine eyes have seen the glory of the coming of the Lord!"

You do have a lovely voice, boy-o, they used to say. They said it in the summertime, they said it in the fall, they said it when the robin pulled the worm. They would sit in the big white Adirondack chairs with their hands on their cool drink glasses, and he would stand and sing for them. He stood still, put his arms to his sides, faced the altar from the middle of the main aisle, and he sang from the very depths of his being, and the song swelled, and the song was grand:

> Last night I lay a-sleeping
> there came a dream so fair.
> I stood in old Jerusalem beside the temple there,
> I heard the children singing, and ever as they sang
> Methought the voice of angels
> from heavenly harps did ring—

No, that was fucked up, the words were wrong. Voice of angels, heavenly harps, oh, give a fuck! Best to sing the song of sixpence, pockets full of rye, 'cause he was only five, and when you're five, Mommy, it's hard to 'member, Daddy, the shadow of the cross, "Jerusalem, Jerusalem, pockets full of rye!"

He would go, eh heh heh heh.

Daddy held me upside down and shook me when I wet my communion suit. "So all who would did enter, then I *close the doors and crush all the people!*"

———

John had never heard anything like it, that powerful, fine tenor belting out "Jerusalem," changing as it sang to the voice of a boy, pure and new, the voice of a child, then the voice of a baby. Now the baby cooed and muttered and smacked, and came looking for him. John wasn't in any shape for this kind of exertion, he was still fighting his own heart and lungs, battling in the sweat of his fear.

But he scurried on. Whoever this was, he very close.

Oh, there he goes, do *wop!* He's got fight in him, this little tasty! He's gonna get it, and get it slow, do wop, time for the question, do the strut, do *wopwopwop!*

Now, wait a minute, isn't that him heading back toward the sacristy? Yeah, better take the far aisle, he's got some definite fight in him, this little honey pie.

He flew, as swift as an owl.

John had gotten behind the altar, he was down low, he was crawling toward the door to the crypt. He had to get in there or he wasn't going to be alive, and he wanted to be alive. It wasn't a matter of thinking anymore, his blood and muscles and bones were doing the thinking. He wanted to be alive, he didn't want to let this happen to him, to end up dead in a dumpster.

Oh, God—listen—he's on the other side of the altar, he's breathing, you can hear it, you've gotta move, hands hurt, pull yourself along, do it, get to that door, look, you can see him, he's right there.

Breathing, breathing. "Do wop," he mutters again. What the hell is it, a phrase in the language of hell? No, he's not even from hell, it's an alien, worse than hell, something from across the black of space, and it's in here and it's after me, it looks like a gargoyle, God help us all!

All he had to do was leap up on the altar, take the monstrance in his fat widdle hand, and *smackaroonie!* Okay, sugar plum, time to die.

Rollemup, rollemup, markem with B
Putteminaoven for baby an' me!

He strutted down the altar, waving the monstrance as he danced. Gee, he'd like a good stogie right now, a nice expensive one like the bishops smoke, one of those Dunhills or—why, Bishop, aren't these *illegal*—a Corona de Corona from Habana Cooba.

Doncha jus lovem, puttem ina oven
fer baby an' me!

God God God he was touching the door, his hand was around the cool good handle, it was turning, then crypt air and he was in! Oh, *yes!*
Somebody moaned.
He's in here too, he's right beside me!
No, no, it was John himself. *He'd* moaned. Oh, that was a relief! He'd moaned, and why not? he wanted to scream, but he mustn't. "Now, be quiet, you old fool," he whispered. Oh, yes, better. This was better. He got up, waving his hands over his head for the chain-pull switch that would light the lights.
He found the chain, yanked. Nothing whatsoever happened.

"It's quiet. Yeah, too quiet. Whaddaya mean? I mean the chicken has flown the bazoosis, das what I mean, mothafuka!"
Now, how'd he do that? John knows his church, he's very good, it's a fine hunt!
So how'd he, where'd he . . . ? Has to be the crypt. Why, this was wonderful! This was just completely so-o chawmin', massa, jes you hie on down to dat dere crypt, and you open dat coffin, and you puts dat wormy squirmy leatherback in dere wit dem bones!
Okedokie!

Without warning, something very hard slammed into John's face. He waved his hands wildly around him, a pitiful attempt

at defense. Some seconds had passed before he understood
that he'd walked into a wall.

He stood still. Silence for a moment, then the creak of a
door. Then, from the top of the stairs: "Fe fi fo fum!"

Frantic, he blundered on, coming to one of the old tombs,
his fingers dragging against the marble. Carefully he moved
around behind it, crouched down.

Ah, smell that leather—the odor of old skin and the Gestapo.
"Where are you, Johnnie? I'm a-scared of the dark!" Oh, yes,
sweetheart, you're a peach, you're a pickle, you just don'
wanna be caught!

Enough was enough. He hefted the monstrance. He was
going in.

John saw it moving in the ink, a flickering gleam, the light of
a cold and distant sun. It was floating, a disk of gold, coming
slowly toward him, gliding, slipping across the darkness, drifting closer, closer still.

All at once John knew: Maria had been killed with the
monstrance, the very repository of the Blessed Sacrament, the
primary vessel of veneration.

John saw the monstrance gliding in the dark, heard the
crunch of her forehead, saw the monstrance gliding back.

He lifted it high, and as he did, saw an extra glimmer on its
golden surface. He held it at his full extension, hesitant, wondering. That glimmer shouldn't have happened. The crypt was
as dark as the depth of a cave, he'd turned off the circuit
breakers himself. So where was the light coming from? He
turned around, looked up the stairway. Uh-oh.

Or no, it was car lights shining on the windows as somebody turned down Morton Street. Sure.

Okay, good. Get it over with. "Now, be still, Mr. Head,
here comes Mr. Monstrance, and he's ma-a-ad!"

Even fear has a border, and as the monstrance rose up over
him, John went beyond that border. He crouched, huddling in

the leather. He closed his eyes. Each detail of the moment presented itself like a tiny intricate flower. First, the rustle of leather as he raised his arm against the coming blow. Then the long smooth intake of breath. Then the tingling that spread across his forehead, as if the base of the monstrance had identified its target with a stroke of chalk.

What the fuck *is* that? That's a goddamn fucking flashlight coming down the stairs, that's what that is!
    Move. Now.

19

J OIN THOUGHT ONLY ONE THOUGHT: LIFE. THE FOOTSTEPS CAME
closer. Life.

"Okay, buddy, get up outta there!"

Life.

A foot probed into his back. "Come on, move it!"

Life.

Hands grasped his leather cloak, pulled. Instinct resisted
and he was tumbled out of the cloak into bright shining
light and the gleaming barrels of pistols.

"Freeze, mister, you're under . . . Jeez, Father!"

He stumbled forward, seeing then the young shaven faces
and the blue uniforms. He sank down before the young men,
grabbing for the nearest cop's chest, his belt, to support himself. Then he was just so grateful he was crying, bawling in
fact, and the strong young man was lifting him up.

"Get a chair over here, Tim, it's one of the fathers!"

Another policeman came with a folding chair from somewhere and John sat down on it. "Christ," he muttered. "Oh, Christ, help me!"

Detective Dowd moved quickly across the crypt, his face hard and tight, his small eyes flickering in the beams of the flashlights. "Got him?"

"No, sir."

Dowd stopped, spoke into the walkie-talkie he was carrying. "Seal it up. The perp is not located. *Repeat, seal it up!*"

Looking past the detective, John saw that the monstrance was standing on the tomb of old Father Thomas Geary. Inside he could see a host.

His priesthood reasserted itself at once. He got up, hurried over to the precious object, started to take it in his hands.

"Don't touch the damn thing," Dowd rasped. "*He* had it, *he* brought it down here."

"He was going to hit me with it."

"Probably the Julien murder weapon too. We had forensics look for traces on every candlestick and chalice in the place. They were all clean. That was clean." He sighed. "But brass is easy to wipe."

The detective got another folding chair and brought it over. He sat facing John. "You want to answer a couple of questions?"

"I—"

Dowd closed his eyes, as if in pain. "Don't say no."

"Please, ask me."

"Description of the individual you saw?"

"Very thin face. Big, bulging eyes. Long nose, narrow lips. The ugliest face I ever saw."

"Familiar?"

He shook his head. How could they ever understand? "In no way familiar."

"That's a pisser!"

"How did you . . . ? I thought I was going to die here."

"We got the whole plant under twenty-four-hour observation. We saw you go in. You shouldn'ta been wearin' that Phantom of the Opera cloak, we were sure you were the guy.

Shit, you're lucky you didn't get shot." There came into his eyes an expression of hurt, but his tone was snide. "Gettin' sentimental about your leather goddess?"

Before John could respond, there came another voice, low and infinitely gentle, and Frank appeared on the steps in the company of another uniformed officer. "The Blessed Sacrament," he said as he moved toward the monstrance.

"Don't touch that!"

Frank was so concentrated on the condition of the host that he grasped the monstrance before he realized what Dowd was saying.

"Shit almighty fire, that's the murder weapon!"

"This is Our Lord," Frank said. "I've got to take care of Him."

Dowd shook his head. "Metal like that takes such good goddamn prints, but they're so friggin' fragile. You just fucked us to the wall, Father Bayley!"

Understanding at last, Frank released the monstrance as if it had shocked him. "Oh, sorry! Sorry!"

"Take your Blessed Sacrament and eat it or put it to bed or whatever you gotta do with it. We might get lucky, find a stray print that isn't one of yours." He laughed, a sound like a laboring engine.

"Oh, John." Frank came over, his eyes swimming. He embraced him. The smell of Afta made John queasy. He drew back, pushed at the big shoulders. Frank released him. "Sorry, John!" He looked hurt.

He could not forget the tone the younger man had taken with him earlier. It had profoundly changed things. There had been in it a shattering echo of truth. John sensed that Frank had revealed his real feelings in those few seconds.

Frank opened the lunette, removed the host, and broke it down the middle. He regarded John, and his eyes were as guileless as a boy's. "The Body of Christ," he said. John took the half offered him and put it in his own mouth.

They ate their communion together.

Lord, John said in his heart, Lord, Lord, Lord.

Frank's voice was cream. "He's terribly shaken, Mr. Dowd. We need to take him upstairs, get some coffee in him."

"You realize that the perp's still in here."

Frank went quite gray. "You're kidding."

"He's here, he's gotta be. We got every single entrance covered."

"The school?"

Dowd nodded. "The whole plant. Right now they're getting ready to do a detailed search of the premises."

"Is it dangerous for us to be here?"

"It ain't safe."

"Then perhaps—"

"You can probably survive a trip to the kitchen for coffee, I come along."

With the halting steps of a stranger, John followed them upstairs and into his own familiar kitchen. He sat at the table and counted the red oilcloth squares until Frank started working on the coffee. Then he watched him.

"I gotta ask you both a few things," Dowd said.

"Shoot." Frank was brisk, efficient, composed. He wore his blue robe and a handsome pair of slippers that John hadn't seen before. They looked warm and expensive. Maybe he'd gone out and done a little shopping, in celebration of his victory.

Dowd turned to John. "First off, why were you wearing the cloak?"

He was too drained to say anything except the truth. "I don't really know. I saw it at Maria's . . . perhaps I wanted to understand something. Wearing it seemed to make sense at the time."

"You were supposed to be goin' up to Holy Cross retreat center for ten days."

"Well, I don't want to go up to Holy Cross retreat center for ten days! So I went the only other place I could."

Frank turned to him. "You were at Maria's?"

"I'm going to live there. It belongs to me now."

Dowd gave him a sidelong look. "The will hasn't been probated yet. The apartment's not yours."

"What're you gonna do, arrest me for breaking and entering?"

"I got no problem with where you went. It's none of my business. I just hafta know what happened here, is all. So you put on the cloak, you come over to the church. What gives, I gotta ask, it's eleven o'clock at night?"

"I wanted to pray. I wanted to say my evening prayers on behalf of those who have died here."

Frank unplugged the percolator and poured coffee into the mugs. John found that he wanted it badly.

"So you come into the church for sentimental reasons. Even though it's night and this is obviously extremely stupid. Then what?"

"I prayed for some little time. I don't know how long. Eventually I became aware of someone else in the church. I heard breathing." He told the whole story of his experience.

"How about you, Father Frank?"

"I made myself some supper, watched some TV, then went upstairs. I was reading my breviary when the officer knocked."

"You heard nothing beforehand?"

"I had the door to the church locked. Even the basement passage."

"Very wise. Unfortunately, we've got to assume that whoever's doing this has keys to all the doors, and is aware of any tunnels or anything like that. Where is Father No-Say-Um, by the way? He usually pops up at times like this, looking like his eyeballs are gonna take a flier."

"He's not in the rectory," Frank said.

John was surprised at that. "No?"

"I think he's gone to the Georgian brothers down on Sullivan Street."

"He's known Brother Harold for years," John said. "If he went anywhere, he'd go there."

"You see him leave? Either of you?"

"No," Frank said. "Not actually. I just presumed—"

"You know George Nicastro, I think?"

"Of course," Frank replied.

"His wife reported him missing at noon today."

John watched his fellow priest go slowly white. His own throat felt like it was closing. He could have gagged.

The detective continued. "He came here two nights ago. He never returned home."

That hit Frank where it hurt. "The smoke—no!"

"We don't know anything more."

"Oh, Jesus, help us! Help us in this time of need!"

John's impulse was to envelop the younger man in his arms. He had not often heard such despair in a human voice.

"We watch the church constantly," Dowd said. "But we didn't observe Nicastro enter the church on the night of his disappearance. Maybe he had family problems."

"He was an exemplary Catholic."

"Catholics run away from home. Believe me, they do."

The plainclothes officer standing in the doorway, a stocky black man wearing an insulated down jacket and a pair of corduroy pants, scuffed his foot along the floor. "I want to know if you have any other way to move around besides the doors."

John spoke up. "There's an iron hatch at the back of the old coal cellar that connects it with the school. That was done so they could trade coal back and forth and cut down on the number of deliveries. If you knew about that door, you could move between the rectory and the school."

"But not the church?"

"No."

"Fuck," the plainclothesman said with quiet intensity.

"Don't cuss in the church, Hal. Oh, I didn't introduce Hal Hawkins. Hal, these are the fathers."

The man in the down jacket smiled. "I'd recommend that you fellas vacate the premises until we've got this guy under arrest."

"That's unfortunate," Frank said.

"You certainly can't stay here, Frank."

"No." He gave John a steady look. "I could be with you."

John thought of what he had seen in the church, and decided that he would very much like companionship—even Frank's. "You'd be welcome."

Dowd drank off the last of his coffee. He seemed about to say something, but then decided better of it. He buttoned his leather jacket.

"You want any more coffee?"

"No, thanks." John felt an actual wave of sickness come over him. The coffee had been strong, and his stomach had gone quite sour. He coughed hard, almost choking on his own bile. Part of him wanted to be alone, to curl up in Maria's bed and forget this dark time, to bury his face in the memory of her smell.

Dowd was watching him. "Need help?"

John did not want their solicitude. What he actually wanted was to somehow edit out what he had witnessed in the church. "He kept singing a children's ditty," he said. "His voice—it was quite remarkable. Complex. He would sound like a baby, like a boy . . . then he suddenly began singing that old hymn, you might know it, 'Jerusalem.' " John remembered the echoing perfection of the voice. " 'Jerusalem, Jerusalem' . . . how wonderfully he sang."

Frank came to him, reached down, clasped his hands. "My friend," he said. John was startled to see how deeply moved the man was, startled and unexpectedly touched.

There was a loud creak and a thud and at least six uniformed police clomped past in the hall. One of them stuck his head into the room. "Clear to this point," he said.

Frank watched them move off toward the upper parts of the rectory. "I don't want to be here if they find him."

That brought John to his feet. "I should say not!" The idea of being within fifty feet of the man he had seen in the church almost tipped him to panic flight.

"Why don't you two guys take off," Dowd said.

"And if you got an overcoat, I'd ditch that thing and wear it," Hawkins added. "That thing ain't gonna go down too well in a precinct on the lookout for a maniac."

"Then you think he's left the plant?"

"I think we ain't found him yet, and the precinct's on alert. Do yourself a favor and ditch the funny costume."

John waited in the foyer for Frank to pack his overnight

bag. They left together. John was in an old raincoat, and he huddled against the sharp wind.

"All I can say is that I'm sorry," Frank said as soon as they were alone. "I can only plead pressure."

"It's all right. I know you have a temper."

"I went to see Rich Hidalgo today."

They crossed Seventh Avenue. Maria's building came into view on Waverly Place. John hadn't spoken with Frank's spiritual adviser in five years. "How is he? He must be pushing a hundred."

"Well, he still looks about fifty-five."

"He's looked fifty-five since he was twenty. Guys used to describe him as a pipe wearing a face."

Frank chuckled, clapped John on the shoulder. John even felt an echo of the old camaraderie.

Two or three minutes later they entered the flat, and were embraced at once by warm air and a particularly funereal atmosphere.

"You didn't leave on a single light."

"I didn't think to. I was eager to get to the church."

Frank turned on the switch and the living room was filled with soft light. "I couldn't have gone in there at night. I don't know how you managed it."

"I thought I was safe because it was early. I was foolish, obviously." John threw off his coat, then dropped onto the couch. He rubbed his face. He was absolutely exhausted. When he closed his eyes it felt as if the room was beginning to turn round. Again he saw the gargoyle sitting on the altar. His mouth went dry, his hands began to shake. How could somebody *look* like that?

A minute passed, three minutes, five. Still he sat. He passed the time ranging his mind across the years, drifting.

"Hey."

He blinked, astonished at first to see Frank standing over him.

"Shouldn't you consider going to bed?"

"He danced, Frank. He seemed . . . terribly fast when he

moved. I thought he was going to kill me. I thought my life had ended."

Frank went to a concealed bar and brought out a large bottle of Black Bush. "A good stiff drink, and then bed. Sound acceptable?"

John took the drink from his former curate, sipped it.

"Now, wait a minute. I think this is more appropriate." Frank tossed his back, poured himself another. "A sin with Black Bush, I know, but given the circumstances . . ." He drank his second drink at a gulp.

John took his like medicine too. The liquor warmed him, and he began to feel somewhat better. "Bed," he said, "at last! Is the door locked?"

Frank nodded, but John went and checked it anyway.

A moment later he had closed the bedroom door and thrown himself down on the bed. He expected to fall asleep instantly, but that is not what happened. There is a kind of sick exhaustion that prevents sleep. Instead of welcome unconsciousness, memories from the church crowded in on him. Once again he saw the monstrance gleaming, smelled the damp concrete odor of the tomb where he had hidden.

Soon he opened his eyes. Being on an alley, the room was quite dark. He fumbled for the lights, did not find them.

It was when he sat up that he saw the shadow on the floor. It was about the size of a large dog, and it appeared to be moving toward the bed. For an instant he was literally transfixed by it. He blinked, he could not quite believe that it was real.

Frantic now, he groped toward the bedside table. His fingers located the lamp at last. He fumbled, found the little round switch, twisted it. Light.

There was nothing there, of course. He let out his breath, dropped back down, and stared at the ceiling. In the morning he was going to call Dr. Morris. He couldn't bear tension like this. And he was definitely going on the retreat at Holy Cross. Tiny rooms, plenty of people, a well-hidden campus: it now sounded absolutely wonderful.

He considered reading, but instead took out his rosary and said a decade. Then he turned off the light, pulled the bed-spread around himself, and turned over.

A minute passed, then two. At last John began to drift.

Again he was disturbed, this time by a single sharp intake of breath, quite close to the bed. Another false alarm, he was sure. But perhaps the simplest thing was to sleep with the light on.

When he opened his eyes, he saw that terrible waxen face, the rigid grin, the teeth gleaming and imperfect.

O nightmare.

The head jerked back and the eyes regarded him, dark pins in pale cream.

An unbidden scream burst out of him; a hand stayed it. He flailed, but he was no fighter. In an instant he was caught, held from behind, his mouth firmly covered.

There came the softest, sweetest tenor in his ear, "Oh Jesus, hide and shelter me . . ."

He went numb, his mind trying to sort out the extent to which his nightmare had invaded reality.

"Oh, Johnnie, oh, Johnnie, how you could love!"

Then he smelled cologne, and knew that it was Frank's cologne.

"Wanna do the strut?" Frank asked. His tone was affable, pleasant, you could hear the smile in it.

John was completely at a loss. Frank? That terrible face—that was Frank?

Dear God, of course! It was Frank in extreme pain, in extreme terror, Frank in mystical torment.

John kicked, he bit, he threw himself about like a landed fish, but there was no breaking the man's sprung-steel grip. This was incredible, it was horrible. Frank, Frank—

"Bake me a cake, Johnnikins, quick as ya can!"

Good God Almighty.

"No problem, I'll bake it myself. I know where she keeps the matches." He dragged John from behind. "I decorated this place, Lambkin. Hunca-Munca and me. Oh, yeah . . ."

John twisted, jerked, fought until his muscles seemed ready to be torn from the bones.

"You fucked her, you bastard! You fucked my baby!"

"What?"

"Maria! You fucked her!" The woe in the voice, the sheer woe! John had never heard anything remotely like it.

"I didn't!" John hadn't had the courage.

"You're a liar!" His strength was absolutely prodigious. John felt like a leaf in his grasp. " 'The Holy Inquisition served important political ends as well. Indeed, its political ends were the primary reason it was tolerated by those states where it entered and took hold,' do wop."

Behind him Frank began pulling his arm up, pulling it higher and higher. Great waves of agony swept his shoulder, his chest, his whole upper body. He was almost off his feet, only his toes were touching the floor, he thought he was going to pass out from the pain if it didn't stop.

Falsetto, Spanish accent: " 'Oh, oh, sirs, loosen me and I will say what you want, only loosen me and I will say it, oh, please, sirs, loosen me and I will say all you tell me to say!' "

Then he was hoisted completely off the floor. An inch from the floor, he had the impression that his toes were kicking in the black eternal. Amazing agony pulsed through his shoulder and chest and neck. His other arm slapped impotently against Frank's well-developed torso.

"Anything to say?"

The hand over his mouth loosened. John tried to cry out for help, but all that came was an inarticulate bellow.

The hand clapped back and the pain got far worse.

"Tell me," Frank said, "do you believe in the Communion of Saints?"

John's screams were a stuffed music.

"Now, Johnnie—she called you Johnnie, you bastardo— if you don't want your arm torn off, and I don't think—stop that shrieking and listen!"

John wanted to stop, but it didn't work.

"You listen!"

He fought himself, held his breath.

"That's better. Now I'm going to let up a bit, and you're not going to yell, you're going to talk. Right? Nod!"

John nodded. He nodded and nodded, this agony had to stop, it was too great, it was the greatest single thing he had ever known, it had to stop!

At last he got himself under control. He hung there, silent and still, seething.

"Okay, you keep quiet. Honestly, you sound like a petulant canary when you scream."

He couldn't bear it, he was going to start again, the pain was so terrible, it was like somebody splitting his bones inside his body. Desperately he began to try to make articulate noises against the hand. "Stuu—uu—" One leg did a slow kick, then the other. He fought the scream that was coming, finally quelled it by making himself go limp.

"Tha-a-t's better! See what we can accomplish if we try?" Then he was on the floor in a heap. His left arm didn't work, it was a rag dangling from his shoulder, it was still blasting with pain. But not for long. It got cold and started going numb. He tried to move it. A ghost arm came up, but the ruin at his side didn't budge.

"Angel fuckers are heretics. It's heresy, what you did!"

"I told you I never cohabited with her. Never!"

"Her name was Zophiel and she was an angel and you fucked her, you *bastard!*"

John hadn't wanted to look at him, but then a sound made him glance up. Frank was tearing the pages of the precious Hilda Dolittle book into strips. "We're going to burn this," he said, "since it's a symbol of your sin." The voice was eerie with familiar charm. He came over to John, folded his arms, looked down at him. The smile was gentle, kind. "Then we're gonna burn you."

20

Y OU STRUGGLE, YOU FIGHT, YOU HATE YOURSELF UNTIL
you're sick of it. Your remarkable acts, so sterling and
so awful, are not a *doing*, they are a *releasing*.

You let the childhood memory that says "no-no" sink into
the silky center of you, deeper and deeper, until it simply slips
away. The conscience goes, your head gets quiet, you begin to
hear the birds again.

Right now, you feel so good you'd like to just cut loose
and dance.

"Too bad we can't do the strut, Johnnikins." You feel your
voice in your mouth, a wooden food.

Look at that long face, he might as well be a big old hound.
"Houn' dawg!"

John was thoroughly tied to a kitchen chair, tied and
gagged.

You look at your hands, human hands, so very *able*. They
once were soft hands, pale when they first inflicted pain, first
brought pleasure.

All priests are crazy!

Except him, the stinking *piece of shit!*

You're calm, just a li'l condescending . . .

"So, okay, we might as well get on with it." He pulled the chair back into the kitchen. "Got work to do," he murmured. "Fun work, too!" He got a metal bowl out of the cabinet where Maria kept her baking dishes, and laid the strips of the John-book in it. Ceremoniously he put the bowl on the kitchen table. In the bottom of the bowl he poured an inch of Amoco. Whee.

Behind the gag John made a growling, gobbling sound, then shook his head. It was an interesting process. Frank thought he was probably bawling.

He looked John in the eye, cleared his throat, and spoke. "Today's lecture will concern barbecue. The most creditable authorities feel that the Inquisition burned between thirty and forty thousand helpless human beings at the stake. But esti-mates range from the official, which is a couple of hundred, to that of the feminist witches, which is five million."

He lit a match, held it over the bowl of gasoline-soaked paper scraps. John chewed.

Closer and closer he moved the match. John's eyes fol-lowed it. "I suspect that everybody who gets condemned to the stake becomes fascinated by fire. And what do *you* think, Father Johnnie? 'In the beginning was the word, and the word was with God and the word was God'? No, that's propaganda, believe me. In the beginning, there was fire!"

Whoomp!

John threw his head back.

"There, there . . ."

Frank watched the book burn. "It's John's favorite," she had said. And indeed, he'd had it out. He must have been looking through it, remembering.

"I fucked her frequently, Johnny. I know that must tear your heart out. But the truth is, we used to go to her place up in Ulster County. Did you know about that place? My God, we fucked sometimes for days." He laughed, thinking back. "The fake family was my idea. I thought it was rather good. If we wanted to spend a weekend fucking each other's brains out, Bishop Bayley called for me to come out to Chicago and her mother got sick."

The loathing in John's eyes angered. Frank pointed his finger at him. "You'll burn!"

To Frank's delight, he jerked furiously against his bonds.

" 'Oh, Johnny, oh, Johnny, how you could lo-o-ve!' The thing is, she loved you but she just fucked me and I am so-o-o jealous." He laughed the bishop's favorite little chuckle. It was a lovely little chuckle, eh heh heh heh. "People like me are supposed to come from dysfunctional families. You know the phrase, of course. In her attempt to understand me, Maria . . ." It was too funny, he had to stop. She'd been kneeling there praying when he did it. *Bonk.* Her eyes crossed and her prayer changed to babble. Flabble-babble. He shouldn't laugh. Flibble-flabble babble. A snort escaped though his nose. "Maria had my number," he squeaked. Then he threw back his head and roared until the tears came. "She knew!" He roared again. "She knew who was hiding in here!"

John got very still.

"Maria blamed me on my fambly. But I was loved. Very much loved. Happy home." O the secrets of the happy home, the very happy home. "My mother and father were such a lovely pair."

Listen to yourself prattle on. You're toying with John, and that's not kind. Time to get him fired up. He took another match from the box.

I am not guilty! Not, not, not!

The match between his fingers, the red head, the white tip.

Friction destabilizes phosphorus, oh yes it does.

A demon is between your fingers, between the worlds, living down in the fissures of your vast soul. You are a world of deserts and towers, and your canyons glow red with demon light.

It hurts to burn, it hurts so bad!

Something got in me and it's bad.

So, okay. That's cool. I'm good. It's all under the soft ocean of silk that hides me.

Satan is so extremely huge that he expels every single small misfortune among the twenty billion galaxies and all that were and will be and he hides so well that—

"It's funny, Johnnie, I don't feel crazy now. When I'm in the church all alone and it's dark, I feel very crazy. What's it like? It's fun! Glorious fun. I swear to you, there's something in what I do—an incredible secret. Beautiful stuff! You can't imagine how it is to be totally free, to do things that nobody dares. It's sweet!" He remembered the kick kick kick of feet, the sneezy whistle of collapsing windpipes, the hiss of the incinerator. "It's testing the limits of human experience." He drew himself up, looked into the indictment of John's eyes. "I don't like your eyes," he said. "Close them."

He didn't. Gee, what gall.

He struck the match, waved it toward John's face. Instantly the eyes closed. He began to bring the match closer. The nostrils dilated. " 'Coming to the stake with a cheerful countenance and willing mind, he put off his garments with haste, and stood upright in his shirt.' Do you know that? Any of it? Tell me, Father, do you know *any* Church history? Have you got the courage to come to the stake with a smile on your face? With a smile!" He got his jar of gas and refilled the bowl, which had burned itself out. "Smell it, Johnnie? 'Fire being now put to him, he stretched out his right hand and thrust it into the flame, and held it there a good space, before the fire came to any other part of his body; where his hand was seen of every man sensibly burning, crying with a loud voice, "This hand hath offended." ' Do you know that passage?" The match went out. He held the gasoline near John's face. The eyes began to open. "Keep 'em closed!" He lit another match.

"I've memorized the whole history of the Inquisition. I felt I ought to, since it's the central reality of the Church."

From behind the gag there was an explosion of what Frank assumed would be clerical dialectic.

"We burned what was good, suppressed what was beautiful, and now we live in the glow of the coals. This is the clerical twilight, Johnnikins, and I'm here to help make sure the sun goes down."

He lit another match, dropped it into John's lap. The eyes popped open when he felt the flame bite his thigh. From behind the gag came a sound like an electric motor tearing itself apart. His face was more red than the flames.

Then he threw back his head and went to screaming wildly, the sound muffled in the gag. The smell of burning skin filled the room, like an overdone Thanksgiving turkey. Frank grabbed his leg, snuffing the flames.

"Calm down! Come on, you can't be that much of a coward! Bishop Cranmer gave a sermon from the stake. He calmly gave a sermon! And it was better than most of *our* sermons, darling."

Frank went to the kitchen sink, drew a glass of water, and poured it on the smoking hole in John's pants. "We love each other, you know. That's why we're involved in this together. Good man, bad man. There's a famous attraction." He lit another match.

When he saw that rising pearl of flame, John's eyes rolled back into his head.

Frank knelt beside John's chair, stroking his head and singing softly in Latin, " 'Aeterne rerum conditor noctem diemque qui regis—' Do you know that one, Johnnikins? Now, don't just sit there." He brought the match close to John's sweating face. "You must respond."

John's eyebrows knit. Was he thinking about the question, or just trying to appear pitiful? "It's a Laudian hymn written by St. Ambrose before the end of the Roman empire. Isn't that amazing, we've preserved a thing like that all these long years? 'Hoc excitatus lucifer solvit polum caligine'—'Through him awakes the morning star,' John. Lucifer. The star of new beginning. Do you think the creation is simple, that God is the only light of the world? There's another light, John. That's why they call me Son of the Morning."

He was so tempted to just pour the gas down his fucking

shirt and drop a match on him and leave. But that wouldn't be right. Morally wrong in part for all. He slapped John's wounded thigh with all the might that was in him.

The noises from behind the gag were ferocious.

Frank waited for calm to return. "You don't want me to do the other leg, do you? Roast thigh?"

Burn the priest, burn the priest. They chanted, they sang, they made it into a bossa nova, into a waltz. Burn the priest. "Oh, Johnny," he said, "oh, Johnny, how you could love." *Look* at him!

21

WHILE HE WAS TIED IN THAT CHAIR JOHN RAFFERTY FOUND out some secret things about suffering, how the body itself despairs and this is why you quake when you are in agony, how at first fire gnaws enough to drive you mad with the pain, and how it later feels cold, and that is more hideous because you know it means you are being devoured.

He also learned what it's like when a human being discovers a mission that he must at all costs complete—and then begins to die.

Frank was a boy again, he was flying on the wings of youth, the bright blood of the child tumbled about in him. But there was dark, old blood too, and he could feel its weight and in every cell of it an entrance to emptiness. He was hate made flesh, he called himself the very Satan.

His was an extraordinary duty; he must not fail. From this one small incident Father Frank Bayley would enter myth, he would be whispered about for a hundred years.

———————

They were dancing together, a dark dance, something beyond the frontiers of affection and hate; John sensed there was a potential in it for change. When Frank began pouring water on his leg, he even hoped for something transcendent.

"See there, Johnnie-boy, just a little bit of third-degree burn at the center of the wound. This is mostly second-degree pain, Johnnie." He caressed his face with a damp cup towel, then dried his wounded thigh, cleaning it with the clipped gestures of a well-practiced nurse.

He embraced John, stood up. John was watching him with total concentration. Every detail of Frank's face, the slope of the jaw, the easy lips now being moistened by a busy tongue, the fast, liqueous eyes, even the stand of moisture across the forehead—all of it at once fascinated and revolted. How the mind could alter a man's appearance was astonishing to see. But the muscles, the way they were held—you could understand, almost.

"Oh, Johnnie," Frank said, sounding like a girl in pain of love. "This is . . ." He hesitated as if considering his next words with unusual care. He cocked his head. "Just a taste, my darling." With that he slipped away.

Frank stood in the alley with his coat collars up around his ears, watching Maria's window for the flicker of flame that would tell him his work was done.

To give himself the minutes he needed to make his escape, he had devised a simple time bomb. He'd put a sheet of paper over the wide mouth of his jar of gasoline, and set Maria's iron down on it, turned up to high. The warming of the iron would cause the paper to burn, and then the gas would explode. The contraption stood on the back of the couch. Plenty of fuel there for a nice fierce fire.

"Be patient, my love . . ."

John watched the iron—its angles fascinated, the stumpy aesthetic of the brown handle distressed, the little red light glowing on its snout made his stomach churn. He rocked, he twisted, he jutted his chin toward it. But the bomb was across the living room, much too far away for him to reach.

He could see the heat tremble in the pale air.

He tried to scream, but the gag was down deep in his throat and the sound didn't carry. The pain from his injured leg was slamming into his solar plexus.

He watched the iron.

With his tongue he pushed at the gag. He tried to hop the chair, but stopped when he thought he might knock himself unconscious in a fall.

The sound of the fire starting was as soft as a child's sigh. The flames went high, then settled into the jar where they had begun. As John watched in absolute horror, the plastic jar buckled, the iron twisted and pitched, and suddenly a gush of flaming gasoline poured down behind the couch.

In the dark window, Frank saw a worm of yellow. It crawled along the glass, gaudy in the fragile dawn. God, to see John, to actually *see* him in there waiting, watching—to hear his fevered prayers, taste his despair . . .

John watched as a flame rose out of the glow, began doing a hopping dance along the back of the couch. Then it was joined by more flames, until the whole top edge of the couch was burning and the wall behind it was blistering, blackening, erupting.

The smoke came in the kitchen door, high, rolling across the ceiling as the sea rolls up the sand, dropping long strings of congealed plastic ash wherever it went.

The flames became a general red glow in the living room, hidden in thick smoke. It had an awful stink, like the unforgettable reek in the clothes of a burnt old woman to whom John had once given the last rites.

Then an idea came to him, a *wonderful* idea! The door was thirty feet away, beyond the living room, on the other side of the foyer. But the kitchen window—maybe ten feet!

He hopped, he struggled, he tried to rock the chair. In his terror he had forgotten the peril of doing this, that he could fall and knock himself senseless.

He thought only that he could get to the window, break it, cause people to notice! He hopped. The chair swayed, teetered, slid about an inch.

The smoke came lower. The chair reeled.

All of a sudden Frank was crying like a child of three, and there was absolutely no reason for it at all. Why cry? You're happy, you're safe.

As a matter of fact, it was time to go have a cup of coffee and get ready to meet the day.

He had a parish to run.

John crouched low, threw himself up and back with all the strength he had remaining. The legs of the chair shot out from under him and he slammed down onto his back so hard he lost his breath. He lay there gagging and gasping, fighting the pain.

The idea of getting to the window left his mind. He'd never get to the window. In fact, he wasn't going anywhere. This was where he would stay.

The air down here near the floor was marginally clearer. He had only the hot little meteors from the burning couch to contend with now. When he was breathing again, he turned his head toward the doorway.

There were springs glowing red in the back of the couch. The whole wall behind it was aflame. John realized that he had done all he could. He must make his peace, for his time was upon him.

His poor neighbors!

An awful gnawing started along the side of his body exposed to the air. A settling spark had set his jacket aflame. He rolled over, smothering the fire. He could not roll again, though, the chair he was tied to made that impossible. This was as far from the fire as he could get.

He screamed and screamed and chewed the gag, screamed
and banged his head against the front of the oven, he thumped
the floor, did everything he could to make some noise, and
knew that it wasn't much.

The smoke was coming ever lower. It had entirely ob-
scured the doorway, and the kitchen light was a dull point.
Great soft bulges of smoke came down, and when they touched
him they were warm. He thought that he might pray, but then
found he preferred silence. When the smoke settled around
his head, a single brief breath caused a wild spasm of coughing.
Its effect was appalling; it made a sensation like knives in the
lungs. He twisted and turned, trying to find a last pocket of
good air.

His next breath would be deep, and it would be smoke.
He prepared himself, wishing that he had access to the sacraments. He would have given much for a final Eucharist, for
the blessing of the last rites. His prayer consisted of imagining
the Virgin as she had always been in his mind, a young, pure
woman with that very gentle smile. When I die, I'm coming
to you, I'm coming!

She was before him, radiant in the fire.

There just had to be a little more he could do. He
had neighbors, after all, he had to help his neighbors! He
twisted his hands, he banged his head, he screamed again in
the thick gag, and all of a sudden his left hand was at his own
throat.

The hand moved to the gag, pulled it off. "Fire," he
shouted, "fire fire fire!" He raised his head and the heat closed
around him like raging hornets. He slammed himself back to
the floor. Then he pulled his body along, still attached to the
chair. He had to get to the hall, had to warn the others, and
never mind anything else. Only when he reached the doorway
did he realize that he could get rid of the chair by simply
untying the cords around his waist. But he fumbled at the
knots, he began to choke again, he feared he might miss escape
by the thinnest of margins.

———

The sound of the siren was at first so faint that it hardly penetrated Frank's thoughts. Then he heard it grinding down nearby. Jesus God, they'd come fast! Another look at the window showed bright flames. Was John dead yet?

Frank left the alley, hurrying to the corner of Seventh Avenue. Two more fire trucks were coming.

Was John dead yet?

He had to stay, to find out. Quick—find a place to hide. He wanted to shrink, or to fly—oh, free, swooping high . . .

Then he saw behind a high fence the winter-gnarled shrubs of the Jefferson Market Gardens across the street. Oh, yes, a lovely spot.

As quick as a leopard he scaled the twelve-foot chain-link fence that surrounded the gardens. He spread his arms and leapt. The ground rushed up, he rolled easily, rattling through the tumult of leaves. When he rose, brushing himself, he saw the brown Plymouth that told him the detectives were here too.

Well, of course—the report of a fire in Maria Julien's apartment building would bring them running.

He shrank back into the shadows as a hook and ladder and another pumper appeared. Take it easy, boys, don't get there too damn soon!

John did not remember getting out of the apartment, he never remembered that. Nor did he remember going up and down the halls banging on doors.

He had been staggering, totally disoriented when suddenly a hard object was clamped over his face. It pinched his cheeks, and he recoiled.

"Take it easy," a voice said, sounding like it came from a tomb. "Breathe! Come on, man, breathe!"

The air smelled of rubber, but he took fierce gulps anyway; he couldn't see much of anything, but he knew that this was an oxygen mask and a man in a black-and-yellow slicker was pulling him toward the window at the end of the hall.

There were people everywhere, in robes, in nightclothes,

carrying dogs, cats, children, one woman lugging a live plant and cursing deep blue. They came like shadows through the smoke, one after another, and he was being carried and the air he was breathing reminded him of the seaside. John strove for words. "Ah, ah!"

"We gotcha," the fireman said. He reached down and lifted him up. "Look, I'm gonna take you down over my shoulder. Just close your eyes and fer Chrissakes relax. We're goin' out the window and down a ladder to the street. Don't move!"

The fireman picked him up and carried him to the window, which was already open. John obeyed instructions as best he could. There came new air, cold and blessedly fresh. He pulled the oxygen mask away and breathed deeply. A glimpse revealed bright lights and figures moving in the street far below. He heard the fireman's hard breathing, the sound of his boots scraping on the aluminum ladder rungs. He heard pigeons making busy noises on a ledge. How soft they sounded with the rush of water, the hammering of engines, the dangerous bustle of the flames. Then the man put John down, laying him gently on a stretcher. Another oxygen mask was pressed onto his face, and a black man with a big beard leaned close to him.

Then everything went out of focus.

Exactly eight minutes after he had left the building, Frank saw the body coming out.

The face—the face—it wasn't covered! Frank's eyes bulged, he hissed, he would have spit acid had he been able. The bastard, he was still alive! Pattycake—catch me if you can!

He saw black towers burning, the old bricks tumbling, heard the screaming of his own heart.

Now they were installing a damned I.V.! Here came Kitty Pearson and that great scarecrow Dowd, swooping down on the old scum like a couple of buzzards.

He growled low, twisting a naked sapling between his hands. The drama of the fire played itself out, the crowd of people in robes began to filter back into the building, dawn expanded in the east, the sky waxing gold behind the black mysterious silhouettes of buildings.

He scaled the fence again, hurried over past the Riviera Café and up Seventh Avenue. All of a sudden he didn't dare enter his own fucking rectory by the front door! As he went closer he had a glimpse of the facade of Mary and Joseph. Sacred place, *clean* place. He retched, bent full, gagged, then recovered himself and hurried on.

"Breathe! Breathe! Breathe!"

The voice was so far away, it seemed to matter so little.

"CPR!"

Somebody hit him. He tried to talk, couldn't. Why were they hitting him? It was warm here, it was nice.

"Swelling of the airway!"

"Get him moving!"

"You gonna be all right," somebody said, and John thought that was just fine.

People were singing, but why? People didn't sing at fires. "He fightin' me," somebody said. How far away was he? Sounded like a hundred miles. "Jes take it easy, I ain't gonna tie you up!"

Never, never, never!

"Christ, he strong."

"He's scared, man. Okay, pop, you're gonna be fine. Just relax." A hand began stroking John's forehead. "You is breathin'," he said.

"Can he talk? What happened, Father?"

Who was that, now? A tall man, all folded up in the ambulance.

"Ambulance . . ." Was that his voice, that squeak?

"Thas right, you in a ambulance! You on your way to St. Vincent's Hospital."

Kitty glared at him. "What happened, John! Where's Frank?"

Poor Frank, it was so sad.

"You old, you like my pap." The hand stroking his forehead felt good, and he closed his eyes.

"Shit," she yelled, but that was in another world far away, and had nothing to do with him.

"Deep in thy wound, Lord, hide and . . . hide . . ." His voice went like a motor, his eyes darted here, there, looking for the quick eye of the cop, the gun, the bludgeon.

Blood, blood, blood, whole oceans of blood, tear them apart, bring down the houses.

His tower was falling, its bricks arcing silently across the gaudy winter dawn.

He knew all the passages and doors, all the corners and crannies and holes.

Down like Alice, into the rabbit hole, down where my love lies dreaming . . .

So much is lost; the world is tombs.

He entered the far end of the school, moving quickly now, the serpent in retreat. But there were holes and quiet, fissures where he could hide. . . .

Mary and Joseph's abandoned school did not extend quite to the end of Morton Street. There was another building there, three apartments above a store. For years it had been a small grocery selling Italian specialties. Recently it had become an art-glass boutique with the revolting name of Chrystalis.

If you went down the iron steps that led from the sidewalk to the cellar, you found a fire door that hadn't been used in a long time. The parish owned the storefront, and there had been a key in the box John kept in his desk.

The basement, which had stored canned goods when the grocery was open, had recently been emptied. Chrystalis had plans to create more gallery space here. Frank moved confidently through the dust, beneath the low, swayed ceiling, down a hallway that in the very distant past had led to a root cellar. The plaster was peeling, the floor was in ruins.

He went to the far end of the root cellar, where there was an opening in the bottom of the wall. Like a prisoner, he wormed his fingers through the grate. "Jim O'Shea was cast away," he sang as he loosened it, "upon an Indian isle."

He stopped the murmured song, lifted the grate up and out. He'd known it would work, he'd done it before. He had been very, very careful.

The grate bore the legend "Stuyvesant Gas Illumination Company." Inside were old iron gas pipes. They gleamed in the beam of Frank's penlight. He crawled in.

"If you lak-a me lak I lak-a you, and we lak-a both the same, I lak-a say this very day I lak-a change your na-a-me . . ."

The song carried him along his way. As a boy he'd sung often for Bishop Bayley, who had always laughed and clapped his hands. He hated the old fuck, hated him, *hated him*!

When John woke up he thought hours must have passed, but they were still bandaging his leg. He understood that he was in the hospital. He even recognized St. Vincent's emergency room. "He's awake, officer."

Kitty Pearson's face appeared. "John?" Dowd was right beside her.

"I'm sorry. I'm so damn sorry."

She reached down, took his hand.

He thought again of the neighbors. "Was anybody hurt, was the building destroyed?"

"Where's Frank? He wasn't in the apartment, was he?" According to the fire department, there was no sign of a body.

"Frank—no!" Black, black, black . . .

"This man is in shock," the doctor said.

Soon Frank reached another grate, put his hands on the bars, and pushed, snatching it before it banged down to the linoleum floor. He emerged into a corner of the old school kitchen. Here were enormous institutional stoves of archaic design, massive range hoods, sinks where generations of nuns had washed dishes for generations of young Catholics.

He spread his hands at his waist, he danced, and mine is the dance of death, struttin' out smooth.

"An' if you love-a me, one live as two, two live as one, under the bamboo tree!"

The kitchen, like the rest of the school, had been left in a heartbreaking condition of readiness. All you had to do was walk in, turn on the old stoves, take the yellowing catechisms out of their boxes, and intone, "What is the Communion of Saints?"

"If you lak-a me lak I lak-a you and we lak-a both the same . . ."

John was looking at something magnificent. He loved the light, just to look into it, the beautiful light, so bright, so white . . .

"Father?"

Now, who would that be? Who would want to talk when all you had to do was just look and look . . . ?

"We need you, Father!"

"You people have got to go easy. This man is exhausted. You let him rest. Come on, get out of here."

The light went off. Now, how could that have happened? If the Light of the World could just be turned off like that, then maybe—

He realized that he had been staring at a ceiling fixture, and all of a sudden he was wide-awake. "Hey!"

The door flew open and they were there, and he poured his story out. "Get him," he concluded, "for the love of God, get him."

He wanted to tear somebody to pieces, to rip out a wet heart with his own dear hands. How the hell had this happened, how had the old *bastard* made it out of that fire alive?

This is damnation!

It can't be happening like this, no. I'm so brilliant, I'm so careful, why did I torture him? Just a knife to the heart, kitchen knife. Why did I take this risk?

"Run, run fast as ya can, ya can't catch me, I'm the gingerbread man!"

—Don't cry now, little boy, just because you're totally screwed.

I worked for this parish! I have a right!

Pattycake pattycake.

Ever so carefully he pushed the door.

The rectory was silent. Good. He had to hide and he needed food. Wanted his razor too.

I eat, I shave, I have a bed, and I have followers. I have people who kneel at my feet and I give them false communion.

"Willie Fitzgibbons, who used to sell ribbons, and stood up all day on his feet—"

"Hi, Father Frank!"

Trish Moltash stood in the doorway to the kitchen.

Gentle, sweet tone, grave smile. " 'Morning, Trish."

"I came in early to put the old missalettes back out. Everybody loves 'em, it seems." She laughed a little.

Kill her?

Yes. She'll tell the world.

No. Let her carry a deception. "If I get any calls, I'm out," he said.

"Yes, Father. Sure."

"Any calls. Remember that. I'm out and you have no idea when I'll come back."

"Are you really going somewhere?"

He nodded. "Far away," he said. "Very far away."

22

J OHN'S LEG THROBBED, HIS ACHING ARM IMPEDED EFFORTS TO get comfortable in bed. Three nights at home had done nothing to ease the pain. In the hospital he'd been drugged, he'd slept black malformed sleep and awakened feeling vile. There were no drugs now, except for the painkillers Pete had given him. But they made him woozy and talkative; he'd reverted to aspirin.

Worse than the physical discomfort, though, was the storm in his mind. That fine young priest! If a young man as good as that could turn out to contain such unspeakable horror, then for John Rafferty something essential was changed in the meaning of not only of the Church, but of God and the world. In the works of the God he served, he had perceived order and the shadow of a kind presence. Even the upheavals of earthly life had until now supported his belief that the City of God must be fashioned to a placid and glorious design.

He twisted, groaning, and threw off his thin blanket. He sat up in bed. There lingered in the room a thin smell of cigarette smoke, and he wanted a cigarette. His tongue touched his lips as he imagined the warmth of it, the inner settling that would accompany the first puff.

He was dwelling on this mundane desire when he suddenly sat up straight, smelling a sharper smoke. Slowly, warily, he stood. He went to the door, pulled it open slightly. Kitty had pulled Frank's office chair into the hall and sat leaning back. Assuming herself to be unobserved, she dangled her legs like a little girl. She had just lit a match, and was applying it to a cigarette.

A burning match.

An image of the demon's face floated into his mind's eye. He felt like he was falling back and back, into the dark medieval depths when they hid such faces in the eaves of their great cathedrals.

What did they know?

It had been so loose and . . . sleazy. The face of a vicious libertine. It was a face that made some part of you filthy, simply because you had seen it. The eyes, though—the eyes sparkled with life. He had been enjoying himself!

What was possession? Did it mean that Frank was a sort of act put on by the demon . . . or had the demon displaced the man?

No, seeing it close, John realized that it was a much more complex state. The function of the demon was to emphasize the man's monstrous potentials and paralyze all in him that was good.

Kitty Pearson coughed. She was looking up toward the ceiling, leaning far back in the chair.

The real Frank might not even know he was possessed.

He couldn't have known. Looking back, the man who had prayed with him, prostrate on the altar steps, and the man who had burned that poor creature in the nave a few hours before could not have been the same.

God help him, help him regain whatever he has lost that is essential to being human.

Kitty hefted her breasts with her free hand, then came lurching forward. Her feet hit the floor with a thud.

John closed his door, not wishing to intrude on the woman's privacy any longer. He looked toward his bed. What to do? He had a long day tomorrow, and he needed sleep. Perhaps he should go downstairs and get a drink, a nice brandy. There was some brandy in the cabinet in the dining room.

But then she'd see him in his pajamas and robe. He didn't like that. He sighed, eased himself onto the bed.

It seemed only a moment later that he was in the church again, moving slowly up the aisle. It's not a dream, a voice behind him said. At first it all seemed the most normal thing in the world.

Then it didn't. A shock like a blow went through him when he saw the tall, immensely dignified figure standing before the altar. He was in shadow, but John knew exactly who this was.

How remarkable! All of this time, he really existed. He was a form, a figure. He had all of history flowing in his face, you could see it in the downturned mouth, in the wry and terrible cast of the eye.

John remembered the literal gust of evil that he had felt, and the astonishing sadness. It was a divine sorrow, not a human one, the sadness of somebody for whom eternity has proved to be a trap.

The figure could not have contrasted more completely with Frank. He had always been such an unprepossessing young man. His burly arms, his open face—it was not a dignified presence. This man was so tall, so grave, so awesome that John found himself bowing his head.

A breeze came down from the altar, stinking like rats stank when they died in the walls. Then there was a sparkle, a hiss, a blooming spiked flower that dazzled his eyes.

With a gasp of confusion and surprise, he awoke. By reflex he sat up, and pain raced up and down his leg, shook his arm.

After all, a dream.

But not quite that, not quite. . . .

His eyes widened, he stared into the dark corners of the room. Was that thick shadow . . . ? No. No, it was only the radiator pipe. Of course.

Was it not Satan rushing through the night, looking for a tunnel into another soul?

"Frank?"

No answer, of course. The door was black, its pediment looming and angular. The sick terror of the dream returned. That odor! Had he been in here, leaning into John's face?

He had to call Kitty, to tell her. No, don't, you old fool. It was just a dream. You've been profoundly shocked, such reactions are inevitable.

With sudden urgency he turned on his bedside lamp. He could picture Frank waiting in the closet, Betty Communiello's cleaver raised high over his head.

How would it feel to have your skull split by such a thing? A terrible pain, a flash, the curious dripping away of the soul.

The closet door seemed full, as if a weight was pressing it from within. Of course it seemed that way; he was terrified. His heart rattled like an old Ford. A stinging came into his right eye: sweat had mixed with the tears.

There was nothing for it: either call her or solve this fear. He approached the closet. Frank wasn't in there, he couldn't be. The thing was too shallow, there was barely room for his clothes.

He put his hand on the doorknob. It was warm. But of course, the whole room was warm. He pulled.

There was a swift movement, he reeled back, his arms windmilling, he started to cry out—and his brand-new homburg fell at his feet with a dry thump.

Now, look at that! He picked it up, adjusted the brim. Who had put it in here? Betty Communiello, no doubt, assuming that he wouldn't want to actually use such a fine hat.

Dressed or not, he was going to go downstairs, put the damned hat back where it belonged, and get a nice stiff drink. He would sit in his own parlor listening to music and sipping brandy until he felt sleepy. Maybe he would say a prayer or two. A nice comforting prayer.

Satan was so much stronger than nice comforting prayers! Why, if he came, did not the Lord also come? "Lord, why?"

He did not try to be quiet as he pulled open his door. No doubt she would come with him, loaded gun in her hand. Fine, and so much the better. Let her see a priest in tattered woolen pajamas. What difference did it make? She'd been there when they were dressing his wounds; she'd probably seen him naked.

Hat in hand, he stepped into the hall. She lay slumped far back in the chair, her head lolling, her throat pale in the dim hall light. A long expiring breath made him think . . . But no, she was only asleep.

He should wake her.

No, let the woman sleep. He'd be gone and back in two minutes. She needn't even know. Her worry was that Frank would climb the walls, after all, not that he was lurking somewhere in the plant.

He crept past her, started downstairs and stopped. The stairway was an open pit. He stood at the top looking down, listening to the clock's great ticks echo through the silence.

Oh, old man, you're so scared. "What is death, then, that it so oppresses me?" Old man—what has happened to you in your life, in your church? It's all being ruined and made ugly. This was the intention of the demon all along.

He thought again of Frank, Frank with Joanie McReady, Frank saying his Mass, Frank at prayer, Frank laughing over the dinner table, Frank dancing with a younger, happier Betty Communiello and making her shriek with laughter, Frank confessing, baptizing, giving out communion.

Determination replaced fear. Step by step, he forced himself to go down to his own parlor. He lived here, this was his home, and here he would stand. He reached up, flipped a switch, and flooded the whole foyer with light. There was nobody here, of course. Nobody in the rectory at all, with the exception of him and Kitty. Such a fine young woman. He could feel God hungering for her love. How hard it must be for God to live so very close to each soul, to feel in such awful detail the tide of indifference that is engulfing the world.

Why be a priest? Somebody's got to help God. Somebody's

got to turn some souls in God's direction, make his love worth-while. We are not alone, we don't know what it is to be alone. But what about God, the outsider?

He intended to do the work of God, and to do it in this rectory and in this church. John yanked open the hall closet and put the homburg on the shelf where it belonged. Very good. His heart was no longer fluttering, he was more in con-trol. He went into the dining room, and it was like going among ghosts.

They were around him, the men of the church who had sat at this table, his friends. He remembered Tom Zimmer when their days were yet young, and all the jokes and the laughter. The lights would be bright, the table piled high . . . and young Frank Bayley blushing to the tips of his ears at some of the jokes that passed. This was the worst room, because of all the happiness stored in its walls.

John remembered a few toasts out of this very bottle of Hennessy. It was at least a year old; there wasn't a great deal of drinking at this rectory. He poured what proved to be the last drink it contained, then took the bottle out to the kitchen, rinsed it, and dutifully dropped it in the recycling bin.

He was sipping his drink when he heard from the kitchen the hiss of a blooming match. He could not move, could not breathe, could not make a sound. Something deep within him closed itself; he heard the sigh of a cassock swirling about, the fainter crackle of the match as it burned.

He waited for the *whoomp* of flaring gasoline, the calm, matter-of-fact voice.

He waited.

He was left with nothing but the flutter of his breath and the ticking of the clock.

A chastened man hustled up the stairs, past his sleeping guard, and into the darkness of his own room. At this point he could not know whether or not what he had just heard had been real. Could Frank really be in the rectory?

John saw in flickering outline the intimation of a plan. He remembered his dream, and knew suddenly who had laid that plan and what it was, and what he must do.

He lay back on his bed. I'll never sleep, he thought, never again. There was a great deal of work to do. He would have to at least learn the basics of exorcism. He hesitated, though, to attempt a ritual which seemed so fundamentally unconvincing to him.

But he had seen the demon. He had *seen*.

How could you affect a thing like that with a few prayers?

It wasn't that he didn't believe in the ritual. The truth was, he didn't believe in himself.

"Bless me, Father, for I have sinned . . ."

Absolution must not only be given but also accepted. The true secret of the confessional is that it takes a strong man indeed to let go of his sins. We fear our sins, and because we do, Satan's argument that we condemn ourselves by revealing them is most persuasive.

He could not imagine himself performing the old ritual . . . and anyway, hadn't Tom Zimmer tried and failed?

Tom Zimmer, who was now posted missing along with George Nicastro.

Outside there came a stir, the creak of the chair, a snort. She was waking up. Good, she ought to wake up.

He drifted to the edge, where dream and truth become one another. Frank . . . why Frank? The conventional explanations were insufficient. A hurt childhood was not the only ingredient of evil; everybody carries within him a damaged child, but we are not all murderers.

John's mind drifted . . . deeper into the question.

How long had Frank been like this? He had seemed so comfortable with his state. The worst obscenity was his casualness. The evil came not in the moment the match was lit, but before, when his hand drew it indifferently from his pocket.

"Why, Frank?"

Was that not laughter, laughter in the walls?

23

AFTER SIX MISERABLE HOURS OF DOZING IN A CHAIR, KITTY wanted a cigarette, but she still didn't feel comfortable lighting up in the church, at least not during the Mass itself. When your body expects a cigarette every ten or fifteen minutes of your waking life, a forty-five-minute Mass is a noticeable ordeal.

"Let us proclaim the mystery of faith," John said. His thin voice reached the timbre of high drama. The impact of it was startling: this man *believed*. "Dying you destroyed our death, rising you restored our life. Lord Jesus come in glory."

Damn him for making her mad. That meant she cared, and she didn't want to care. Truth be told, she even felt sorry for Frank, and he was . . . well, God only knew what the hell he was.

John looked miserable. Tired, in pain, scared. Yeah, look at the way he fumbled with the chalice, trying to use his sprained arm.

His vestments were shimmering, his altar was drowned

in flowers, his bald pate was glowing with exertion. The church was jammed. The media coverage had brought in lots of outsiders, which made her even more nervous.

He reached the communion rite and soon was standing before his altar with two deacons, giving the Eucharist to the throng. Almost everybody wanted to receive the sacrament, and the length of time the process was taking added to her unease.

The image of that black shape moving up the back wall of her house came again to mind. Yesterday she'd made the time to go out to her place and examine the wall inch by inch.

All of a sudden she realized that she was on her way up to communion. She'd just gotten up with the rest of her aisle. It had been sort of automatic.

No it hadn't.

Her communion was a big crumb of pita bread. She preferred the mysterious little wafers of childhood. It was a lot harder to believe that Christ could be contained in pita bread from some Lebanese deli than in one of those perfectly white little wafers.

Back in her aisle she tried to say a prayer. "Hail . . . bread of our fathers . . . trespass . . ." She got a little booklet from the pocket on the back of the pew in front of her and read. "My soul is thirsting for the living God, as the hind longs for the running waters, so my soul longs for you, O God."

There was that hind again, still in there from when she was eight years old. But what the hell is a hind?

She watched John struggle back to his altar. It was painful to see. This man needed more than an overnight in the hospital and a fat patch on his leg. He needed rest and counseling and support. And above all he needed to be away from here.

Why the hell did you come back, you stupid jerk?

Now her prayer came, her real prayer, right out of the center of her soul, from so deep she probably didn't even know she was saying it. Where is he, God? We gotta find this guy. I mean, it's your Church he's screwing up. You get my drift? Your priest he's gonna off. Help me, for Chrissakes!

Frank had done one hell of a disappearing act. Astonishing. She lifted her eyes, gazing into the rafters. Last night she'd dreamed that there were things peeking out of the windows in the friggin' bell tower.

"Go, the Mass is ended," John said. The congregation's reply was a generalized rustle, the practiced voices rising to give the correct response, "Thanks be to God."

He turned and went through the door into the sacristy. Kitty followed at once. She watched silently as his deacons removed his vestments, listened in anguish to the awful little sounds he made when they raised his hurt arm.

She'd come to like the old guy a good deal. Even if she hadn't liked him much, she hated to see people suffer.

She was now desperate for a cigarette, but wasn't sure if it was any more proper to smoke in a sacristy than in the church itself. In any case, there wasn't a sign of an ashtray. The thought of using the chalice crossed her mind. You have a sick sense of humor, woman.

"Father, we gotta talk."

"So, let's talk."

She glanced at the deacons. "Elsewhere," she said.

She followed him through the door into the rectory. "How's the leg?" she asked as he maneuvered himself painfully into the lounger in the parlor.

"I'm praying to St. Jude for faster healing, but so far he seems to be busy on other cases."

"Father, you're insane to come back here."

His reply was to sit there blinking at her. How could such a bright man manage to look so utterly stupid?

"Father, you've gotta leave. You *cannot* stay here overnight."

"No."

"Oh, come on, you've got a thousand places you could go! Any one of your parishioners'd put you up in a minute. Plus there are other rectories, other places a priest can stay." She took out a cigarette, offered him one. He shook his head.

"This is *my* place. And I've gone through a hell of a lot to get it back."

"I'd sooner sleep in a cage full of tigers than stay here."

"That bad, eh?"

"Do you realize that we don't have a single worthwhile lead—and that's with national publicity."

"I know. The publicity's been tragic."

"On the contrary, the media happens to be doing a damn good job. Considering all the interest, it's incredible that there hasn't been even one good sighting. Not one!" A little voice inside her said: What do you expect? The man can climb sheer walls. God only knows what else he can do.

John's slight smile never wavered. "I think we'll be hearing from him."

"Look, at least tell me why you want to stay here. Give me one good reason."

"If I stay here, openly conducting the affairs of this parish, he's going to show up. Sooner or later."

"I knew it! You're damn well setting yourself up as bait. This, Father, is what is so crazy."

"If he escapes, he becomes a legend, a myth. He's already hurt the Church enough. Something has to happen that'll let people put this behind them."

"God damn you, John!"

"Where did you learn to speak English, dear lady?"

"In the fucking sewer, and don't try to get me off the subject. If you don't get out of here on your own, I'm going to start condemnation proceedings."

"On what grounds?"

"The place is infested by a fucking demon!"

"Oh, come on—"

"No! You and I both know he's—"

"The word we use is 'preternatural.' Above the natural, below the supernatural."

"Fill 'im fulla Thorazine and he won't be preternatural anymore."

"Probably not. But we don't have him in our possession, so we can't. If I left I'd end up having to stay away until you caught him. No offense, but that might be rather a long time."

At last, an opening! She plunged. "Give us two weeks.

Just two weeks. If we don't have him in custody by then, you can come back."

He looked his officious best. "No can do. The parish is in turmoil. I'm needed here now."

"I thought you'd been fired!"

"After the pasting the chancery took in the press, they've backed off on that." The little smile broadened just slightly.

"Wipe that smile off your face! That has to be one of the most annoying things I've ever seen a human being do. If you had a wife she'd—I don't know what—beat it outta you!"

He laughed then, and the laughter was kind.

She decided to try another approach. "Okay, look. If you stay here, then the police department is going to respond by having guys crawling—and I mean crawling—all over this place. We'll be on the roof, in the basement, under your damn bed, Father! We'll have five guys in the toilet when you take a dump."

"And therefore you'll never get another shot at Frank. I'm telling you, unless I'm here to lure him back, he's gone. Until the next church, that is."

"They all get caught sooner or later. All of them!" She said it to reassure him, but she knew perfectly well that it was very far from true. His face told her he was aware of the lie. "Goddammit, John, I'm scared for you, don't you know that!"

"I'm an old man, I've done more than my fair share of living. If my last act is to stop Frank . . . well, I can think of many a less worthy death."

"You arrogant bastard!"

His smile could also be devastating. She found herself momentarily at a loss for words. She'd been mistaken to think that she was still dealing with an innocent man. In his new depth abided something that she had never seen before, and it awed her. She gave way before it, there was no other choice. "So this place is going to be a trap, and you're the bait."

He said nothing.

"The thing is, if you're alone in here, and there's nobody to help you—"

"I won't be alone." He regarded her steadily. "If Satan is real, then so is God."

"What's the idea, then? You just live your normal life, and we *wait?*"

"I doubt if it'll be long." There was light in his eyes now. He knew that he'd won. "Considering that he's still here."

"I can't buy that."

"It's true."

"Nah, he's on his way to California. Canada. You name it."

John shook his head.

"You have proof of this?"

"I know what he's going to do. What he *has* to do. He's here, he must be."

"We searched the whole damn place."

"Let's do it again. If you have a weapon."

She raised her purse, which contained the .38. Then she glanced toward his leg. "If you can."

A dreadful look came into his eye, and she realized that the little smile was nothing but bravado. He was in great pain, and he was absolutely terrified.

She hauled him up out of the chair. They went to the bookcase, which had behind it a door into the school. She dragged the case back.

"Don't scratch the floor, please."

"Relax. I'm a careful lady." They entered the principal's office. John groped his way to the far wall and turned on the light. A small bulb cast a stingy glow. She already knew that they'd taken out most of the light bulbs, using a few low-wattage replacements to provide the minimal light an abandoned school might need. It was a shadowy, silent place.

"The day I closed the school we still had over four hundred kids. My nuns flew the coop on me. I was faced with hiring twelve lay replacements over a single summer. Couldn't swing it." He sighed, threw open a box on the wall. "This is the main lighting panel."

"I know. And three-quarters of the bulbs are gone."

"Light is money."

"I want every light you have turned on and left on."

"Incidentally, does your boss know you're shacking up with a priest?"

She'd not so much as hinted that she had plans to stay another night. "No," she snarled.

He laughed a little.

"Let's start at the bottom," she said. "We'll work our way up."

Everywhere you turned you saw evidence of childhood, the yellowing decorations in the classrooms, the little desks, even the bits of chalk still in the runners on the blackboards. This was not a dead place, but one held in thrall, as if by a malicious spell.

Somebody hoped to get this school running again, that was why it had been left furnished and ready. She watched John's bowed back as he rolled slowly along.

At the far end of the cafeteria was a small black door. She knew that it led into an ancient conduit filled with gas pipes, they'd seen it in the plans. But there was no exit. Just to satisfy herself, she pulled the door open, shone her penlight into the gloom, and then closed it. "When the place had gaslights," she said.

"The school never had gaslights. It was built in 1923."

"Then they were for what was here before it. Anyway, the conduit's a dead end. Nowhere to go from there."

They turned away, not hearing the tick of breath among the pipes.

They went then to the first floor, moving more swiftly, looking into each classroom. The second floor was the same. "I don't like to come here," John said. "This is my failure."

"Half the Catholic schools in New York are closed."

"Half are open."

"Don't blame yourself. You're dealing with something a lot bigger than one parish and one school."

They reached the third floor, where the nuns had had their residence, when he stopped her with a gesture.

Then she heard it too, faint laughter. They listened, but it did not repeat. "I think it came from outside," she said.

"I hope so. Because if it didn't, he's living in the walls like a rat."

"Don't say that. It's too creepy."

"I heard laughter like that once or twice before."

She'd never heard *anything* like that, and didn't care to again. She shook her head, as if expelling the residue of the sound.

Then she noticed a small door in the wall. "I wonder if anybody looked in there."

They were in the nuns' dining room.

"It's the dumbwaiter, so the food doesn't have to be carried all the way up from the kitchen." John pulled the door open. Inside there was a rope leading down into darkness.

She reached in, touched it. There wasn't enough space in here for a man to hide. She shone her penlight up to a wooden ceiling three feet above. The pully mechanism was suspended by rusty screws. Peering down, she could see something at the end of the rope. "That's interesting," she said.

"What?"

She gave him the penlight. "You know what I think that is? I think it's a plastic garbage bag lying on the dumbwaiter."

"If that's what it is, it's recent. Plastic garbage bags weren't allowed into my plant until Mrs. Communiello threatened to quit over the issue last year." He pulled on the rope with his good arm. The mechanism was stiff, and it took both of them to haul the dumbwaiter up.

"Heavy, whatever it is," she commented. About three feet short of the opening, everything stopped. She shone the light down. The garbage bag had slipped partly off the edge of the platform and lodged against the wall.

"Lower it a little," John said.

But it wouldn't go anywhere. "What the hell is it?" She leaned in, reached down.

"Careful, the pully's not exactly stable."

"If I could give it a tug, maybe it'd come unstuck." She

realized too late that the sill around the opening was rotted. Before she could react, she was toppling forward amid a shower of wood dust. "Shit!"

She felt a hand grab her dress. He stifled a groan of pain as he broke her fall.

"Careful, Father!"

"I'm okay. Let's try it again. I think it's loose."

Recovering herself, she grabbed the rope and heaved with all her might. She was totally unprepared for the ease with which the dumbwaiter rose, now that the obstruction had been cleared. It shot up toward and past them and slammed into the ceiling of the shaft.

The plastic bag burst like a banana skin and black objects cascaded down around them, hitting the floor with loud thuds.

There was a moment's silence, then John saw and all he could do was scream, he could not control it, he could not stop himself. For an instant Kitty was confused, then she saw the blackened, jawless human skull that lay on the edge of the dumbwaiter. And another one was in her lap, the cranium caved in.

She completely lost it, for the first time in the Job.

She wasn't a detective anymore, not a cop, only a human being, disgusted, outraged, terror-stricken.

Then she saw a white flash, felt herself losing balance, tripping back against the dining table. "I'm sorry," John said, "I'm so sorry!"

"You hit me!"

"I'm sorry! You were—"

"That's from the movies, damn you. Hitting people to bring them to their senses."

"Are these . . . old?" He gestured toward the bones.

She felt freezing cold, she hunched her shoulders, clasped herself. "How should I know? Look, we gotta get the Job moving on this pronto." He tried to hold her, then stepped away, defeated by his inexperience with close physical contact. "Come on," she added, "let's get back to the rectory and phone."

They came yet again, the squad cars, the forensics experts, the medical examiners. John made coffee and she took a big mug with her back to the crime scene. This time there were additional cops on duty outside to control the horde of press people, who were showing signs of turning into an out-of-control mob. Photographers had to be pulled off fire escapes and gutters, so desperate were they to get pictures of the skeletons for the early editions.

"A photog's got five hundred bucks for anybody'll let him in," Dowd told Kitty as he hurried up the stairs. "In case you want to become corrupt at last."

She shook her head. He clapped her on the shoulders. "Hey. You look like you've been to dinner with a vampire."

"It's so horrible, it's just . . . Christ! This is beyond me, it's more than I can fucking well *take!*"

"There's a Bishop Bayley in town. He's called the precinct wanting to talk to us. He wants to talk to St. Johnnie too."

"*Bishop* Bayley—who is he, the father?"

"Now, now, don't get bitter in your old age. He's the loving uncle. The mother's checked into a hospital in Chicago because of her heart. Daddy lives in a basket. Stroke a couple of years back."

"Probably worried about his kid."

"I doubt it. These cases, the perp is always a surprise."

"Parents sense things."

John returned from the rectory. He was lugging a big aluminum coffee urn, which he put down on the dining table. Flashbulbs were popping as police photographers recorded the crime scene. "I'll get more mugs," John said, and left.

"Christ, I wouldn't drink that stuff," one of the forensics technicians commented when he was gone.

"These are definitely burn victims," the medical examiner said. "I'll bet the father's coffee is good."

"Laced with wolfbane, probably," a uniform replied.

"That's for werewolves," his partner said. "This here was done by a ghoul."

The medical examiner, a tiny woman with a huge purse,

came up from the pile of bones. "Two dead people here. Probably both guys. And it's recent, is my guess."

"You're certain it's two? Not more?"

"I'm not certain of anything. But it looks like two."

"I got a feeling we just located Tom Zimmer and George Nicastro," Sam said.

"They must have found him out."

"Don't assume anything about his motives."

"Where'd he do his burn?" the M.E. asked Kitty.

"There are ovens in the school kitchen. An incinerator in the rectory."

"Let's get to work," Dowd said.

She was grateful that this also meant getting away from the skeletons. She'd never seen one before, hadn't understood how it would affect her. This case was eating away at the careful distance she had learned to maintain between herself and her clients. Cases are not supposed to be people, but to Detective First Class Kitty Pearson these skeletons were entirely human.

She led Dowd to the kitchens. "This is where the dumbwaiter comes out." He lifted the latch on the wooden door with a pen. There was nothing to be seen in the shaft except the rope and a falling smatter of particles as somebody above worked on the platform.

They turned to the ovens, which were big and old, four of them in two stacks. Their doors were black iron, embossed with the words "Royal Rose." Kitty wrapped a handkerchief around her hand. Steeling herself, she started to open the first one.

"No. Me." Dowd opened it, peered inside. "Clean."

So were the other three. Then she saw why: the gas main was turned off and sealed. Con Ed puts a seal on a gas line that's still live but disconnected. If anybody had lit these ovens, the seal would have been broken.

"That leaves the incinerator," Kitty said. They went back up into the rectory, where Father John was fussing in the kitchen. "We're going to check out the incinerator. It's still functioning, isn't it?"

"Oh, yes. We use the incinerator. We have a permit."

"When do you use it?"

"Every couple of days Lupe does a burn. We know it pollutes, but it's a lot cheaper than a carting service, and the city won't cart C.O. refuse."

"C.O. refuse?"

"Garbage generated by charitable organizations."

She took Dowd down the narrow basement stairs, the boards moving beneath their feet. The place stank of garbage and wet ashes . . . and a faint singed odor. She knew at once that they had found the site of the burning.

As they reached the bottom of the stairs Father John appeared in the doorway above them. "Stay there," Kitty said over her shoulder. He started down anyway.

"The incinerator's ancient. It's dangerous." His eyes said that he was afraid for them.

Dowd lifted the iron bar that closed the double doors, then swung them open. He shone his flashlight into the black firebox. "This is weird."

"How so?"

"Somebody's cleaned the interior of your incinerator."

"Why would they do that?"

Dowd snorted. "You never told the super to do it?"

"Never in all the years I've been here. It never occurred to me."

"No. But it occurred to Father Frankie, who burned people up in here, then got rid of the ashes. Almost."

"Excuse me, but don't call him 'Father.' The creature that burned his victims here is not a priest. He isn't even a human being."

"That's your belief, Father."

"I saw his face!"

For the next half-hour Kitty performed her professional duties, made her report, finally sent Dowd away. The place slowly emptied of cops, of life, of sound.

At last all was still. John was lying in the big recliner in the sitting room. "They've closed it out for the night," she said. "You're going to bed."

He opened his eyes. "I could make more coffee."

"You get up those stairs and get to sleep or tell me why."

He shuffled off. It made her thigh hurt just to watch him work his way up the stairs.

She felt that only a firsthand witness to Frank's abilities would be able to mount an effective defense against him. You could tell people he could climb walls. You could certainly tell them.

You could not be prepared for a thing like that if you hadn't seen it.

Maybe not even if you had.

24

SUDDENLY IT WAS LIGHT AND SHE KNEW SHE'D SLEPT FOR hours. She leapt up from the office chair she'd been hauling out for her vigil. John was safely asleep; thank God he hadn't been destroyed while she shirked her duty. She let out her breath. He lay legs akimbo, arms thrown out at the shoulders. Little Mikey, her brother's three-year-old, slept like that.

He took a long shuddering breath and turned his head toward the wall. She went to the bedroom window. At the curb she could see a squad car with two uniforms inside. They had coffee cups in their hands, they were talking. One of the benefits of cop life is cop talk.

To wake Frank up there was only the scuttle of the roach, the whispering movement of the rat.

The Frank who opened his eyes was not the one who had closed them, who had come here, who had done terrible crimes.

The priest woke up, stretched first one leg and then the other, then sat up—and got a knock on the forehead that laid him back with a thud.

For a moment he was completely mystified—why in the world was he here?

Then he shuddered, flashes of memory coming up from the depths of him. "Oh . . . no. No. No!"

—Maria is flopping like a fish. Her tongue is smacking in her mouth.

She is scared, amazed.

But she knows, she has to die! She knows! And she's a whore, she fucked that scumbag John.

No, that isn't me thinking like that. That isn't me!

Maria runs, she runs toward the door, the street.

"No!"

The monstrance glides toward her forehead. Frank, she says, I've been waiting and waiting—Good God!

She dies.

Tom Zimmer, the white fire.

Do I do pattycake?

What the hell is the strut?

And do wop?

My sister played do-wop records, she loved do wop.

He threw back his head and screamed into the thick silence of the crawlspace.

Then he stopped, clapping his hands over his mouth.

—They know what you do.

—They're looking for you.

You're a ba-a-a-d boy!

So don't be fucking stupid. Be fucking quiet.

John gasped as he became conscious of the black shape before his window. It moved, and suddenly Kitty Pearson was there, looking down at him with a twisted, uncertain smile on her face. "You need coffee?"

He tugged at the sheet, trying to cover himself more adequately. Not only was he a very modest man, he treasured his time alone, and early mornings had always been precious. Even the hospital had been quiet between six and seven. He wanted his breviary, his rosary. This was a time for prayer and contemplation, not social contact.

Watching him snatch at his sheets, she wondered if she created mere uneasiness, or actually caused his flesh to crawl. She struggled to retrieve the moment. "I'm gonna make some," she said. "Coffee's more important to me than food." She also wanted a cigarette, but she didn't add that. She'd light up in the kitchen. "I'll make you some breakfast while I'm at it."

When he still said nothing, she marched off to the kitchen. It was safe enough to leave him alone now that it was light, and that was obviously what he wanted her to do.

He-e-re's Frankie!

A funny thing happened to me on the way to the crypt, I died. Eh heh heh heh.

Uh-oh, fellas, knees up—boner patrol!

"If you lakka me lak I lakka . . ."

I'm in a hole hurting to piss, Momma, 'cause I kill Hunca-Munca mouse people. Mouse-Father Johnnikins, oh, I . . . I . . . I shoulda putta knife in his chest. Let him look at it, o ho ho ho.

He swung the hatchway open and dropped down into the cafeteria. A little light came in the high windows, making the rows of tables and empty chairs gleam softly.

"I am the Lord of the Dance, said he. Dance, dance, whoe'er you shall be!"

Gotta pee.

John shaved meticulously. Afterward he removed the dressing from his wound, as he had been taught. He covered it with the lotion Pete Morris had prescribed. Tonight he would have to wash it in the iodine soap, a prospect he found unsettling. It had hurt a great deal when the nurses washed it, and he was afraid he would cause himself far more pain than they had.

Hard as it was, he dressed in a suit. These days anything

could happen, and the suit was more serviceable if he had to go out. After he was dressed he found himself opening Frank's medicine cabinet.

He took out Frank's Afta and splashed some on his cheeks. Normally he never used after-shave, but today he wanted some. He noticed that the razor was gone. Carefully, he looked for it among the neat rows of unguents and salves. Frank was a meticulous man, and the razor was very definitely missing.

Indeed.

While the coffee was perking and the bacon was frying, Kitty called Dowd at home, hoping he'd have heard some news about the identity of the skeleton. She was not a kitchen person, but she wanted to give Father John some food, the man looked so cadaverous. She watched the bacon warily as it sizzled and congealed on itself. It took six rings for her partner to answer.

"I'm standing in the kitchen cooking Father's breakfast and I wanta know if they made the skeletons."

"You slept?"

"A little, toward dawn. But baby's still fine."

"You can't really believe the perp's still there."

"No, but he could sure as hell come back."

"Be hard and dumb, considering the surveillance."

"He could get past it."

"They haven't made the skeletons yet. They're waiting for dental records on the two logical candidates. So nothing's new except the fact that you're cooking breakfast for yet another man you don't have to worry about getting involved with."

The problem with Dowd was that he didn't miss enough.

Little bitty itty little-boy urinals where they used to compare their tallywackers, oh, dear, I am so lost. Golden flow, bridge into the black sewer. If only I could follow thee, golden flow, down and down where freedom's cesspool lies.

You consecrated the host, you heard confessions, you baptized.

He was a sword pointed at the heart of the priesthood, do wop.

John was determined to get the parish rolling again. Everything had stopped, even the soup kitchen. For a while he was going to have to do a great deal of it himself. He doubted very much that Bob Quindlan would give him a curate even if there was one available. He glanced at his watch. Six-fifty. In five minutes he would go over to the church, open the doors, and say the morning Mass.

As he read his breviary he became aware of the smell of coffee coming up from the kitchen, mixed with an odor of burned food. Crashes and white-hot curses made it difficult to concentrate on his prayers. He glanced at the general calendar. St. Blaise had come and gone, the blessing of the throats. How long ago that seemed, and it wasn't ten days. And look at that: tomorrow would be Ash Wednesday.

Maria had planned to observe two hours of silent prayer each day for Lent. She had been fascinated by the idea of penance.

From the ceiling there came a creak, very soft.

"Ole bullfrog down the yankity-yank, jumpin' back an forth from bank to bank!"

Wee Willie Winkie lives up here in the attic. Hey, Wee Willie, you got big black eyes you see always forever up and down in and out, you see the *emotional world*.

Sing a song of sixpence, hopping back and forth from beam to beam.

Attics are neat.

They have trapdoors that dummies tend not to think about. *They* don't look up. Bad habit.

He crouched down beside the trap that opened onto the upstairs hall. In a little while he would drop into John's world, a spider on a thread of air.

25

THE MAN STANDING ON THE RECTORY STEPS WAS TRYING TO smile and making a mess of it. The sun made his hair seem like white smoke clinging to his temples. Even though he was wearing a hat, scarf, and heavy overcoat, his body was trembling visibly. John recognized an archdiocesan car at the curb behind him. "I'm never leaving here," John said, "if that's what this is about."

"I'm Bayley," the man said. John stepped back and pulled the door open wide.

"Come in," John said, "please." Bishop Bayley must be eighty, and an old man feels the cold.

Frank pulled the trapdoor open. Nice and quiet. He looked down into the upstairs hall. Empty. Coming up from below, voices—John and another man. He craned his neck to listen. A policeman? No, the voice was lacking in authority.

He leaned farther out, careful not to unbalance himself.

Who had come a-calling, who?

As the bishop entered the rectory, John realized that his expression wasn't a smile at all, but a permanent grimace. He stood
in the middle of the foyer, working with the buttons on his
coat. It took John a moment to understand that he could not
open the coat. His hands were twisted, the knuckles gnarled.
He was arthritic, horribly so. It must have taken enormous
effort for this sick old man to come all the way here from
Chicago.

John helped him. "There's coffee," he said.

Now Bishop Bayley managed a genuine smile. "I've been
with the police," he said. "They floated me in coffee." He
looked toward the parlor. "I won't stay long, Father. I know
you have many duties."

Then, quite abruptly, the old man was crying. John put
his hand on his shoulder. "Age," the bishop finally said, "is
a dreadful betrayer." Pulling at a handkerchief with the frantic
delicacy of the arthritis victim, he managed to extract it from
his jacket pocket. He blew his nose noisily.

Frank dropped in his stocking feet to the floor. To absorb the
shock, he squatted. Then he stood to full height, reached up.
Yes, he could get back with just the slightest of jumps, grab
the edge, vault over.

In three long steps he was at the stairway, looking over
the banister.

The *sambiento* was a tunic of cheap undyed material,
usually wool, on which were inscribed symbols of the heresies
committed by the prisoner. There was also a conical miter, the
coraza. In the case of those to be burned, both *sambiento* and
coraza were decorated with flames.

An das de word ob de *Lawd*!

Earlier John had said morning Mass, consulted with Tina, and
begun to reconstruct his calendar. There were already six appointments set up for today, covering everything from the
logistics of taking over Frank's Confraternity of Christian Doc-

trine class to arranging a Mass schedule that would still serve the parish and wouldn't result in the pastor dropping dead. "I have a busy day," John said.

The bishop waved a twisted hand. "I'm sure."

John drew the old prelate into the parlor. Ed Bayley sank gratefully into the easy chair. For a moment he closed his eyes. "His mother and father could not come here. The father is completely helpless from a stroke. The mother has a delicate heart. I hope you understand."

"Of course."

"Father, I'm assuming that you think my reasons for meeting you are selfish. Perhaps that I'm here to plead for my nephew."

"Plead with the police. I can't hurt Frank, and I doubt if I can help him."

The bishop closed his eyes. "I fear that nobody can, but I love him still."

That voice! It was impossible, he was retired, hopelessly crippled, he couldn't have made it here. But no, it was him, pattycake pattycake. Frank sprang to attention. When he sang there must be only the smallest whisper, he must not be heard. But he *had to!* "Sure, a little bit of heaven fell from out the sky one day, and nestled on the ocean in a spot so far away . . ." Now, now, shhh. Oh, please let me sing, let me sing for Eddie the B! Oh, you loved me so much you used to kiss my head and hold me in your black arms, O Uncle Edward, Ed, Eddie, call me Eddie when we're alone, markem with a B, a fella can't go on alone forever, Eddie, hold my hand, do wop. The torch was given to the prince, and he thrust it into the pile of faggots, then watched as the flames . . . "I'll take you home again, Kathleen, across the ocean wide and wild." The flames moved up his tightly bound legs.

Gotta dance!

John's injury was aching, and he shifted uncomfortably in his chair. He found himself wanting a drink. At this hour, most unwise.

The bishop continued. "I remember those early days so fondly and so well. Frank's father had been a sad case. His first wife had died, leaving him with a seven-year-old daughter. For two years my brother faded, as if the light was just seeping from his soul. Then he met Angela. She brought the sun back in." Then he laughed a little laugh, "Eh heh heh heh." His eyes clouded.

"Frank spoke of his parents, but more often of you."

"Angela Holmes was a radiant girl. She was twenty-eight." His voice went high, began to shake. "You cannot imagine the beauty, the remarkable decency—my God, she was wonderful."

"Do you have any advice for me, Your Grace?"

"Don't make the mistake of thinking you're dealing with something . . . natural. That's what I've come here to tell you." The bishop looked as if he wished he had not lived so long.

"He must have had a hard upbringing."

"We did nothing to harm Frank! He was raised with love and kindness in an impeccable household. Look at his older sister—she's a successful businesswoman, she's been happily married to the same man for eleven years, she has two lovely children."

Oh, Eddie, tell him what we did! Tell him about the nights and the songs. Tell him, Eddie! I'm coming, Eddie, pattycake pattycake, oh, Eddie!

"My nephew was a lovely boy. Like his mother, Franklin could sing. He was like a little bird. We would sit out amongst the trees of a summer night, and he would sing all the old songs. His voice was as pure as a mountain stream."

"It still is."

"When Franklin was eight years of age, something happened, something odd and appalling."

John wanted to shake it out of the old man. He forced himself to wait.

"One Sunday morning Franklin slept in. He didn't want to go to church, he felt ill. When his parents returned home, there was a dreadful smell in the house. Out on the back patio they found that Franklin had built a stake and tied his sister's white rabbit to it and burned it to death."

"So you got him psychiatric help?"

"We viewed it as a satanic intervention, so we prayed. There was no recurrence. Frank was a happy boy, outwardly at least. In his adolescence there were a few incidents. A girl complained that he climbed into her bedroom stark naked one night, then slugged her when she woke up. From time to time neighbors reported seeing a naked man creeping about in the late hours. But . . . well, when he announced his intention to become a priest, we were quite naturally delighted."

"Get him off your hands, I suppose. Was the seminary told about his troubles?"

"The incident of the rabbit was ugly, but he was also a mere child. As for the other matters, he said they had nothing to do with him, and we chose to believe him."

Frank wanted to sing out, sing to the roofbeams, sing to the stars, "I believe in you!" Eh heh heh heh. Sing out! Eh heh heh heh. Sing out! Eh heh heh heh.

He would just walk right in, sit right down, and remove their hearts.

"When he first came to me, he was absolutely wonderful. A wonderful young priest."

"He *is* wonderful!" The tears threatened again.

"I might have wanted somebody a little more liberal, but Frank was always fair and just too damn good a priest for me even to consider it."

"Did anything ever . . . happen?"

"He had a temper. I'd even consulted with his spiritual adviser about it. He would scream at me from time to time. But that isn't what this is about. Let me be plain. You're a sophisticated man. Myself as well. We do not believe in primitive superstitions. But I must be honest with you. Frank changes so completely, so utterly, that . . . well, his face even changes. You can't recognize him."

"In what way does it change?"

"I can't even begin to describe it. Horrible! Inhuman. The difference between the good and evil sides of him is so profound that I believe it is, in effect, a dual personality."

The bishop closed his eyes, obviously in great pain. "Perhaps."

"You said you had something to tell me. I don't think you've quite done that yet."

He regarded John from the heart of the mystery.

How dare you, old man, I am your ever-lovin' puttem inna oven *nephew* and you say, you imply—oh my—that I'm crazeee.

So solleee!

"Shut—" Oops. That was loud. He clapped his hand over his mouth.

Bishop Bayley froze. "I heard him." His eyes went to the dark doorway. "Out there—now!"

"Calm down, Your Grace."

"No, I will not calm down! He's here, I'm sure of it."

"I'll take a look."

The bishop went to his feet. "No! Don't move! He's out there, I know it! Listen, I haven't told you everything. There was a ritual—a joke, really—but something happened to him . . . Oh, it was sacrilege, what we did—but as a *joke!* Dear God, it changed him. Somehow."

"So you did know something was wrong with him when you sent him off to the seminary. Do you think that the Lord really invests the sacraments in such a man?"

"The sacraments . . . I don't know. I hadn't thought about the sacraments."

"I cherish the sacraments, Your Grace, even if you do not. People come to us for the sacraments. The rest is just so much stuff and nonsense."

"If the Lord could stand Judas the Apostate, He can stand Franklin."

"What was this ritual?"

The bishop shifted in his chair. "Nothing important."

"Aside from the fact that it might have opened the gates of hell."

Bayley's eyes flickered toward the door. "Franklin?"

"He's not here!" John knew that this was probably a lie.

"He's here and you know it damn well!" So did the bishop, it seemed.

By stealth the inquisitor would approach the accused. He would come upon him suddenly whilst he was unawares, and then put the question to him with great force.

There came a rattling noise from down the hall. Tina had rolled the chair back, and now that ticking sound—her heels were tapping the floor, she was in motion, she was coming out of the office!

John heard the rat-tat-tattle of Tina's footsteps crossing the foyer. "Father?" She peered in.

"Yes, dear?"

"I just wanted to see if you were all right."

"We're fine. I think you should go home, Tina. I don't think you should come in the rectory again until this is resolved."

Frank took shallow sips of air. If you were careful, you could make the oxygen in a closet like this last a very long time indeed. As he listened to the bustle of Tina's departure, a tear formed in his right eye and rolled down his cheek.

Bishop Bayley had called the initiation a joke, just children at play. There is a door that leads downward, and that door is everywhere.

Din'cha know that?

"Your Grace, I would like to know what you did. What was the innocent ritual—the sacrilege?"

The bishop's hands were shaking, and the tremor obviously caused him a great deal of pain. "The children were studying Satan. You know, I believe in evil. But I must tell you, I do not believe in an actual devil. The devil was a medieval invention—a way they had of discrediting the pre-Christian gods."

"What did you do?"

"I undertook to demonstrate to them that Satan did not exist by calling him in an ancient ceremony known as the Raising of Asmodeus. There are certain words—I took the children into a cave—and I said those words. I called Asmodeus."

And I wuz born! Aw, shucks, and it hurts to be born. It hurts, Onkle Eddie! They will lay the flaying paddle first against the skin, and ask ye the question: Do thou repent? Then they will cut the line. Do thou? Then they will push the flay inside. Repent thee now? Then they will lift the flay. Take a breath, stop. Stay stopped. Take another. They suffocated the nuns and priests by a place they had wherein they were walled up and given food and drink through a hole. There were in that room spaces for twenty and seven of them to die in the walls.

John regarded the old bishop. "That doesn't satisfy me," he said at last. "That isn't enough. People play with rituals all the time and nothing happens."

The bishop looked at the floor. When finally he spoke, his voice was low. "It was horrible, the way we lived! There were so many things that were wrong. I . . . I . . . ." He emitted a long sigh that John had heard many times in the confessional. Now it would come. "I am afraid that I loved him . . . physically . . . I—"

The anger took John by surprise, almost caused him to lash out at the old man.

"He never knew! I swear to God! I went to him in the night. Late. I would kneel there . . . he was like someone come down from on high. I'd never had a child and I just . . . My love became something foul."

"You say he never knew! But it's in the depths of the night that he goes out and strangles people and burns them. He strangles *you*, he burns *you!* A thing like that is never unnoticed, you damn fool! The child noticed, and he feared and he hated! *And he hates!*"

The bishop was turned in on himself, twisted and contorted and now sobbing the bitter sobs of a shattered human being. "I never thought I would have the courage to confess this sin."

John should have given comfort to this poor devastated sinner, but he could not, it was beyond his power. "It's too bad that he didn't burn you, Bayley. Then maybe he wouldn't have burned the others."

There followed this statement the laughter of the demon. But it was not physical laughter, echoing in the walls and the rafters, but something far more awful, that trembled in the soul and made it feel small, and robbed it of its power.

I am coming, Johnnie-John, with my bells a-ringing and my nails as sharp as razors and my wonderful flowers of fire.

26

THE PARISH MADE A TUMULT OF DEMANDS, THE PRESS BAD-gered him, his leg and arm tormented him, he remained exhausted. He received the tragic news that one of the skeletons they had found was the mortal remains of harmless old Tom Zimmer. The other one was still not identified, but the Nicastros weren't holding out much hope.

Thank the good Lord that neither funeral would be held from M. and J.

Now he was facing another crisis. Kitty was standing at the door with her overnight case in her hand, preparing to spend yet another night in the rectory.

He blocked her way. It had become obvious to him that Frank wouldn't make a move as long as others were around. Given his powers, it was also clear that he wouldn't be caught unless he revealed himself.

"I'm staying right here, John Rafferty!"

He held his hands up as if warding off a blow. "Temper," he said in the most buttered tone he could manage. "I just don't think I need a police presence inside the buildings anymore.''

"I'm not a police presence, I'm me.''

What could he say to her? They both knew perfectly well why he wanted her to go. "It's my home.''

"I've already made an asshole out of myself doing this. They're laughing at me. The guys are saying I want to seduce you, to put a fine point on it.''

He touched his injured thigh. "I cannot imagine how I could perform the required gyrations.''

"Which is why I've got to stay. You need a bodyguard.''

"I do not.''

"He can climb walls! He's . . . well, he's . . .'' She lowered her eyes. "We know what he is, you and I.''

Once John would have scoffed at what she was implying. Now he did not. "Remember that he's also a human being. A victim.''

"You know what he can do.''

"I'm an invalid, it's nearly ten o'clock at night, and I need my sleep.''

"You can't force me to leave!''

"I can, hon. Sam.''

At the sound of his name the tall detective came out of the kitchen. At John's request, he was here to help if necessary. "Let's go out and knock back some coffee, lady.''

Kitty Pearson knew when she'd been outmaneuvered, and she now sought to preserve her dignity. "Okay,'' she said, "coffee it is.'' Without another word she left. Dowd hurried after her.

John went to the door, closed it behind them, and locked it. He leaned against it, his eyes shut.

The Lord is my light and my salvation,
Whom shall I fear?
The Lord is my life's refuge;
Of whom should I be afraid?

The clock in the parlor chimed ten. John spoke into the silence that followed. "We're alone now," he said. "It's just you and me."

His mouth tasted like metal, his hands shook as if he was palsied. He felt the racing flutter of his heart. The fear made fists and pressed them into his throat, as if its very spirit wanted to choke the life out of him.

With a heavy step he moved through the downstairs, turning out lights. It was an incredibly hard thing to do, but there was no choice.

Frank was in here, of that he was certain. And nobody on this earth could locate him, no matter how hard they tried.

He had to be lured.

John was the bait. The baited hook . . . hopefully.

He checked the front and back doors. Frank would want to be assured that they were securely locked.

Then he crossed the hall, moving toward the great oak door that led into the sacristy. Never had it seemed so tall, or so extremely ugly. The very shape of the pediment seemed to speak of some vast coiled evil.

He unlocked it and went through. The silence within was profound, so total that it communicated a sort of dignity.

But it was not a natural silence. There were no horns honking outside, no city whirling on its busy way.

He smelled the faint familiar smell of candles burning in the nave. He'd relit them himself, saying a prayer each time he struck a match.

The tall mahogany closets where the vestments were kept stood silent. He went out into the sanctuary, pausing at the altar. The shadows were deep, the only light coming from the votive candles, and from the sanctuary lamp. He'd relit it after evening Mass, when he had consecrated the single host that he intended to use on this night.

The sacral candle glowed in its ruby glass, the flame stable and strong. He unlocked the tabernacle and removed the chalice. He took the host in his hands and kissed it, smelling the ancient scent of the unleavened bread.

He looked up sharply. He'd felt . . . But no, the place was full of drafts. That's all it was—a draft.

He returned his gaze to the host.

How could man possibly be saved by a piece of bread?

But if Satan actually existed, then the Lord must too.

Oh, no, a voice said inside him. Look at the world. The works of Satan straddle time and history. But where are the works of the Lord?

He laid the host back in the chalice and went for the monstrance, made now even more sacred to him because of the awful work to which it had been put.

Somehow, he was going to exorcise Franklin Bayley. He'd read the rituals, but it was not ritual that did it—the form of words wasn't the important part. The demon isolated the soul from the body, leaving it in darkness. To the victim, possession is simply a black unconscious emptiness.

The body runs before the whip of the demon, while the soul sleeps. . . .

He had created his own exorcism, just for Frank. The point of the thing was to awaken the soul of the possessed. Then it would come forth in all its hidden goodness, and drive the demon as the angel does, over the cliffs of life and into the pit.

He must keep on, though, he must not stop and consider, not for a moment. Otherwise he would run, he would dash screaming down the aisle, he would race through the streets crying for safety, but there would be no safety, not ever again, not for the man who knew the demon.

He hurried down the aisle to the doors, and shook them hard. Well locked, and he knew that nobody would be opening them, not on this night. To make sure that he himself didn't try to escape at the height of his fear, he threw his keys off into the dark.

Then he began his examination of the church. It must be empty of police.

First he ascended the stairs to the choir loft and looked among the dusty pews, then made his way into the bell tower. Above him he could hear the whirring of the electric works that controlled the bells. There were ropes, too, so they could be rung manually. As he mounted the stairs he kept one hand on the ropes to guide himself.

It was profoundly dark here. He could see nothing at all, and he was high and there was below him a sickening sense of depth, and he felt something slithering up his leg.

He took in breath, emitted a high, choked scream—and fell a good three feet before he was again clutching the ropes.

It was more like a very, very long finger than a mouse or a roach. "Frank?"

Then it was gone, and he could see ahead of him again. Light came in the clock face. He paused there and looked through the crooked glass at the crooked image of the city.

Then he went down from the spire, satisfied that the whole church was empty. Next he must search the crypt, and that was going to be very hard.

He had to be certain, though, that there was not a single outsider intruding here. Just one, and Frank would know, and he would not come.

"Frank, I want you to come."

When he opened the door and smelled that familiar damp concrete odor coming up from below, he realized why he had put the crypt off until last.

He looked over toward the altar, to the monstrance flushed by candlelight. His heart swelled, and he thought: Thus do I taste of the love that has no end. The sacral candle reminded him of the light of life, and its flame of how we spin and dance and go.

He took a step into the crypt, paused, then took another. The blackness was absolute. He reached up and out, trying to find the light switch. Finally his hand contacted the ancient pull. When he flipped it, the sound echoed among the tombs below. This time there was light.

He saw that Dowd had been good to his word. There were no police hiding here either. He saw, also, that the two empty tombs had been opened, and that was as it should be. Frank obviously intended one for Tom Zimmer.

The other was for the one who lost.

Normally it would have filled him with peace to imagine himself among the priests who had expended their lives here. Not now. He intended to drive out the demon. He had to. Any other outcome was unthinkable.

He touched the cool marble of one of the tombs. Then he looked about, sure there had been a rustle.

The walls seemed ready to fall in on him, the ceiling to come down. Even the air, which had possessed a timeless coolness, seemed to grow thick and oppressive. You will walk, he told himself. But he could not, he broke and ran, taking the steps in clumsy twos, until he was out of the crypt and the door was shut.

He leaned against it, his eyes closed, breathing hard. The more his tension grew, the more his injuries hurt. He returned to the sacristy, went through the door into the rectory. The phone was ringing. Of course, this was a busy parish. Somebody had been born, somebody else had died. As he grabbed the instrument in the front hall, he glanced at his watch. Ten-twenty. That eternity in the church hadn't even lasted half an hour. "Mary and Joseph."

"It's Tina."

"Hi."

There was a silence.

"What is it, Tina?"

"Just . . . I worry about you, Father. The press calling in the middle of the night, that sort of thing."

Her tone said she was worried about much more than the press. "Thanks, Tina, I'll make sure to let the machine get it."

"Father?"

"Yes, Tina."

"We love you, Father. All of us!"

"And I you." He hung up quickly, worried that she would detect the fear in his voice if the conversation continued. Then he went upstairs. "I'm going to get ready," he said. He was as nervous as he had been when he was preparing for his ordination. He would bathe himself, present himself in as fresh a condition as an old man could. "It's up to you now."

He went into the bathroom, dropped off his clothes, threw

them into the hamper for Betty to sort and wash. Naked, he opened Frank's medicine cabinet and took out his shampoo and his soap. Then he ran the shower.

The shampoo had a powerful perfume that sickened him, the soap felt greasy. But he craved this closeness with Frank. He had lived in the same house with him for five years, had seen him pouring his heart and soul into this parish. The good part of Frank might be captured, but it was still there, John could never believe otherwise. It deserved love, it deserved compassion, it deserved help.

The whole point of this exercise was to appeal to that good part, to use the sacramental moment and the grace of God to bring it forth, to enable the good to banish away that which had captured it.

He knew as he lathered himself that a shadow had come into the bathroom. He pressed himself against the back wall of the shower. The shadow withdrew and did not come back.

"Thank you," he said, when he saw that a garment had been left. This was the first overt sign he'd had that he was tilling good ground.

The garment was roughly cut from one of the wool blankets M. and J. gave away to the homeless. He took it from the small table beside the basin and unfolded it.

Like a chasuble it was formed of a single piece of cloth with an opening in the center. It was intended to hang down over the back and front. He examined it. In the middle of the chest and back there had been painted a red X, the symbol of the apostate. Along its lower borders were orange and yellow flames.

From his Church history he knew this garment. It was the sambiento, the rough covering that the heretics wore to the auto da fe, the act of faith. "If a man abide not in me, he is cast forth as a branch and is withered and men gather them and cast them into the fire, and they are burned." Poor old St. John, he probably never realized the horror that would be born from those words. The whole Inquisition had been spun out of John 15:6.

Rolled up beside the sambiento was a morgaza, a gag

dipped in gall. He touched it, tasted his fingers. Vinegar, perhaps urine. He did not ask for deliverance, nor for help. In faith there is a critical condition of surrender to God that is beyond prayer. Such who enter it are marked as martyrs.

It does not mean that they will fear less, or suffer less.

He threw the *sambiento* over his head, tied its woolen sash around his midriff, and took the *morgaza* in his hand. When he went out into the hall, he saw once again the Virgin of Guadalupe. He sensed, also, that the trapdoor that led into the attic was open. He could not make himself look up.

The Virgin gazed at him, and her face was very different from the way it had appeared to him before. It was still as pure, but this was also a face of knowledge. She knew terrible things, the eyes said, but even so remained as pale as the rose.

He went to the top of the stairs. Rather than a sound behind him, there was a quick movement of air. It was him, oh, yes. My dear friend, my fine young man.

They descended together. "Do not look at me," he said.

"Why are you doing this?"

There came an animal sound. "Why does the snake go in the path, why does the flower grow?"

Because they must, John thought.

"Exactly," said the rough, sighing voice.

John felt sick at the thought of those eyes looking inside him, at that terrible mind regarding the works of his soul. How unspeakably horrible he was. The evil was thick about him, as thick as quicksand.

"How can you think me evil—because I seek to destroy this Christ of yours? Perhaps I'm a doctor in the land of souls, and he is your sickness."

"No."

As they reached the foot of the steps, the phone rang again. Its jangling froze them both. It also created an issue. John looked toward the nearest instrument, visible across the foyer. When a hand came down on his shoulder, he jumped, stopped himself. The hand patted gently, the fingers brushed his cheek. As the message machine in Tina's office began talking, the hand withdrew.

They moved across the foyer and John heard Kitty: "Why aren't you answering, John? Goddammit, I've got to talk to you! I've *got to!*" Then a click, a buzz.

From behind him there came the voice. It was so strange, a growl, the movement of wind, some dark memory: "Why do you fear me? I didn't invent myself. We are all victims of creation."

"You committed your sin."

"What sin?"

"For example, you've possessed the body of my friend."

"I am your friend."

How cunning was the art of this lie. The impression grew to a certainty that he was in a most august and dreadful presence. Paradoxically, this renewed his hope. If there really was such a thing as possession, he had a very distinct chance of rescuing Frank.

The demon, having come by lies and cunning, may be evacuated only with a subterfuge. So the old books said, if they did not lie.

"I cannot come to you without a body, or you would overlook me."

"Which would be fine."

"You cannot free yourself from the concept of evil until you understand me."

"Another lie." John struggled to lift his hand to open the sacristy door. His arm felt heavy beyond belief. This was the famous weight of dread that made it necessary for men to be carried to their executions.

As if sensing John's terror, his companion once again patted his shoulder. "There is no friend so true as one with whom you share a vice."

John did not feel that he was speaking with Frank. "I share no vices with you," he replied.

"Not pride?"

Of course it was true. The ease with which he had been brought to this realization made him uneasy. He wavered inside . . . just a little.

"Do wop. And hurry. The lady cop's already on her way."

When he tried to force himself to move faster, he pranced the fuzzy prance of a marionette. "I'm sorry," he said.

"Never mind, my friend." Again the fingers touched his cheek. They were dry, and startlingly warm.

John managed to open the door into the church. Behind him there was a pause. "It's empty," John said. "I even checked the crypt."

"The tower . . ."

"Empty and locked."

"Then go to the back. Put on the hat you find there, light the taper, and come up the aisle."

On his feet John wore only his carpet slippers, and they made no sound as he drifted along. Once he stumbled, the soft thud reverberating through the nave.

The hat was what he had known it would be, the *coraza*, the tall miter of the heretic. Like the *sambiento* it was rimmed with painted flames. Frank had made these things in the school, John realized. He pictured the art room a long time ago, full of the littlest ones and their finger-painting sets, the sunlight streaming in the tall windows and tiny Sister Anne trying to organize the hullabaloo.

With a heavy sigh he put the *coraza* on his head. It was made of *papier-mâché* on a frame of chicken wire, and the ends of the wire pressed into his scalp like some absurd parody of the crown of thorns. The taper was a red sacral candle. For a moment he didn't know how he would light it, then he saw the box of matches lying beside it.

Matches. His hands shook so much that he could hardly get one out. As it was, they spilled across the floor.

The flame of the candle quivering before him, he began his procession to the altar. He saw him standing there in golden vestments, a white miter on his head and a homemade bishop's crook in his hand. He'd chosen the simple miter reserved for funerals.

He sang in that clear, pure voice of his, the voice of the lost boy:

O saving Victim opening wide
The gate of heaven to man below!
Enemies press at every side;
Give us aid, thy strength bestow.

How many times John had heard *O Salutaris Hostia*, but never sung with such grace or feeling as this. Some of the wonder of it even survived the rather wooden English translation. As if sensing John's wish, he shifted to the Latin, and the hymn soared.

Uni trinoque Domino
Sit sempiterna gloria,
Qui vitam sine termino
Nobis donet in patria.

The closer John got, the more the light of the candle began to flicker on his rival's face.

This was the hardest part, seeing the way his face changed. The departure was so radical, so impossible—the mummy-taut skin, the eyes gone huge, swimming in their own tears, blood popping from the pores.

When the thing spoke, the pure child's voice gave way to something like the screaming of a crow. "You filthy whore, straighten your back! You who spread apostasy, who ram lies down the gullets of the faithful, I excoriate you, I anathematize you!"

The viperous sting of the words shocked John deeply. The Frank he sought must be very far from the surface.

"Unfortunately we have no *quemadero*, but this church you have rendered filthy with your vile presence will be burning ground enough! The flames will cleanse it, the flames will make it good again, and your ashes will become holy soil! Son of a *prostituto*, filthy *sodomite*!"

"Frank, you can defeat this. All you have to do is try." The words sounded thin and improbable, and they got the response they deserved: a gust of laughter. John thought: I've made a terrible mistake. Then: I've got to get out of here! But the door was locked and he'd purposely denied himself the option of a key. He decided to try to be cunning too. He would attempt a trick. "Frank, listen! You're not possessed. It's a sickness, Frank. In the name of God the sick can be healed!"

John could sense the laughter. "Wanna do the strut?"

"No I don't! I don't even know what it is."

He started toward him. "I'll teach you."

"No! Stay there! Listen to me, I know what you're feeling. You're terribly hurt and angry—"

Again there was a burst of laughter, as sharp and hot as a slashing blade. Something moved beside the altar, quick like a rat, as big as a large dog. John told himself that he hadn't seen it, that such things were impossible. Frank snickered. "Your pride brought you to us. Your pride is your destruction."

John spoke to the man he was increasingly afraid was no longer there. "Frank, nothing, *nothing* will convince me that you don't want to escape from this."

He hurled his bishop's crook like a javelin all the way down the aisle. It clattered against the door. Then he was holding something else, a tall thick object. There was a sparkle in his free hand, and suddenly what he was holding was a torch.

The flames danced in the windows and down the walls. "Frank, if you can't talk, reach out your hand, reach out to me!" He forced a shaking hand toward the still figure. An instant later there was terrible agony—the torch was thrust against his open palm. He snatched his hand back, he howled. "Oh, *Jesus!*"

Again the torch was thrust at him. "Some of them became so convinced of the rightness of their verdicts, they themselves took the torches from their executioners and thrust them into the wood stacked at their own feet. Others set themselves afire with their candles. It is said that the flames felt cold to those who self-administered them." Grinning so tightly that his skull rose in his face, he offered John the torch.

"Get it away! Get it away from me!" How stupid he had

been, what a fool. There wasn't the faintest hope that the old Frank could return.

John dashed down the aisle and began to work on the locked door. The enemy had two torches now, and came along behind, dragging them across the backs of the pews, spreading a line of fire from each. With a roar like some bull animal, he flung one of the torches straight at John. It came *whoom*, twirling, *whoom*, and sailed right over his head, so close that it knocked the insane headdress to the floor.

The torch hit the doors a reverberating blow and exploded into a thousand globules of flaming gel. John backed away from the wall of fire.

Then Frank was thundering down the aisle like a great mad ape, two more torches in his hands. One of them he hurled straight up into the air. It splashed against the ceiling, caught in the rafters, and sent white-hot drips cascading everywhere.

"Not my church!"

"Do *wopwopwop*!" He raced round the perimeter of the nave, dragging two more torches behind him, leaving a trail of fire. Back at the altar he tossed these torches high, and they flew like comets into the choir loft and lay sputtering there.

Two more torches exploded to life in his hands. John made a dash he realized would probably be his last. He raced for the sacristy.

"If you don't want to dance, would you perhaps care to play pattycake," Frank asked in a tone so completely reasonable that it was hideous.

John raced into the sacristy and through the door to the rectory. He slammed it and locked it. He went to the phone, hit 911, but even as he did it he heard the sirens starting. They were here, of course. They'd been outside all the time. Thank God for you, Kitty. You stubborn woman, you would not give up on an old fool!

He grabbed his overcoat and threw it around his shoulders. With one of those peculiarly detailed afterthoughts that characterize moments of great catastrophe, he took down his new hat, put it on his head, and carefully adjusted it before racing outside. He'd also grabbed the ancient fire extinguisher from the pantry, and carried it before him as a child might an offering of flowers for Mary's May altar. The water in the old device sloshed as he ran.

The windows of the church glowed with the light of inhuman life: Joseph capered before the Babe in the Manger Window, Mary gyrated through the Seven Dolors in the Mysteries Window.

A phalanx of fire trucks was blasting four abreast down Seventh Avenue, scattering tough New York traffic like a gust of leaves.

Then he was being grabbed, somebody strong was taking him in his arms. He was astonished to see Bobby Quindlan, his face bright red, his eyes all wild, and behind him the gnarled form of Bishop Bayley emerging from a limousine. Then Kitty burst out of her car. "Jesus H. Christ," she yelled.

"I'm sorry. It was pride, the sin of pride!"

"You say a thing like that at a time like this! Come on over here, let me look at you." She held him by the shoulders. "You idiot, you've lost what was left of your eyebrows."

"I'm sorry."

"We never should have let you out of the hospital."

"I'm not going back!"

As the fire grew, its reflection turned her face a horrible orange. She hugged him. He could hear the flames now, even over the uproar of the arriving fire equipment. He pulled back from her, started to turn around.

"John," she said, "don't."

Sirens ground down. Voices began shouting in electric bullhorns. An eerie whistling sound joined the steady crackle of the fire. "Yes," John replied, "I have to."

A spear point of flame ascended from the bell tower and strove for the night sky.

"Move back," a fireman shouted at them through a bullhorn. "Get back across the avenue!"

John had remembered something that made the importance of orders from bullhorns fade to nothing. When he had first conceived of this effort, he had visualized reconciliation, a moment when he would have shared the host with Frank, broken the bread of life with him, and thus begun the healing that would lead him to confession, to a mental-health facility, to rehabilitation.

This was why he had consecrated the host, why he had left it on the altar.

It was there now, standing in Satan's own monstrance.

John thought: Because I thought I was better than him, I will die here. I have indeed been destroyed by my pride.

He stared at the burning church, sick with dread over what he must do. Under no circumstances—and no matter the danger—a priest could not allow the Blessed Sacrament to come to harm.

27

"SANCTUS, SANCTUS, SANCTUS DOMINUS DEUS SABAOTH. PLENI sunt whatchamacallit, oh yeah, caeli et terra gloria tua, hosanna in excelsis. Benedictus qui venit in nomine Domini, and a whoop de doo, another consecrated shoe."

Consecrate and reconsecrate, so much consecrating to do! He pulled a broken cigar from the pocket of his pants and put it on the altar beside his consecrated shoes. He consecrated the cigar. My, it was hot in here.

John came back in, as he'd known he would. "You're gonna have to eat everything on the altar," he told the man. "I've consecrated it all. Maybe you can boil the cigar and the shoes together. Consecrated-shoe stew."

Steam was rising from John's clothes, and it caused him to suppose that he was burning. "Dear boy, that's nothing. My miter's been on fire for at least five minutes. Honestly!"

John struggled closer, snatched at the monstrance.

"Need some light?" his opponent asked, holding out a burning sleeve. "How do I do it? you ask. Where I come from, fire's no big deal. We're used to the stuff!"

The man inside felt it, though. There was pain around the eyes, pain in the little edges that define the set of the lips.

"Come with me, Frank."

"Gimme that fire extinguisher, I can consecrate it too. I'd *love* to see you and the Dead Bishop eat a fire extinguisher."

"Your uncle is not dead. He's outside."

"Nonsense, he died when he fucked that bitch."

"He what?"

"That Irish setter of his, sweetheart. Fucked me too, *the old bastard!*"

Where did Satan end and Frank begin? John had counted on there being a division. What if there was none? He could actually *feel* the filth, the corruption, the hate pouring from the man. How dare he touch the Body of Christ! "Give me the monstrance!"

"Fire buggin' you?"

"Give it to me!" John clawed for it, batting at the flames that were beginning to consume the altar cloth.

He held the monstrance just out of John's reach. "No, no, not yet. I wanna consecrate a few more things. Could you drop me a load, by any chance?"

John grabbed his shoulders, tried again. "Frank, wake up!" He shook him with all his might. "In the name of God, awaken!" Give me this soul, John cried within himself. Even though I'm weak and full of pride, give me this soul! "Awaken, in the name of the Lord!"

"Shakedy shakedy shake shake shake!" He let himself flop back and forth until John stopped. "The guy you want isn't available right now. He had to go to his room."

There, that was something, that was acknowledgment that he existed! "That's right, Frank, that's a first step! He's in there, you know it, you just admitted it!"

"Nobody in here but us debbils, Johnnie-boy!"

"I want you, Frank! I want you!"

He pushed John away, hid his face for a moment, then peeked back over his shoulder.

The face was wet, red, the veins pulsating on the surface. It appeared to have been turned inside out. John's whole body convulsed, his own scream sounded to him as fragile as the cry of a bird. Then it went dark.

He knew exactly what he had done. He ought to just let the old fool cook. But there was still more that could be extracted from him. "Oh, come on, you're not any use to me like that!" He picked up the fire extinguisher, pumped it a few times, then sprayed soda water in the old man's face.

John sputtered, staggered away.

"Let's strut together, we'll look pretty in the fire. Can you dance in fire? Where's your *sambiento*, I worked hard to make that! Art class is my funnest one! I made a gallows and they said turn it into an oil derrick, eh heh heh heh. And Bishop Eddiekins *is* dead, by the way. Ever look in his eyes?" He danced round and round, the sparks flying off his vestments.

Now John would try his own exorcism, would make his appeal to his friend. His voice, when he spoke, was a whisper. "Frank, please come back. You can. I know you can."

"Eh heh heh heh!"

"We're going to die here if you don't!"

"Gonna strut?"

"We'll burn! Both of us! Because I can tell you one thing, unless you *do* come back, you're not getting out of here alive. I won't let you escape into the world. I won't let you!"

"Rollemup, rollemup, markem with a B!"

John held out his hands toward Frank. "I abjure you to leave this man and go back into the depths from which you came!"

"Puttem ina oven—"

"Frank, my friend. My dear friend!"

Frank's face seemed to sink into itself. His raging eyes dimmed, his flaring nostrils closed. "John?"

"Oh, Frank!" John's hands came, grasped his, held them tight.

"John?" The face became a blur, then went soft. Suddenly there was a hurt man here.

"Thank God, thank God!"

"I . . . Where . . . ?" He looked around him. His eyes opened wide, an expression of absolute disbelief and horror came into his face. "What have I done?"

"Frank, we've got to run!"

"I didn't do this! I couldn't!"

The pain in his voice was almost unbearable. The words were so astonishing that they stopped John still. They had not a moment, the fire was raging, but he stood staring at his poor friend. "You didn't know?"

"I did this?"

John nodded. At that moment the pain of his burning reached Frank's consciousness. His whole body shook, his skin showed red cracks when he writhed, his muscles knotted, his bones twisted in the heat.

He threw back his head and bellowed.

John struggled to direct the fire extinguisher on him. A huge orange wall of flame swept over them and both men suddenly were burning.

It took Frank's last bit of strength to grab the extinguisher and spray John properly, to douse him, to try to save him, and then to take the hot monstrance and remove the lunette and hand it to him with a hand dripping flesh.

"Come with me, Frank, it's dead, the demon is dead!"

He jumped away. "The hell it is, Johnnikins!" The good priest gathered his last bit of energy, placed himself between John and the wall of flames before the altar. "Come, demon," he said.

He delivered himself to the fire.

It took John a moment to realize that the lunette with the host was in his hand.

"Oh, Frank," he whispered, staring down at the precious bread within.

Showering sparks, the miter fell from the head. Then the face slowly twisted back to its rictus, made the more hideous by the busy action of the flames.

An immense effort began, a body trying to move, to function, in blue fire.

John took a step back just as a charred hand swept past his face. He wasn't seeing this, Frank was dead, he could not still be moving, not all burned and destroyed. This was the heat doing this. He wasn't seeing this.

The hand clawed at his face again, and this time he leapt away. Scorching wind rushed past him as he retreated to the sacristy. He slammed the door.

The screams on the other side seemed to go on and on and on, and they were so awful that John screamed too.

The door shuddered, shook, rattled.

Oh, God, what was in there, what mystery? He saw that he hadn't even begun to understand. Frank had not died entirely, only the good man. This thing—how could it be struggling, how could it be screaming, when the body was nothing but a blackened shell?

The shaking of the door became a pounding. It bounded on its hinges. John lay against it, but it jumped and cracked. It was getting hotter and hotter, it would not hold long. John's hand went to the deadbolt, the door shuddered, the screaming would not stop.

"In the name of God, begone," he cried. If anything, the pounding got harder, the screaming more furious. He tried to throw the bolt, but it was warped by the heat. The pounding grew to a crescendo, the screaming to a roar. "By all the saints and angels, by the power of the Lord—"

The door would not hold, the issue was lost.

Then, silence. A little boy's voice began weeping. John shook his head, he refused to listen, but the weeping went to piping cries, and the little-boy voice cried out, "Mama, I got fire on me, Mama, help, oh, help!" Then, louder, older: "Let me out!" Fully mature: "Let me fucking *out*!"

The door creaked, the pounding started again, John wept, John shuddered, John pressed the door closed with all his might and main, John prayed as best he could, halting, confused snatches of every prayer he had ever known.

On and on the pounding went, rising and falling. The door grew hotter, the hinges groaned, John struggled.

A woman rushed at him, all ancient and bent, and dug her nails into his wounded thigh. He shrieked in agony, he called the name of God, and she went with a hiss into the dark.

He thought of the host in his breast pocket, he tried to believe that its presence mattered, that it would help him. For a man of faith, he felt weak indeed, weak to the test.

He was near the end of his ability to resist when he realized that the pounding had stopped. He waited, but nothing came from the sanctuary save the complicated sigh of fire. The door was hot, and John stood away from it. A single burning ash drifted down from above. He dashed for the rectory, put another door between himself and the inferno.

His face stung, his coat was scorched, his hat singed, and he was dripping with water from the fire extinguisher.

With the host safely in his pocket he went outside. The cold air felt like new skin. Up the block he could see a crowd behind a line of policemen. Mary and Joseph presented a tragic spectacle, flames pouring from every window. As he watched, the tower swayed and went twisting down into the street, landing with a great shower of sparks before the church.

Firemen clamored and ran, hoses surged, torrents of water were pouring into the holocaust.

John could not have stayed in there another moment.

He crossed the street and went up the sidewalk. Kitty and Dowd burst out of the crowd and ran toward him. "John!" Kitty was screaming, her feet pounding. A fireman tried to intercept her. "Move your tail, fire boy," she roared as she went past.

"This man is burned, ma'am!" The fireman was trying to get him toward an EMS unit.

"You're burned, oh, you're burned!"

"Actually, not to put too fine a point on it, I'm singed. Frank saved me with a fire extinguisher."

She looked toward the church. "Is he dead?"

"He's . . . not intact."

She hugged him, pressing her cheek against his chest. How

small she was, how light! She took his hand and led him like an official into the black Cadillac.

Her hand gave his a final pressure and she was gone.

Bobby Quindlan's face was smeared with tears, his eyes were black sockets. "John—"

"Bobby, it's not necessary."

"I'm so damn sorry."

John looked past him, at the developing ruins. "I'm a lot sorrier, Bobby."

Bishop Bayley gave him a thin smile. "John," he said, "you'll rebuild. You'll find that the people are still there, waiting."

"They're waiting for us," Bobby Quindlan added, "waiting until the Church catches up with them. I learned that from you, John."

"What about the cardinal?"

"The Church has room for you."

John looked to the old bishop. What could he say to the man? This was one of the creators of Frank Bayley. This fragile old ruin had inflicted critical abuse.

The bishop covered one of John's hands with his own pitifully gnarled paw. "We'll raise a fund, we'll return her to her original glory, young man! Her original glory!"

John shriveled within, to feel that reptilian touch.

The twinkles that had been flickering in Bishop Bayley's eyes fled.

Bob Quindlan was beginning to frown. The bishop closed his eyes. There was amazing pain in his face.

At that moment the entire central structure of the church collapsed in on itself with a tremendous roar, and a great moan went up from the crowd.

The rectory and the school remained intact. There would be something left for him, for the parish. Some little bit.

John did not know if he would ever be able to put it back together. He wanted to, though, and he was willing to spill his blood if he had to, because his success meant the defeat of the demon.

More people were coming, figures running up the streets, breaking away from the idle curiosity seekers, their faces flattened by shock.

The parish was gathering.

"I've got work to do," John said. He launched himself out the door of the car, leaving Bob to contend with the weeping, shattered bishop.

All in an instant John thought of Frank and his suffering, and the suffering of those he had killed, and the tormented soul in the back seat of that Cadillac, and how it is that the undoing of evil is always the same: even its worst destructions uncover hidden gold; grace flows from the cracks it makes in the world.

Maria's face appeared before him, and he saw that a freedom had been offered them, a grace of woman, and had been rejected and not understood, and all this horror had followed.

He crossed the street, went under the yellow tape that marked the police barrier. "Mass in the rectory when the fire's out," he shouted. He held up the lunette. "I have the host." They pressed forward. Hands clasped hands. This was what was eternal, this was the Church: the host, the seeking hearts, the people of God.

He went among them.